MICHAEL JECKS

City Of Fiends

**SIMON &
SCHUSTER**

London · New York · Sydney · Toronto · New Delhi

A CBS COMPANY

First published in Great Britain by Simon & Schuster UK Ltd, 2012
A CBS Company
This paperback edition published by Simon and Schuster UK Ltd 2013

Copyright © Michael Jecks, 2012
First chapter of Templar's Acre copyright © Michael Jecks, 2013

This book is copyright under the Berne Convention.
No reproduction without permission.
® and © 1997 Simon & Schuster Inc. All rights reserved.

The right of Michael Jecks to be identified as author of this
work has been asserted in accordance with sections 77 and
78 of the Copyright, Designs and Patents Act, 1988.

1 3 5 7 9 10 8 6 4 2

Simon & Schuster UK Ltd
1st Floor
222 Gray's Inn Road
London WC1X 8HB

www.simonandschuster.co.uk

Simon & Schuster Australia, Sydney
Simon & Schuster India, New Delhi

A CIP catalogue record for this book is available from the British Library

B PB ISBN: 978-0-85720-523-0
A PB ISBN: 978-1-47111-181-5
Ebook: 978-0-85720-524-7

This book is a work of fiction. Names, characters, places and
incidents are either a product of the author's imagination or
are used fictitiously. Any resemblance to actual people living
or dead, events or locales is entirely coincidental.

Typeset by Hewer Text UK Ltd, Edinburgh
Printed and bound in Great Britain by CPI Group (UK) Ltd, CR0 4YY

Michael Jecks gave up a career in the computer industry to concentrate on writing and the study of medieval history, and he is now the author of over thirty medieval mysteries. A regular speaker at library and literary events, he is a past Chairman of the Crime Writers' Association. He lives with his wife, children and dogs on northern Dartmoor.

Also by Michael Jecks

The Last Templar
The Merchant's Partner
A Moorland Hanging
The Crediton Killings
The Abbot's Gibbet
The Leper's Return
Squire Throwleigh's Heir
Belladonna at Belstone
The Traitor of St Giles
The Boy Bishop's Glovemaker
The Tournament of Blood
The Sticklepath Strangler
The Devil's Acolyte
The Mad Monk of Gidleigh
The Templar's Penance
The Outlaws of Ennor
The Tolls of Death
The Chapel of Bones
The Butcher of St Peter's
A Friar's Bloodfeud
The Death Ship of Dartmouth
The Malice of Unnatural Death
Dispensation of Death
The Templar, the Queen and Her Lover
The Prophecy of Death
The King of Thieves
The Bishop Must Die
The Oath
King's Gold

This book is for Andy, Jenny,
and all the BERTS Frangles,
for ales, for Morris dancing, for cycling,
and for all the fun.

You are the best of neighbours.

GLOSSARY

Bratchet	a diminutive form of 'brat'.
Coffin	a pie-case of pastry.
Deodand	the fine exacted for the value of a thing that occasioned death. Deodand finally disappeared after a train killed a man in the nineteenth century, and the full value of engine and train was charged to the company.
Deofol and **Foumart**	two terms of opprobrium.
Gegge	term of contempt for man or woman.
Leman	lover or sweetheart.
Lurdan	sluggard, vagabond, rascal – also implying dimness.
Misericord	small wooden projection set into choir stalls for monks and canons to rest upon to ease their legs during long services; also a long, narrow-bladed dagger for the *coup de grâce*. Both implying compassion, pity, or mercy.
Parnel	wanton young woman, harlot.

Recusant   one who refuses to submit to authority.

Scanthing   very small, insignificant in size.

Strummel patch   term of contempt.

Villeiny-saying   speaking slander of a person.

CAST OF CHARACTERS

Sir Baldwin de Furnshill   Keeper of the King's Peace and keen investigator of felonies.

Edgar   Sir Baldwin's loyal Sergeant.

Simon Puttock   once a bailiff of Dartmoor, now a farmer near Crediton and friend to Sir Baldwin.

Edith   Simon's daughter.

Peter   Edith's husband.

Henry   Edith and Peter's baby.

Hugh   Simon's servant.

Sir Richard de Welles   Coroner in Lifton.

Sir Reginald   Coroner in Exeter.

Sir James de Cockington   Sheriff of Exeter.

Luke Chepman   a successful merchant and member of the Freedom of Exeter

Sir Charles of Lancaster   the loyal servant of the Lancaster family, he has become a committed supporter of the former King, Edward II.

| **Ulric of Exeter** | servant to Sir Charles. |

Cathedral & Religious

Adam Murimuth	Precentor and Canon at Exeter Cathedral.
Fr Laurence Coscumbe	Vicar within the Cathedral.
Fr Paul	Vicar of Holy Trinity at the South Gate.
Janekyn Beyvyn	porter responsible for all the gates to the Cathedral Close.

Paffards

Henry Paffard	a wealthy merchant in Exeter.
Claricia Paffard	Henry's long suffering wife.
Gregory Paffard	eldest son of Henry and Claricia.
Agatha	the second child, with the most business acumen.
Thomas	the third child, a boy of six years.
John	old bottler to the family.
Benjamin	Henry Paffard's apprentice.
Alice	maid to the Paffards.
Joan	younger maid.

De Coyntes

Bydaud de Coyntes	Gascon merchant.
Emma de Coyntes	Bydaud's wife.
Anastasia	Bydaud's eldest daughter.
Sabina	Bydaud's younger daughter.
Peg	maid to the de Coyntes family.

Avices

Roger Avice   a dealer in good wines, who has suffered from debts.

Helewisia Avice   Roger's wife; a determined woman from farming stock.

Katherine   their daughter of sixteen.

Piers   their son, who died two years before.

Marsilles

Juliana Marsille   a widow, who struggles to survive.

Philip   her eldest son, who is trying to build up his family's business again.

William   aged sixteen, he is determined to help his brother and mother.

AUTHOR'S NOTE

The idea for this book came to me while I was researching what I had intended to be a very parochial little story about four families in Exeter. Why is it that, when sitting in a darkened library, so many curious little diversions always occur to me?

This one came about because I was looking into that strange period after the capture, and escape from captivity, of King Edward II.

The kingdom must have been in complete turmoil. Many men were keen to try to spring Edward from his prisons, first at Kenilworth, then at Berkeley, while others were more than happy to see him languish in gaol, letting his son rule in his stead.

Despenser, at last, had been removed. But in his place was the ever more avaricious Mortimer, who took every advantage. Some believe he was hoping to take the throne for one of his sons. I don't believe that myself, but there is no doubt that he grabbed all the money, lands and authority he could lay his hands on.

And in the middle of all this, poor Bishop Berkeley suddenly died.

The facts are few and far between. We know that the good Bishop was elected, and confirmed on 8 January 1327. He left no Register, or other record, apparently. About the only document we have from him was a letter to Adam Murimuth, on 12 January, appointing him his Official-Principal.

It is thought that he was enthroned soon after 25 March, and then, following the precedent of his immediate predecessors, he went on a tour of the ecclesiastical estates. Proof of his determination to be a good administrator, I suppose.

But his journey was cut short by his death.

It is Murimuth's chronicle that tells us that he died at Petreshayes, in Yarcombe, on 24 June. A shockingly sudden death.

What could have led to such a brief episcopate? Was he merely unwell?

I suspect not.

Generally, it is true that men, whether bishops or lords, could die while travelling from one manor to another. Their entourages generally used up all the resources of a manor quite quickly, after which they would move on to the next. However, if there was even a hint of ill-health, they would stay put, since there was no point in hastening a man's demise by forcing him to cover twenty miles on horseback.

Be that as it may, there is other evidence that must be looked at.

Berkeley's successor was Grandisson, one of Exeter's greatest bishops. According to Wikipedia there was mention in Coulton's *Social Life in Britain* of a section from *Grandisson's Register* that said Berkeley had been murdered and his estates despoiled.

I am not convinced. This is the only mention I have seen (in Wikipedia, I mean) of this murder and despoilation. Looking in

Coulton's book, which was published in 1918, there is a foot-note on page 27 that reads: *Grandisson succeeded (after a very brief episcopate of John (sic) de Berkeley) to that Bishop Stapeldon whose murder is recounted in the* French Chronicle of London *(Camden Soc. 1844), P.52.*

I do wonder whether the mention of murder and the vision of rampaging hordes which it brings to mind are due to some-one's misreading Coulton's book when they put the comment up on Wikipedia.

Don't get me started on inaccurate quotations on Wikipedia!

However, although this researcher may have had a problem, there is no doubt that Berkeley's contemporaries did view his death in an especial light. For several years after his demise (and to the disgust of Bishop Grandisson, according to Professor Nicholas Orme in his *Death and Burial in Medieval Exeter*, Devon & Cornwall Record Society, 2003), pilgrims went to pray at his tomb. This cult lasted until the 1340s, after which it dwindled.

So, I was left with the idea of a bishop who was revered by his people, even to the extent that they would travel to visit his tomb under the disapproving eye of his successor. A man who had died suddenly – and a man with the magical name of Berkeley – just at the time that King Edward II was being held by Berkeley's brother at the castle that still holds their name. And also, of course, at the time when certain men were trying to free their King from that castle. *And* when the Dunheved brothers had succeeded in doing so.

Is it any wonder that a fiction writer would be attracted to this story?

As always, my gratitude goes to my copy editor, Joan Deitch; to my marvellous editor, Jessica Leeke; my agent Eddie Bell; and the many people who have contributed (knowingly or not) to the story: Jules Frusher, Kathryn Warner, the excellent Ian Mortimer, and all the many others whose research I have shamelessly pinched!

My greatest thanks must go to my wife and kids for their patience and fortitude during the writing and editing of yet another book. Love you all.

And as ever, any errors are my own.

Unless they were caused by my mislaying an important note after being called out to liberate a cricket ball from the barn roof . . .

Michael Jecks
North Dartmoor
July 2011

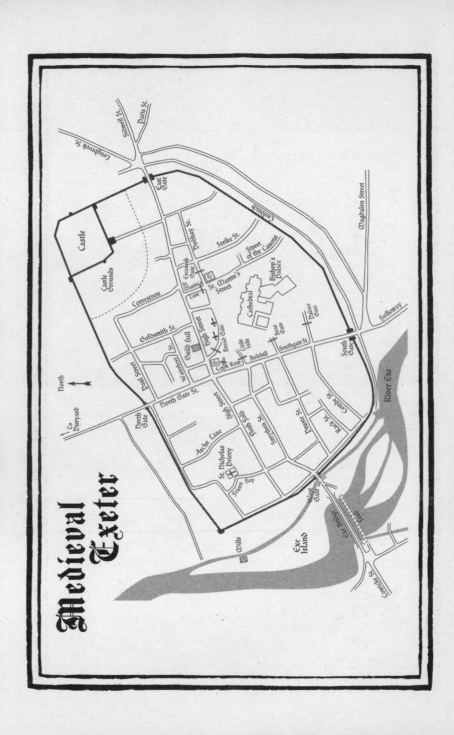

Medieval Exeter

North

To Duryard

North Gate
North Gate St.
Dual Street
Goldsmith St.
Correstrete
Castle Grounds
Castle
East Gate
Longbrook St.
Sidwell St.
Paris St.
Crollop

St. Ereneck Gate
St. Martin's Lane
St. Martin's Street
Dobbay St.
Strike St.
Street of the Canons
Bishop's Palace
Cathedral
Bear Gate
Palace Gate
Magdalen Street

High Street
Bread Gate
Little Stile
Bolehill
Southgate St.
South Gate
Holloway

Waterbeer St.
Guild Hall
Cook Row
Stepcote Hill
High Street
Smythen St.
Preaus St.
Rack St.
Combe St.

Arche Lane
St. Nicholas Priory
Friern Hay
West Gate
Exe Island
Mills

Exe Bridge
Leat
Combe St.

River Exe

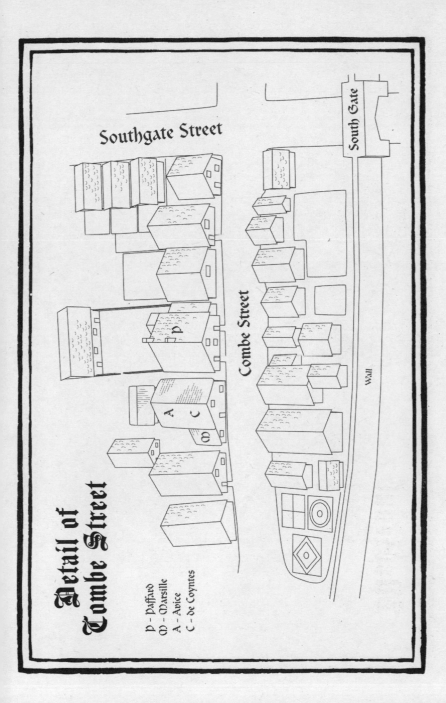

Detail of
Combe Street

Southgate Street

Combe Street

South Gate

Wall

P – Paffard
M – Marsille
A – Avice
C – de Coyntes

PROLOGUE

Relationships are always changing. Sometimes their adjustments are so gradual, we hardly notice them; occasionally they are shattered by shocks that devastate all concerned, but whether they alter with glacial or lightning speed, the effect can be profound.

In a family, in a village, in a city, the connections that matter most are those with our nearest family and friends, yet they are the ones which are tested daily. These are the people whom we can most easily upset – and yet they are the very ones upon whom we most depend.

Disputes can occur at the drop of a hat: a misinterpreted expression, a careless word, a hand held too long – all can lead to sharp words, bitterness and rancour.

Reconciliation may be straightforward if attempted with speed, but it is less certain when allowed to fester. It is better, so they say, not to sleep on a quarrel. But all too often men and women lie weeping into the night over cruel words. Words which were uttered in the heat of the moment and which were never intended to have a lasting impact; or worse, words which were precisely considered – and all the more vicious as a result.

In the year 1327, all over the kingdom people went about their business in a state of constant worry because they feared what the future might bring.

Their King, Edward II, had been forced to abdicate.

The uncertain political situation affected everyone: the merchants and traders of Exeter, just as much as elsewhere in the realm. In such a climate, even mild-mannered people became uncharacteristically quick to take offence; disagreements abounded and could grow into outright feuds, petty disputes into fist-fights. Even murder.

In one street in Exeter that June, an argument that arose from an ill-considered reckless threat grew to dominate the lives of all about and escalated into a disaster that would overwhelm them all with hideous acts of violence. All for love, for loyalty, or for honour.

And none of those who were intimate with the victims or protagonists would be untouched by the consequences.

CHAPTER ONE

Feast of the Nativity of St John the Baptist[1], first year of the reign of King Edward III

Petreshayes Manor, Yarcombe, East Devon

The smoke could be seen clearly from half a mile away. In the still air of the summer's evening, the columns rose from the manor's fires like pillars supporting the sky.

'Hold!' commanded Sir Charles of Lancaster, peering ahead. There was no sign of alarm. A wood on their left offered some protection, while to the right there were some fields, pasture, common land. All ideal for pursuing their victims, should they escape.

'Here we are, boys,' he breathed.

His men stared. There was a heightened tension, the awareness of an imminent fight. Breath rasped, and he heard the soft hiss of a blade being drawn, the jangle of bit, the squeak of leather, the hollow clop of a hoof.

1 Wednesday, 24 June 1327

'That's the manor,' his guide said. Wat Bakere was a rotund, smiling man, but he wore a scowl today. 'You'll find it easy to overrun. Kill them all.' He was pointing at the church and manorial buildings over at the other side of the dirt road. It curled about the line of the manor, which was a prominent landmark.

'You're sure they are there?'

'Ulric told you, didn't he? He said they would be,' Bakere said, jerking a thumb at the lad behind him.

Sir Charles nodded.

He was a tall man, fair and handsome as a Viking, and ruthless as a berserker. During the last civil war he had fought against the King for his lord, Thomas of Lancaster, and when Earl Lancaster was executed, Sir Charles had been exiled. That was five years ago, and when he begged for a pardon for his offences, his King had been gracious. He was rewarded with positions of trust, and given a living once more.

He asked for no more; he had given his word and his hand to his King, so when Edward II was captured by his enemies, Sir Charles became a recusant knight. He would not renege on the new oaths he had given his King. Instead he left the comfortable billet in the King's manor at Eltham where he had lived for the last months, and rode into the twilight to take up arms on the King's behalf.

Now the King's son had taken the throne, Sir Charles was a renegade. A felon. Because he would hold to his vow.

Today, with his band of warriors committed to the King, he would begin the fight to return Sir Edward of Caernarfon, as he was now labelled, to his natural place on the throne of England.

Sir Charles looked at Ulric of Exeter. He was more trustworthy than Wat Bakere. Bakere had been given to him by Stephen Dunheved, a man who appreciated the value of good information, but it was Ulric, the merchant's fellow, who had brought the details. Returning his gaze to Bakere, he nodded.

'You were the baker at this manor?'

Bakere rolled his eyes impatiently. 'Yes. I told you – I'd been here two years when I left a fortnight ago.'

'But even then you heard that the Bishop and his entourage were to come here?'

'Yes.' Wat looked up at him, his eyes creased in sardonic amusement. 'You don't know what it's like. They hear their lord's coming to visit, and all hell is let loose! Rooms must be cleaned, beasts must be slaughtered, money must be counted and recounted, food stores checked so the master can see nothing's been lost or stolen . . . there's no peace for anyone. As soon as his visit was announced, the villeins were driven lunatic by the steward's demands. So was I. I needed more flour for their food, and the steward was never willing to—'

'What makes a man like you become disloyal to his master, I wonder?'

'I owe them *nothing*!'

'I see,' Sir Charles said languidly. He suspected that Wat had been found with his hand in the food bin. Bakers were notorious for making undersized loaves, keeping back the excess flour to sell, or making their own loaves larger than those for others. A greedy little man, this Wat.

He turned his attention back to Ulric. The scrawny wretch was looking miserable. It was he who had brought confirmation that Bishop James Berkeley was heading this way, and now he knew the consequences of his report, he was regretting it. The lad was too young; he needed his spine stiffened.

Sir Charles studied the road ahead and soon made his dispositions. The men for the woods dismounted, the youngest boys taking the reins while the older men shifted their weapons on their belts, bound quivers to their hips or backs, laced their bracers, and strung their bows. There was little sound from any. All knew their part.

Those on foot were to work their way to the north of the manor and drive the terrified workers south, to where the horsemen could cut them to pieces. After that they would head for the manor itself. Easy prey, these, although it was best not to be complacent. Sir Charles had once been all but bested by a pathetic-looking chaplain who had displayed a ferocity in fighting that was more suited to a Teutonic Knight.

The men were disappearing into the trees already. When the last was gone, Sir Charles nodded to himself. He would wait until he saw the first signs of panic in the fields, then race down and destroy the peasants.

Wat's eyes were fixed on the scene ahead. 'They don't realise what's going to hit them,' he said with glee.

'Few ever do,' Sir Charles smiled.

Wat was about to speak again when the knight's fist caught him in the chest. He jerked with the slamming shock, then hunched to save himself being thrown over the cantle, and glared at Sir Charles.

'What's that for?' he gasped, but even as he spoke, his eyes fell to the mailed fist at his breast.

Sir Charles pulled his hand away, tugging the long-bladed dagger free, and Wat's mouth moved without sound as he gaped at the knight. Then his body convulsed, his head snapping back, and he fell from the saddle, twitching and thrashing on the ground in his death-throes.

'That, boy,' Sir Charles called to Ulric, 'is what happens to rude sons-of-whores who are disrespectful to their betters. Remember that. And also remember, I distrust those who are dishonourable and faithless.'

He smiled, and Ulric, who had been staring at the body lying on the ground, found that smile more terrifying than any outburst of rage.

It was like the smile of the devil.

Marsilles' House, Exeter

William Marsille nodded to his neighbour Mistress Emma de Coyntes as he walked home up the alleyway from Combe Street, and was surprised when she ignored him.

Pretending not to notice her manner, he pushed his door open, saying to his brother as he entered, 'Emma's pissed off about something again.'

'What is it this time?'

His brother Philip, two years older at eighteen, sounded grumpy. He spent half his life snapping at William now. Perhaps it was the hunger.

William reached the sideboard – which was one of the few items of furniture that they'd rescued from their old home – poured himself a cup of wine from the cracked earthenware jug, and drank. 'No idea. She just ignored me. You know what she's like. 'Er wouldn't 'cknowledge me if I 'uz on vire,' he added with a grin.

His attempt at humour failed.

'Pathetic!' Philip muttered with a viciousness that surprised William. 'We spend our lives trying to soothe her ruffled feathers, but we always end up with the sharp end of her tongue, the stupid bitch!' There was something alarming in his over-reaction.

'She was all over us like a rash when we were rich,' William agreed. 'Now we are poor she can exercise her contempt for us while she tries to suck up to the next lot of fools. We can live without her sort of friendship, Phil.'

'Yes, she was always hanging around like a wart when we

7

had money,' Philip ranted. 'Why can't she give some peace now? That's all, just a bit of peace!'

'I think I prefer her like this,' William said. 'Philip, are you all right?'

Philip nodded. His normally animated features were pale. 'It's nothing. Just . . . Oh, God's teeth! Just leave me alone,' he said, and wiped his hand over his face, as though remembering a disaster that pained him. Then, with a gesture of despair, he blundered from the room leaving William staring after him.

Petreshayes

Sir Charles could make out his men at the edge of the woods as the light faded. Shortly the fight would begin. He enjoyed the feeling of liquid fire in his belly. A sharp battle, the slaying of his enemies: he was looking forward to it!

He drew his sword, held it before him and bent his head a little to the cross, kissing it. He was doing God's work today, upholding His will.

'Ready!' he roared, lifting his arm so the rest could see his sword. He heard the slither of metal being drawn from all around him, and was about to give the order to canter towards the manor, when Ulric gave a cry.

Sir Charles followed his pointing finger. There, on the road curving across from their right, was a raggle-taggle line of men. A great flag moved in the air above them; there was a strong contingent of men-at-arms, walking men, carts, a wagon – all in all at least fifty men.

He threw a look at the lad beside him. 'Well?'

'It's *them*. They must have been delayed on their way here,' Ulric said.

'You are sure?'

'I know the Bishop's banner – gold chevron on a scarlet

background with ten crosses. Anyway, look at the men there! Most are clerics.'

Sir Charles gave a wolfish grin. Thinly on the air he could hear the shouts and screams of peasants dying under the first flights of arrows. The manor's peasants would be fully occupied in protecting themselves, and would pay no heed to the attack on travellers.

He stood in his stirrups and gestured with his sword. 'There! There! To Bishop James of Exeter! Ride with me!'

Cooks' Row, Exeter

The sun was sinking as Joan hurried back down Cooks' Row into Bolehill with her loaf of bread, the limewashed buildings on the other side of the road drenched with an orange glow. The colour reminded her of bodies writhing in the firelight, and the thought made her shudder. She averted her head from the buildings, from the pictures in her head, her belly curdling.

There was a crunch from an alley, and she felt her heart pound like hooves at full gallop. She turned reluctantly, staring, only to see a baker's boy breaking up staves from a broken box for firewood. He glanced at her without interest before returning to his task.

She hated the city, with its tiny, narrow alleys and reeking, clamorous streets. The rich lived well, the clergy better, but for the others who eked out an existence, it was horrible. She was fortunate that she at least had a place in a merchant's house, but if for some reason she upset her master, she would be out on the streets in an instant, and probably forced to join the other women in the stews.

At first it had been exciting, being away from her bully of a father, with his cidery breath, and the sting of his belt, away from the cold, dismal hovel, but just lately, for Joan, Exeter had become a place of fear. Walking the streets was unsettling; the people were so brash, so threatening. Only last morning she had felt a man's hand on her arse as she passed by an alehouse, saw his other hand reaching for her breast. He could have pulled her into an alleyway, like some common draggle-tail. She'd only escaped with difficulty.

But there was worse here than the streets. Here there was the terror of the soul.

If Joan could, she would return home. Apologise to her father. She had run away in a fit of pique after an argument, and wished she could go back, admit that her dreams of finding a husband, an easy life, in Exeter, had failed.

She couldn't. Her father was an unforgiving man, who would never let her forget her failure. Her life would be made unbearable.

It had seemed such good fortune when she found a position in the home of Henry Paffard. Their last maid had run away, and she was lucky to be settled so quickly.

That's how it had seemed, anyway.

Steps. She heard steps – a panicky, bolting sound – and she darted into a darkened corner, eyes wide in sudden fear. A man came hurtling around the corner, arms slamming back and forth in his mad rush, his robe flying high. A priest, then, and running away from the Paffards' house. She watched as he pelted up into Southgate Street, then away, out of sight.

Petreshayes

Their surprise attack threw the weary men-at-arms into disorder. They had not expected an ambush here, so close to the manor.

Sir Charles bellowed with joy as he cantered into the guards about the Bishop. There was a man on his right, and he hacked at him with his sword, saw a gout of blood, and then he was at the next, a terrified-looking fellow with a heavy riding sword. Sir Charles knocked his blade aside and thrust his pommel into the man's face, feeling the bones crunch, before spurring on to the Bishop.

Bishop Berkeley was no coward. He had a sword of his own, and was as experienced as any nobleman. His blade was up, and he rode on to aim at Sir Charles with a roar of anger.

Sir Charles turned as the edge flashed past his shoulder, rolling back to slash, then used the point.

It caught the Bishop in the throat, and Sir Charles felt his sword jerk in his grip. Looking over his shoulder, he saw his victim huddle as if to hide from the assailants, but then one of his archers slammed down with a war-hammer, and the Bishop was thrown off his horse. The hammer rose and fell – and Bishop Berkeley was dead.

His banner was already trampled on the ground, and as Sir Charles turned, he spotted the remains of the Bishop's guard galloping off towards the manor.

'With me, with me!' he roared, and hared off after them, his soul singing with the joy of the encounter.

Yes. Today, he was doing God's work.

Alley beside Paffards' house

She was panting. The sight of that priest's terror was enough to bring back all her own terrors. Thank the Holy Mother she was close to the house now. The mass of the South Gate was in front of her, and she turned right, along Combe Street. Only a very little way to go now.

The house was imposing, with its great height on three levels, yet narrow. Steps were cut in stone before it, bridging the filth of the gutter. Today the area stank even more than usual.

Someone had left the corpse of a dog in the road, and now, trampled and squashed by cartwheels and hooves, it rotted half-hidden beneath the bridge where it had been kicked.

To the right lay one door, which opened onto the place of work. Here the merchant plied his trade, while the other, to the left, was where he would invite his guests, clients and friends. They would enter to his welcome, drawn along the passageway to the hall behind where his fire would cheer any visitor.

These doors were not for her. She was only a maid: the lowliest servant in his employ, not even the equal of Alice. She must use the alley on the farther side. This led to the rear of the house, where servants and apprentices were expected to gain entrance, but from here, it looked like the entrance to hell. She hesitated. She always did. It was like the little copse of trees back at home, where it was said a woman once hanged herself. All the children knew that place, and all avoided it. This had a similar brooding menace.

There was little light here, between the buildings, and she kept her eyes ahead as she hurried down the alley. If she looked about her, she might see something, and it was better not to dwell on *that*. There was a skittering of claws, and she imagined rats scurrying.

She had to keep away from the wall's edge on the left here, she remembered. A dead cat's corpse lay there, and she didn't want to carry the reek of carrion on her shoes.

At last she saw a lighter patch a few yards away, and grunted with relief. This was the little door in the wall that gave into the garden behind the kitchen – *sanctuary*. Without conscious thought she increased her pace but, just as she was about to reach the gate, her foot caught on something and she tumbled to the ground, dropping her package and breaking her fall with her hands, grazing both on the stones and dirt of the alley floor.

'Oh, what . . . ?'

She clambered to her feet, and saw the head she had tripped over. She took in the fixed gaze from those dimmed blue eyes, the bright, red lips with the small trickle of blood, the golden hair surrounding the young woman's face, and began to scream and scream as she desperately scrabbled for the door handle, to get her away from that hideous stare.

CHAPTER TWO

Paffards' House

In his bed, six-year-old Thomas Paffard heard the maid's screams, and his eyes snapped wide. He didn't dare move until he heard men shouting. The knowledge that other grown-ups were there made him relax slightly.

'Mother?'

His bed was low, and he pulled his legs up to his chest as he listened. He couldn't recognise the voice of the person screaming. It almost wasn't human.

'Mother?'

He had heard a dog being killed once. Thomas had found it wandering in the streets, when he was only four years old, and had brought it back to the house here, concealing it out in the yard in a small lean-to that used to hold the family pig. After his meal, he took pieces of bread and some meat to it, and fed it, and the dog had been grateful. It had wagged its tail, and it made Thomas feel happy. His heart seemed to grow bigger, and he knew he loved it.

His family had never owned a dog. Most of his friends had a little dog of some sort, and he couldn't understand why he didn't. He was sure his mother would let him keep this one, if he told her about it, but Father and John, their bottler, didn't like dogs. He couldn't see why. It didn't make sense to the young lad. So he didn't tell anyone.

But it is difficult to conceal a dog.

That night, while Thomas slept, it had escaped from the makeshift kennel and began to bark and howl in the yard. That had sounded scary, too. Thomas had heard it, and the noise woke him in the end. He sat up in bed, rubbing his eyes, and then felt his whole body grow cold as he realised that if it had woken *him*, John might hear it and go down and hurt it.

Thomas quickly climbed from his bed and stole to his door, hoping to get outside before anyone could waken. And then, as his finger lifted the latch, he heard a horrible, wet sound, and the barking changed into a screech of agony. There was that wet thudding sound again, and then once more, and the noise died.

He never saw his dog again. There was a patch of redness on the dirt by John's old shed, where he stored the ales and wines in their barrels, near to where a plank had been badly scratched. It looked to Thomas as though the little dog, *his* little dog, had been scrabbling to get in there, under the raised floor, to escape the spade of the bottler.

Thomas had never brought another dog home. He couldn't bear to think of a second being killed.

'Mother?'

'It's all right, dear. Go back to sleep. It's nothing to worry you,' his mother called from the next room, and with renewed confidence, knowing that she was there, he rolled over in bed and closed his eyes.

But in his mind, he still saw that poor dog. His darling little dog.

Alley beside the Paffards' House

Standing in the gloom, Henry Paffard tapped his foot impatiently as the neighbours gathered. A boy with a horn lamp shed a pale glow over the scene, his own eyes fixed on the corpse.

Henry had been standing here since the first alarm. It really was time they got on with things. A man of his status shouldn't be forced to wait out here like a peasant.

'Where is Juliana Marsille and her boys?' he demanded, but nobody answered. His wife looked at him, then glanced away. She was shivering with cold.

Henry Paffard was tall and strong, with the blue eyes and fair hair of a king, but today as he looked along the alley at the huddle of death, he felt the sadness again. Poor, sweet Alice.

All his life he had been fortunate. He had sired two boys and a girl: the boys to secure his future, the girl to bring him a noble connection. Agatha would one day be a useful bargaining chip. The boys, meanwhile, were healthy and intelligent. Not like others. He had not even suffered the loss of a child.

Only this maid, he told himself with a frown. Only Alice.

The watchman who had been sent to beat on the Marsilles' door at last returned with Philip and William.

Philip looked as peevish as ever, Henry reckoned, while his younger brother William was his usual self, ducking his head in polite acknowledgement to the others before glancing down at the body with every appearance of sorrow.

The reaction of his brother was shocking, womanish.

When Philip recognised Alice, he seemed to crumble, his face a mask of anguish. It was ludicrous behaviour, Henry Paffard thought impatiently. Most lads his age would bear up, show a little backbone. Not Philip Marsille. He'd simply fallen apart after his father's death. While his brother held himself like a petty baron, Philip was going to pieces.

Henry sighed, deeply. They really should hurry along. Poor Alice couldn't be helped by any of them now.

'Let us get this over with,' he called.

The watchman nodded and looked at the four neighbours. 'This girl is dead, and I believe she was deliberately killed and left here. You are the nearest families. Do you recognise her?'

It was a formality, of course. As the boy with the lamp held it to the girl's face, they all recognised Alice, maid to the Paffards. Henry mumbled his assent, while a lump grew in his throat. It was hard to speak with the sight of that lovely face so spoiled. However, he had no intention of displaying any emotion in front of these churls.

'Good. I name Joan, maid to Henry Paffard, to be First Finder. You know what that means, maid? When the Coroner arrives, you'll have to come and tell him how you found the body.'

'I know.'

'You are all to come as soon as the Coroner is here,' the watchman said more loudly, staring at the men of each household in turn. 'Any who don't come will be attached and fined. All understand? Right, then. You will need to guard this body. Who volunteers?'

Henry avoided the man's look. It was a bit much to expect a man like him to stand out here in the alley all night. He was relieved to hear William Marsille say he would stand guard for the first half of the night, his brother for the second. They were younger, after all. Better suited for this sort of duty.

There was a sharp cry from behind him, and Henry turned to see Juliana Marsille pelting down the narrow way.

'What is this? Oh, God, no!' she cried as she saw the body, and looked as if she might faint at any moment.

'Mother, it's fine,' William said quickly, stepping around the body and holding out his hands. 'Don't worry. We'll guard her till morning. That's all.'

But Henry had seen the way her eyes had gone to her sons – accusingly, or so he thought.

Petreshayes Manor

Sir Charles walked about the manor with the excitement of the battle still thrumming in his blood.

He had been alarmed when some of the men had formed a wall before the manor's doors, but it took only one charge of his mounted force to shatter that, and soon all the villeins were dead, while a few of the manor's lay brothers were captured. Two were too badly injured to be of any help, and Sir Charles motioned to his men to finish them off. They died quickly.

The others soon led him to where the Bishop's accounts and money were stored. There was a good strongbox in a locked cellar, and the key on the dead steward's belt opened both.

'Bring the Bishop's carts in here,' he shouted at the men milling in the open yard area before the manor, and walking inside again.

The buttery had a small barrel of good Bordeaux wine, and he broached it, filling a horn he found on a shelf. Draining it, he topped it up and walked to the hall.

Ulric was in there, sitting with his back to the wall, arms about his knees.

'Boy! You will keep this horn filled for me.'

Ulric looked up, but said nothing.

'I can understand your feelings,' Sir Charles said. 'You think

I have forced you to betray your faith, to make you complicit in the death of the Bishop.'

'I didn't know I was sent to ensure my Lord Bishop's murder!'

'No. I daresay you didn't,' Sir Charles said. He sipped. 'But in reality I have not. I have helped you to ensure that God's will is done. Would you gainsay His wishes?'

'No!'

'The Bishop was installed after the death of Sir Walter Stapledon, who died in London last year, and the Canons of Exeter elected Bishop Berkeley. But the Pope did not. The Pope was hoping for another. And the Pope is God's own vicar on earth, is he not? Quite.'

'He was the Bishop, though.'

'He was the brother of Lord Berkeley, who is holding your King in his gaol. King Edward, who was anointed by God as King of England, was captured by traitors, and even now is in a cell, while his son has been told to take his throne from him.'

'How does killing the Bishop help?'

Sir Charles was becoming irritated. 'His death will begin to bring Lord Berkeley to reconsider, I hope. Berkeley has betrayed his own oaths to his King, and this is but the first of his punishments. And meanwhile . . .'

'Sir?'

'Meanwhile, my horn is empty, boy. Fetch me wine!' Sir Charles rasped.

There was no need to tell Ulric about the other force, led by the Dunheved brothers, who even now would be trying to release the King from his prison at Berkeley Castle.

For the death of Bishop Berkeley was only the beginning. Soon, armed men would rise up all over the country, working to destabilise this inept and illegal government, and return King Edward II to his throne.

Paffards' House

Joan sat on her palliasse, her arms wrapped about her legs as she shivered, staring at the door.

She had a vision rising up before her horrified eyes: Alice's body. But even as she saw her friend's dead face another picture intruded: naked bodies writhing on the floor beside the fire, the orange flames illuminating their passion. It was so shocking, she had gasped.

And then Gregory Paffard heard her; he looked up and saw her and his little brother Thomas watching, and there was rage in his eyes. The sort of rage that promises punishment and retribution.

She was petrified.

Morrow of the Feast of the Nativity of St John the Baptist[1]

Precentor's House, Exeter Cathedral

He was not fussy, he told himself as he sat at his table, but he did like things *just so*.

If asked, Adam Murimuth would have described himself as an affable man in his fifty-second year. His face had the look of one who had never known hunger or hardship. He had spent all his adult life in the Church, and was a Doctor of Civil Law as well as being a priest. He enjoyed the trust of the Pope and of kings, and his friendship was sought out by bishops – which was why he was simultaneously a Canon of Hereford and Exeter.

For some years he had clambered up the ladder of promotion in the Church. He had taken patronage where it was available,

---

1 Thursday, 25 June 1327

buying positions when he could, retaining friends who were powerful, discarding those who could embarrass him. He was a highly respected figure – and yet here he was, scrabbling about, trying to find a knife for his quill.

It was annoying. When he came to his table this morning he discovered that his little penknife was missing, and that his ink had been mixed weak. His quill, a good new one, was unprepared, and how on earth could he write his journal without a decent pen?

He had begun to write this little memoir twenty years ago. Of course, then he had still been a callow young man, without the experience that life could bring. No man, he believed, should contemplate recording a life until he had lived one.

At last he found his knife on the floor, where it had fallen beneath the table. He stripped the fletchings from his quill and began laboriously to shape the pen's end. Satisfied, he dipped it into the insipid ink and stared at the greyish staining on the nib with distaste while he prepared himself to write. For some moments he did not move, holding the quill over the paper, staring at the window ahead of him, the strip of parchment as blank as his mind.

Mornings like this were infuriating. There was nothing much to note. Little happened in this quiet little Close. There was some bickering about how the Close was looking, scruffy and unkempt, with horses wandering over the grass, men standing and haggling over deals, or gambling or brawling – even women plying their unsavoury trade. He had found one rutting with her client behind the Treasurer's House last week – a disgraceful site for fornication!

But these were not the memories he wished to record. Ach!

Setting the quill on his desk, he rose and walked around his room, head down, contemplating, and then as inspiration suddenly came to him, he resumed his seat and picked up his quill once more.

The door opened and his steward slid around it like oil under a gate. Adam looked up irritably. 'What on earth is the matter? You know that this is my time to write.'

'Sir, I am sorry, but Janekyn would like to speak with you.'

'What about?'

'Something to do with the murder last night.'

'Murder? What – here?' Adam hadn't heard of a killing. 'In the Close, do you mean?'

'No, sir, out along Combe Street, I heard.'

'What of it? It's a city matter. Oh, never mind. Show him in,' Adam said grumpily. He put his pen back down and stared at the empty sheet. Today, he felt sure, he would never write a thing.

Soon Janekyn Beyvyn, the porter from the Broad Gate of the Close, entered, shooting little glances all about him with that expression of nervous awe that servants so often exhibited. They were unused to such magnificence.

'Porter, my steward tells me you want to speak to me. Well?'

Janekyn nodded. 'Sir, last night there was a maid killed. It was a way away, but as I was closing the gates, I heard running.'

'Did you see the man?'

'No, sir.'

'So, then? What of it?'

'My fear was, where the footsteps went.'

'Explain yourself, man!'

Janekyn cleared his throat. 'I think they came into the Close, sir. It was someone from the Cathedral.'

CHAPTER THREE

Combe Street, Exeter

It had been an unprofitable day for William Marsille. Again.

He had set aside thoughts of Alice lying dead in the alley as soon as he had risen, and had come here to the Cathedral in the hope that his prayers might succeed in winning him work with the masons. He must earn some money somehow, and he had tried every other possible avenue.

He had hoped that sheer determination and persistence would persuade a mason or carpenter to hire him, but they only laughed at him.

'Come here, boy,' one had called, a heavy-set man a clear six inches shorter than William. He'd been to a barber recently, so his beard and head were well shaven as he pinched and prodded William's arms. 'Did you ever have a muscle on them, boy?' he laughed.

Another man was behind him, and he squeezed the flesh of William's thighs and buttocks hard enough to hurt. 'He couldn't carry a hod, and those spindleshank legs of his won't drive the treadmill.'

The first was eyeing him up and down. 'Give me your hands ... thought so. You've never done a day's real work, have you, boy?'

'I can add, write and read, and I'm used to accounting.'

'Then go and speak to someone who has need of such skills. We don't. We need carpenters, masons, plumbers and all the others who can help build a cathedral, not parchment-scratchers. Well?' he said, standing back, arms akimbo. 'Go on, get up there.'

'Where?'

The mason pointed to the nearest ladder. 'There. That one'll do.'

William stared at it. The thing was immensely long, reaching up to the third level. The larch poles of the scaffolding had some kind of rope that bound the cross members to each other, and while William had heard that sailors tended to be used for lashing the poles to each other, he could see clearly that the ladder had nothing to hold it steady.

'What ails you?' the mason said, and the others all laughed.

He walked to the ladder, set his hands on the rough rung, and began to climb. He did so with a steady carefulness, and a rising panic as, after ten or twelve feet, the whole contraption began to bounce. It felt as though he must be catapulted from it, and his speed slowed as he approached the middle. Here it was terrifying. He clung with knuckles whitened, as the ladder sprang in and out, towards the new cathedral walls, and away again. His thighs turned to water. He could no more climb than jump, and he must set his entire body flat against the madly bouncing contraption, his eyes shut. Surely it would fly away from the wall at any moment.

Looking down, he saw that all the masons had left. He was alone, desolate in his failure. Slowly, he let himself down to solid ground once more.

Thrusting his thumbs in his belt, he walked down the Close and went out by the Bear Gate. While there, he saw the old beggar woman who had her post there. Reaching into his purse, he was about to throw her a penny, when he realised he had nothing. She had more money than he. With a mumbled apology, shame firing his face a dull beetroot, he scurried past her, and out to Southgate Street.

Here he almost bumped into someone. William tried to apologise, but his tongue clove to the roof of his mouth.

The man was his height, with pale, waxen features, and a long, straggling beard that reached to his middle-breast. His clothing was a mixture of tattered shreds: there was a once-good tunic that was sorely worn, a fustian cloak, and hessian sacking covered his legs. In a bundle he clutched to his chest were all his worldly belongings. But it was his eyes that caught William's attention. They were wild, terrified. The eyes of a man who had lost everything, and knew that life would never improve. He must walk, and hope to find food. That was his entire life.

William stared after him. That sight, he felt, was a revelation. An appalling picture of how he might look in a short time, if he and Philip could find no work and money: a desperate vagrant dependent upon the alms of the Church just to exist.

Petreshayes

Sir Charles stood at the gateway and donned his worn riding gloves as he watched the three men. They were gathering with their torches about a brazier. The two survivors of the manor were in the doorway, hands bound, and Sir Charles nodded to the two guards with them.

He turned and took his horse's reins from Ulric. 'Watch,' he said, slipping his boot into the stirrup and springing up into his saddle.

25

The lad was still looking very pale. Sir Charles had almost expected him to fly from the place in the dead of night, and it was with a vague sense of pride that he had beheld Ulric's earnest features this morning.

Sir Charles knew what was happening without watching. The two men took their daggers and stabbed, one quickly thrusting in his victim's back, the other sweeping his blade about the man's throat.

Ulric winced, and tottered as though he was going to fall, but then threw a look at Sir Charles. 'What, are you telling me you will do that to me in a moment?' he said hoarsely.

'No, my fellow. I am merely showing you what will be happening all over here soon. The King will be fighting for his kingdom, and all those who stand in his path will die, like them. It is the way of war, the way of the *chevauchée*. When there is war, men-at-arms will ride all about the country, creating fear and panic in the hearts of those who stand against them. We must do this now. And while we do, others will take up arms against us, and they will terrorise our friends and family. If you want, you can go back to the city, and live there.'

Ulric looked down. The man with the slashed throat was squirming ever more slowly, his blood staining the ground. At his side, the other man was already dead, an expression of surprise on his face.

'Choose, then. Are you with us, with your lawful King, the man anointed by God, or not?'

'I am with you,' Ulric said dully.

'Good! Mount your beast, boy,' Sir Charles said with a smile. He glanced at the three with the torches and jerked his head. In a moment, all three had lighted their torches and then flung them in through the open doorway. There was a *whump* as the oils drizzled over the floor and beams caught fire, and almost immediately a thick, black smoke roiled from the door and open window.

Sir Charles eyed it with satisfaction. 'Come, my friends! It is time to visit terror on Devon!'

Rougemont Castle, Exeter

Adam Murimuth walked in at the red sandstone gate and peered about him. ,

He did not like this castle. As Precentor, he had had to come here on various occasions. The last had been in the spring, when there had been a fight in the High Street near the Guild Hall. Two servants of the Cathedral had been rightly infuriated to see a Dominican preaching to some folk, and had remonstrated. The friar loudly rejected their justified arguments, and a small crowd gathered.

As the dispute grew more heated, locals joined to take sides, and in the end it was necessary for some men-at-arms to come to cool tempers. Not that they had succeeded. The ensuing fracas had been ended only when a few sensible traders managed to calm the troubled folk.

And the cause of the escalating violence? The preacher and the servants were abusing each other in fluent Latin, the locals had interjected in their mixed languages, some in Celtic, some in English, while the castle's men had reverted to Norman French when they lost their tempers. In the babel that ensued, it was only when three merchants fluent in a variety of languages had interposed, that peace was restored.

The castle was a symbol of the power of the Sheriff, and Adam resented the man and his authority. However, thankfully Sheriff de Cockington had no control over the Cathedral or its staff.

'Sheriff,' Adam began when at last he was permitted to enter the hall itself, 'I fear that there has been a death in the city.'

'Aye, a maid was murdered. What of it?'

'I wished to know what the Coroner thinks of the matter.'

The Sheriff gazed at him. He was a pompous fellow, this James de Cockington, Murimuth thought. He remembered his pale eyes staring at him before, with that same look, when they were discussing the fight in the High Street. Even then, he had been certain that the man was searching for a way to request a bribe, rather than seek resolution.

'What is a murder in the city to do with the Cathedral, Precentor?' he asked smoothly.

'Probably nothing. But it occurred near enough to the Close for us to hear it. When will the Coroner be here to review the matter?'

The Sheriff sucked at his teeth. 'Perhaps the day after tomorrow – maybe not until Sunday. He has been away, down at Ashburton. A tin miner was found hanged down there, and the Coroner left yesterday. It is a full day's ride to Ashburton, since the roads are appalling. I would think he would hold his inquest today or tomorrow, and return Saturday.'

'Good, good,' Murimuth said.

'You will wish to send a witness to hear the evidence?'

'Perhaps.' Murimuth ducked his head, preparatory to making his exit. He disliked dissembling. There were situations in which he felt comfortable, but this was not one of them. The Sheriff never impressed him with his intellect, but the man was the King's own representative.

'It would almost seem as if you knew something about this murder, Precentor,' the Sheriff said. 'Do you know who was responsible?'

'Certainly not!' Murimuth said. 'If I did, I would say so, to prevent another innocent being accused. Murder is a grave matter.'

That was the fact that absorbed him as he left the castle. Murder was indeed a serious affair, and if Janekyn was right, the murderer could have been one of the Cathedral's inhabitants.

He stopped at the High Street. There were some people coming into the city from the East Gate, and he saw a watchman on the gate push a man leading a packhorse against the wall, while his companion began to search the panniers on the beast's back.

Nothing there, thank the Lord, and the sumpterman was soon on his way again, but it was just another proof to Murimuth of the tensions all felt. The King had been forced from his own throne, replaced by his fifteen-year-old son, and gangs of men were now ravaging the land in the old King's name. One such had breached the castle at Kenilworth, trying to free him, a few months ago. All the guards here, and elsewhere, were on tenterhooks, expecting a fresh upsurge of violence.

He made his way back to the Cathedral feeling depressed, convinced that there would be more bloodshed. There were too many men like the Sheriff who were out to seek personal advantage from the realm's troubles.

Until the kingdom was stabilised, with the new King grown to maturity, there would be no peace for anyone, only increasing disorder.

Well, that may be so, he told himself. But the disorder would only increase if men felt they could get away with it. It was vital to uphold the law, and show that justice would swiftly follow a crime, be it large or small.

He must do all he could to bring justice to the felon who killed that poor young maid.

Paffards' House

Benjamin, Henry Paffard's apprentice, had been to the church that morning, offering prayers for Alice. He would miss her. She had been a part of the household.

When he first arrived at Exeter, the boy had thought himself fortunate to be apprenticed to Henry Paffard. The latter was known as the best decorator of pewter in the city, but the glorious engraving for which he had made his name was a thing of the past. The work he performed today was at best pedestrian – when he could be bothered to visit the workshops. Henry was living on the reputation he had forged years ago, and Benjamin was hard-pressed to recall a single day during which he had learned anything from his master.

In those early days, before disillusion set in, everything had seemed possible. Benjamin was sure that, once he was ready, he would soon be made a pewterer in his own right, that he would set up his own little business, and start to earn his fortune. And over time, when luck allowed, he would meet a woman to marry, and he would raise his own family. And when he did, he would remain loyal to his wife.

But he had not done any of those things, and while he got on well enough with the other apprentices, there was none he could call an especial friend. Most, he suspected, looked down on him.

Of course, they all knew about Henry Paffard's nocturnal visits to Alice in her chamber, the trysts they held when they thought no one else was listening. Henry should not have insulted his poor wife by taking a maidservant as a lover. And when Claricia remonstrated with him, Henry had beaten her! That was not Christian. But nor was Alice's behaviour, and the couple's flagrant adultery brought disgrace to all in the house.

Henry Paffard's unseemly behaviour meant that Benjamin

would be forever remembered as the apprentice who lived with the reprobate – and *not* as the skilled artist of pewter which he hoped to become. His reputation was ruined before he could carve it out for himself.

For some weeks now, the pleasure he had once gained from working metal, the joy he had experienced at the sight of a perfectly rendered decoration cut into the metal, was lost to him. His disappointment gave him a bleak view of the future: he now was convinced he would never find a woman, never have children with her, never know the joy of a professional career.

In this bitter mood, he went to the buttery to fetch himself a strong ale, but the small cask there was low. He dared not empty it. Perhaps he could fetch a pot of ale from one of the barrels in John's locked storage room at the rear of the house? The keys hung on the bottler's belt usually, but today Benjamin had seen them resting on a protruding wooden peg. He hesitated, but then snatched them up. Pox on what the bottler might say!

Striding to the storage room, he unlocked the stiff door and tugged it wide. The cool interior always had a strange smell, like meat left drying for years, enhanced by the malty sweetness of the ales stored here after each brewing.

He stepped on the elm flooring, his feet echoing hollowly in the shed, and went to the nearer barrel, tapping it. There was a good, wholesome sound to it, and he fetched himself a mazer.

The bellow made him almost drop the cup. 'What are you doing in here?'

'John! Hell's teeth, you could have killed me!'

'I still may,' John said, his hand dropping to his knife. 'Why are you in here? Are you robbing our master?'

'God's honour, no! I was thirsty.'

'Thirsty? That's why you stole my keys? I put them down for a moment, and when I turn my back, you steal them and come to fleece my master! I trusted you, apprentice, and this is how you repay me?'

Ben was regretting his impulse now. 'I was thirsty,' he repeated, 'and you weren't there. I thought it was better to come and drink from here, rather than from the cask in the buttery. It's almost empty.'

'Oh,' grunted the bottler. He seemed to accept the lad's explanation and calmed down.

'I am sorry, Benjamin,' he said. 'We're all on edge, after what has happened. Just remember your duties, and all will sort itself out. Our lives are devoted to service, and that is how we shall be measured.'

'Yes. I'm sorry I took your keys,' Ben said contritely, passing them back. 'I won't do it again.'

'I hope you won't,' John said. He rubbed a hand over his face. 'I didn't mean to shout, boy. That young maid's death has affected us all.'

'Yes. Yes, it has.'

CHAPTER FOUR

Precentor's House

Adam Murimuth remained sitting at his desk when Janekyn Beyvyn entered with the vicar behind him.

'Come in and stand before me, Father Laurence,' the Precentor said. 'I wish to hear what you have to say.'

He was a good-looking fellow, Murimuth thought. Father Laurence Coscumbe was tall and ruddy-complexioned, with powerful shoulders and arms. He had the sort of face that would have suited a knight more than a man of God: square, rugged, with strong brows over intent, green eyes – a face that could have snared many a maid's heart. However, today there was a pained look about him.

'Do you know why you are here?'

'Janekyn saw me at the gate, Precentor. But that murder was nothing to do with me. I had been with Father Paul in his church, and when I realised how late was the hour, I hurried back. That is all.'

'Did you go into the lane where this maid was killed?'

'I didn't kill her, Precentor. I happened to be passing by on my way back from the Church of Holy Trinity, that is all. I would never harm a maid.'

'You didn't go up the road there?'

'Are you accusing me of kicking a maid to death?' Father Laurence demanded with spirit. 'Look at me! I am no felon, Precentor. I have never had an accusation of any kind against me. It is simple villeiny-saying to suggest I could have had anything to do with her injuries.'

Precentor Murimuth remained gazing at him for a long time, but the vicar stared back stolidly.

'Very well,' Murimuth said at last. 'You may go for now, but I think it would be well, were you to remain within the Close for some days. At least until after the inquest.'

'Yes, Precentor,' Laurence said. 'You may be right.'

Church of the Holy Trinity, South Gate

Father Paul watched as his little congregation drifted away from his church, and then made his own way from the nave into the small room at the north side.

He had a large chest here, and he pulled off his vestments and stored them carefully within it. The alb was showing its age, he thought, as he folded the long white linen tunic; and so were most of the other ceremonial items. His daily robes, too, he thought, glancing down. But it didn't matter, not today. He had other things on his mind.

Last evening, he had seen Philip Marsille out in the road. He knew the Marsilles, and how desperate was their plight, so he went to speak to the lad.

'Philip. Are you well?' he asked gently.

Philip looked up at him with eyes raw from weeping. He was a tall, well-favoured lad with a shock of fair hair and blue eyes in a pale face. 'You couldn't understand, Father. It's a matter of love between a man and a woman. Or not!' His eyes filled again, and he bent his head to his hands. Through them, he choked, 'She doesn't love me.'

There was the sound of a door opening, and Father Paul saw that Henry Paffard and his family were emerging from their home. Henry's son and daughter walked out, then his wife, all following after him like servants in a Canon's *familia*, descending the short flight of steps one by one.

Philip stared at them, his face working. The eldest son, Gregory, glanced back at him without emotion, as if the poor boy was beneath his dignity. The master of the house peered briefly at him, but Philip was his tenant, and what interest would a man like him have in a fatherless son, after all?

The lad should pull himself together, Father Paul thought. It was ridiculous that he should be so, so . . . overwrought.

It was then that Philip had hissed the words that so alarmed Father Paul.

'You bastard, Henry! You son of a pox-ridden whore! I'll kill you!'

Hearing of a murder in Combe Street, Father Paul had immediately assumed that Philip had gone ahead with his stated purpose: to strike down Henry Paffard. He had knelt in front of the cross, hands clasped, knowing he could have done nothing to prevent the crime, but rocking with the guilt nonetheless.

This morning, he had heard it was a maidservant who'd been killed – some wench trying her luck as a tickle-tail no doubt, and the relief had been overwhelming. If it had been Paffard, he would never have forgiven himself.

There were many such women selling themselves, tempting men with their leering and lascivious teasing. Only two weeks ago, one outside the Cock Inn had bared her breasts at him, offering him a tumble with a wink and a wriggle of her hips. He had flushed in an instant, and had gone back to the church as fast as he could, to pray for himself, and for the whore.

They were all women who had fallen from the path of virtue – he must try to remember that. Kindness was more important than condemnation.

He drank a cup of wine while he set his pottage over the little fire, and sat on his stool stirring; he was still there when the knock came at the door.

Rising with an effort, he went to open it. Outside were two women from the stews. 'What do you want?' he asked.

'It's not what we want, my lover,' slurred one. It was plain that she had been in an alehouse for hours. Sarra was typical of her kind, Father Paul thought – blowsy, red-faced, and with a cap that had slipped sideways to show her thick, coarse hair.

'No! We wanted to give you something,' the other said. She was younger, with a slight cast in one eye and a lop-sided grin that exposed a pair of broken teeth. He didn't know her name. Both were as thin as rakes.

Father Paul looked them up and down, and then sighed. 'Come inside.'

Friday after the Feast of the Nativity of St John the Baptist[1]

Combe Street

Juliana Marsille, a slim woman of almost forty, with greying hair and flesh drawn tight over a heart-shaped face, was walking back from the baker's, a tiny loaf held carefully in her hands. It was all she could afford.

1 26 June 1327

She was unhappy. Two days ago she had lost Emma as a friend, and nothing she could do or say would repair the damage.

It had been one of those days. Juliana had been trying to talk sense into Philip, her son, but he paid no attention. It was *important*! She'd been talking about money, saying that he needed to find work, and when she saw him ignoring her, she had been infuriated: she slapped him, just to make him listen.

He had snapped. Catching her hands, he stared at her as though he didn't know her. For a moment, she had seen utter wildness in his eyes and knew he could have broken her neck without regret.

It was a shocking revelation, but she was not stupid enough to deny it. Philip was a man, not her darling little boy any more, and if she were to push him, he might strike back.

He was weak, that was the problem. He had no idea that for the family to survive, each must do their part. He was the head of the house now her poor, beloved Nicholas was dead.

She missed him so.

A pig's bladder skittered by, and the figure of Thomas Paffard darted past in pursuit, a thick-set little boy of six with a thatch of tallow hair above a face moulded into a frown of determination. With that fixed concentration on his features, he could be mistaken for a serious-minded child, but Juliana knew him better than that. His face was more usually broken almost in half by his broad grin. His blue eyes were seemingly designed for joy and for inspiring it in others. He was the sort of boy who could make any mother wish for a child again, just to enjoy those years of merriment and laughter.

'Hello, Thomas,' she called as he ran behind her to fetch his bladder.

He looked and gave her a shy smile that quickly faded, before returning at full pelt to his companions.

It was enough to make the breath catch in her throat, to make the sob begin deep in her breast, when she thought of her own older boy and what he had become.

Cock Inn, South Gate

The tavern was full of noxious fumes from the poor quality logs. The hearth was a small pit filled with ashes in the packed soil of the floor, and every now and again there was a loud crack from a splitting log, and a spark would be hurled over onto the rushes that lay all about. No one bothered to stamp it out, for with the amount of spilled ale, spittle, and urine from the host's dogs, there was little likelihood that the sodden flooring could catch light.

Philip Marsille walked in, feeling resentfully that everyone was staring at him as he made his way to the far side where the barrels were stacked.

They didn't understand what it was like. No one did. He had loved Alice with the honest conviction that she was the only woman he would ever love. All he needed to do was to rescue her from her life of servitude, and she would have adored him with an equal passion. That was all. He had planned his campaign, he had set his charm to work upon her, and he had been sure that she had begun to reciprocate his feelings . . . and then she threw it all back in his face.

She had *laughed* at him; she laughed at his endearments and promises of undying affection, she was scathing when he told her of the house he would have when he had made his fortune.

'Where is this house, Master Philip? Is it in the High Street near the Guild Hall, or behind it, where the goldsmiths work? Or is it in a small alley off Combe Street, here, where there're more rats than men, where cockroaches wander over the tables, and the walls are rotten and flimsy? You'll marry me and make me rich, you say? You don't know what "rich" is!'

'I love you, Alice. I can make you hap—,' he had begun, but she cut him off.

'I don't want your love. I am happy without you, so thank you, master, but I think I'll carry on alone.'

'You don't understand,' he attempted patiently.

'No, *you* don't understand. I am well off where I am. I get food, I get my bed, and I'm content.'

'But a life without love is a poor one.'

'What makes you think I live without love?' she retorted. 'But I will not be content with a poor fish like you! What do you have? You rent a foul hovel from Henry Paffard with your mother and brother, and you want me to join you there?'

Her contempt made him recoil, but still he had to try – he felt sure that if she only realised how deeply he felt for her, she must reconsider.

'Alice, if you would only . . .' he mumbled, and reached out to touch her hand.

She pulled it back with an expression of disgust. 'Keep away from me! If you touch me again, I'll tell my master about this. A word from me, and the whole pack of you will be out on the street. You want that? No? Then leave me alone!'

Even now, the memory of her words and the scorn in her eyes was enough to bring the hot blood to his face.

Combe Street

Juliana was almost back at the alley when she caught sight of Helewisia Avice.

'He's a pet, isn't he?' Helewisia said with a wistfulness in her tone as she eyed Thomas.

Juliana shot a look at the woman. Helewisia was tall, heavy

in build, with large breasts and a well-padded backside. In her youth she had been much sought-after for her looks, but they had flown when she and Roger lost their son, Piers. He had fallen into a well in a silly accident. Helewisia had watched other boys with jealous longing ever since.

'He is.'

'Hard to imagine such a lovely fellow born to that bastard Henry!'

Juliana was not surprised by the venom in her voice. 'Even the most miserable old sinner can father a saint.'

'You believe that? Well, I say a man's blood runs in his son's veins. Perhaps the boy is not his.'

'That is a dreadful thing to say,' Juliana gasped. 'Such villeiny-saying could get you into trouble, Helewisia.'

'Perhaps.'

Juliana was unsettled by her comments. Still, it was better than dwelling on Emma, the friend she had lost.

The event that had ended their friendship occurred soon after Philip had threatened her. She had been outside, and Sabina, Emma's young daughter, had been singing the same tune, over and over again, until Juliana had snapped. A combination of anxiety about money, and then Philip gripping her like that, which had shaken her badly, made her screech at Sabina to *just shut up*. The girl had fled, and now Emma ignored her. There was nothing she could do to put things right. Emma was the sort who would put up with anything, but not unkindness to her children. She would never talk to Juliana again.

Helewisia was staring at Thomas still. Juliana said, 'Is there any more news of the poor girl?'

'Alice? No. Nobody knows what happened.'

'The Coroner has been summoned?'

'Of course. But he's not in town. He'll come when he may.'

'It's horrible to have her left out there like garbage.'

'Aye, well. She was only a maid without honour.'

'Helewisia!' Juliana remonstrated, crossing herself. 'Don't speak ill of the poor thing.'

At that moment Claricia Paffard opened her door, a basket crooked in her arm. Seeing the two women, she joined them. She was of middle height, with hazel eyes in a sharp face that reminded Juliana of a ferret. On the surface, she was easy to dislike, with her money, her easy life, her affectations of superiority – but in fact she aroused sympathy in the hearts of many women in the neighbourhood. All of them knew of her husband's womanising. Today her whey-coloured features filled Juliana with compassion. To have had her maid murdered, and so near to their home at that, must have been horrible.

'Good morning, Gossips,' Claricia said.

The two nodded and muttered greetings, both wary in the face of their landlord's wife. She continued along the road towards Southgate Street while Juliana and Helewisia watched.

Neither noticed Emma approaching.

'So: have you worked out who killed her yet?' Emma asked when she was closer. She stood nearer Helewisia, and might have been unaware of Juliana's presence for all the notice she paid her.

'Us?' Helewisia burst out with surprise.

'Why not you?'

'I haven't heard anything,' Juliana said. She was relieved that Emma had come to them. Perhaps she was going to forgive her, after all. Holy Mother Mary, but she felt the need of a friend just now. Never more so.

But Emma paid her no heed. 'Helewisia, have you seen the Paffards' apprentice? He looked awful. You don't think he could have killed Alice, do you?'

'Surely not! Benjamin seems a pleasant fellow,' Juliana protested.

'When I went to Mass, I heard something interesting,' Emma said without apparently hearing Juliana. She looked at the children before adding quietly, 'They're all talking about it at the Cathedral. It seems the porter heard a man running after Alice's body was found.'

Juliana felt her heart begin to pound unpleasantly. She dreaded to hear what Emma might say next.

Emma leaned towards them. 'The man ran up the street and into the Cathedral, is what I heard.'

A shiver ran up Juliana's spine, and she almost had to catch hold of Helewisia to support herself.

'Are you all right?' Helewisia asked, seeing Juliana's face.

'Y-yes. Just the thought of that poor child lying out there. It's horrible to have to walk past her.'

She tried to pull herself together. She could hardly tell Emma and Helewisia how relieved she was: that until that moment she had suspected that her son Philip had killed the girl.

CHAPTER FIVE

Cock Inn, Southgate Street

'Brother, are you paying?' William had joined Philip, and he stood tugging at the fingers of his gloves as he eyed the others in the room. 'There are few enough in here with a penny for a pair of hardworking merchant's sons.'

'What of it?'

'I want to work, brother. I want to learn all the aspects of business our father was trying to teach us.'

'And how will you go about finding new clients?' Philip sneered. 'We're sons of a failure, Will. A *failure*. Nobody cares to remember Nicholas Marsille, and that means they won't be interested in us.'

'Well, I think that's where you're wrong. There are plenty of men who would help us, in memory of our father. He was well-liked.'

'If that's so, why are we in this state?' Philip had attracted the attention of the wench, who now deposited two green-coloured drinking horns before them. She was a slim girl, with ringlets of raven-black hair straying from beneath her wimple. She smiled at William as she waited to be paid.

William glanced at his brother with frustration, and finally reached into his own purse and dropped carefully counted coins into the maid's hand. 'There, Sal, but next time I want a kiss too,' he said.

She grinned and slapped away his hand as he allowed it to casually drop towards her thigh. 'Look but don't touch, Will Marsille!'

'Would you grudge a poor orphan boy a moment's solace?' he pleaded mock-seriously.

'You want that, go and find a girl at the stews. It'd only take you a moment, I'm sure,' Sal declared. 'She wouldn't be able to charge you much for her time.'

'Sal, Sal, I'll die for your cruelty!'

'I'd better take away your ale then,' she returned smarthy. 'Wouldn't want to waste it, would you?'

'Your heart is made of ice.'

'Aye, and it won't be melting any time soon.'

'Christ's ballocks, leave her alone,' Philip snapped. 'She's got work to do.'

Sal winked at William before striding away.

'Why take it out on her?' Will said without thinking, and then rolled his eyes. 'Sorry, Philip, I didn't consider what I was saying.'

'I take it out on her because she is a parnel from an inn. And not even a very good one. Offer her enough and she'll be your wife for the night, I have no doubt, but don't expect me to listen to your maunderings. I have better things to be doing.'

'She's not like that, Philip. She's a good woman. I know you're upset because of Alice's death, and—'

'*Alice?*'

'I know you loved her, Phil. I'm sorry she's dead.'

'You think I cared about that strumpet? The wench was nothing to me. In fact, I hated her.' Philip was drinking grimly, and his red-rimmed eyes were bleak.

'Buy me another drink,' he said, draining his drinking horn.

William shook his head and stood. 'We can't afford it, brother. Come on, let's get back.'

'You wander back to that shabby little midden if you must. I need air,' Philip said.

He rose and blundered from the room, pushing past a man with a muttered oath. It made William wince to see it. He didn't want to leave his brother alone in his misery, but could see no alternative. It wouldn't help either of them to come to blows.

Cook's Row

Walking about the market with her basket on her arm, Claricia Paffard tried to maintain the smile upon her face, but it was not easy.

Early on, their marriage had been perfect. Henry had been the successful apprentice of Master Roland de Witt, a master craftsman from Bruges who came to Exeter when young and decided to stay. The decision had been a sound one, for Exeter had no pewterer to compare with the fine work he could produce, and soon he had taken over almost all the market. In his workshops Henry had learned much about the mingling of the two metals, lead and tin, the forging and engraving, and while he was not as skilled at the actual mixing of the metals and the production of lustrous, gleaming pewter as Master Roland, his engravings had been so transparently superior to all the other workers in the city that he had grown his business very quickly.

Claricia had been happy. When they were first wedded, Henry had been engaging, exciting to talk with, and funny. He charmed her into his bed, and every day he had something extraordinary to share with her; whether it was to do with a design he had just thought of or some intriguing means of creating a new effect with the metal, hadn't mattered. She had enjoyed listening as he planned how he was going to enhance his work, where he would have his shop, how many apprentices he would employ, and how he would take the city by storm with his ideas on running the markets. And astonishingly, he had never lost that ambition and drive. All through the lean years when he was still scrabbling about for money to invest in a larger workshop, or tools, or when she fell pregnant with Gregory, Henry still had the vision of what he wanted to do firmly fixed in his mind, and exactly how he was going to do it.

The first betrayal had hurt so much, the second too; the third had been devastating. He should have come to terms with his life, and with her by then. How many affairs had he had? Claricia could count five that she knew of in the last twelve years. It was as if he could not control himself. He was like a dog smelling a bitch in season when a woman caught his eye.

She took her purchases and set off homewards.

All women had to grow accustomed to the fallibility of their men, she supposed. But accepting his behaviour did not mean she had to approve of it.

Ottery St Mary

The small manor had been unprepared, just as Sir Charles had hoped. They came across it early in the afternoon, after riding quickly without attacking anyone else in the vicinity, so that there should be no warning of their arrival. He had led his men at a trot, smiling and nodding to the lay brothers on all sides, before drawing steel and charging at the last moment. All the men had been killed.

'Go and check the undercrofts. See what there is to eat and

drink in this place,' he ordered as he entered the yard before the hall. There was a collection of farm buildings over at the far side, and the fish ponds looked as though they would be full. A net had been discarded at the side of the water. 'Some men have escaped, so keep your eyes open for someone who may seek to challenge our right to be here!'

He dismounted with relief. They had spent much time in the saddle in the past two days, but their sweep across the country had been successful. He had added three carts of booty to the ones he had taken from the Bishop's party, and gold and silver rattled merrily wherever they rode.

'Ulric, come with me,' he said.

Later, he would wonder if there had been some divine interference in that. He did not know why he called to Ulric to join him, it was a mere whim. But Sir Charles of Lancaster was nothing if not religious, and later events would make him wonder why the fancy had struck him.

Ulric walked along behind him. He still did not look like a warrior, but there was a sullen pugnacity about him that Sir Charles rather liked. Like a cur, whipped, but still loyal and ever hoping for a display of affection.

'You have never killed a man, have you?' Sir Charles asked.

'No.'

'The first time, it is quite hard. I was fifteen when I had to kill my first – a Scot who was riding into my Lord's lands to steal cattle. I remember him still, a foul-faced man with a black beard. I struck first because I knew if I didn't, he would kill me. So I drew, and with God's aid, I managed to stab him. He died. It took me some time to stop shaking. The next time, I was in a line with companions, and that was easier. It was a cruel war, that, but we won over. The Scottish are always ferocious fighters, boy. If you meet with them, you strike first.'

'Will I live long enough?' Ulric said directly.

Sir Charles had not expected him to be so forthright. The fellow's manner had led him to anticipate an unwilling obedience, as from a serf forced to work an extra week on his demesne lands.

After a moment's reflection, he said, 'If I learn you are seeking to harm us, I will destroy you without compunction. But if you are true to me, I will deal with you honourably, and you will share in my largesse. I am an old-fashioned man: I believe that those who are loyal should be cherished by me. If you are faithful, so too shall I be.'

Ulric nodded, and Sir Charles walked in front as they crossed the threshold into the hall.

It was a large room, with a tall ceiling, and a fire ready-made on the hearth. A dais at the far end of the hall held a large table and chairs, while benches and trestle tables sat at the walls. Sir Charles wandered about, looking at the room with a twisted smile on his face.

'The tapestry will be taken,' he said. 'I like hunting scenes, and the colours here are superb. The hart held at bay – it will look splendid in my own hall.'

'Where is your hall?' Ulric asked.

'I have none yet. I used to have a manor in Lancaster, and served my lord at the Scottish March, but I trust that when the King is returned to his throne, he will allow me a manor of my own. A small place near Bexley, that would be good. Close to London, but in the country. He has many little manors about there. And then I could live out my days in peace. You could join me, Ulric, hey? You and some few of the men here. I have always intended to set my lance in a rest and take up the sport of politics at some point. Perhaps when the King is returned, that would be my cue?'

He laughed then, an easy chuckle as he walked along the dais, his hand brushing the tapestry – and it was as he was past the scene of the hart that Ulric saw it.

There, at the point where the tapestry ended, he spotted the tip of steel, and he shouted as he flung himself at the weapon.

For a long time afterwards he asked himself why. Sir Charles was a fierce creature who would slay any man without remorse, wild and untameable as a boar, and yet Ulric threw himself forward and wrested the arm away from the knight's back before the blow could fall.

It was a servant of the manor, a young lad, scarcely old enough to shave, and he fought with despair rather than skill, flailing with his hands and a dagger, and Ulric felt its edge mark his forearm before he grabbed the fellow's wrist and clung to it with grim determination, while his face was buffeted by the other fist.

Sir Charles turned with a stunned expression to see Ulric rolling on the floor, grappling with the boy. Then he drew his sword and thrust quickly.

'Ulric, give me your hand,' he said, and helped him up. Then he grinned, holding Ulric's hand in his fist so that it was raised before both their faces. 'From hereon, you are mine. I will protect you as you have protected me. We are handfast, my friend.'

Saturday after the Feast of the Nativity of St John the Baptist[1]

Paffards' House

Old John the bottler tested the cask and found that it was quite empty. Lifting it from its chocks, he rolled it along to the passageway and thence out past the kitchen, the dairy and the

1 27 June 1327

brewing room to the yard behind, where he left it, rocking gently on the paving stones by his storage room, while he fumbled for his keys.

The door opened to a dark, cool chamber. Underfoot, the floor was planks of wood, and up ahead were the two large barrels of ale. Both had the expensive metal bands about them, while the smaller casks of wine were like his little one here, bound with woven willow to hold the wooden staves together, and watertight. He brought the empty cask inside and set it beneath the tap on the left-most barrel, opening the tap to fill it. It held a pair of gallons or so, and he stood there for a few moments, watching the ale drool into the cask. It was a wonderful sound, a lovely sight and smell. He turned off the tap and pressed the bung back into place, slamming it home with the heel of his hand, thinking how useful this little room had been to him. Then, rolling the cask away, he noticed a small pool of ale that had stained the floor beneath the barrel, and he tutted. He didn't want it to seep below the floor and make the chamber stink. That was a sure way to attract rats.

Rolling the cask out, he shut and locked the door, reminding himself that he must be more careful in future.

CHAPTER SIX

Taunton, Somerset

At the castle gates, Sir Baldwin de Furnshill stood a moment, pulling on his gloves and adjusting his sword-belt before preparing to mount his horse.

'Feeling stiff, Baldwin?'

'I'm not so old as that,' the knight growled. He set his foot in the stirrup and heaved himself up with a grunt. 'But I confess, the thought of my own bed is most attractive.'

Sir Baldwin was a tall man. His chest was broad, and while his eyes were kindly and brown, there was a scar on his cheek that spoke of his youth when he had been a warrior-pilgrim defending the city of Acre in the last days of the Kingdom of Jerusalem. He wore an unfashionable, neatly trimmed beard that followed the line of his jaw, but where once it had been black, now that he was in his middle fifties it was liberally salted, like his hair. Although he looked most unlike a modern knight, with his faded green tunic and tatty cloak, he was comfortable in himself. He had never had much patience with fads and fashion.

His friend, Simon Puttock was a tall, lean man of forty years, with dark hair and a rugged face. His grey eyes had always looked out on the world with confidence, but the last years had hit him hard.

Puttock had recently returned to his old family home near Crediton, and was coming to terms with his newly straitened circumstances. His skin was leathery from hours in the open air and on horseback, but the lines of anxiety Baldwin had noticed earlier in the year were steadily being replaced with those of laughter. It was good to see that.

'HAH! YOU READY, THEN?'

Both Baldwin and Simon winced at the booming voice of Sir Richard de Welles, a jovial companion, built like a bear, with appetites and voice to match. The man had the appalling habit of telling lewd jokes at full volume, no matter what the company, and it was all but impossible to embarrass him.

Taller even than Simon, his belly, however, was huge – protruding before him over the top of his black sword-belt. His grey beard was long and straggly, framing a heavy face, but the eyes hidden in among the creases were shrewd, and while he always smiled, his mind was as sharp as any. Coroner to the King's Manor at Lifton, he was an important local official who had lately been with Baldwin and Simon at Berkeley Castle, where the three had been instructed to guard the King's father, now known as Sir Edward of Caernarfon. But rebels led by the Dunheved brothers had attacked and gained the castle, riding off with Sir Edward.

It was a tragedy. Sir Edward had reigned as Edward II, but his rule had proved a disaster for the realm, and many were relieved when he was forced to surrender his crown to his son. The endless round of fighting between barons, the lawless thefts and bribery, the wanton destruction and corruption at every level of government had at last ceased – or so Simon hoped. He himself had suffered badly at the hands of the King's friends, the Despenser family, and for his part he was glad to see an end to the reign that had brought such misery.

Baldwin was ambivalent. His oath had been given to the King anointed by God, and he was reluctant to be forsworn. Once he had been a warrior monk, a *Poor Fellow Soldier of Christ and the Temple of Solomon*, a Knight Templar, and he detested the idea of casting aside an oath. If Sir Baldwin gave his word, he held to it. Yet Sir Edward had voluntarily abdicated, and Baldwin felt that absolved him from the responsibility of protecting his King.

In any case, the escape of Sir Edward while in their care was a disaster, since his supporters might now, at any time, launch an attack on the young King Edward III. The latter might even have to defend his throne against his own father, which was not a prospect Simon or Baldwin wished to contemplate. The young King ruled under a council of regents, who advised him at every step, but Baldwin felt sure that news of the release of his father must inevitably lead to recriminations against those considered responsible – himself and Simon – since their failure could lead to a renewal of civil strife.

Many, like Simon, did not understand how anyone could seek to release the old King. Others believed that past crimes could be pardoned, or perhaps they acted for their own financial gain, by removing Edward III and replacing him with his father. Some thought that removing God's anointed King was an atrocious crime, and could lead to the realm being placed under anathema, as had happened in Scotland when the Bruce rebelled; Baldwin himself had some sympathy with this view.

All he did know for sure was this: if Sir Edward of Caernarfon were to attempt to regain his kingdom, there would be bloody civil conflict. And he did not wish for that.

They had reached Taunton the previous day after riding hard, and now, breakfasted, and having attended Mass in the castle's chapel, they were ready to continue. They must ride to Exeter to inform the Sheriff of the escape of the King; so far, with God's grace, news of Sir Edward's escape had not become widely bruited about. And then they could at last return to their homes. Baldwin had gained a strong dislike for travelling, and he knew his wife must be anxious to see him again, just as he was to return to her.

Having travelled for many leagues together already, the three companions had used up their stock of conversation. Being men of action, all preferred to tend to their thoughts rather than airing inconsequential comments. Simon jogged along with a smile on his face, thinking of his wife. Sir Richard peered ahead, as if seeking out a memory of a joke in the views between the trees. For his part, Baldwin was glad of the time to consider his position. This should have been a delightful journey. The sun was shining, and with his mastiff, Wolf, trotting on ahead, his friends nearby and his servant Edgar close to hand, he should have been able to relax. But he could not.

'You look weary, Baldwin,' Simon remarked.

'I am, Simon. I have been Keeper of the King's Peace for more than ten years now, and I have had enough of it.'

Like other Keepers, he held a warrant to chase felons 'from hundred to hundred, shire to shire', with the posse. It was a basic premise that people must see justice in operation, if they were to maintain any faith in the King's laws, and that meant bringing men to the courts where their guilt could be proved.

'You would give up the job?'

'Possibly. I took on the role in gratitude to others: to you, and to Dean Peter of Crediton. I carried on, really, for Bishop Walter.'

'He was a good man.'

'I revered him. Since his death I have lost much of my motivation.'

It was not only the Bishop's death. If Baldwin were honest, it had been a gradual realisation that he was too aged. His body was old, even if his mind was unchanged. His right ear had lost all hearing, his hips ached when he spent too long in the saddle, and there was a stiffness in his back that was often painful. Hurtling over the countryside in search of malefactors was work for younger men. As for his other duties: sitting in judgement on others had never held much appeal for him, and seeing men convicted and taken to their deaths gave him no pleasure.

They had passed by Wellington and were continuing southwards when they saw two men on horseback riding towards them at a gallop. Baldwin and Simon glanced at each other. There was no reason to suspect danger, but since the escape of Sir Edward, both had been extra vigilant. Sir Richard trotted up to their side with Edgar, and the four waited together.

'You ride in a hurry,' Baldwin said as the two came into earshot. 'What speeds your journey?'

'We're from Dunkeswell Abbey, sir. We have urgent messages to take to Taunton.'

'Urgent?' Sir Richard said. 'How so?'

'I fear the Bishop of Exeter is dead.'

'Sweet Jesus!' Sir Richard muttered.

Marsilles' House

Juliana Marsille entered her home and stood in the doorway, staring about her with a feeling of weariness.

It had been here, sitting at her table over there, that Philip had caught her hands and left her convinced that he could kill her. She had been too harsh, perhaps. But he *must* grow used to the fact that he was their breadwinner now. He must snap out of this ridiculous melancholy!

Nicholas had died but two years since. Two years, and yet in that time she and her boys had lost everything. Oh, God, she wanted him back so badly!

Nicholas Marsille had been a kindly soul. He'd never managed to join the higher ranks of the city, because he was not born into the sort of position that conferred ready acceptance into the Freedom; it was a particularly exclusive club within Exeter. But Nicholas had been a genial soul, and his generosity and reliability had made him popular with his peers. He had made Juliana very happy all their married life, and his ventures had been generally successful. Until that last one.

He died in a silly accident, and that was the worst thing he ever did to her. Walking along the High Street, he saw a mother stumble and fall, and her baby tumble from her arms into the path of a cart. Nicholas darted out to rescue the child but, unsettled by his sudden lunge into the roadway, the carthorse kicked out. A hoof stove in his skull, and her lovely Nick was gone.

Other families in such circumstances would have been able to call on friends or relatives, but when friends tried to help, Juliana proudly refused them. She would not take alms, she said. Her parents were peasants on Lord de Courtenay's lands down at Topsham, and had no money. She couldn't turn to them. And without any other means of supporting herself or the boys, she was forced to sell their house. Henry Paffard had helped, yet even so the price she received for the place with all their belongings had been pathetic. As Henry explained, Nicholas had owed considerable sums. Now, with the proceeds mostly gone to creditors, there was only a paltry sum left, and they must all live on that. Her only hope was that one of her sons might make his fortune. It was too much to hope that either could marry into wealth – those with money would not wish to wed their daughters to the impoverished.

Which was a shame because Juliana was sure that Katherine Avice would have appreciated Philip's advances. Her eldest son had been pining for a woman, she knew. At first she had dared to hope that the object of his affection was Katherine. Only sixteen, and perhaps a slightly froward young vixen, but if Philip could marry her, all their problems would be over. As it was, the fool seemed to have lost the desire to find his own way in the world. How he hoped to win a woman without the means of supporting himself, let alone her as well, baffled Juliana.

She'd be better than Anastasia de Coyntes. Juliana wouldn't want anything to do with Emma's family, not after the way Emma had behaved towards her. Well, Juliana didn't need her friendship.

With a flare of anger, she kicked the door shut, walked to the table and dumped the loaf down.

Yes, if he could have taken Katherine, they would have been secure for life, but oh no. Instead, he had fixed his eyes upon the Pafford's maid – that silly little tart Alice. Even though the girl had made it clear that she had no interest in him, he had continued to plague her, until she had been forced to demonstrate, in no uncertain terms that she had no feelings for him.

Which was why Juliana had feared that he could have been responsible for the maid's death.

It was such a relief to hear that the killer was from the Cathedral, and therefore could not be her son.

Road south of Wellington

Simon looked at Baldwin. They had all dismounted, and the messengers were happy to break their journey and share some crusts of bread with cheese.

'How did it happen?' Baldwin asked.

The two messengers exchanged a glance, then one admitted, 'I don't know, sir. I wasn't there. But I was told to ride to Bath to let the Bishop know, and to stop in Taunton and pass it on there, too.'

'I see.' It was natural enough that there should be messengers sent hither and thither on the death of a Bishop, but he was surprised that the man did not know how the Bishop had died. What Baldwin did know was that the Bishop would be sorely missed. He had taken on the Bishopric only four months before, a popular choice amongst the Canons of the Cathedral who elected him, and to lose him so soon, only a matter of months since the murder of Bishop Walter II, would be devastating to the Cathedral.

'What is happening to the good Bishop's body?' Sir Richard asked mildly. 'He'll be taken back to Exeter, no doubt?'

'Yes, but the progress will be slow, naturally, out of respect.'

The messengers could add little more. Soon they had remounted and were riding away again.

'It seems a terrible coincidence for the Bishop to die just when Sir Edward has been released from his brother's castle,' Baldwin said as he climbed on to his own horse. 'Almost as if one was punishment for the other.'

Sir Richard cocked an eye. 'You believe that sort of twaddle?'

'What, a divine intervention? No, I think God has more important matters to interest Him,' Baldwin said lightly.

Simon was frowning. 'I suppose that those messengers

would have had companions leave for Exeter at the same time as them?'

'Yes, so they ought to arrive in Exeter before long,' Baldwin said.

'I was only thinking', Simon said, 'that while we have to ride to Exeter and give news of the King's escape, it would be easy enough to let the Dean know what we've heard. We may arrive before the messengers.'

'Good idea!' Sir Richard declared, a beatific smile spreading over his features. 'I would be pleased to test the hospitality of the Cathedral for an evening.'

Baldwin nodded. 'It would be more to my taste than the castle's gaol, in any case,' he muttered. 'So long as we can return home soon.'

CHAPTER SEVEN

Sunday after the Feast of the Nativity of St John the Baptist[1]

Church near Broadclyst

Ulric shivered as he walked into the church, looking about him at the devastation.

The body of the priest who had stood at the door to refuse them entry had been dragged outside now, only a smear of blood showing where he had been cut down. Inside, the simple altar had been sent flying, and the cross and rich hangings from behind had been taken away and packed in a cart, while men ransacked the small chamber beneath the tower.

It was sacrilege, and Ulric was all too keenly aware that he was now a part of this band of desperate felons. He had saved their leader, and was now viewed as Sir Charles's personal squire. If he could, he would have fled, but to where? He knew he was miles from Exeter, but he had no

1 28 June 1327

idea of the land about here. He would be caught before he had ridden a mile.

That was his difficulty. He was no trained outlaw, he was a merchant's assistant from Exeter. God, the memories he had of Paffard's house. He ought to be there now, helping measure the white tin and lead, melting them to make the pewter, working it – not here, wallowing in blood.

However, there was a thrill to being one of this band, he couldn't deny it. Being one of a group for whom the usual rules and laws did not apply was scary but intoxicating too. He had begun to feel as though there was nothing he could not do.

But in here, in this little church, he felt all the old doubts. He did not want to die on a felon's tree, his body spinning in the wind as the hemp tightened about his throat, and then be sent to hell to suffer torments at the hands of the devil. Surely for aiding those who killed the priest, he would one day pay.

'Come, Ulric,' Sir Charles called. He was sitting on a bench near the altar. 'You see this little church, and you think you have been brought to the brink of ruin, eh?' he continued when Ulric was standing before him. 'No, my friend. We are doing God's work here.'

'It is not God's will that we should kill innocent priests and rob their churches!'

'It is God's will that His order be renewed. The removal of a King is His responsibility, and His alone.'

'But to kill a Bishop, and a priest, too.'

'The Bishop of Exeter was the brother of the man who captured and held the King, brother to the man who told the King he must surrender his throne, against all the laws of man and God. Berkeley must be forced to realise his error in setting his face against God.'

'You cannot succeed with this,' Ulric said with miserable

certainty. He looked at the altar once more and felt like weeping. 'God will punish us for this.'

'Oh?' Sir Charles said. There was a shout from outside, but neither paid it any heed. 'Ulric, for once and for all, get it into your head that the men who caused this are the men who took the stern decision to forswear themselves. They were servants to the King, and broke their oaths. There is nothing for them when they die but the pits of hell. We are serving God by our—'

There was a fresh cry from outside the church, and Sir Charles muttered a curse before bellowing, 'What is it?'

'Men coming here!'

Sir Charles rolled his eyes. 'Of course there are,' he said with a long-suffering sigh. 'This is their church.'

Exeter Cathedral

Adam Murimuth felt a vague disquiet. It was the expression on the face of Philip Marsille. The poor fellow was plainly upset by the murder, as a man should be – and yet there was something more than sorrow in his expression.

He squirmed as unobtrusively as possible, his legs already aching. For his part, he had spent much time considering whether he should take matters further with Father Laurence. The fact that the vicar had denied absolutely any part in the girl's murder should have reassured him, but Murimuth felt that there was something shifty at best about his behaviour. Perhaps he himself had not been involved, but had seen someone else in the road who could have been?

From here in the choir, Murimuth faced the altar, looking along the heads of the choristers towards the newly-built eastern half of the Cathedral. It was warm, and there was a fug of humanity that incense could not subdue. Murimuth himself could feel the itching of sweat at his beard and the stubble of his tonsure. It had been some days since his last visit to the barber, and he felt slightly unclean as a result.

Father Laurence himself was always clean and fresh. He belonged to that category of men who were always washing themselves, as though it was some form of ritual in its own right.

Murimuth suddenly had a vision of a man washing away blood from his hands, as though he could as easily wash away his guilt. Cleanliness as proof of a crime? No, that was nonsense! At least the Coroner should soon be able to open his inquest. Murimuth rested his backside on the little carved *misericord* behind him and tried to ease his legs. It would be a good thing to rescue that poor child's body from the alleyway in which she still lay, and see to her burial. There was no excuse for leaving her out there any longer than necessary.

He would make some notes later. Perhaps that would help clear the fog in his mind. Because for now, he felt such a heaviness of spirit.

It was as though his soul was telling him that Father Laurence *did* know something of the maid's murder.

Church near Broadclyst

Sir Charles was on his feet and halfway to the door before Ulric had registered the call. There, Sir Charles motioned to a pair of his men. They were rugged-looking fellows, who wore leather bracers like archers, and had the appearance of experienced fighters in the way that they stared through the open doorway with calm concentration, showing no anxiety.

'Are they Bishop's men?' one of the men asked as Ulric reached their side.

'No. Looks like the congregation is on its way to the church for Sunday worship,' Sir Charles said with a chuckle. 'Get the men ready to greet them.'

One of the archers hastened away to the side of the church where the rest of the band were waiting with the carts and horses. There was a muttering of quiet orders, a slithering hiss of steel, and then nothing more.

Ulric looked at Sir Charles and the other archer. There were another six men in the church, and Sir Charles nodded his head to them. 'The people are coming. Make haste!'

In the blink of an eye, the men concealed themselves about the church, while Sir Charles and the archer took their positions at either side of the door. Ulric was motioned away, impatiently, and he darted to the wall behind Sir Charles.

There was a chattering of voices, and then the door opened, and a tall, grizzled man entered. He was clad in good scarlet, and Ulric instantly thought he must be the vill's bailiff. Behind him was a short, buxom woman, and a couple of young fellows who looked like their sons, and Ulric saw more people behind them, thronging the little entranceway.

Whoever he was, the man was no fool. In an instant he took in the sight of the altar thrown against the wall, the blood on the floor, and he roared a warning, setting his hand to his hilt, but even as he made to draw steel, Sir Charles had rested his blade on the man's shoulder, the steel against his throat. 'You'll wait, man.'

Outside there was a sudden commotion as the congregation was herded inside, the archer and two others grabbing any weapons from the unresisting peasants as they came.

It was all so easy. Ulric gazed in wonder to see the people brought in and forced to kneel on the ground, while Sir Charles's men moved amongst them, cutting away purses and pulling rings from fingers. Some rich, most poorer, men with sullen eyes, women with fear in their faces, holding children to them, terrified of what might happen, all pushed to the rear of the building while Sir Charles's men took up positions around them.

And only then, when Ulric glanced at the grim faces of the men from Sir Charles's party, did he feel a leaden fear in his belly.

Exeter North Gate

It was already late when they finally reached the gates to the city, and Simon knew that they must hurry if they were to get to the Cathedral before the Close was shut.

'Simon,' Baldwin said as they rode under the city gates, 'there is no need for you to come as well. If you join us at the Cathedral, you will be held up there and may not escape this night. Do you go to your daughter's house instead, and we shall come to meet you tomorrow morning as soon as we are free. We can visit the Sheriff tomorrow, and then head for our homes.'

It was a welcome plan. Simon grasped Baldwin's hand, waved to Sir Richard and Edgar, then called to his servant Hugh, and trotted off in the direction of Edith's house.

Baldwin watched him, then grunted to himself as he and the others carried on down the street to Carfoix, and along the High Street to the Fissand Gate.

'Sirs, the gates will be closing soon,' Janekyn Beyvyn called from his stool just inside. He was eating a husk of bread, and Wolf, Baldwin's great tricoloured mastiff, went and sat in front of him, his eyes fixed earnestly upon the crust as his jowls drooled. Janekyn glowered at him.

'Aye,' Sir Richard agreed. 'But we have urgent business with the Dean.'

'I'm afraid Dean Alfred is not well,' Janekyn said. 'He has been bled, and is away resting. I think the barber took too much blood. He's not a young man, but the surgeon wouldn't listen to anyone.'

'Well, the Precentor will do,' Baldwin said. 'Porter, could you send a boy to tell him that Sir Baldwin de Furnshill and Sir Richard de Welles regret interrupting him at this sorry time, but we have some grievous news to impart.'

'Sorry time, sir?'

Baldwin gave a quick frown. 'Have you not heard?'

'Simon was right, then,' Sir Richard said. 'Please send to the good Precentor, porter. We have bad news for him.'

Monday after the Nativity of St John the Baptist[1]

Cathedral Close

Adam Murimuth walked from the Cathedral in a state of shock. So much effort had gone into selecting the new Bishop, and to learn from Baldwin and Sir Richard that he had been murdered was devastating. Already he was thinking of the messages that must be sent: to the Archbishop, to the Pope, to the King . . . there was so much to be done.

He had walked from the West Door and was halfway to the Charnel Chapel before he realised he had no idea where he was going. He scarcely even recognised where he was. For a moment he thought the ground was bucking beneath him, like a violent sea, and had to close his eyes to steady himself.

He had lived here at Exeter for some little while, and in that time he had seen many disasters. When the news of the murder of Bishop Walter II was brought to the Cathedral last year, it was he, Adam, who had arranged matters as best he could.

1 29 June 1327

When the dispute arose about who would replace Bishop Walter, it was Adam who had negotiated and persuaded until Bishop James was elected. It had not been easy. And now, a scant three months after his enthronement, Bishop James too was dead. It was a disaster for the See. For the Cathedral, it was a catastrophe. The Cathedral needed a Bishop, never more so than now, with a King who was under-age, and a Pope who sought to take over ancient rights and customs. The next Bishop might be selected not in Exeter but in Avignon.

The noise of the masons brought him back to his senses. The hammering of chisels on stone, the rasp of saws, the creak and rumble of the treadmill slowly hauling rocks to the top of the new walls, and all around the bellowing of the hundreds of men involved in the building works. He had almost walked into a massive stone lintel, curved to form a part of an arch.

To hear that Sir Edward of Caernarfon had escaped, that was shocking enough — dear God, to think that so many men could wish to see him return to the throne! – but it would surely mean little to Adam down here in Exeter. Whoever was King, the taxes demanded from the Cathedral would not change. But to lose the Bishop – that was a substantial blow.

Enough! His duty was to keep the Cathedral working so that it could perform its sacred duty of caring for the souls in the city. He must pull himself together so that others could do their job.

Meanwhile, Adam had been responsible for the administration of the Cathedral when Bishop Walter had died. During this latest interregnum he would very likely be asked to take up that function again. His task was to manage the diocese, after all. He must look after the income and expenses until a new Bishop could be elected. The work involved was a great burden to be shouldered.

No matter that a Bishop had died; God's work on earth continued.

The Precentor set his jaw. There was also this other matter of the man who had been heard running as that girl was killed. Should he report Father Laurence, or merely question him again? He would have to think about what to do.

Standing at the edge of the cloister, he stared up at the towers. He tried to imagine this marvellous building without the lattice-work of scaffolding, without all those masons and plumbers, carpenters and labourers, who swarmed up and down the ropes and beams like so many monkeys, and it was as he stood there, marvelling at the insanity of the men dangling precariously so high above the ground, that he saw Sir Baldwin and Sir Richard ambling from the guests' chamber by the Palace Gate. They were on their way to see the Sheriff, he remembered.

With a sudden sigh of relief, Adam saw how he could delegate one task at least.

CHAPTER EIGHT

Rougemont Castle, Exeter

Baldwin and Sir Richard stood in the small room before the hall. They had been waiting for some little while already. Edgar lounged at the doorway.

'The Precentor was very keen for us to have a look at this dead woman, wasn't he, Sir Baldwin?'

'I think he has much on his plate, what with our news of the Bishop and the affairs that must inevitably attract his attention,' Baldwin said.

'Aye. So you think it's fishy too, then, eh?'

Baldwin smiled. 'It is possible that there was something else about this matter that he forgot to tell us,' he said, tickling Wolf's ear.

'Hmm. The inquest will be this morning, he said, so we should hurry.'

'If the Sheriff will permit us to leave him,' Baldwin agreed, looking out through the window at the shadows.

Sir Richard followed his gaze. 'We've been waiting a long

time already. Do you think they forgot to tell him we were here?'

'No. I think he intends to show us how unimportant we are,' Baldwin said.

'Eh?' Sir Richard asked, baffled. Such rudeness was incomprehensible to him.

'He demonstrates that he has lots of important business to get through, and we do not measure compared with his other, more pressing matters.'

'Ah, he does, eh?'

'And in case there could be no doubt, I am sure that he has a scale of time for which to hold men up without seeing them. Perhaps a squire would be so long, a knight a little less, a peasant still longer.'

'But we *said* we have very important news,' Sir Richard growled. 'And we have an inquest to attend, since the Precentor asked us to witness it for him.'

'Only for a murdered maidservant. All the more reason for him to keep us waiting, my friend.'

'God's blood, the arrogant puppy!'

Baldwin smiled. 'There, I admit, I have to agree with you. Sir James de Cockington dislikes me. I was responsible, in part, for arresting his brother last year. I fear he believes that I have a feud against him and his family.'

'Well, can't let the fellow get away with that,' Sir Richard said, and there was a gleam in his eye. 'Come, sir.'

'Where are we going?' Baldwin asked as his companion began to clump his way to the door that led to the yard.

In answer, Sir Richard bawled at a page and beckoned. When the boy had joined them, Sir Richard glowered down at him.

'It would seem your master the Sheriff is too busy to see us at present. We have urgent business, so tell him he can come to us when he is ready. We'll be at the inquest at Combe Street. Please also tell him it is a shame he doesn't have time to hear news which involves the security of the Cathedral here, and even of the Crown itself. Now, Sir Baldwin, we must hurry if we are to reach the inquest, I suppose?'

Combe Street near Paffards' House

Emma had arrived early with her husband, but the jury had already gathered at the entrance to the alley. They couldn't all fit inside, for there were sixteen men all told, none younger than fifteen.

The men were almost all known to Emma from the parish: a cobbler there from Combe Street, his brother who lived next door, a merchant who had once accused her husband Bydaud of defamation, damn his soul, but Bydaud had already won over too many friends in the city, and the fellow was forced to withdraw. Yes, looking over the grim faces, she knew them all.

'Gentlemen, I am glad to see you all here for this sorry duty,' the Coroner said, but quietly. He looked about him with a scowl as if daring any to ask him to speak more forcefully, and Emma tutted, wondering if this was his first inquest. He looked barely twenty. He was certainly younger than her.

'Who's he?' Juliana asked. She had walked up behind Emma, and stood staring at the Coroner.

Emma was tempted to ignore her, but with all these people about, she had no desire to show herself mean-minded. 'I've no idea. I'd have thought it would be better to have a man with a little more experience for this kind of task. This one looks as though he's not yet drawn his sword in anger. He's so *young*!'

'Aren't they all?' Juliana said. 'That's probably why he hasn't been called away to the King's war.'

'Lucky him,' Emma said shortly. 'We never win against the Scots. Not since the old King died.'

Helewisia Avice joined them, and Emma gave her a smile of welcome, which Juliana noticed. She felt a stab of hurt at the affirmation of friendship. Helewisia for her part greeted both with a reserve suited to the occasion. 'You were talking about the old King?'

Juliana nodded. King Edward I, 'the Hammer of the Scots', was well-named, but since his death twenty years ago, the Scottish had always maintained the upper hand, even in Ireland for a while. 'Who are those two?'

'No idea,' Emma said, following her pointing finger to stare at Baldwin and Sir Richard. Edgar lounged behind them, and Emma was suddenly shocked to observe that he was giving her an appraising look. He smiled languidly and she felt her face colour as she hurriedly averted her gaze. She was a married woman, and wanted no attention from a man like him. In any case, this was no place for dallying. They had a stern responsibility here.

The inquest was formal, the Coroner's Clerk murmuring quiet instructions every so often when it appeared that the Coroner was becoming confused or lost, and then they reached the point where the girl must be viewed.

'I have already viewed her body,' the Coroner said. 'Perhaps we should bring her out here, so the jury can study her?' he added, glancing at his clerk.

The clerk, a weasely little man, gave a sharp frown and opened his mouth to speak, but before he could do so, Sir Richard interrupted. His voice was like the rumble of a wagon on a poorly-made road, Emma thought; her ears ringing.

'GOOD SIR REGINALD, WOULD YOU MIND IF WE TOOK A LOOK *IN SITU*?'

'Who are you, sir?'

'I am Sir Richard de Welles, Coroner of Lifton. I have some little experience of matters of this sort.'

The man scratched at his beard, and then when he shrugged and stood aside, the two knights and their escort walked past him and up the alley.

'What can they hope to see up there?' Juliana whispered.

Alley near Paffards' House

'Bit dark in here,' Sir Richard rumbled as they stepped over the rubbish.

'It is hardly congenial to an investigation,' Baldwin agreed.

The alley was a mess. Baldwin saw the body of a cat lying in a corner: it was clear that the scavengers had not cleared through here in weeks, which was a surprise, bearing in mind that Paffard was a wealthy man. Such fellows tended to receive better service.

There was a City Bailiff standing by the body, and Baldwin nodded to him. He thought he recognised the fellow from a previous investigation, but for now his full attention was fixed on Alice.

She lay on her left side, half-covered by a cloak, her legs against the wall. Her torso ran at an angle from the wall, while her head reached out almost halfway across the alley. He could see one arm, her right, which lay over her breast, the hand on the ground in a natural manner, as though she was asleep. Sir Richard wandered up, and stood over her sadly.

'Very young, this maid, eh?' he said to the Bailiff.

'Yes, sir. Seventeen, I think.'

'Where was she from?' Baldwin asked.

'Not Exeter, I know that. She's one of these girls who come in looking for work. You know what it's like. There are hundreds of them each year, thinking the city's paved with gold. They all reckon it's the place to come and find a little work, have some fun, snare a man and live happily ever after.'

'Most of them don't have such a happy experience, do they?' Baldwin said, crouching at her side.

'No, sir. Too many end up at the stews, and if they're unlucky, they die there. Thank God some come to their senses and go home.'

'But many don't have a home to return to,' Baldwin noted.

'What of this one?' Sir Richard asked. 'Was she a whore?'

'No, sir. She lived here. Got a job with the Paffard family,' the Bailiff said, jerking his thumb over his shoulder at the merchant's house. 'She was just unlucky. Probably caught the eye of some drunk, and he followed her and killed her here.'

'Perhaps,' Baldwin said. He rose, facing along the alley towards Combe Street. 'She has been stabbed twice in the breast. Not a frenzied attack, then. Her hands have defensive wounds, you see, Sir Richard? So she tried to beat him off, but presumably he wasn't taking no for an answer, and when she still refused his advances, he stabbed her and let her fall.'

The Bailiff nodded. 'Could be.'

'We should examine her in the light,' Baldwin said. 'Edgar, would you go and inform Sir – what was his name?'

'Sir Reginald, sir.'

'Well, let him know we are finished and that the body should be taken out for the jury.'

'Sir.'

Baldwin stared down at her. He breathed in the stench of decay; felt shards of broken pottery snap under his boots.

Hers was a grim resting-place.

Four men returned with Edgar. Two took up an arm each, a third her legs, and the fourth followed unhappily as the three lugged Alice's body along the alley back to the inquest.

'It is almost as though,' Baldwin said, 'she was placed here deliberately, along with all the rubbish.'

Road east of Exeter

The roadway here was ideal for an ambush, Sir Charles thought. He would have to keep that in mind.

So far, their campaign had met with considerable success. They already had four carts containing rich cloths, gold and coin, and a number of plates and jewelled or enamelled work. He could not remember a ride which had provided such profits.

His companions were a raggle-taggle bunch – some peasants, two men who he was sure should long ago have been hanged, one renegade priest and a few who had been committed to the old King – but on the whole they seemed reliable. Yesterday in the church he had tested them and all had proved satisfactory.

Ulric was different. He had no place here. His only duty had been to bring news from Exeter about the Bishop's travels, but he had had no idea that his intelligence was to be used to kill Bishop James. Sir Charles was very content to have him as squire, untrained though he might be. The lad had saved him in that hall.

Besides, this untrained squire had very light duties, since Sir Charles possessed little in the way of equipment to be cleaned and maintained. It was his fervent wish that he might renew his fortunes by this meandering ride through the Bishop's estates. The thought of the armour and mail he could buy when he had the King's favour was almost enough to make his mouth water. The proceeds of this ride must be desposited with the King's backers, of course, but there should be a trifle left over for him.

A fine spitting rain began, and he pulled his hood over his head. He was used to such weather. The main thing was to ensure that one's sword and dagger were safe from the damp, and so he tugged a fold of his cloak about him as he rode, covering their hilts.

Yes, there should be a good profit. For now, he must continue with his little campaign, and then get to the man in Exeter who was to take all the goods and sell them. Ulric's master, a merchant called Paffard, would be happy to take all this from him for a good fee. And then the money could be taken to Sir Edward of Caernarfon and the Dunheved gang who had released him from his gaol, to help fund his return to the throne.

Aye, Sir Charles thought to himself, life was good. And there, three miles distant, was another manor ready and waiting to be despoiled. He smiled contentedly.

Combe Street near the alley

Sir Reginald looked petulant when the two knights finally emerged from the alley, Emma thought. For all the sombre mood of the gathering, it was tempting to giggle at his grumpy expression.

'Undress her,' he commanded, but there was no movement from the watching crowd. 'Come! Someone must undress her.'

There was such a tone of hurt in his voice that Emma wanted to pet him. He was little more than a boy in a man's office. He glanced down at the clerk as if seeking support, but the clerk was writing in his rolls still, and made no effort to assist.

'Helewisia,' Emma said, 'come and help. We can't leave the poor chit to some carter or tanner. Better that we do it.'

Her neighbour nodded, and without speaking, they both went to the figure and knelt beside it.

Alice had been set down a short way from the alley, and her body was cold and flaccid, which was a relief; the two woman could undress her without too much difficulty. They gently removed her clothes and piled them neatly to one side, and then moved away.

It was sad to see her naked. Emma knew it was essential that the corpse should be exposed to the full view of the Coroner and his jury, but still it seemed as though the girl was being humiliated after death. She crossed herself, and realised a tear was forming in her eye. She wiped it away crossly. Tears should be saved for the funeral itself, not expended here.

'I find that she has been stabbed twice in the breast,' the Coroner declared loudly, studying the slim body. 'Once in each. It's . . .' He broke off and turned away.

'As if she was being deliberately marked in the breasts,' Sir Richard finished for him.

CHAPTER NINE

Alice had always been a pale girl, and naked in death Emma thought she looked like a figure carved from marble.

On her pure flesh the stains of blood about the two elongated diamond-shaped stab wounds stood out clearly, as did the discolouration of dead flesh where her body had lain. About her wounds, the blood had dried black, and flaked off as a powder. But other signs stood out on her body: Emma could see the marks, one on the left side of her throat, another pair on her breasts. Not bites with teeth, but the marks of love. Sucking kisses that had drawn the blood to the surface of her skin like large bruises. Seeing them, Emma knew what the girl had been doing earlier on the day she died, as did all the other adults there.

Baldwin stared thoughtfully at Alice's body. He looked like a man peering at accounts in a ledger, not at a dead maid.

'Do you object to my studying her?' he asked the Coroner. 'I have been asked specifically by the Precentor of the Cathedral to aid you as I may.'

'Sir Baldwin? My apologies, please, do take all the time you need. I know of your reputation, sir.'

'I am grateful,' Baldwin said as he crouched by the body. 'The two stab wounds are quite clear,' he went on. 'Both were from the same blade. It is a blade some one and one half inches broad, and it is less than eight inches long. The blade appears to have penetrated to its full depth.'

'How do you know that?' the Coroner asked. Emma thought he looked baffled.

'The cross of the guard has slammed into the girl's flesh here, over the breast, and bruised it. Yet it did not pass through her body to her back, so it cannot be as long as her body is deep. If I insert a finger . . .' Baldwin stuck his finger into the wound. 'Yes, it passes down slightly, but not steeply. So the knife-blade is longer than my finger. It was no eating-knife, but a dagger with two edges. The wounds are clearly diamond-shaped, and they penetrated the tunic which she wore.'

'I see,' the Coroner said, and Emma saw that the clerk was scribbling quickly as he tried to note all Sir Baldwin's comments.

Baldwin considered, wiping his finger on a fold of her skirts. 'She made love not long before her death. These marks on her body,' he pointed out the bruises Emma had noticed on the neck and breast, 'these are not the marks of a rapist.'

Sir Reginald's clerk was unconvinced. 'A rapist driven by his lust may have brought her here for himself and made those marks on her body, and afterwards she pulled her clothes on in modesty before he slew her. Men in the heat of their passions can be brutal.'

'You suggest that the rapist stood by as she donned her clothes, and then slew her? The stabs were through the material of her chemise, so she was clad when killed.'

The Coroner was nodding, as though impressed with the

logic of Baldwin's reasoning, but Emma guessed that professional awe was tempered with irritation at being shown up before the jury.

'Consider this,' Baldwin said, holding Alice's head and studying her. 'I am sure you noticed this, Coroner: her lips are bruised. One may think she was grasped there, to prevent her calling out? But there are no finger-marks at either cheek. If I saw a maid silenced in such a manner, I would expect four bruises on one cheek and jaw, and the thumb-mark correspondingly on the other, but there is no such mark here. Which is peculiar.'

'What else would bruise her mouth?' Sir Reginald asked.

'Her teeth are firmly fixed. It was not a punch,' Baldwin explained. 'But now I have seen her body, an explanation is to hand. If she was kissed violently, passionately, that would possibly lead to her mouth being bruised. So this lover was an ardent fellow.'

'But you don't think she was raped,' the clerk said.

'With a pretty maid like this, I would always look for signs of a rape,' Baldwin agreed, 'but she had recently lain with her lover, so how could we tell whether she was raped afterwards?'

He stood, and pulled her arm to roll her gently over onto her stomach. Her back was smooth and unblemished, except for the staining where blood had pooled.

'There is no evidence of a blow, a slap or punch, to her face,' Baldwin said. He stared down the length of the figure. 'I should have expected that, if she had tried to fight off an assault. And obviously she was not raped here in the alley.'

'Why not?' the Coroner asked.

'Her back,' Baldwin said, 'is not marked. Consider: if she were forced to lie among the stones and filth of the alley, she would have abrasions, and her clothing would be stained from the dirt. There are no such indications, so I doubt that she was raped out here. That does not mean she was not raped somewhere else, perhaps on a comfortable bed, but not here.'

'I don't understand – why would someone kill her and dump her body here?'

'To distract a Coroner, to conceal the killer's identity, or to avoid paying fines. Wherever a body is found, that community will pay the fines for infringement of the King's Peace. If it were moved, someone else would have to pay.'

'Well, since there are none of those signs, perhaps she was not raped, but merely killed there in the alley,' the Coroner concluded.

'For what reason?' Baldwin asked, rifling through the pile of her discarded clothes.

'Robbery,' said the clerk.

Baldwin looked at him. 'This was a maidservant, not a merchant. Would a cut-purse think her likely to wear a gold necklace, or hold a well-filled purse?'

'What do you think, then?'

Baldwin had picked up her chemise, and was studying it closely.

'There is no way to tell, as yet. Perhaps we shall learn more when we hear what she was doing on the day she died.'

Rougemont Castle

He had been in a good mood that morning. Sir James de Cockington, the Sheriff of Exeter, had been entertained by a young woman from the local tavern, and her skills and athletic ability had first delighted, and then alarmed him. He had woken to a mild headache and that inevitable fuzziness that comes from a lack of sleep, and the wench was gone – without robbing him, he noted.

He made his way down to his hall, and called for food and drink, considering his future. It was uncertain.

Only a few weeks ago he'd thought he must lose his position here. The new regime would not appreciate his efforts on behalf of Sir Edward of Caernarfon, and he was as aware as any that his post would be a perfect gift to many of those who had spent the years trying to unseat the King. This position of Sheriff of Devon was a ripe plum ready to fall into any hands which had been supportive of the barons opposed to Sir Edward.

But nothing had happened.

Sir James reckoned that at first there had been too much going on around Bristol and Wales, let alone London, for those in charge to worry about him. King Edward III was still not yet fifteen, and the land was controlled by the council of the leading barons of the country. And behind all there stood that wily dog, Sir Roger Mortimer.

He was the real power in the land. That was clear enough to any man with a brain. And Sir James had a particularly astute mind when it came to seeing where was the safest haven in troubled times. He hadn't got to be a Sheriff without understanding the details of politics.

Hearing that Sir Baldwin was waiting in his antechamber had sent him into a minor paroxysm of panic. Last time he had met Sir Baldwin, he had not enjoyed the experience.

Then a thought took him, and it was a happy thought.

Sir Baldwin, whom he had always considered a grumpy example of a rustic knight, had always appeared to consider himself the equal of Sir James. More, in fact: Sir James felt sure Sir Baldwin looked down upon him. Well, times had changed now, hadn't they? Sir Baldwin's influence at court was ended. He had been loyal to the old King, to Sir Edward of Caernarfon. And now that King was gone, and in his place was the council and the new King. Sir Baldwin's position was built on sand – while Sir James was held in some esteem by the new government, clearly, because he was still in post.

Refreshed with his musings, he took a leisurely time over breaking his fast. It was balm to his soul to know that, as he drank two mazers of watered wine, the older man was outside cooling his heels. There was probably some little favour he wished. A rural knight like him was little better than the peasants who wallowed in the mud. Certainly Sir Baldwin would not fit into the circle of friends that Sir James had assiduously cultivated. He wiped his lips and poured a third mazer before motioning to his steward to remove all the debris.

'Tell Sir Baldwin I will see him now,' he said, stifling a belch.

The steward gave him a baffled look. 'Sir Baldwin?'

'He is waiting for me in the antechamber.'

'No, sir, he had to leave. He has been gone since before Nones, sir,' he said, and gave him Sir Richard's message.

The steward did not particularly like his master, so it was a cheerful man who left the swearing Sheriff a few moments later. He shut the door behind him and made his way to the buttery, where he had to laugh aloud at the memory of the Sheriff's amazed expression.

Combe Street

Joan, the young maid at the Paffards' house, was the first witness, since she had discovered the body. The Coroner stood at the side of his clerk and asked her what had happened on the fateful Saturday evening.

'I just tripped over her head. I didn't see her down in the alley. There was no light there. She was just lying there, and I fell over her. I couldn't help it.'

'Ah! Did you trip over her face? Perhaps you bruised her lips in the way Sir Baldwin noted?'

'I don't know. I just couldn't see in the dark, else I'd have seen to avoid her.'

'Yes, quite,' the Coroner said patronisingly.

'May I ask a question?' Baldwin said.

Joan liked the look of this knight. He was neat and precise in his manner, and when he fixed his dark eyes upon her, she felt as though he could see right into her soul. Not in a nasty way, not like Henry Paffard, nor accusingly, but with sympathy, like he understood what she was going through, standing here with all the men staring at her like she was a murderer just because she had found poor Alice.

'Maid, you worked with Alice. Were you friends?'

'Yes. It's hard to live in the same room and not get close.'

'Was she in love? Girls will talk of their men, I know. Did she confide in you about any man in particular?'

'No. Not at all,' Joan said. Alice had never said anything about her lover. There had been no need.

'She had no one?'

'She wouldn't have betrayed the master,' Joan said primly, face reddening.

'That is curious,' Baldwin said, and she could not help glancing at the master. Henry Paffard was watching her, his face devoid of emotion. She couldn't tell whether he was pleased or angry.

'Another question,' Baldwin said, drawing her attention back to him. 'Why were you walking along that alley? It is very unpleasant there for a young woman as the light fades. Surely you would have been better served to use the front door?'

'It's just a rule of the household that servants will enter the house by the rear door,' she told him.

'I see,' was all Baldwin said, but the look he gave Henry Paffard was as black as thunder.

Edith's House, St Pancras Lane

Simon had woken to the sound of his grandson bawling his head off, and he rolled over in his bed to listen with a smile on his face.

It was good to wake in a real bed again, and better still to know that he was here with his daughter's family, safe with people he loved.

He rose and dressed, making his way to the hall.

'Good morning, Father. You slept well.'

'Yes.'

'I wasn't asking! I could hear your snoring through the floor!'

'I didn't keep you awake, did I?' Simon said, crouched beside the cot in which his grandson was lying, his face red as he opened his mouth for another bellow of rage. 'Your mother is unkind to your old grandpa, isn't she?'

Edith laughed and offered him some meat and bread to break his fast. Simon knew that she was showing off, but he accepted with alacrity. Soon he was sitting at the table, a pewter plate filled with honeyed larks and slabs of fresh cheese before him, and a goblet of wine at his side.

'You do yourselves well here,' he commented, sucking the meat from a lark's thigh.

'Peter hopes to be accepted into the Freedom of the City,' Edith said.

'I never thought to hear my daughter with such a smug tone!'

'I'm not smug, Father. Just proud, that's all.'

'Aye – proud as a popinjay! I am very happy for you, Edith.'

He was. From here, he could see the tapestries on the walls, the picture at the far end of the chamber. She had a better house than he, by far. His room last night was a separate chamber beneath their solar, and this hall was huge compared to his own, the screens decorated with emblems of the city. Much money had been expended on the place from the days when it was owned by Edith's father-in-law, Charles, and he and his wife had left it for Edith and Peter when they had their new house built near the Guild Hall. It was only natural that she should be proud of all she had acquired.

'When do you expect Sir Baldwin to arrive?' she asked.

'Hmm? Oh, not late. I daresay he is still having some discussions at the Cathedral,' Simon said.

The light tone did not reflect his mood. It was still uppermost in his mind that there would be consequences flowing from the escape of Sir Edward of Caernarfon, and that was a source of grave concern to him.

He had no idea how this was going to affect him – and his family.

CHAPTER TEN

Combe Street

Baldwin glanced at Sir Reginald. He did not wish to take over the inquest, but the Coroner gestured assent, so he continued, looking at Joan. 'Maid, did you see a man near here that night?'

'Yes. A priest,' she said.

'Where?' Baldwin asked.

'Out in the road there,' she said, and explained how she had hidden, fearful of encountering a man so late.

Baldwin glanced over his shoulder. The Coroner was looking up at the sky, measuring the sun, and Baldwin thanked the girl for her evidence then stepped back to Sir Richard's side.

'I find that this maid Alice was killed by a man unknown,' the Coroner began, and read through the facts of the case. 'The knife which killed her was a knife worth about one shilling and sixpence. I shall enrol that as deodand. Is there anyone here to present Englishry on this maid? No? Then I will impose the Murdrum fine. You, Joan, must attend the court when this affair is brought before the judges. Your master must pay sureties to my clerk here. Also, the families nearest must also be attached: Roger Avice, Bydaud de Coyntes, Master Philip Marsille, and Henry Paffard. You are all attached to attend the court. Pay your sureties too.'

'There! That's all done with,' Sir Richard said with contentment. 'We should find a tavern and buy a little wine or ale.'

'There is one more thing I should like to know, first,' Baldwin said. He walked over to Paffard's apprentice, Benjamin, as the jury and witnesses began to disperse. 'Master, Joan said that after she found the body, you were next into the alley. Is that correct?'

'Yes, me and our bottler, John. Joan was in a terrible state, screaming and screaming – there was nothing I could do or say that would calm her, but John managed to get her away and into the house.'

'I see. It was strange that she should be walking about the city so late.'

'John sent her to buy some bread.'

Baldwin looked at the man he pointed out. John was a little older than Baldwin himself. He was not tall, and stooped, which made him look even shorter. He had thick white hair, but dark brows that looked curiously out of place. He was dressed in a thin woollen tunic of dark brown, with a white chemise beneath. A broad black belt was bound at his waist, a purse, keys and a dagger hanging from it.

'You sent her?'

'We needed bread for the servants' meal.'

'I see. What of Alice? Who last saw her?'

'She was well enough that evening. She was there when the master left for the Cock with his family,' John said.

'All the family?'

'Yes.'

'What did she do after that?'

'I don't know. I was in the buttery, after sending Joan for the bread, and then the apprentice and I met for a mazer of ale in the yard later, and we were there when we heard Joan's screams.'

Baldwin nodded. A short way away, he saw Paffard. The merchant was tall, with rather gaunt features. There were lines about his face and brow, but his brown eyes looked clear and steady.

Just now he looked like a man who had been insulted. In fact, he had the demeanour of a felon who had narrowly escaped the rope, but who felt that an inquest into his behaviour was unreasonable.

Seeing Baldwin's eye on him, he turned abruptly and strode away.

'What is it?' Sir Richard asked, seeing Baldwin's expression.

'Probably nothing. He has lost a maid. It is a disturbing event for a man. But his manner is curious, nonetheless.'

Road east of Exeter

Ulric watched Sir Charles drop from his horse and study the land closely with one of the two archers who were always close by him. The rest of the cavalcade remained on their horses, chatting among themselves.

He had nothing to talk about with them. Yesterday, in the church, he had seen them . . . Those scenes wouldn't fade. The women, pulled from their children and forced to the ground while the men took their pleasure, the children squealing in terror, men gritting their teeth and watching with despair on their faces, until one man, a tall, grey-haired fellow of perhaps fifty summers, launched himself at the nearest guard.

The guard was a weasel-faced fellow with a cast in his eye,

who had been watching the nearest woman's torment with a grin of anticipation, and didn't expect an attack. He fell under a blow from a fist like a block of timber, and his dagger and sword were snatched up in an instant.

A shout, a scream as the sword was thrust in a man's chest, then a roar of fury as the old man lunged at Sir Charles's second archer. The man side-stepped like an acrobat, and the sword missed him. A second guard sprang to his side, and the desperate man was forced to block both their weapons while the rest of the menfolk watched, held back by a ring of steel.

When a woman screamed, it was enough. There was a general movement by all the men in that church to break free of their captors, and Ulric watched as they leaped upon the weapons hemming them in. He saw the young men nearer Sir Charles gripping his sword with their bare hands, trying to yank it free of the knight's grip even as their blood flowed down the fuller. Others ran forward, only to be spitted on their enemies' blades; a few were shot with arrows, some beaten about the head with a steel war-hammer, and when the madness was done, there was still only one trio remaining: the older man and his two opponents.

At a nod from Sir Charles, the man with the war-hammer went to them, and with one blow from his spike, ended the man's battles forever.

Afterwards, while the bodies of their menfolk cooled all about them, the women were forced to lie in their husbands' blood while they were raped.

Ulric could not close his eyes all night, for fear that those tortured faces would return to haunt his dreams. And now, in the daylight, as he watched Sir Charles walk about the lane here, gazing at the trees with the eyes of an expert tactician viewing a new ambush site, all Ulric could think of was somehow warning people about the band. Surely he could get news of the men to someone before more died?

But he could not think how to do this. Escape was impossible, and without flying from the men, he had no hope. Already he could feel their eyes upon him. He had not helped when they killed the villagers, but had stood back at the wall, clutching at the stones to stop himself falling. Now many of them viewed him as an enemy in their midst. They were watching him all the time in case he tried to run.

The only man who viewed him with any fondness was Sir Charles. The knight appeared to consider him like a slightly wayward boy, to be treated with an amiable tolerance. He would not forget that Ulric had saved his life.

But it did not help Ulric. He was sure that soon he would die. Whether at the hands of the men here, or those of a posse, it made no difference. He had no hope.

No hope at all.

Near alley at Combe Street

Baldwin and Sir Richard waited until the body was released for burial.

Glancing down, Baldwin noticed that Wolf had been distracted. The huge dog sat at the wall of the Paffard house, panting happily, while a young boy cuddled him.

It was a sight to make a man smile. In the midst of this pain and suffering, it was good to see that there were still boys who behaved as boys. Baldwin could recall when he had been young. In those days he had spent more time with his dogs than with his family. They had been happy days.

Happier than these, certainly, he thought.

A boy was sent to the Cathedral to instruct the Fosser to dig a new grave, and to bring a cart of some sort to transport the body. The Holy Trinity was the local parish church, but the Cathedral had an absolute monopoly on funerals, and Alice would have to be taken up to the Close.

The Coroner was relieved to be done, chatting to his clerk, but for his part, Baldwin was dissatisfied. He left Sir Richard where he was for a moment, walking over to Emma and Helewisia where they knelt beside the girl's body, wrapping her in a winding sheet.

'Mistress, I should like to ask you a question.'

Emma looked up at him with suspicious eyes. 'Why? The inquest is over, isn't it?'

Baldwin drew her away from Helewisia. 'Yes. I didn't wish to embarrass you before the jury. This young woman died a vile death. The matter is less about her, than about the man who was prepared to do this to her.'

'I don't know what you mean,' Emma bridled, immediately on her guard. This man had dark eyes that fixed on her with a curious intensity; it was alarming, as though he could see through her foolish defences to all the secrets she held in her breast.

'You are a clever woman. You know she had a lover, don't you?'

'Perhaps,' she allowed.

'Madam, I do not wish to slander her now she is dead, but I have to know the truth if I am to discover her murderer. Who was her lover? Was it a man from about here?'

'I couldn't say,' she said, and refused to look away, staring up at his face with firm resolution. He couldn't force her, after all, and she would not lose her house and home just because of this man.

Helewisia had been watching them both talking, and now she stood a scant ten paces from them.

'What of *you*, mistress?' Baldwin asked, seeing Helewisia as though for the first time.

'Me?' she echoed.

Emma could see that Helewisia was flattered to be asked, the silly woman. She was easily flattered. She deserved sympathy, but there was a limit to the compassion owed even to a woman bereaved of her child, when she behaved so ridiculously.

'This maid had a lover. Do you know who he was?'

Helewisia did not look at Emma, but instead stared over her shoulder. 'If you wanted to learn, you could do worse than question Henry Paffard's son, Gregory.'

Baldwin turned and followed her pointing finger.

Gregory was a boy of middle height, with a chubbiness about him like his mother. He wore a long tunic, fur-lined cloak and warm felt hat as he entered the hall. His eyes were deep and brown, and he had a habit of blinking rapidly, Baldwin saw. Perhaps it showed he was upset, but in the past Baldwin had known such signs to be proof of guilt. He cast an eye over the lad, saying, 'You have seen them together?'

'No, it's just that he's a wastrel who spends his time in frivolous enjoyment instead of working. You ask him, if you want to know who she was with before she died.'

'He was with his father at the Cock,' Baldwin said.

'And came back before his father.'

Rougemont Castle

Sir James de Cockington was a man of power and authority. He commanded the Posse of the county, he was responsible for the main strategic sites, such as Exeter, and he upheld the law across his demesne.

And yet Baldwin de Furnshill had disappeared.

He had no right to go when he had been told to wait for Sir

James to call him in. He was *Sheriff*, in God's name, not some tradesman who could be expected to remain waiting for a knight to return at his leisure.

But there had been that cryptic comment about the King. He didn't like that. There was something threatening about it, and it was not for Baldwin to threaten his Sheriff. That was not his place. It was insulting.

'What is that noise?' he demanded of his page-boy.

Outside there was the sound of bells rising up from the Cathedral.

'I don't know, sir,' the boy said, quailing at the sight of the Sheriff's anger. He was used to being beaten or kicked when things did not go well for the Sheriff. Today he was safe, however. Sir James had other things on his mind.

'Go and find out. And while you're there, also find out where in God's good name that damned fool Furnshill has got to! Find him, and demand that he come here and explain himself!'

Combe Street

Gregory watched the knight talking to that busybody Helewisia, and when she turned and looked at him, he knew it was his turn to be questioned.

He stood firmly, refusing to be antagonised. 'Yes?'

'I am Sir Baldwin de Furnshill. Precentor Murimuth asked me to learn about this maid's death, if I may.'

'So?'

'Were you her lover?'

Gregory stared at him, then gestured down at the body. 'With *her*? You have a poor opinion of me, if you would accuse me of *that*. No. She was not my lover, neither willingly nor unwillingly. Besides, you heard: I was with my father and mother at the Cock.'

'Others think you a wastrel.'

'People should be careful whom they insult,' he said, his voice lower and angry. 'I would not take kindly to such smears being bandied about.'

'It is hard to keep secrets in a small house.'

'Is it?' he said. 'How interesting.'

'Did she have a lover inside the house? An apprentice? Another servant?'

'I never saw her with anyone,' Gregory said firmly. 'If I had, I would have spoken to her and her lover. I wouldn't want a promiscuous maid in the house.'

Baldwin nodded, and then looked at Wolf. The boy was still cuddling and petting him enthusiastically. 'You like him?' he said gently.

Thomas looked up at him and seemed about to reply, but then, seeing his brother, he rose to his feet and slowly backed away.

'My brother Thomas is very fearful of all people since Alice's death,' Gregory said coolly. 'It shocked him.'

'As it must,' Baldwin said.

But there was something in Thomas's manner that jarred. The young lad looked less alarmed by the corpse which had been the focus of their attention, and more by his own brother.

CHAPTER ELEVEN

De Coyntes' House

Bydaud de Coyntes was glad to be away from the alley. Every so often the breeze had turned and brought with it the distinctive stench of death, and he had almost gagged.

His house was at the other side of the alley from Paffard's. It was small, more or less the same size as the Avices' house, but better located, bordering Combe Street. Of course, both were a great deal smaller than Paffard's. That was enormous, as befitted one of the city's wealthiest men. But that did not matter. Bydaud was rich enough, he felt. Emma was a good woman, his daughters were the pride of his life, and he had money enough to keep them all warm and fed. There was little more a man would wish from life usually.

'Peg, bring me a flagon of wine, and mazers for me and Emma,' he called to the maid as he squatted at the fireside, poking the embers until sparks gleamed and burst into the air. He blew gently, and flames erupted along the length of the logs resting on top, until he could feel the heat.

It was bright outside, but in here it was always gloomy. He took a taper and lit the candles in their great iron stands, then the smaller candles on the spikes in the walls.

He needed light to drive away thoughts of death. Since the unrest last year, when the King had been captured and imprisoned, there had been a lingering sense of unease about the city, and Alice's murder only served to underline the tension.

'Husband, to burn so many candles is expensive!'

'I know, woman. But I enjoy the light.'

Emma sighed and shook her head. 'We should save money, Bydaud.'

He blew out the taper and dropped it into the pot hanging on the wall by the door, then dipped his finger in the stoup of holy water and crossed himself, before going to his chair and sitting. 'Come here.'

Emma scowled. 'This is no time for—'

'Woman, come here.'

She gave an exclamation of annoyance, but obeyed him and sat on his lap.

He placed his arms about her waist. 'There, that's better.'

'You should be working.'

'I have a meeting with Henry later at the Cock Inn. I will be working then. All work and no pleasantry would make for a tedious life, wife.'

'Oh? Get off me!'

He withdrew his hand from her bodice as she slapped him, but then clasped her in a tight embrace, and this time kissed her until she put her hands on his head and pulled him closer. He was utterly maddening, but he was kind, considerate, handsome, and she loved him.

And while the maid from Paffard's was dead, Emma wanted to celebrate life, as though by making love with Bydaud she could eradicate the memory of the other girl's cold, lifeless flesh.

Precentor's House, Cathedral Close

Baldwin was standing and tickling Wolf's ears in Adam Murimuth's chamber when the door opened and the vicar entered.

After the inquest, Baldwin had suggested to Sir Richard that they should inform the Precentor of the outcome. It was there, in Murimuth's hall, that the Precentor had told them of the man suspected of running into the Close after the murder.

'I am sure he is innocent,' Murimuth said unconvincingly, 'but I would be remiss were I not to tell you.'

'I should like to speak with him,' Baldwin said.

Adam Murimuth nodded with sadness as he sent for the vicar.

It was some minutes before Father Laurence entered, and Sir Richard gave him a quizzical stare, commenting loudly, 'They build vicars more heftily here than at my home.'

Murimuth was already feeling guilty, as though he had surrendered Father Laurence to the hangman. Laurence was the son of a baron near Axminster. It was unthinkable that he could have had anything to do with the murder of some maidservant. Out of the question. He sat on a stool with a sense of misery that he could ever have thought Laurence involved. And yet . . .

'Father, there was a murder in a yard out near Combe Street last Saturday,' Baldwin began.

'In the alley,' Father Laurence said calmly.

Sir Richard said, 'You saw the body?'

'I almost fell over her. As soon as I realised she was dead, I was struck with fear lest I should be thought to be the killer. I ran, I'm afraid.'

'Which way did you run?' Baldwin said.

'Down to Combe Street and back up Southgate Street. I knew that Mark on the Bear Gate would let me in.'

'So you didn't see the woman who was declared First Finder?' Baldwin said.

'I saw no one. Or didn't notice. It was late, so—'

'Yes,' interrupted Baldwin. 'It was late – so why were you there?'

'I was visiting a friend.'

'Who?'

'Father Paul at Holy Trinity.'

'And after that you walked up to Combe Street?' Baldwin asked. 'Why turn up there, instead of heading into the Cathedral Close?'

'I was thinking of things.'

'Such as?'

'Private matters that concern only me,' Father Laurence said quietly.

'So, you found her. Why run? It was your duty as a priest to pray over her. You were derelict in your duties, surely?'

'I was. I went to her, and saw who it was, and that scared me.'

Laurence was pale, but composed. Baldwin thought it was strange to see the man accepting his failure without trying to defend himself.

'Was there a reason for you to fail in such a dramatic manner?' Baldwin asked.

'I panicked.'

'Was she your lover?' Sir Richard demanded.

'No,' he said, and there was a slight movement of his lips, as though he was close to smiling.

Sir Richard said scornfully, 'It ill behoves you to run away at the sight of a poor young girl's corpse.'

'Why were you in the alley?' Baldwin pressed. 'It leads nowhere, but to the Paffards' house.'

'I had a lot on my mind, as I said,' Laurence said, and now he glanced at Adam Murimuth. 'I was in the church with Father Paul, and he gave me many things to consider, so I went outside to think through all he said. It has nothing to do with this murder.'

It was clear that the man was determined to stick with this story.

Murimuth peered at him anxiously. 'Is this a matter for the confessional, Father?'

The priest looked at him, and there was pain in his eyes. 'No. There has been no sin on my part. Only a foolish hope.'

Baldwin did not get the impression of guilt from Father Laurence's appearance. In his experience, a guilty man would look away, would nervously fidget, would twitch. This vicar stood resolutely, like a man-at-arms waiting for a cavalry charge: with trepidation, but with courage. Yet some men who were guilty did not think their crimes a felony. Perhaps this was one such man.

'I will ask one last time: why were you there? Will you not answer?'

'There are some things even a vicar may hold to himself. Things which hurt no other. I will not tell you more. It is my affair,' Laurence repeated.

'No doubt,' Adam said, 'you feared that the murderer might still be there in the alley, and your life could also be in danger.'

It was a good excuse. Baldwin could have kicked the Precentor for supplying it, but Father Laurence shook his head.

'No, I will not lie. I had no such fear, yet I was anxious not to be discovered, so I ran away.'

'I will inform the Coroner of your story,' Baldwin said heavily. 'He will have to know.'

'Please!' Laurence turned an anguished face to him. 'If you do that, it will be bruited about the city. I would rather it was kept private.'

'This is not a private matter,' Baldwin said flatly. 'This is an enquiry into a maid's murder. I would have the truth, and if not, I would certainly not help you keep secret the little you have told us.'

Laurence threw a look at Adam Murimuth. 'Precentor, could you not intercede for me? There is nothing that can assist the matter of this girl's murder. Can you not ask that it be kept secret?'

'Why on earth should I? Really, this is the most ridiculous situation I can imagine,' Murimuth said tetchily. 'You deny guilt, but refuse to aid the good knights here, and then demand that I help you? No! Certainly not! I suggest you go at once and pray, because your heart must tell you that this silence is shameful. You are concealing something, Vicar, and I would have the truth confessed. You have failed in your duty to your cloth.'

Baldwin turned back to Wolf as the vicar left them.

'What's ailing the fellow?' Sir Richard muttered. 'Cannot make sense of him. Denies all, but refuses to tell us anything that could corroborate his story.'

'I wish I knew,' Murimuth said. He had walked to his sideboard and filled three goblets. 'He is a good man, I know: dutiful, honourable, and kind to all whom he meets. I cannot understand this attitude of his.'

He passed the wine around, musing that if he could, it would be tempting to force the man to confess to what he knew. Murimuth had enough to contend with already without the recalcitrant vicar.

'He is troubled,' Baldwin said musingly. 'He was firm, reluctant, but not defensive. A strange mixture. Precentor, could you ask this Father Paul if he recalls the conversation with Father Laurence? Especially if there was any means of telling when they parted. And I would ask that you have Father Laurence watched. Carefully: there is no need to worry him further. I would not wish him to compound his crime by fleeing the Cathedral. Meanwhile, perhaps I should speak to Henry Paffard too, just to ascertain whether there was any possible infatuation that the maid had for the priest? Paffard may, possibly, have heard something.'

'Yet his son is rumoured to have had an interest in the girl,' Sir Richard rumbled.

'Yes,' Baldwin said with a frown. 'But Gregory appeared scathing about such an idea. He was most emphatic on the point. Whereas his father looked more deeply shocked. There is something troubling Henry deeply, which may possibly have a bearing on the murder. If he thought she was having an affair of the heart with a vicar, he could be ashamed or fretful, I suppose. She was in his care.'

'Something troubling him?' Adam Murimuth said with a sarcastic laugh. 'I think there is enough to trouble all of us just now, wouldn't you?'

Holy Trinity Church

Father Paul was recovering from a bout of coughing when the Coroner's Clerk arrived.

'Father, the wench's body is ready for you now. The Fosser is coming to take her to the Cathedral.'

The vicar rose and wearily went outside. His fit had ceased, but it had left him profoundly exhausted, and his head was aching now with a steady, thundering beat that made him wish to close his eyes.

It took little time to walk to her, and as soon as Father Paul arrived, he found only a few men standing about idly, some little bratchets staring with goggling eyes at the form beneath the winding sheet. The Fosser from the Cathedral and Benjamin, Henry Paffard's apprentice, were lifting the body onto a small handcart.

'Stop that snivelling, Ben!' his master snapped.

Father Paul glared at Henry. 'Master Paffard, it is right that the boy should mourn the passing of the girl.'

'She's dead, and that is an end to it,' Henry stated callously, but there was a distinct redness in his eyes. He looked like a man who was mourning the passing of his maid, no matter how he spoke.

Watching the men place the body on the cart, Henry jerked his thumb. 'Ben, fetch my wife and the others. Then you may return to your duties.'

'Benjamin must come with us, Master,' Father Paul said. 'He grieves for her too.'

'Be damned to that!' Henry said hoarsely. 'I have a business to run, and Benjamin and the other apprentices have work to do. There is an entire set of plate to be made for the Sheriff, and a pair of bowls and goblets for the de Tracys. I cannot have my boys leaving their duties when there is so much to be done.'

'The child here was under your protection,' Father Paul said, resting his hand upon the shrouded head of the corpse. 'It is your duty to her to see that she is properly buried, and that means her friends from amongst your household should be there. She requires their prayers.'

'Oh, very well, if you insist,' Henry said, waving his hand in irritation. 'But hurry, Ben.'

In a matter of minutes, the Paffard household was gathered. Father Paul watched as Claricia Paffard and her two sons came down the steps to join her husband, their daughter Agatha a pale figure behind her. After them came the family bottler, then Benjamin and two other apprentices, while Joan brought up the rear, wiping her eyes all the while. Father Paul stood at the front of the column and they began to walk to the Cathedral behind the Fosser and his cart.

The hill to Carfoix was not steep, but in recent times the vicar had found it intolerable. Today, rather than be forced to endure a second coughing fit, he ordered the Fosser to turn into the Bear Gate, and from here they entered the Cathedral Close, walking with a slow, respectful tread to the great West Door, avoiding the masons' tools and the other men working on the rebuilding. Father Paul could not but help a quick glance about him.

He felt that same poignancy that so many others must have, whenever he surveyed the Cathedral. It was such a massive undertaking, to pull down the old building so it could be built up stronger and larger, ever more beautiful. Many Bishops had striven to make this glorious building still more magnificent, and all had died before seeing the fruits of their ambitions. Paul knew that he must die before this was complete, just as they had. There was no possibility of its being finished during his lifetime, sadly.

They brought the body to the hearse in front of the Chapel of St Peter, and there set her down, and while Father Paul spoke to one of the vicars, arranging for candles and incense, the Paffard household stood silent. There were sniffs from Joan, and from young Thomas, Father Paul noticed, but all the others stood with restraint in every line of their faces.

It was so sad to see them like this. No demonstration of sadness or affection, but from the youngest and the closest. All others were mute.

Father Paul stood before them, staring at the cross for a long time, and then, before he began the service, he allowed his hand to rest once more on the dead girl's head.

'Poor child,' he murmured, and his voice was clogged with tears.

CHAPTER TWELVE

St Pancras Lane

Baldwin and Sir Richard stood outside Edith's home with Edgar standing respectfully a little way apart.

The door opened at Baldwin's knock, and the maidservant Jane stood, warily watching Wolf as he padded past her, walking straight to the fire and dropping before it with an audible thud.

'Sir Baldwin!' Edith cried on seeing him. She ran the first steps over the floor, just as she had when a child, and then catching sight of Jane's disapproving face, slowed to a sedate maidenly pace, before throwing her arms into the air, beaming, and hurtling over the last few feet. 'It is so good to see you again!'

Baldwin smiled as she took his hands in hers, but then she was looking over his shoulder, once more the lady of the house.

'Sir Richard, you are very welcome. I hope I see you well?'

'Hah! My lady, how could any man not feel well at the sight of such loveliness?' Sir Richard rumbled, walking into the room and bowing. 'You grow more beautiful every time I see you, and I can only assume God smiled benevolently upon your father when you were conceived, for clearly He has turned his face from Simon since then, if his own appearance is any form of evidence!'

'You flatter me, Sir Richard,' she said. 'But you must both be hungry. Will you not join us in a meal?'

'No, Edith. We are fine,' Baldwin said, ignoring the mumble of disagreement from Sir Richard. 'Is Simon awake? I would appreciate his assistance. And perhaps your husband's, too.'

'Peter is in his father's counting-house this morning, Sir Baldwin. My father could take you there, I'm sure. He knows where it is – but he's out in the yard with my son just now.'

Baldwin and Sir Richard waited in the hall, and soon Simon was with them.

'I hope you slept well in the Cathedral's guest rooms?'

Baldwin grimaced. 'It would have been better without the snoring.'

'Snoring?' Sir Richard demanded.

Baldwin ignored him. 'There has been a murder, Simon – the killing of a maid who works for a man called Paffard. He's a wealthy city merchant, and I thought your son-in-law or his father might know him.'

'I see. Well, we can walk around there if you like.'

It was only a short way. Charles, Edith's father-in-law, had a new house only a stone's throw from the Guild Hall, and as soon as Baldwin and the others were shown in, Peter rose from his table to greet them.

He was a good-looking young man, still very boyish in appearance, but with a coolness towards Simon, Baldwin noticed. While Edith had been pregnant, she had been captured by men on the orders of Simon's enemy, and Peter himself

107

arrested and held in gaol. The memory still rankled, plainly. Still, he was polite enough to the two knights and Simon as he begged them to accept wine and cakes.

Sir Richard smacked his lips after an enormous gulp that all but drained his mazer, while Peter spoke to Baldwin.

'Henry Paffard? Yes, I know him well. He is a member of the Freedom of the City, as is my father. I hope to be a member too, one day. But that will be some while, obviously. It tends to be for men of proven acumen.'

'There has been a murder in his household – a young woman who was his maid.'

'He is a very honourable man. A leading merchant in the city, and one of the most important clients of my father,' Peter said.

'You do not need to fear that we will embarrass you with your father's client,' Baldwin said with a faint smile. 'It is already thought that the man who committed this killing was heard fleeing. The porter at the Cathedral heard him. But sometimes it is possible to glean something about a maid from the household. I was wondering whether you would be able to introduce me to him? It would be rude and thoughtless to go to a house that was mourning a dead maidservant, and begin to ask questions, but if an introduction could be made . . . ?' He left the question hanging.

'Oh, well, I suppose that should be no difficulty,' Peter said. 'So long as there wouldn't be any trouble with my father's business.'

Baldwin shook his head. 'I foresee no reason for an altercation. It is only an enquiry into the maid's death.'

Rougemont Castle

Sheriff James de Cockington span on his heel when the knock came at his door, and when he saw the nervous features of the pageboy, his expression darkened instantly.

'You have Sir Baldwin with you, eh? Bring him in immediately! I will not have my—'

'Sir, I am very sorry, I haven't found him. However, I—'

'You haven't found him? Is this a guest-house for the bored and lunatic that you come here with that news? I want Furnshill here *now*, and you don't come back until you can deliver him to me, you son of a whore!'

'Sir, I . . .'

The boy was shoved aside and a tall, lean man in blue particoloured clothing walked in. He gave a cursory bow, as one might to an equal.

Sir James gritted his teeth, recognising the uniform. 'You are most welcome, my friend. You have messages from the King?'

He motioned to the page to close the door, flapping his hands, and then changed his mind. 'Call my steward to me, boy, and then go to find Sir Baldwin. Understand?'

'I only have a short time,' the messenger said coolly when they were alone. He walked stiffly, as would a man who had spent much of the last week in the saddle, opening his little satchel as he went. Withdrawing a scroll, he passed it to Sir James.

The steward had arrived, and now, taking a quick look at the Sheriff's face, he bowed deeply and went to fetch wine.

'Where have you come from?' Sir James asked, his eyes on the scroll, and then, as the words sank in, 'Christ's ballocks!'

'The King is at York,' the messenger said suavely. 'It was fortunate that I happened to be riding to Berkeley with other messages, and was made aware of the situation.'

'Sir Edward of Caernarfon has been freed? Does my Lord de

Berkeley have any idea who was responsible?' Sir James continued, reading furiously.

'It was the Dunheved brothers with a gang. The castellan was convinced of that. My Lord de Berkeley is on his way to join with the King to attack the rebels in Scotland, so the castellan is doing all he may. Men are riding all about the area, but no sign has been discovered as yet. The gang managed to break into the castle, ransacking the place, before taking the knight with them. Several men were killed, including a banker from the House of Bardi. The castle was in a terrible state when I reached it.'

'Dear merciful heavens!'

'So, the castellan asks that you ensure that all are aware of the dangers, and that the city's bailiffs are told to keep a firm lookout for any large parties of men riding about. Also, that you inform all the officers of the law in Devonshire of this, and that they should listen for any clues as to the whereabouts of the man who was King, of the Dunheved brothers, of William Aylmer, and all the others listed in that report.'

'Yes, of course,' Sir James replied, reading through the names carefully. Twenty-one had been hastily scrawled under the note.

'If you would provide a clerk to copy the message, I will continue on my way.'

'Naturally,' Sir James agreed, and bellowed for his clerk. Soon he had sent the latter to copy the message, while the messenger was taken to the hall for food and drink.

When Sir James was alone again, he sipped wine pensively as he considered the letter with its alarming news.

He always prided himself on being with the men who were in power. It had occasionally been a delicate balancing act, but he had survived when weaker men would have allowed despair to overtake them.

But this new situation would take some thinking through . . . What were the chances of Sir Edward of Caernarfon managing to gather enough men under his banner to wrest the crown back from his son? And would he be able to force his son to submit?

Because if there was the remotest chance of that, Sir James de Cockington would want to be with him.

Paffards' House

It was a relief to be back from the burial, Henry thought. Such a sad, horrible service, made all the worse by the body lying before them, a constant reminder of guilt, and his wife staring at him with resentment and contempt.

Returning to his hall, he sat in his great chair and gazed at the wall with unseeing eyes.

Alice's death had been a shock, and was all the more unwelcome because of his other ventures. He knew that at any time soon, Sir Charles of Lancaster could arrive, and when he did, he would expect payment for the goods he had with him. That had been the original bargain. However, there were no funds in the house, not since his acquisition of the house up in Stepecoat Street. Still, it should be easy enough for him to persuade Sir Charles that he could sell the goods and find finance that way. He had no choice, in any case.

He was still sitting in his chair when Thomas walked in. The youngster said nothing. He merely peered at his father with his pale, fretful eyes, and then trotted out of the room again.

It was so out of character, it tore at Henry's heart. Thomas Paffard had always been an unruly little fellow, but with a smile so engaging that it was impossible to be angry with him – not for long, anyway.

At six Thomas had already learned the basics of much of his schooling. He was quick to comprehend the figures on the sheets, and appeared to enjoy his sums so much that he had taken to carrying a wax tablet with him wherever he went. On it he would make calculations, and have his father's clerks check his results. It was delightful.

The lad was not merely a scholar, though. He was very much a normal boy, with the energy and noise that went with that class of creature. All through the day he would run and stamp, shout and slam doors: always happy. Loud, boisterous, exuberant, and intelligent, he was the perfect son for any man.

But the noise had stopped a couple of days ago. The boy had been fond of Alice, as had they all.

No, not as they all had. Henry had known her especially well.

Henry covered his face with his hands, and wept for the loss of his lover.

CHAPTER THIRTEEN

Paffards' House

'What is the matter?' his older son asked.

Henry hadn't noticed Gregory walk in, and he couldn't answer for a moment. He just turned and looked at him, while in his mind's eye he saw Alice, her lithe body, her spirit. 'Do you feel nothing for her?' he managed.

Since the death of Alice, Gregory had been blinking a lot. It was surely because he missed her too, but his demeanour was not that of a bereaved man, but rather of a child who'd lost a favourite toy. Lazy, ineffectual and unbusinesslike, he was not the man Henry had hoped he would become. Henry had wanted a strong son, one who was dedicated to the family and the business. Instead, he had a boy who was spendthrift, and possibly worse.

'She was a good maid, I suppose. *You* were very fond of her, weren't you?' His tone was pointed, his manner accusing, and Henry felt a sudden anger.

'Don't speak to me like that! At least I grieve for the poor girl.'

'Yeah, well, I suppose we all do in our own ways. Even you're quieter than normal, Father.'

'Don't insult me, Greg. I can still take a belt to you,' Henry snapped. 'She was a good maidservant, that's all.'

'Yes, Father. *That's all*,' Gregory said slyly. 'You'll need another maid soon. We can't have the place getting into a mess. That's all that matters, isn't it?'

Henry ignored his sarcasm. There was a lot to forgive just now. Gregory was almost nineteen years old, and when he was younger he had been as affectionate and warm-hearted as Thomas; it was only in recent years he had grown into this peevish youth.

'Perhaps I should feel remorse at the way I raised you, Gregory,' Henry said heavily. 'I haven't, perhaps, served you well. You've always had a good brain, just like your sister, like Thomas too. I should have ensured that you had more opportunities to use it.'

'I use it all I want.'

'For what? Gaming and drinking?'

Henry set his jaw. It was Claricia who had failed them, as usual. It was the way she'd cosseted Greg that had spoiled him. She should have forced him to work more. Instead she had indulged his whims, and it was her fault that the fellow had turned out like this: more interested in his clothing than in the business that gave him the money for his fripperies.

'I enjoy gambling and drinking,' Gregory smiled.

There was a malicious gleam in his eye. Henry saw it, and rage heated his blood.

'I never sent you with the ships, did I? Because I knew sailing was dangerous, and I didn't want to lose you. There are always ships sinking, because of shipmasters' incompetence, or piracy, or sometimes the monsters of the deep which break ships apart. There are many perils on the waves and below. That was why I never sent you abroad.'

'You never bothered to ask me for my opinion, but as it happens I didn't *want* to go. I have no desire to learn your trade. What is it to me that wine comes from Bordeaux? Send your agents to find it and bring it back, but don't expect me to do so.'

'It was the ships that persuaded me to move into other ways of making money. A little loan here or there at good interest rates, purchasing properties and renting them out again . . . There are any number of ways to make money if you are bold. I had hoped you would see that. I had hoped you would learn a new trade to bring to the business.'

'What do I want with a trade? I'm happy as I am.'

Henry bit back an angry response. Gregory needed an occupation. That was the reason for his ill-humour. He had a good mind and needed to use it more. And Henry could use a good brain. His son was not adept at pewter-working, but he might still have a financial brain suitable for importing wine, or for negotiating with sellers and buyers.

'You spend too much time in idleness and in frivolity. You should spend more time with me.'

'Father, I have no desire to do so.'

'*Desire* has nothing to do with it, boy. This city is a place of wildness and danger. You don't realise how lucky you are! As my son, you've been protected. Most men and women go through life worried to death about where their next meal will come from; about their work, and whether they will earn enough to keep them in their house. Look at the Marsilles. Once they were almost as wealthy as us – but now? Nick died, and his family have to scrape a living as best they might. Emma de Coyntes has told me that they have been upsetting her and her daughters. They haven't paid the rent for weeks either, so I may have to evict them. The Marsilles' lives are teetering, and can soon fall into ruin.'

'They are so lucky they have you to protect them,' Gregory said.

Henry shot him a look, seeking cynicism or deceit, but couldn't be certain. He resorted to a bland, 'Yes. It could be worse for them.'

'Anyway, I have no interest in the business,' Gregory declared. 'I cannot run the place.'

Henry had to clench his jaw to stop the bellow of rage that threatened to burst from him. At last he forced a grin to his features. 'Really? You have no interest. That is good. So, when I die, I should leave it all to your brother? Leave you destitute, perhaps? You would prefer that?'

'There is more to life—'

'Don't speak to me like that! You try to tell me about life?' Henry shouted. 'You think I'm a fool? You have no idea about life, or the world. It is nasty, it is dangerous! You have to fight every day, you have to grab what you can, snatch it from your enemies if possible, pry it from their dead fingers if necessary, but you must take it *while you can*! I grew up in poverty, and I've come all this way as a result of my efforts, boy! You sit here, pandering to your desires at my expense, and you have no concept of the cost of it all. This house is expensive. If you want to remain here, you need to learn to help support it.'

'No. I think I don't want to know any more. Be damned to the business! What good does it do us?'

'It keeps you fed, it maintains your wardrobe, it—'

'It's just pointless! I'd rather give it all up, and travel to London. Maybe go on pilgrimage.'

'Pilgrimage? You?'

'Why not? Everyone should take up the pilgrim's cross.'

Henry sneered, 'Well, of course, if that's what you want, there's nothing I can say to prevent you. It'd do you good to trudge through mud and rain for a hundred miles or more.'

'I wish you could pass the business to Agatha. She's more interested in it.'

'I wish I could too. Your sister is keen, but she's not a man. I have to pass it on to a man. And you are my oldest son.'

'And I want nothing to do with it! Let her have it – she would be more successful than me or Thomas,' Gregory threw at him.

'Then it is fortunate I may have a different plan for you,' Henry said, all of a sudden.

'What does that mean?'

Henry eyed his son. He had not mentioned the plots to return King Edward II to his throne, but if the plans were as success-ful as he and Sir Charles believed, there would be rewards for all those who assisted Edward. A knighthood for a son was little enough to ask.

'I am negotiating a deal, Gregory. If it comes good, you may be knighted.'

Gregory gaped, and then laughed derisively. 'You think *I* could be a knight? A man needs money and friends to win such a prize.'

'Listen, you fool! You may have cloth between your ears, but when I speak to you of such matters, you will pay attention! If you will achieve nothing else, you will have to accept what I can do for you. And this, I swear I can arrange. In a short time, if all goes well.'

Gregory nodded. 'Yes, of course you can,' he said sarcasti-cally, then marched out of the room.

Henry stood a while, chewing the inside of his lip.

It was possible that Gregory would come to his senses. It

was possible that he would learn to love the business as Henry did, even that he could eventually bring new ideas to it and increase the family's wealth. But for now, all Henry was convinced of was the desire to take a whip to Gregory's backside and beat some sense into him.

The summons came just as Joan was helping old Sal in the Paffards' kitchen. Sal was ancient, wrinkled, and fat as lard, with small, piggy eyes that watched Joan like a hawk. She believed that all were in her kitchen only to filch her best pies or meats, and she eyed all visitors with a suspicion that was searing. Every time her eyes lighted upon Joan, the maid felt her face flush, a reddening that began at her breast and rose inexorably until her whole face was as bright as the sunset on a clear day. It drove her mad to think that a mere glance could do this to her; she knew it only served to make her look guilty, but she could do nothing about it.

She was unused to being called to the hall. There were other rooms into which her duties often brought her, but the hall itself and the merchant's counting-house, plus his small chamber beyond, in which he stored the choicest prizes from his foreign expeditions – rich tapestries, cloth of gold, even some ingots of silver – all were denied to her. Only John, the elderly bottler, was permitted to enter them.

Her legs were leaden as she walked along the passage from the kitchen to the hall. What had she done wrong, to be summoned like this? She could not afford to lose this job. There would be no more for a girl like her before the next fair.

'Joan, come here,' Henry said as she peered round the doorframe.

She walked in, her head downcast.

'Do you know why we've called you in here?' he said.

She looked up, trying to think of any unintentional crime she might have committed, but could think of none. Then she noticed that Claricia was beside her husband. There was no anger in her eyes, only a deep sadness. She was always a timid woman, and the death of Alice had sapped the spirit that remained.

'No, sir.'

He gave a gesture of irritation. 'Child, do you have a brain in your head? How old are you now? Fifteen? You should be able to think for yourself. Our rooms here need a maid to keep them clean. John cannot do all on his own. Alice used to help me in here, but now she is gone – so what is to be done with all the tasks she had? There is nothing for it, but to have you fill in. You will take on her duties as well as your own until we resolve this situation. Soon we must manage to find another to take her place.'

'Yes, sir,' she said reluctantly. 'But . . .'

'There is nothing more to be said. What, would you expect my wife to do this work? For shame!'

'I have many duties, sir.'

'I am aware. We shall attempt to ensure that the additional work is not onerous.'

Not onerous, she thought. Yet she was already busy all week. And he wanted her to take on Alice's duties!

'Well?' Henry demanded. 'Do you have an objection?'

'No, sir.'

'Good, because I would not like to lose you as well as Alice. She was an asset to the house. Be sure that you will be too. You know her duties, I think? In here, in our solar, you are to keep all clean. Make sure that the fire's lit, that the candles are all trimmed and ready . . . You will know. Now, you may go.'

She almost tried to object again, but in the face of his unflinching stare, she managed only a second flush, and with her head hanging, she hurried from the room, heart thudding painfully.

'These idiots!' he muttered. 'God knows where we got them.'

'Oh, *shut up!*' Claricia spat suddenly, and walked from the room.

He was still in the hall a few minutes later, in shock, like a man who had stroked his pet pup only to have a finger bitten off, when there came a firm knock at the door and he heard old John answer it, then announce.

'Sir Baldwin de Furnshill and Sir Richard de Welles, sir.'

CHAPTER FOURTEEN

Paffards' House

Baldwin and Sir Richard had told Simon about the inquest results and that a man had been heard running away from the area.

'So, Simon, with luck we should be able to leave here very soon,' Baldwin concluded. 'Tomorrow morning, I hope to be able to advise Precentor Adam that either the murderer has escaped, or that he remains in the Cathedral and his name is Father Laurence.'

'What is the point of coming here to the Paffards' house, then?'

Baldwin waited while Peter knocked at the door. 'We are merely completing the task. Collecting facts. As you know, it is my belief that a murder is a story like any other. If we can understand what the dead are trying to tell us, we can uncover the truth.'

'But you know the truth, surely. The priest was there: he admits it.'

'Yet he does not confess to murder – even though he would suffer little punishment, for his robes protect him. Why did he admit to being there? If he were the killer, surely he would lie about that?'

'So you think he's innocent?'

'I do not know, but I would like to be convinced that there was nobody else in the alley that night. Did the maid have a lover? Gregory Paffard was convinced she did not, but she did lie with a man the day she died. And then was killed.'

'Priests have taken women before now.'

'Possibly, yes,' Baldwin agreed. 'But that would involve the priest being with her quite some time. How would that be, when he has already told me that he was only free for a short time? Perhaps that was a lie, and Father Paul will expose him. We must speak with the good Father.'

He was still musing on these matters when the door swung open and John the bottler allowed them inside. He led them along a corridor, past a business chamber and a parlour, and out to a large hall beyond.

As they walked, a door opened, and Baldwin saw Claricia Paffard standing there. She was a tall, well-built woman. Outside, Baldwin had scarcely noticed her because his attention was fixed on the witnesses and Alice's body, but now he saw Claricia more closely, he was struck by her appearance.

Once she would have been beautiful. Her hair was restrained decorously beneath her wimple, but her face was well-featured and very pleasing. She wore a long tunic of green velvet, bound about her waist with a belt decorated with enamelled panels. There was rich embroidery at her throat and hem, and the over-all impression was of a comfortable, wealthy woman, but for the expression in her large, lustrous eyes. In them, Baldwin saw a despair that reminded him of something.

That expression nagged at him as he followed the steward into the hall. There, John stood aside to let them all in.

'Ah, Peter! To what do I owe this pleasure?' Henry said, rising from his chair.

Baldwin studied him. He saw that Paffard was under a strain. He tried hard, but could not hide his tension. 'We met this morning, Master Paffard. At the inquest.'

'Of course. Apart from you, I think?' he said, looking at Simon, who introduced himself, and when he had done so, Henry continued, looking from one to the other: 'I am at a loss, I confess. How may I help you?'

'How long had Alice been living here?' Baldwin asked.

'Some two years, I suppose – no, three. She was seventeen, and I recall she came here when she was but fourteen.'

'She was happy?'

'She was assiduous in the tasks given to her. I think she found satisfaction, yes.'

'Did she have many friends?'

'All the servants here would have been happy with her,' Henry said quietly. 'I am sure she wouldn't have lacked companions.'

'But what of men? She was young and attractive. Was there no one wooing her?'

'If there was, I'd have had him thrashed, and if she had encouraged him, I'd have had her thrashed too, and thrown her from my door. I have a daughter of her age. I wouldn't have an incontinent maid under my roof fornicating with all and sundry!'

'You take a strong line on such behaviour?'

'There are many who relax their rules. I do not. It is not merely prurience: I have to consider the security of my house. If my maids were to bring young lemans here, any one of them could be the first of a gang of picklocks who sought to steal in under dead of night to rob me. I will not have promiscuous wenches working here.'

'That is very clear, I thank you,' Baldwin said.

Simon could see from his friend's expression that he disliked this merchant. Arrogant, bullying in manner, he was the archetype of the modern rich men whom Baldwin so detested.

'So, you never saw her bring a friend into the house?'

'Of course not!'

There was a kind of suppressed fury in his manner that intrigued Simon. Something Baldwin had said must have struck home, but he had no idea what that might be.

'Did you see her in the company of a priest?' Baldwin asked. 'A vicar from the Cathedral?'

'I said to you—'

'A vicar is hardly the same as a young apprentice draw-latch, Master Paffard,' Baldwin said bluntly. 'Not many would attribute to a priest the same imperfections you attribute to others.'

'I saw no priest here. No. And she had no need of a vicar from the Cathedral. She was well served by the vicar at Trinity Church.'

'Do you know of a Father Laurence?'

Henry shook his head quickly. 'He's from the Cathedral?'

'Yes,' Baldwin said. 'He actually found the girl *before* Joan – but he denies killing her.'

'The bastard! He denies it? You should question him most vigorously. Put him to the *peine forte et dure* until he confesses!'

'We cannot do that, as you know. I shall definitely tell the Precentor of your suggestion, however. I am sure he will be pleased to do as you suggest,' Baldwin said suavely.

Combe Street

Joan was glad to be out of the house when she was sent to empty the washing barrel. She carried it laboriously down to the street, and gazed into the gutter. There was a dead rat and a dog blocking the way, and she carried the water a little further, tipping the heavy bowl beyond them so they wouldn't dam the flow.

It was hard, doing all this work. Still, it was good to be out in the open air, even if the daylight was dying.

'Hello, Joan. How are you?'

'Peg – hello. I'm all right, but you're about the first person to ask me. My own household are so bound up with the trouble Alice has put them to that they don't give me a thought.'

'It must have been awful. Anastasia's been desperate to get any bloodthirsty clues she can. I've told her to stop playing the ghoul, but you know what she's like.'

'Yes.' Joan shivered. She had herself been a young girl until Saturday, she thought.

'Here, I heard you say the priest was running past. Was it the man from Holy Trinity? He's been less good than he should have been,' Peg said, eager to change the subject now she noticed the sudden greenish tinge of Joan's face. 'Are you well?'

'Yes, I'm fine. What do you mean about Father Paul?'

'He's been entertaining whores, according to two of the stable boys I heard talking about him. Apparently he takes them in at night. He says,' Peg added with a roll of her eyes, 'that he's just praying with them and feeding them. I'll bet I can guess what sort of payment they give in return . . .'

Suddenly John the bottler was with them. 'Well, you shouldn't listen to such gossip, should you, Peg? Joan, back inside, girl, before Sal starts shouting for you. And I'm sure you have work to get on with, Peg, eh?'

125

CHAPTER FIFTEEN

Cock Inn, Southgate Street

Peter left them as they walked from the Paffards' house. He looked troubled after their meeting with Henry Paffard, and Simon felt a fleeting guilt in case it could cause problems for his son-in-law, but then he reflected that the merchant had been rude and hectoring. He probably wasn't used to being questioned in such a manner. It was enough to make him angry when confronted by a trio such as Baldwin, Sir Richard and Simon. In any case, the man had probably forgotten all about them by now, Simon reckoned. He would be sitting at his great table with a silver goblet, thinking about his business no doubt.

And now he looked up with a feeling of impending doom as Sir Richard stopped outside a rough-looking inn with a great sigh of contentment. Simon recognised his expression. Usually it portended a bad headache for him on the morrow.

'You know, it was in here that I was told the jest about the cleanest leaf. Did I tell you that one? Eh? What is the cleanest leaf in the world? Eh? Can't get it? The Holly, because no one would wipe his arse with one! Eh?' He laughed uproariously, and Simon chuckled for his benefit. Sir Richard was a kind man, and while his jokes sometimes missed the mark, to offend him would be like upsetting Baldwin's Wolf. Easily achieved, but mean-minded.

Sir Richard de Welles strode into the inn, narrowly missing the low beam near the door, and stood looking approvingly all about him. It was a large establishment. There were stables behind, which were reached by an alley between the wall and the inn itself, and at the rear of the hall were three large rooms with palliasses liberally scattered for those guests who needs must spend the night here. For those who could not afford a palliasse in the communal sleeping quarters, there was a lean-to with straw spread on the ground.

'I've used this inn on several occasions, and while the bedding charges are usurous, I am very content with the quality of the ale,' Sir Richard boomed happily as he advanced on the host. 'Your best ale, Keeper, and bring it quickly!'

The owner of the inn glanced from Sir Richard to Baldwin, Simon and Edgar with a grimace. 'Can you keep his voice down? He drowns out all my other clients put together.'

'We shall do our best,' Baldwin assured him. 'Although it may not be good enough.'

'Aye. It'd take a charge of chivalry to silence him,' the innkeeper said sourly as he walked to his barrels.

The place was full of merchants and traders who were finished for the day. There was a group of five at the farther end of the room where the innkeeper had his bar, all talking in that loud manner that denoted a good quarter-gallon of strong ale each. A pair of apprentices were playing at merrils nearer the doorway, and in a great huddle stood porters and leather-aproned smiths with cooks and a pair of priests, all chatting animatedly. It was, Simon thought, a gathering that summed up the city itself. There were the men who made money, those learning how to, and the people who moved goods around the city from seller to buyer, and all overlooked by the priests. And there were the women, of course, going from man to man in the hope of winning a few pennies. Wolf looked around once without interest, and lay on the rushes near the fire.

'Could she have come here, do you think?' Simon asked the others, nodding at the women.

Sir Richard looked at the nearest. He smiled broadly and winked, and she gave him an arch grin, making her way over to him.

She was the better-looking of the wenches here, he thought. A cuddly figure, and pretty face, with a tip-tilted nose and freckles.

'Hello,' she said.

'I don't think I know you. What's your name?' Sir Richard said.

'You can call me Poll.'

He eyed her affably. 'Well, Poll, I am glad to meet you. You haven't been here very long, have you?'

'I've been here two months.'

'You are a most welcome addition to the inn,' Sir Richard said.

She giggled and tried to climb into his lap.

'No, Poll. You see, I'm a King's Coroner, and these gentlemen and I are looking into a murder for the Precentor of the Cathedral. Did you know the girl who died on Saturday?'

'Alice?' Poll's grin faded. 'No. Not me.'

'Did she ever come into the inn?'

'No.'

'But you knew her, didn't you?'

'I said no.'

'I know you did. But you're a young lass, and she was, too. Much the same age as you, I'd think. Don't you meet with the girls about here?'

'No, I don't. They don't want to mix with my sort in case they get thought to be in my business.'

'I see.' Sir Richard remained silent, staring at her.

Poll reddened and began to look about her. 'Look, I can't stay here all night.'

'No, of course.'

'I didn't know her.'

'But?'

'Nothing.'

'You didn't know her, but you certainly know someone who did.'

Poll threw him an indignant look. 'I didn't say that.'

'Who is it, Poll?'

She grumbled to herself, then, 'Algar, the stableman's boy. He was very keen on her.'

'I see,' Sir Richard said.

She went away, and he turned to the others about the table. 'I knew it was a good idea to come here.'

The innkeeper returned with their ales and as he was distributing the drinks, Sir Richard leaned back on his seat, which creaked dangerously. 'So, my host, where is this stable-helper Algar? We would speak with him.'

Paffards' House

Claricia Paffard heard the men leave with a mixture of relief and anxiety. Relief that they were going without causing any arguments, and anxiety about her husband's mood after being interrogated.

She had heard much of their conversation, and the tone of Baldwin's voice had shocked her. It was so rude to speak like that to her husband, especially in his own hall! Henry was too important in the city for someone to come and hector him as though he was some pimply lurdan suspected of brawling.

'Mistress? Are you all right?'

She spun around to see that Ben, her husband's apprentice, was staring at her sympathetically.

'Yes, of course I am,' she said huskily, averting her face in shame. He was only being kind, she knew, but the fact remained that he was Henry's apprentice, and she couldn't discuss her troubles with him. It just wouldn't do. 'I am fine.'

'You know if I can help, mistress, I would be glad to,' Ben went on.

She could not look at him: she knew that his eyes would be full of compassion. He hated to see her sad, ever since the day he had found her cowering in the little room off the dairy after Henry had thrashed her with his belt. Ben had covered her back with a blanket and helped her to the kitchen, where Joan and Alice had been working.

Not that it aided her much. To have that *whore* minister to her had been so demeaning. The bitch had been sniggering at her, she was sure. All the time that Joan mixed the poultice, Alice must have been enjoying Claricia's discomfort.

'Once I was able to help,' he said.

'No,' she burst out. 'Leave me!'

'Call me if you need anything,' he said, and would have left the room, but then John entered.

Claricia saw how John's suspicious little eyes went straight to the apprentice. 'Thank you, Ben. That will be all,' she said. Ben nodded to her and sidled past the steward in a hurry, but John kept his eyes on Ben until he was out of the room.

'You need to watch that boy,' he said.

'I know you don't trust him. But he is harmless.'

'You think so?' John snorted. 'He is your husband's apprentice. Devious and dangerous, he is. What if he stores up conversations with you to share with your husband?'

'There is no harm in him,' Claricia said with quiet certainty, and gestured for the old bottler to leave her. Alone, she stood staring at herself in a mirror on the wall. Her eyes were haunted, remembering. Once she had been young and beautiful, the spoiled child of a rich knight. That was why Henry wanted her, for her noble position. Sad to say, after her father died in that inconsequential little battle in Roslin, his lands were sequestered. Without a son, there was little possibility that the family would be renewed, and it was then that she realised she must marry. And she found Henry a good husband. At first, he loved her. It was only in the last thirteen years or so that he stopped giving her that affection that a wife craves. Instead he paid his attentions to others.

Especially that strumpet Alice.

Claricia was not sorry she had died.

She was glad.

CHAPTER SIXTEEN

Cock Inn

Baldwin eyed the boy without pleasure.

Algar was a short, scrawny wretch, with a thatch of tallow hair that appeared to be as full of filth as the straw in the stables it resembled. His grubby face was sly, and Baldwin felt the lad's testimony was unlikely to be reliable.

Sir Richard gave the fellow a long stare, after which he drained his cup of ale, waving it at the innkeeper for a refill.

'So, boy. I think you know why we're here. You knew the girl who was murdered.'

'What girl?'

'Right. We'll begin again, and this time you'll be best served to keep a civil tongue in your head,' Sir Richard rumbled with a genial wave of his hand. 'Otherwise, I will have you taken outside and strapped until you holler for peace. Understand me?'

The boy's expression darkened, but he nodded.

'Now, we are here because we've been told to look into the

girl's death. You knew her, didn't you? We'll have the truth this time.'

'I didn't know her exactly. I liked her, that's all.'

Baldwin was convinced that this at least was true. The idea that this brutish fellow could have tempted Alice was a trifle hard to swallow.

'Did *she* like *you*?' Sir Richard asked patiently.

'Dunno. She was often walkin' past here. I used to see her. She was pretty.'

'Did she come into the inn often?'

'Not at first. But recently she'd started coming in.'

'With whom? She wouldn't enter an inn on her own.'

'I've seen her with her master, Paffard, and his sons – that apprentice of his, too.'

'Paffard used to bring her here?'

'After they'd been about the city. They'd come here for a mess of pottage and ales before returning home.'

Baldwin could imagine them. A cheery group, the father bringing them in to one of the low tables, exercising his patronage with pride, for he was one of the richest men in the city. There were not many who could compete with him when it came to demonstrations of largesse. They would walk in, Henry Paffard in the lead, then his sons, and last of all his apprentice and the maid, these last only to show that their master was so wealthy, he could bring his apprentices and servants with him.

It was curious, nonetheless. Baldwin had not seen many men taking maidservants with them when they went to mess at an inn.

'What of the day she died?' Sir Richard continued. 'Did you see her then?'

'Not here, no,' the boy said shiftily.

'Where, then?'

'It was late afternoon. My master told me to go and fetch a horse from the house of a clerk in Combe Street, and I was leading it back to the stables when I saw her. She was walking out from her master's house.'

'From the alley, you mean?' Baldwin asked.

'No. She was coming out of the main door – as proud as a hen with a new chick, she was. Like she owned the place.'

Paffards' House

Henry Paffard sat at his table for a long time after dark. John had already been in and banked the fire, so that it gleamed dully in the hearth, but John didn't speak to him. He rarely did. John was a servant from Claricia's childhood whom she had insisted on bringing with her, and Henry was happy that the fellow was trained and effective in his job, while not expensive. There were too many bottlers and stewards whom he had seen in his dealings about the city who cost their masters a small fortune.

John had set out a quart jug of wine before he retired, and Henry was more than halfway through it now. The wine didn't help, though. His thoughts kept returning to those men with Peter – Sir Baldwin, Sir Richard and their tatty friend Puttock. It had left him empty and drained when they had finished questioning him. He could see the contempt in their eyes when he spoke of Alice. They seemed to think he had behaved badly.

They couldn't understand. He wasn't like them. Henry Paffard needed more women than others. He was strong, a tiger amongst the men of this city. Where he prowled, others ran or were eaten. He had stronger urges – appetites, passions – than others. He couldn't be measured by the same standard as other, lesser men.

That was their problem, after all. They were looking on him like some sort of equal. They didn't realise who they were talking to. He wasn't some shopkeeper who could be browbeaten. He was Henry Paffard, member of the Freedom of the City, one of the richest men in the whole of Devon. In the country, perhaps.

Church of the Holy Trinity

The knock at his door brought Father Paul back from his reverie.

Since the service he had been thinking about that girl. Alice had been so pretty, it was a shock to think that she was dead, never to be seen again. And Paffard didn't seem to want any demonstration of affection. His sole concern was that, instead of being about their duties, his family and workers were all there at the Cathedral. It was all, from the look on his face, a stupendous waste of time. And yet there were still those unshed tears in his eyes that appeared to belie his hard expression.

It was not only him. Claricia, he sensed, was just as miserable to be there. She had clearly not been fond of the girl – but if Alice was truly, as the rumours suggested, supplementing her income by offering her body – Claricia would scarcely have been glad. A maidservant who flaunted herself, when Claricia had two sons in the household, both impressionable boys, and a husband who must surely have an eye for such an attractive maid, would not have been a comfortable addition to her house. The bottler said nothing, but at least stood staring down into the grave with every indication of sorrow, and when he was called away, he threw a look at Henry Paffard that was so full of vitriol, Father Paul was surprised it did not burn Henry where he stood.

'Yes?' he called as the knock came again. Father Paul slowly rose to his feet, stiff and weary, his mind still set upon Alice's death. The creaking of his joints was louder even than the

135

crackle of his fire, and he grinned wryly to himself at the sound. There was no hiding the fact that he was an old man.

He walked to his door and set his hand on the latch – but then he felt a sudden inexplicable wariness. 'Hello?' he called.

The door instantly burst open, the timbers catching his forehead. He felt the door ride over his toes, pulling the nails from the quick, and would have screamed in agony, but for the man in the doorway.

Father Paul looked up, and saw a tall man with a hessian sack over his face, clad in dark clothing, an old grey cloak hanging tight at his shoulders, who shoved him inside, slamming him against the wall, face to the hard lime-washed plaster.

When he spoke, it was in a rough whisper that terrified Father Paul. 'Shut up, little priest! Shut up or I'll shut you up forever!'

'What do you want?'

'There are stories about you, Father. Stories that you use the bitches from the stews, that you fornicate with abandon, with two or three at a time. Stories I can back up, with witnesses. Remember that, priest.'

'I don't know what you're talking about, man! I don't keep women!'

'What of Sunday? Two whores in here, in the House of God, and you bulling them both, here, in His holy place. You are obscene!'

'My son, you don't understand! I gave them food, and they left. I didn't—'

'You will forget what you saw.'

Father Paul looked up at him. 'Forget what? I don't know what you mean.'

The masked face pressed closer. 'All you saw the night the girl died. You forget all you saw in the street. Don't breathe a word of the people you saw there!'

'For your soul's sake, sit down, tell me what troubles you,' Father Paul said, bewildered. 'Perhaps I can help: let me pray with you.'

The man leaned forward and hissed viciously in his ear, 'You have no idea what this is about. This is nothing to do with you, little man. You worry about others who need your help. Because,' he added, punching to punctuate each word, 'I . . . need . . . none of it.'

He let Father Paul drop to the floor, then kicked him in the belly, making the elderly cleric curl up like a hedgehog, moaning and sobbing with the pain, coughing as the dust clogged his lungs once more. He closed his eyes, then opened them again when he was kicked a second time, only to see a black stain at the corner of the cloak, and a small tear.

'You forget what and who you saw, or I'll tell all about you and the whores, and I will see the church burned down – with you inside it, little priest! Think on that!'

Father Paul rolled over, away from the man, but he kicked again, this time in the priest's kidneys, and then he was gone, and Father Paul sobbed as he tried to raise himself to sit, and stayed there, his back against the wall, whimpering, unable to stand as his foot throbbed and his back pulsed. The wind gusted through his open doorway, bringing leaves and shreds and tatters of rubbish with it. It made his room look as desolate as he felt, he thought, and gradually sensed himself topple sideways; somehow he didn't hit the floor, but fell into a deep, deep pit of pain.

Paffards' House

Joan was asleep when she heard the noise. It took some little while to become aware of what was happening, and then she suddenly snapped wide awake in an instant.

The door was open, and she saw her master standing there in the doorway.

He had been drinking. She could smell his breath even from here, and she knew immediately what he wanted with her.

'No, please, no,' she muttered, shaking her head and pulling her blankets to her chin, but it was impossible to stop him.

He walked in, kicked the door shut, and pulled the bedclothes from her bed, standing and staring at her nudity with a cold rapacity that made her blood turn to water even as she struggled to cover her nakedness.

'You know what I want, wench. It's why you're still here in the house. If you wish, I can throw you from the place right now. Out on the street. You want that?'

She knew he could. He was rich. He was her master.

But all through it, and later, she could not stop her tears.

In his chamber downstairs, John heard his master rise and walk unsteadily up the steep stairs to his solar. Overhead the floor-boards creaked as he made his way along the passageway, and then John heard the complaint of the rusty hinges as a door was opened at the back of the house. The master's bedroom was at the front of the house, and John knew that the mistress slept in that, while her children had the two chambers at either side. But the master had not gone to his own chamber. He had walked to the back of the house, where the maidservants' room lay.

Silently, the bottler rose from his bedroll and stood in the doorway. He could hear the sounds from upstairs, the weeping and pleading as Henry forced himself on the girl, and finally the man's footsteps from Joan's room to the front of the house. Then the door to the master's bedroom was closed, and John returned to his buttery.

In a flagon he had a pint of burned wine that he had bought

from St Nicholas's Priory. He poured a measure into a cup, sealed the flagon and took the cup up the stairs.

She was sitting up, a blanket wrapped about her shoulders, eyes wide and terrified as a rabbit's. John sat on her bed, as far from her as possible, and held out the drink. She made no move towards it, but stared at him as though fearing that he too would attack her in his turn.

'Drink, maid,' he said with gruff kindness. 'It's good for a hurt heart.'

She did as he bid, and pulled a face at the flavour.

'I know what he did,' John said. 'You have to be brave, maid. He will come to you as often as he likes. You can't stop him. You can't do anything. Only stay or leave. But if you go, you will lose all.'

'Why?' she asked in a tiny voice. 'He has his wife, why do this to me?'

But John couldn't answer her. He waited until she had finished the cup, and then he pulled the blankets back over her, and patted her head before leaving.

Later, lying back with his head on his hands, staring up at the ceiling, he could hear her sobbing late into the night, and he wished he could understand. Joan had never given any signs that she wanted the master's attention, he was sure of that.

She was only a poor, terrified little maid.

ChAPTER SEVENTEEN

Tuesday after the Nativity of St John the Baptist[1]

Cock Inn

On Sir Richard's advice, Baldwin had agreed to take a room at the inn. It had been much as he had feared, however. As soon as Simon fled, pleading the lateness of the hour and the need to see his daughter, Sir Richard had begun to bellow for food and drink, and although Baldwin tried to avoid consuming too much, inevitably politeness forced him to imbibe more than he usually would. Edgar remained with them, watching with an amused look in his eyes which Baldwin found intensely irritating, but since they were all sharing a communal bedchamber, there was no earthly point in going to their bed before Sir Richard.

This morning, unrefreshed after a night kept awake by Sir Richard's snoring, Baldwin went to the inn's main room and

1 30 June 1327

called for a watered wine and some bread to break his fast.
Usually he would not eat until later in the day, but this morning
the woolliness in his head and a mild ache were demanding
attention. He sat by the fire and stared into it as a maid unhur-
riedly scuffed her way about the place, eventually bringing him
what he required. He didn't even have the energy to complain
about her slowness.

Edgar appeared a short while later and sat at Baldwin's
side. He eyed the girl and asked for the same breakfast, and
when the wench lazily strolled towards the pantry, he frowned.
Edgar was unused to being treated so discourteously, especially by women.

'What did you think of the boy Algar last night?' Baldwin
asked.

'Sir? The stable boy? He was honest enough, I think, for a
ragamuffin. Why?'

Baldwin kept his attention on the flames at the hearth,
considering. True, the lad had seemed to be telling the truth.
Algar must have lusted after Alice, it was only natural. She
had looks that would tempt the statue of a saint; even in death
she was lovely.

'I think he was, too,' he said at last. 'And if that's the case,
and he saw Alice using the front door, I have to wonder how
often she did so. For all she knew, her master might hear of it,
or even see her himself. Either she was a fool, or she had a
special dispensation that other servants didn't at the Paffard
house. Which begs the question "why"?'

'If she enjoyed the luxury of the front door and pretending
she was no ordinary servant, perhaps Gregory lied when he
said he wouldn't have lain with her.'

'Yes . . . but perhaps there was another reason,' Baldwin
said.

'If he did lie, could it have a bearing on the girl's murder?' Edgar suggested.

Baldwin shook his head slowly. 'There is no indication that young Paffard had a motive to hurt her. Others could have been jealous, of course – servants, perhaps, if Henry demonstrated favouritism. There is another point that niggles at me: why the girl was in the alley. Why should she go there, if she was used to using the front door? Or did she only use the front door occasionally, and tried to maintain a sham respect for conventions at other times?'

'Or she died somewhere else and was placed there,' Edgar said.

'True.' Baldwin was thinking of all the people in the house. Suddenly he recalled Claricia Paffard.

There was something about the expression in Claricia Paffard's eyes that had been oddly familiar. And now he remembered where he had seen it before. It was some years before, when his wife had guessed that he had committed adultery.

With a pang of guilt, he realized that it was the expression he had recognised in Claricia's face: the despair of the betrayed.

Combe Street

Juliana Marsille left the house early to walk up to Cooks' Row in the hope of getting a bargain for their meals. A vendor did give her a couple of day-old crusts as she passed, and another traded an egg, for which she was very grateful. She was holding her prizes carefully in her apron as she entered Combe Street, and then she saw Joan, and gave her a wave.

'Are you all right?' she asked, when the girl drew closer.

Joan was pale and tear-stained, quite unlike her usual self.

'Maid, please, I'd offer you some wine, but we have none,' Juliana said gently. 'Tell me, what's the matter?'

'I can't tell you,' Joan said, her lips trembling. And then a tear ran from her eye.

'Right! Come with me to my house,' Juliana decided. 'You will tell me all.'

'I cannot.'

But her protestations were weak. Soon Juliana had her sitting with her on a step near the alleyway. Joan could not bring herself to talk about what troubled her for a long time. But then, as Juliana kindly chatted on, she felt her barriers tumble.

There was no one near to hear them as Joan gradually began to unburden herself.

'He came to my chamber. Oh, it was horrible! It didn't matter what I said, he wouldn't stop. You do believe me? I couldn't think what to do, and . . .'

There was more, much more, and Juliana nodded and agreed, and on occasion she wept with Joan, and the two sobbed together and hugged, and then wept some more for the misery that was womanhood.

'I am so sorry. You should leave that house,' Juliana said.

'How can I? Where would I go?'

'It is no place for you, Joan. You deserve better.'

'It's a hateful household. You wouldn't believe what else I saw . . . But I have to go. It's late.' She looked frightened.

'Come on – you can tell me.'

'No, no, I can't!' Joan cried.

But her protestations were in vain. She had to share it with someone. She couldn't keep it only to herself and poor little traumatised Tommy.

Precentor's House, Exeter Cathedral

Adam Murimuth set aside his journal and rubbed at his eyes. That was all the enjoyment he was permitted today, he thought. Now for the ledgers – and work.

Any cathedral was a serious enterprise, with estates to administer, courts of law, business ventures and ecclesiastic interests, both great and trivial. There were farms, and issues to mediate between tenants and peasants; there were marital disputes to be decided, up to and including divorce; and then there were the rebuilding works: the purchase of stone and timber, lead and copper, for the fabric of the Cathedral. Not to mention the responsibility for maintaining cordial relations with the Dominicans, and the Franciscans in their new friary outside the city walls.

That was usually the hardest matter, since Cathedral staff would often come to blows with the friars when they met in the city; professional jealousy inevitably caused friction.

For this reason, he was not overly surprised when he heard that the vicar of Holy Trinity had been beaten up. It was probably a friar who had taken offence at some remark made by the priest, he told himself.

The man who brought the news was one of the secular staff: a lay brother from the Palace Gate, Adam recalled.

'Bruised and battered and left in the street?'

'No, he was attacked in his rooms in the church.'

That was different. Adam's brows furrowed. 'No one would dare to assault a priest in his church, surely?'

'It does happen, sir.'

'Did he say who perpetrated this vile act?'

'No, sir. He won't talk of it at all.' The man was visibly nervous.

'Spit it out!' Adam said firmly. 'Is there something else I should know?'

'Sir, only that it's rumoured he had been seeing whores. Perhaps a whore's bully deprecated his attentions?'

Adam wiped a hand over his face. He didn't need this kind of additional problem. Not just now.

Marsilles' House

Juliana had already lighted the fire and set the pot over it. She had a little pottage left from the previous evening, and some oats and barley to bulk it out along with the crusts, but her prize this morning was the egg she had managed to exchange for some old strips of material. The woman who supplied the egg had been happy with the trade, and so was Juliana. It was the first egg she had handled in weeks, and she treated it with reverence, breaking it carefully into the pot, and stirring, watching the orange yolk break into strings of yellow with a hungry devotion, like a priest preparing holy wine for Mass.

'Morning, Mother,' William called and descended the ladder from their sleeping chamber. He stood scratching his head, complaining, 'My head has more life in it than most farms. I've been bitten to pieces during the night.'

'One day when we have some fortune come to us again, we will have a big house with our own bath-tub in the brewery,' Juliana said. There was a strong wistfulness for those long-passed days. Happiness with her Nicholas, the comfort of their lovely house just behind the High Street, the little garden with all her vegetables set out in the plots. She had been so contented there.

'Well, if we're to win it all back, we'll need me to take charge. You heard Philip wants to leave and join the King in Scotland?'

'No!' Juliana cried, and threw a look up at the sleeping chamber.

A tousled head peered over. 'Why not? I could win a ransom and—'

'Are you that stupid? How many men are there in the King's Host, and how many win a prize? Most of the men who find a knight will be killed by him! If not, they'll have their victim taken by their Sergeant or Lord. No, if you go to Scotland, all you will find is a grave, Philip. You mustn't even think of such a thing!' And how could you afford to go up there? You would have to buy food and drink!

'There is nothing for me here,' he said bleakly. 'I've managed to save a little.'

'You didn't think to share it with us, though?' William asked, then blurted out, 'Did you love her?'

Juliana was still. She had never dared to broach the subject with Philip, but she was keen to hear his answer. It even stopped her from beating him about saving money without sharing it.

'Yes. I loved her. And she felt nothing for me. She told me so,' Philip said. There was a dull gloom in his voice that tore at his mother's heart.

William said sympathetically, 'What did she say?'

'She said she was happy.' Philip sighed. He had rolled over, and now lay staring up at the rafters. 'She had a strong man in her master, and she had no need of a callow youth instead. What would she want with a whelp, when she had a sire already? That was what she said. I adored her, but she threw only scorn at me when I offered to marry her.'

'You offered her marriage?' William said, aghast. 'You know she was only Henry Paffard's bedwarmer!'

Juliana listened with her mouth falling open, thinking of Joan's words earlier.

'She was forced into it,' Philip argued.

'No, she wasn't! She was a willing bedmate or she'd have left!'

'It's no matter now. She's dead, and my life is over. Without her, I don't know how I can live.'

'It's because of her you're so languorous?' William said with frustration flooding his voice. 'Man, you should be glad you were rescued! She wasn't worth your time and love, if all she could think of was remaining with her master after you offered her an honourable marriage.'

'You didn't know her. You can't understand.'

Juliana broke in. 'Your brother's right, Philip. If she turned you down, preferring to whore herself with her master, you are fortunate to be free of her. Think, if she had accepted your hand, would you ever have been able to trust her? She was a tickle-tail, no more. If she was married, she would be waggling her arse at other men all the time. Your life would have been miserable.'

'I cannot live for thinking about her,' Philip groaned.

'You need new reasons for living, then,' Juliana said gently. 'Come, have some pottage. There is an egg in it. Eat, and the world will look better.'

She watched him descend the ladder, walking to the bowl and silently ladling a portion into a wooden cup. He sipped, sitting on the stool, while William watched him with kindly amusement, and Juliana felt it best to leave them alone for a while. Perhaps William could persuade his brother to talk some more, and maybe then the two could come to some understanding. Then Philip must try to find work. There was almost nothing left from his savings.

Meanwhile, her mind kept circling about this news of Henry Paffard. What sort of a man would make use of the maids in his house in that manner? Ach, it wasn't unheard of, and Juliana was no innocent, but for him to move straight from Alice to Joan spoke of a determined lust, without any affection. It spoke of his shame, too.

She had a job with a goldsmith's today, which a kindly providence had bestowed upon her. A friend had suggested her to the smith, who was keen to have someone help keep his house. Not a maidservant, but a manager of his household. It was a unique position: his wife had died some months before, and he felt the need of a woman's hand about the house, but not the effort and expense of a wife. Juliana hoped that a second stroke of good fortune could occur. Perhaps he would consider William as an assistant in his business. It was by no means an apprenticeship, but for William it could provide food and a little money. That still left Philip without a means of supporting himself, but Juliana was optimistic.

A knock on the door made all three look up. Juliana was nearest, and she pulled the door wide to find that John, bottler to Henry Paffard, stood with a note in his hand. 'Yes, John?'

He looked from her to the young men behind her, and nodded at them in greeting. 'Mistress, I'm sorry to bring this. I have been told to speak to you. My master has heard you've caused a disturbance.'

'He's heard *what*?'

'About your argument. News has come to him that others here are distressed by you.'

'I don't know what you mean . . . What, has Emma reported me to Henry?' Juliana gasped. 'She couldn't have! Emma was a friend to us for such a long time, I can't believe she'd do such a thing!'

'My master has instructed me to tell you: this breaking of the peace in the neighbourhood, on top of the rents you owe, means you must leave.'

Juliana was still in shock, her mouth gaping. 'No, you can't mean that, John! He's warning us, isn't he? He won't throw us from the door. We depend upon him, you know that. Where would we go if he kicks us out?'

'I don't know,' John said. 'Mistress, if I had a place, I'd offer it to you. I knew your husband, and he was a good man.'

'*Henry* knew him, in Christ's name!' Juliana said. Tears welled, but refused to be shed. She stared at John, then at the room around her as though she had never seen it before. 'He was an associate of my husband's. Nicholas helped him with his business many times. It was for that reason that Nicholas set him to aid us with our affairs. He named Henry in his will. In God's name, what will I do if we are evicted?'

'I don't know, mistress, but—' John began, but already Juliana's face had altered. She listened to no more, but instead thrust him from the doorway, and strode into the alley. Emma's door was only feet away, and Juliana beat her fist on the weak timbers. 'Emma de Coyntes, come to your door! I must speak to you!'

There was a rattle and the door opened. Emma stood in her doorway, her features harsh, arms folded. 'Well?'

Juliana's anger faded. The resolution on Emma's face was too daunting. 'Your complaint to Henry Paffard, Emma. You didn't know, you couldn't know, but he's told us we must go. At once! Emma, come with me, tell him you didn't mean it – that it was just the moment's anger.'

'It wasn't. You upset Sabina, and you upset me. You should have thought of the consequences before you screamed at her. Poor Sabina! She was only singing, that's all. I don't know what right you think you have to insult people!'

'That's enough,' William interrupted. He had followed his mother, and now he stood at Juliana's side. 'We have rights the same as any. Just because we've lost our wealth doesn't mean we aren't still people. We're Exonians, same as you.'

'But you're *not* the same, are you? You have nothing. I'm sorry for you, Juliana. You have had a lot to contend with, but I won't see my family hurt and upset because of you.'

'So you'd see us thrown from our home?' Juliana said, and now the tears did fall. She had trusted Emma: they had been friends. Emma had been the one person she felt she could rely upon when Nicholas had died.

'I'm sorry,' Emma said, and turned away so that she wasn't looking directly at her any longer.

'You *bitch*! *Whoreson's daughter! Strumpet!*' Juliana screamed suddenly, and sprang forward, her fingers clawed.

'Get off me!' Emma shouted, alarmed. She raised her arms, and Juliana's nails raked down her forearm, bringing up three long welts in an instant.

William was tempted to leave them to it. He was sure that his mother would soon have the better of the fight, but he knew that it wouldn't help them, were she to cause an affray. 'Come, Mother,' he tried, and threw his arms about her when remonstrations failed.

'You faithless wastrel! You have seen to our destruction!' Juliana screeched. 'See what damage you wreak with your lies! Dishonest wretch! You have seen us evicted!'

With her son's arms wrapped about her, she convulsed with deep, groaning sobs, and turned to him, hiding her face in her shame. Then she allowed herself to be led back to her room, leaving behind her an ashen-faced Emma clutching her sore forearm.

CHAPTER EIGHTEEN

Holy Trinity Church

The first thing that came to him as he coughed and lurched on his palliasse, was that the pain in his back was as nothing compared to the throbbing in his head.

Father Paul kept his eyes closed as he felt the terrible wounds that bruised his kidneys; there seemed little enough of him that was undamaged, and the coughing only made it all worse.

'Are you all right now, Paulie, eh?'

His eyes snapped open and he found himself looking up into the cider-sodden face of Sarra. 'What are you doing here?' he croaked.

'We came by to see if you had a pot of wine for us. And you might have decided to have a free one on us,' Sarra said with a wicked leer.

'I never have before,' Father Paul admonished, and tried to rise. Instantly he winced and groaned.

'So, some priests can swear and fornicate and even kill, but you won't even try one of them,' Sarra said, laughing hoarsely as she put her hand under his armpit, her younger companion doing likewise at his other side. 'Come on, Father, upsy-daisy.'

He found himself on his feet, and looked down in surprise. 'Have you made a habit of assisting priests to their feet?'

'We help 'em up, sometimes,' she winked.

He reddened. 'I didn't . . .'

'Allow me a laugh, Father, we've been up all night looking after you. Usually my nights are sleepless, but at least I get to lie down. And I am paid for it.'

'You can have . . .'

'No. You give us food. That's enough for us.'

'Well, I am very grateful.'

'Who did it, Father?' the younger woman asked. She was so young she had not lost the beauty that comes from innocence, he thought. That would soon be beaten or worn from her. Prostitutes always lost it, which was partly why he tried to help them from their lives of poverty and disease.

'I don't know,' he said truthfully. The hessian sacking had effectively covered the man's face, and the assault had been so swift, it could have been from one who was five feet or six feet tall. Most of the painful encounter had seen Father Paul bent over in pain, after all. 'He wore a grey cloak,' he remembered.

'Did it have a mark on it? Fur? Embroidery?' Sarra demanded.

'It had a stain at the bottom, on the man's left side. A dark stain,' he added, thinking it was like dried blood. 'And a tear, no more than an inch long. As though he had caught it on something while walking along, and the material ripped.'

'A tear, eh?' Sarra said. 'I don't know about that. But there aren't too many men with simple grey cloaks. Men like that Henry Paffard – he has one . . .'

Edith's House, St Pancras Lane

It was quite late in the morning when Simon heard the commotion. He had been in the hall with his grandson, watching over the little boy dozing, and the noise at first did not register with him, he was so content.

Many years ago, his firstborn son had caught a fever. The poor fellow would suckle, but all the milk passed through him or was vomited up, and he grew fretful, weeping and bawling all the while. Simon and Meg did all they could to tempt him with more food, but nothing prevailed, and Simon was actually glad when the noise finally ceased. A horrible, guilty relief, it was, but he was not so dishonest as to deny it. Perkin's death was many years ago now, and yet the guilty reminder that he was not so good a father as he would have liked remained with him. This little boy reminded him of his first son, and he was resolved never to betray him in thought or deed.

The row in the road grew, and Simon rose to peer through the front door.

There was a short alley leading to Eastgate Street, and he could see many people flitting to and fro; the racket came from there as though the King's own host was arriving in state. Setting his daughter's maid Jane to look over the boy, he went out into the street to investigate.

The milling people were not watching Eastgate Street, however, but were streaming down towards Carfoix, and Simon allowed the crowd to draw him down with it. There was an uncountable press of men and women at the crossroads, and Simon must wait with the others as the noise increased.

'What is it?' he demanded of a man nearby.

'They do say a man's died, who wants to be buried here in the Cathedral, but I don't know.'

Simon wondered at that, and at the angry muttering. He saw a cart, on which three urchins and a maid were standing, watching the High Street, and pushed his way through the crowds towards them. Ignoring their complaints, he climbed up with them and stared ahead.

Then he realised what the fuss was about.

Bishop Berkeley had been brought home to rest.

Paffards' House

Joan nodded as Sal shouted at her, and avoided the wooden spoon that lunged near her head, before grabbing the bowl and darting to the flour chest. There was only a small amount left in there, but enough to make the pastry for the coffins, and she scooped a couple of handfuls into the bowl, hurrying to add the butter and begin to mix it with her fingers.

She shivered. It was still in her mind, last night. Her master's face, red and sweating, eyes bulging. Her own soreness. The memory was so gut-churning, she tried to eradicate it by work, churning the pastry dough harshly.

'Hoi! You stop that, silly strumpet, you'll harden the pastry!' Sal reprimanded her, shoving her aside and thrusting her own dumpy hands into the mess. 'You have to treat a good dough with respect, gently, like, if you want your pies to be good and crisp and crumbly.' She threw a look at Joan, and came to a quick conclusion. 'You go outside and take Thomas with you. He needs the fresh air, and you do too.'

Grateful for the sympathy, Joan nodded. The picture in her mind of Henry Paffard's face was so vivid, she felt sick to the pit of her stomach. Last night she had tried to eradicate it by closing her eyes, but his weight, his stertorous breathing, his rancid odour, had all imposed themselves upon her mind so firmly that she was even now aware of him. Her groin was sore, her breasts bruised and tender, and she felt as if she could never be cleansed.

She wiped her hands on the towel bound about her waist. Looking after Thomas was the last thing she wanted to do, for Thomas was a part of Henry. To look after him, she was looking after Henry Paffard's second heir, the apple of his eye, his pride and joy. It was fortunate that she was fond of the lad. Otherwise she would take one of the flesh knives from the kitchen and cut his throat, just to repay Henry.

It would not be only last night, either, she knew. Henry Paffard was a man of enormous appetites. She had seen that with poor Alice. She had been called to him almost every day, and then afterwards he would go back to his own bed with his wife. He had no shame about his behaviour. The servants in his house were his to do with as he pleased, he thought.

She choked, a sob catching her unawares.

This was her life, then: if she remained here, she must become Henry Paffard's whore. Except no whore would rut without money. What did that make her? A slut. Perhaps she had given him to believe that she would appreciate his advances. It could not have been just that he was convinced of his own power over her, surely? He would not expect another man to treat his own daughter in this way, would he? Agatha must be safe from such a humiliation.

Joan found herself leaning against the wall, face turned to the plaster, weeping uncontrollably. It was the first time she had ever felt so hopeless, so helpless. The abominable truth was, she was ruined now. Henry Paffard had taken something from her she could never replace. She was tempted to harm him in some similar way. But the one piece of information that would hurt him was so dangerous, she dared not share it.

Thomas was standing watching her, and she turned to him

with a kind of relief. His presence forced her to recover a little of her self-control, and she swiped at her eyes angrily.

'Come, Tommy. Let's go outside. The sun's shining,' she said, trying to sound contented, as though the events of the last days had not happened. 'Shall we find your ball?'

He shook his head, but turned and walked with her out into the garden, and there, while she sat on the bench, he stood staring at the wall. She should have gone to him to soothe him, but there was still an instinctive reluctance to touch the flesh of a boy that came from Henry Paffard. His face returned to her, and she flinched.

Thomas noticed, and he shuffled over to her, looking up into her face. 'Was it them?' he asked.

She could have cried to think it. 'No,' she said. 'It wasn't them.'

'When I see the fire I see them,' he said quietly, fearfully.

'You mustn't, Tommy,' she said firmly, and at last a little of her self-possession returned to her. 'Listen, Tommy: you must forget what you saw. It won't help to keep thinking about it.'

'He said to me that he'd—'

'I know. But you mustn't tell anyone. Especially your father,' she pleaded. The thought that Henry Paffard could learn of the two bodies merging in the warmth of the fire that night was too appalling for words. He would want no one to repeat what they saw, after all. It would be disastrous for him, and for his business.

'I don't understand,' Thomas said.

'Nor do I, Tommy,' she said, and drew him to her, her arms tight around his body as she sobbed, '*Nor do I.*'

Combe Street

There was nothing left for them to do.

William was in the chamber, packing their few belongings in

preparation for their departure. That was at least some consolation: Henry had not told them to be off instantly and sent rowdies to hurl them and their goods into the alley's filth. He had shown them that courtesy at least.

To Juliana, it was intolerable. She stood in the alley for a while, staring at the ruin of her hopes, and occasionally giving a distraught glance at Emma's door, but it was too much. She couldn't wait there. Instead she walked down to the street and stood there, looking about her wonderingly.

Her mind could not cope with this sequence of disasters. She felt as numb as a naked woman in a snowstorm. How Emma could have so turned upon her was a mystery. A moment's irrational anger against Juliana for telling her daughter Sabina to pipe down was no reason to see her thrown from her house. It was way out of proportion. And Henry, to send her away when all knew that the widow had nowhere else to turn – that was itself beyond cruel. It was not even fury that brought her here, to the front of the Paffard house, but more a sense of confusion, a desire to understand.

Slowly she climbed the steps to the front door, and knocked.

It felt an age before the door was unlocked and swung open. 'Yes?'

'John, I want to speak with your master.'

'He said he wouldn't talk to you. He knew you would come.'

'Really?' Juliana said, and barged past him.

'Please! Please, mistress!' John protested, trying to catch at her tunic as she hurried along the corridor, but it was no good, and before long Juliana had stormed into Henry's hall.

Seeing her, he gave John a look of annoyed contempt. 'Juliana, I am very surprised to see you here.'

'Send him away,' she demanded, pointing to John.

'Very well.' Henry waved John away. Then he asked, 'What do you want?'

157

'Don't throw us from our house, I beg.'

'It is too late. I'm sorry,' Henry said, and he did look genuinely uncomfortable. 'If you had only left that woman alone, I could have done something, but with Emma de Coyntes muttering and complaining, my hands are tied. You should not have attacked her daughter.'

'I didn't, Henry! I merely chastised her for making a noise. You are supposed to be serving us, my friend. You know that. It's why Nicholas had you nominated to look after our business.'

'But there was so little left,' Henry said sadly. 'You have cost me much treasure, and there is no means of receiving compensation for all I have done. I would do more, truly, if there were means available to me. But you make it impossible for me.'

'You cannot send me away.'

'Why?'

'Because of what I know!' she hissed. Joan had told her in confidence, but Joan couldn't use it. However, it could save Juliana and her sons.

'There is nothing you could say about me that would surprise anyone about here,' he said smugly, unmoved.

'No, not about you. About your son.'

'Shock me.'

His coolness was a spur to her anger, but she swallowed it down and was about to answer when Gregory himself entered with his sister Agatha.

Juliana looked round at them, and then a twisted smile crossed her face. 'You really want me to talk about it in front of *them*?' she said, and then leaned forward. 'I doubt that very much.'

And as Henry saw her glance back at Gregory, he suddenly felt a chill like a block of ice in his gut. He had suspected for a long time . . . 'What do you want?'

'Meet me,' she said, her mouth close to his ear, so his children wouldn't hear. 'Tonight, at dusk.'

'Very well.'

'Tell John to let us stay in our house tonight.'

'I will see you in the alley that runs to the city wall from Combe Street,' he said.

'At dusk. And bring your purse,' she said, and ignoring the others, walked from the room.

CHAPTER NINETEEN

Road east of Exeter

They were moving again.

Ulric rode along like a man with too much wine in his belly. Twice he nearly overbalanced from his saddle, and once he had to jerk himself upright quickly before he fell.

In his mind's eye he saw the villagers again in that hideous charnelhouse that had been their sanctuary, their church. And he wondered how he might bring retribution to the men here, to Sir Charles and his band of devils.

He could see no means of betraying the men without being associated with them, however, and dying at their side.

How had he come to this? He was an apprentice to Henry Paffard, and all he knew was that he was to help inform Sir Charles when the Bishop was intended to arrive at his manor. But now he was an accessory to this band of murderers.

Escape was impossible, but there was still the possibility that he could make his way back to Henry Paffard. Master Paffard could not have realised what Sir Charles and his men intended to do. Surely the merchant would be as horrified as Ulric when he heard about the attack on the Bishop.

But why then had he instructed Ulric to come here to direct Sir Charles to the Bishop?

That was his greatest fear: that his master was in this up to the hilt. That he was a knowing confederate of Sir Charles. He was the only man who might save Ulric, but if he was an ally of the murderers of Bishop James, Ulric was lost.

Then another thought struck him.

What if Henry Paffard were to disassociate himself from Sir Charles? What then could Ulric do?

Exeter Cathedral

Adam Murimuth stood in the Cathedral Close, his head bent, praying for his dead Bishop.

He had a terrible feeling of loss. It was as if he had not yet come to realise that the death of Bishop James was genuine, as if there could be a vague hope still that he would return to surprise the congregation, that wry smile on his face that showed he had enjoyed the joke.

Not now. The procession that had made its way to the Guild Hall was utterly convincing. The grief of the people of the city was unfeigned, and the Sheriff himself had come to pay his respects, along with all the prominent men of the Freedom. All stood solemnly as the cart bearing the body stopped, and the people could see the sad, grey face of the man who had been their spiritual leader for such a cruelly short time.

'Only three months,' Adam murmured.

The man had been so good a Christian, and Adam had enjoyed working with him. To lose him so swiftly was terribly sad, but at least he was in God's care now.

Adam had gone to meet the body at the Guild Hall, and soon

he and the procession were making their way along the High Street, past suddenly silent men and women, and thence into Broad Gate, and from there, down to the West Door of the Cathedral.

Now, while the Bishop's body was lifted and carried solemnly into the Cathedral Church, Adam spied the Bishop's steward, and went over to his side.

'This is a terrible business, Arthur. Was it sudden?'

The old steward turned eyes bleary with misery to him. 'Sudden? Yes. They appeared from nowhere.'

Adam blinked. 'What do you mean? Who did?'

'The force that attacked us. I still don't know who they were, even.'

In his shock, Adam's mouth moved without speaking for fully ten beats of his heart. 'I don't understand, Arthur. What do you mean? I thought he had an accident, or a brain fever.'

'No. We were attacked. The men who killed him ambushed us as we arrived at the gates to Petreshayes. There were thirty or more of them, and they were in among us, slashing and hacking – and when they rode off, my Lord Bishop James was dead on the ground, along with two Brothers and his squire, while they went on to plunder the manor. We cleaned him as well as we might, once they were gone, but that was that.'

'Who would do such a thing?' Adam breathed. It was incomprehensible, but his shock was already giving way to anger. 'Who would *dare* do such a thing?'

'Whoever it was, they knew what they were doing. They cut all the way through us until they reached him, and when he was dead, they just took everything they could, and rode off. It was awful, Adam, awful. My poor master!' And the steward burst into tears, wiping them from his cheeks with a bitter grief.

Avices' House

Helewisia invited Emma in as soon as she saw the state her neighbour was in.

'Come, take a seat,' she said calmly, motioning to her servant to fetch some strong wine. Weaker stuff would not do, she guessed.

'You heard the screaming?'

'Of course I did. It must have been most unsettling for you.'

'Oh, Helewisia, it wasn't that. I just couldn't believe the look on her face. It was all twisted, you know? I was sure she was mad. I thought she might pull out a knife and kill me there. It was horrible.'

'She is losing everything, Emma, all because you told Henry about her bad mood the other day. What did you expect from her?'

'I know. I wish now I hadn't. But I couldn't *not* tell him. It upset Sabina so much.'

'Well, soon they'll be gone, I suppose,' Helewisia said, taking the cups from her maid.

'I just hope I did the right thing,' Emma said, staring into the cup. She took a sip. 'I do feel bad about her and her boys.'

Helewisia said nothing. She was thinking that it was good to regret injustice, but better to avoid it in the beginning. And besides, she had more in common, she knew, with Juliana than with Emma. She herself had wanted to collapse after her lovely son, Piers, had died. Trying to get them food because they were so hard up for money, he had climbed the church spire to catch roosting pigeons. One slip, and he was gone forever.

Father Paul had tried to comfort her by telling her he was alive in heaven, and that he would be there waiting when she died too. He was trying to be kind to her, reminding her of the miraculous salvation granted to those who died in innocence, but his words gave no succour. In fact, they made her furious, because why should God have taken her little boy from her? Piers was hers, he was here for her to love and cherish and watch grow, and when she was older, he would look after her, and she would love him all her days. But God had taken him from her, leaving her nothing.

Of course she had become accustomed to the tragedy, as all mothers must. She had striven for another boy with her husband Roger, and the two had mechanically tried every month, but it was as though little Piers had dried her womb when he had been born. There was no joy in their lovemaking, and no success. After two years she had desisted. Occasionally when Roger had been out with his friends and returned drunk, she would allow him to use her body, as the marriage vow insisted, but she found no pleasure in it. She would avert her head and try to think of other things.

But life returned to its usual tenor. She had a daughter to raise, even if her darling boy was gone. Katherine was a good girl, by and large, and Roger had his successes in business, so they were comfortable. But their lives had for those few years known such happiness that all their days remaining were a reminder of how good things once had been.

'I feel so bad now. Juliana's mind nearly broke, Helewisia.'

Helewisia said nothing. Emma wanted her sympathy for her own cruelty to their neighbour, and Helewisia could not give it. Her sympathy had all been used up years before.

Precentor's House

Adam Murimuth had aged ten years in the past few hours, Baldwin thought as he walked into the Precentor's hall. His usually cheerful face was haggard, his mien sombre.

It was normally a cosy room, this. A bright fire was always

lighted in the hearth, and the windows allowed plenty of light to fall inside. But today it was a cheerless place, without fire or candles to bring relief.

Simon was sitting near the Precentor's table. 'You've heard?' he asked.

'The Bishop's body is brought back, I hear,' Baldwin said.

'It is terrible news,' Adam said. 'We had thought it was a sad accident, or perhaps a sudden malady – it had never occurred to us that it could be simple murder!'

'Tell me what happened,' Baldwin said. He stood before Adam while Sir Richard sat down beside Simon, and Edgar took his post near the door.

Adam sighed. 'It would seem a party of men attacked him at the gates to Petreshayes,' he began, and told all he had learned from Arthur. Finishing, he looked about him mournfully. 'I do not know how any man could attack the good Bishop in so violent a manner. It is incomprehensible.'

'I fear it may be all too comprehensible,' Baldwin said. 'Our good Bishop was James of Berkeley, was he not? Therein lies your answer. For the last months, Sir Edward of Caernarfon has been held at Berkeley Castle, under the guard of Lord Thomas of Berkeley. Many in the kingdom still support Sir Edward. Someone has chosen to ride to the Lord's brother, who was less well-guarded, and slay him in revenge for Sir Edward's incarceration.'

'But surely no one would kill a Bishop because of his brother's actions?' Adam said plaintively.

There was no need to answer. All knew that the kingdom was bubbling like poison on a fire. The new King was too young to rule, and must submit to his council of regents; his mother remained a dangerous, wild creature who sought power for herself; and her lover, Sir Roger Mortimer, controlled more men than any other, many of them Hainault mercenaries who were loyal only to him. At such a time it was no surprise that some supporters of the old King might take revenge for the imprisonment of their leader.

'To think that he was cut down while trying to visit the religious houses in his demesne as a good Bishop should,' Adam grieved. 'He was innocent of any crime.'

'Many are, who have died in these troubled times,' Baldwin agreed.

'You must go and seek these murderers,' Adam said suddenly.

Baldwin smiled a little. 'Me? Go to Petreshayes? And what should I achieve there?'

'You could find them, bring them here to justice. See them punished for their abominable crime.'

'I am sorry, Precentor, but I am afraid that the felons who committed this evil deed will be long gone from Petreshayes. It would be a similar group to those who attacked Berkeley Castle and freed Sir Edward of Caernarfon. They too are flown, as well as all their retainers. I must remain here, in Devon, to see whether it is possible to find Sir Edward, if I am so commanded.'

'You have a duty to your Church!' Adam countered passionately.

'No,' Baldwin said flatly. 'I hold a warrant from the King, and I am duty bound to obey my orders from him. And while I would help if I may, the Bishop died far away from here. It is up to the local officials to investigate and pursue these felons. Precentor, I am truly sorry. I can do little to assist you.'

Adam was not content, but he could see there were no words that would tempt Sir Baldwin to undertake this mission.

'I shall have to do what I may, then,' he said at last.

'There is much to do when a lord dies,' Sir Richard said.

'All the servants must be warned or let free. Many will never find work again. I trust the Bishop had made his will,' Adam said, his mind racing. 'There are the peasants on all his estates, and others who will want to pay their respects.'

'Aye. Since he was murderously slain, there could be even more comin' to see him,' Sir Richard said. 'You should buy a new strongbox.'

'What do you mean?'

'It's the way of things. If a good man like Bishop James is to die before his time, then many will think him worth commemorating – like a martyr, I mean. You could find the place swarming with the godly before long. You'll need a new chest to store all their gifts.'

'Pilgrims? To Bishop James's tomb?' Adam said. 'No, surely not. What nonsense that would be.'

But there was a pensive look in his eye as Baldwin and the others left.

CHAPTER TWENTY

Paffards' House

Claricia was startled as the door opened, but it was only Gregory with Agatha. The two had taken to walking about the house together, and Claricia thought it was good to see them getting on so well. They were very close.

'Mother, are you all right?' Agatha asked.

'Yes, of course I am. What a silly question!'

'You looked so anxious just then.'

'I wasn't expecting you, that's all,' she said with a firmness she didn't feel. It was impossible to share her concerns with her children. She could never confide in them. Not ever. 'Where is Thomas?'

'You know what he's like these days,' Gregory said shortly. 'Probably skulking in his room.'

Claricia felt her brow furrow. The little boy was so unhappy now.

It had started pretty much the day that Alice had died, and he had remained in the depths of misery ever since. Alice had been his favourite among the servants because she always played with him, no matter what. It was easy for them both. Thomas could take time from his tutor when he wanted, and Alice could play because she knew full well that no one would dare tell her off. Not while Henry was sharing her bed. 'You should try to talk to him,' she said. 'He needs someone to take an interest in him.'

'Like Father's next wench?' Agatha said cynically. She walked into the hall and perched on the table. 'We all know what Father's doing, Mother. We heard him last night going to Joan's room. I'll bet she never thought that when Alice was gone, she'd have to take over Alice's extra duties, did she? Poor chit, there she was, probably jealous of Alice's easy chores during the day, and all the time not realising that she'd be called upon to perform herself, were Alice to disappear.'

'You mustn't talk like that about your father!' Claricia said, scandalised.

'Why ever not, Mother?' Gregory was leaning nonchalantly against the wall, eyeing his fingernails. He put a finger in his mouth, running the nail over a tooth to clean it. 'Hmm? We all know that our blessed father is fornicating with the maids. He exercises his *droit de seigneur* as he wishes. And there is nothing you or we can do to stop him, but that doesn't mean we have to pretend it doesn't happen. Did you hear Joan weeping late last night? We did.'

'You should tell him he must stop, Mother,' Agatha said angrily. 'You cannot let him keep insulting you in this way. It's demeaning to us as well as you.'

'What can I do? This is his house. I am his, you are his. We have no rights.'

'What of Joan?' Agatha demanded.

'She can leave if she wishes. But while she remains within

169

the house, she is under the patronage of your father. He can treat her as he sees fit.'

'He doesn't have the right to rape her, Mother. Not under the law. If he were denounced to the Church, he would be—'

'Don't even think of such a thing!' Claricia said. She closed her eyes in terror.

The first time she had raised the subject with Henry was also the last time. He had been drunk, and it had been days before she could walk without pain.

Continuing, her voice scarcely more than a whisper, she said, 'You know how he treats me when I displease him. If you were to speak to the priest, he would blame me and beat me again. Please, don't do anything that could tempt him to do that again.'

'Mother, I don't want to, but nor do I wish to see you suffering like this,' Agatha said. She was a resolute young woman, and there was a light in her eye that Claricia recognised: determination.

'For God's sake, Agatha, don't antagonise him,' she pleaded.

'He destroys all he touches,' Gregory said. He eyed her dispassionately. 'How many other people do you want him to hurt?'

'He is your father. You must not disgrace the family.'

'You think I don't know that?' Gregory suddenly burst out, and to her shock, there were tears in his eyes. He was always quite emotional, but this was somehow more alarming than his usual little tirades.

He stood stock-still for a moment, his entire being focused on her, and then he seemed to sag, and he turned away from her.

'This is what he's doing to us, Mother,' Agatha hissed. She walked to Gregory's side, put her arm about his neck, pulling his head to her shoulder. 'This is what he's doing: he's destroying us all with his moods and his despotism. This isn't normal. *He* isn't normal. One day, if we aren't careful, he'll kill us. And I don't want to die like that.'

Marsilles' House

William looked up as his mother came in. 'Well? Did you get yourself thrown from his door?'

'William, don't be so silly.'

She had a fretful look in her eyes, and William tried to sound reassuring. 'Don't worry, Mother. We will find somewhere else to live. It won't be impossible. We must pack and—'

'No. We *don't* pack. We aren't leaving here.'

'But John said—'

'I've spoken to Henry. He will see me tonight. Until then, he won't evict us – and he won't afterwards, either.'

'Why? What do you mean?'

'I have secret information that will make him want to keep us here,' she said. And although she was worried, she was convincing.

'What do you know?'

'Something about his boy. His son. And he *won't* want it bruited about the city,' she said grimly.

Precentor's House

Simon was glad to leave the atmosphere of the house. Coming out, he saw that the Close was already filling with men and women from the city.

'It's started, then,' he commented.

'Eh?' Sir Richard eyed the crowds with mild interest.

'All these people are here to view the Bishop's body. The clergy will have to get it ready as soon as possible,' Simon said.

Some would be coming to pay their respects, some so they could say that they had seen his body, while others were coming out of simple loyalty to their lord. James of Berkeley had been a kindly, popular Bishop in the short time he had been here at Exeter. People appeared to have developed a genuine affection for him that was unusual for a man in such a remote position.

'Look at them all,' Simon said. 'They're queuing all the way to the Broad Gate, and with that lot up there, you can bet St Petrock's will be impassable too.'

'Let us go out by the Bear Gate,' Baldwin suggested.

There was a rumble as Sir Richard cleared his throat. 'I would think the Palace Gate would be well enough for us. And we could call in at the Cock on the way for an ale.'

Baldwin winced, and the sight brought a smirk to Simon's face. He had often been forced to accompany Sir Richard on his forays into alehouses and taverns, and Baldwin had routinely found Simon's suffering the following mornings to be hilarious. It was, Simon felt, a joy and a justice to see that Baldwin himself was at last paying the price of Sir Richard's friendship.

'Yes!' Simon said. 'Let's go and see the inn. I have a happy memory of the place.'

'Should we not go to your daughter's to let her know what is happening here?' Baldwin said hopefully.

'Ah, if you wish you may send Edgar to let her know,' Simon said with a mischievous grin. 'After all, we ought to speak to others at the inn to see if they too heard anything on Saturday night, or if they have any more information about the girl who died.'

'I would have thought we spoke to all of them before,' Baldwin grumbled, but he gave in with a bad grace, and walked with them to the Cock.

It was less packed than on their last visit, and as they entered, the maid Poll who had served them last night came to them, wiping her hands on her towel. It was bound about her waist with a cord to serve as an apron, but it was so discoloured by spills of food and ale that its original colour could only be guessed at.

'What can I fetch you, gentles?'

Sir Richard gave her his most dazzling smile. 'Maid, I think we should have a quart jug each of your best strong ale.'

Combe Street

Juliana disliked doing this, but she had no other option open to her, since Henry Paffard had threatened her with eviction.

Poor Nicholas. She missed her husband every single day. They had been that rare thing, a couple who were actually in love. It warmed her heart to see him smile. It was a slow smile, a lazy smile . . . she had never been able to resist him when he smiled at her.

At least she had been lucky enough to know Nicholas and enjoy him. He had given her Philip and William, and that alone was a comfort in those terrible days after his death.

Philip tried to be strong, but he was not the man his father had been. Nicholas had built his business from nothing, and Philip didn't have the wits to do that. His plans were hopeless. If they had to rely on Philip, disaster would surely follow.

No. It was better that she took charge. She would do anything for the protection of her family.

Even blackmail.

She turned down the alley off Combe Street; he had agreed to meet her before curfew.

It was dark, with tall houses shadowing the pathway. Ahead rose the great mass of the wall, while overhead she could

173

glimpse the sky between the houses, occasionally concealed by wafts of greyish-black smoke from a seacoal fire nearby. A ringing of hammers came to her ears from the blacksmith further up Combe Street. At houses all about, women and cooks were preparing food, and the odour of stews and pottages nipped like pincers at her nose, she was so hungry.

There was a snort, and along the alley she saw a snotty little churl aged nine or ten with scruffy chemise and hosen that were more holes than material. He gave her a disinterested glance, then returned to stare at his charges, two hogs, each of which was considerably larger than himself.

She wanted time to marshal her thoughts, and the presence of this little tatterdemalion was distracting. What's more, his pigs were blocking the way.

She squeezed past. One snuffled at her leg and Juliana pushed it away. Hogs had been known to carry off babies, and she wasn't going to have it bite her. She glared at the boy, but he was too cold and hungry to care.

Master Paffard wouldn't be long, she hoped, and then he would hear what she had to say about his oh-so-perfect son.

It had not been warm all day, and she was chilled to the marrow as she waited. It was a strange area, this, at the foot of the wall. Men used the wall as their toilet, and it reeked of urine – but it was the coolness she noticed more than the smell. There was a special kind of chill at the base of the walls. Even in the depths of summer the sun did not reach in here. Nor did the paths ever dry, for several gutters ran here, and ordure accumulated until the rain washed it away.

She turned, hearing a slight slap, like a man's boot striking the mud of the alley. She peered through the murk. Above, it was still daylight, but down here, it was hard to see. She heard another sound – and the idea that she was being hunted suddenly sprang into her mind and wouldn't leave. She became aware that this was a good place for a trap. There was no one to help her even if she were to scream; someone seeking to hurt her could do so with impunity.

Memories of stories of ghosts walking the streets came back to her. Tales of the dead – of men who had been buried, but who retuned to terrorise their neighbours, making the dogs howl, rendering the very air putrid, drinking the blood of the living . . . And with a sudden horror, she thought she saw something there in the alley before her.

Her tongue clove to the roof of her mouth, and her heart beat fast like a lark's. And then she saw the bloated, ugly face of the hog as it turned to her, snuffling, and she almost collapsed from relief.

And then her relief turned to anger. Henry Paffard had not come. Why, did he think she was tugging his cloak when she threatened to tell all she knew about his son? Did he think she was joking? The man would learn that a woman with nothing to lose could still *bite*!

Setting off, she tried to put all thoughts of phantasms and vampires from her, and strode along resolutely, back to the safety of Combe Street.

Until she came to the corner, and the figure appeared before her.

CHAPTER TWENTY-ONE

Church of the Holy Trinity

Father Paul had completed his last service of the day, and his vegetable garden was looking as good as it could after the depredations of pigeons and rats. Still, even a feathered agent of destruction had its merits. He had loosed a stone at one, and broken its wing. It had tasted glorious. The flavour had distracted him from the pain where the door had ripped at his toenail's, and the bruising that still throbbed so in his belly and his back.

But no matter what he did, he could not remove the memory of the girl whom he had buried: the Paffards' maidservant. Why had Henry Paffard come to his house and beaten him and threatened him? It was ridiculous of him to think that he could remain incognito with a sack over his face when his cloak was so distinctive.

There was only one conclusion that the priest could reach: Paffard wanted him silent because of something he had seen on the night Alice was killed.

He recalled Alice now. A pretty little thing, all large, liquid eyes and a body that made even a priest think of earthly delights. He remembered that the first time he had seen her, he wondered that the angels themselves didn't get tempted to fall from the sky at her feet. But he was an older man who had been truly celibate for many years now, and he could look at a young woman, daydream about her, imagine her kisses and caresses, and still not feel the need to try to bring the vision to reality. A consummation would inevitably bring disaster for him. And after so many years of fidelity to his calling, he would not wish to throw it all away.

It was astonishing, Father Paul thought, that any man could have wished to destroy so pretty a woman. There must be a hideous urge at the centre of any man who could desire something so much that he would break it into pieces, annihilate it, so that no other could possess it. Other priests, he knew, had seen men kill just so that the object of their own desires might be forever their own, and it was surely the same when a man slew his wife because she had been taken by another. It was that sinful sense of pride and possession: once defiled by another, she was ruined forever. So perhaps it was natural that a man might as easily seek to murder the focus of his affection, in order to save her from being sullied?

This was not a happy reflection.

It was a curious coincidence that the very day young Philip Marsille had threatened to commit murder, was the same day that poor Alice was slain. Perhaps the death of the girl had dissuaded Philip from his evil plan, but somehow Father Paul doubted it.

The incident had occured in the road outside the Paffards' house. Father Paul had seen Philip out in the lane, and both had witnessed Paffard walk through his door then stand a moment, preening himself, as he waited for his daughter, son and wife to join him.

'You bastard! You evil, raping bastard,' Philip had breathed, adding, 'I'll kill you for stealing her from me!'

Father Paul had been appalled, and would have gone to the boy, had Philip not then blundered away to his home. Perhaps he should make the effort to find Philip now, take the time to speak with him. It could not hurt, and it might serve to ease his anxiety about the lad's apparent intent to kill Paffard. That would surely be better than to sit here worrying at the mystery of his attack by Paffard last night. Besides, as he told himself, Sarra could have been mistaken. She spent much of her life looking at the world through a fug of strong ale or cider. She could have got men confused, cloaks confused. After all, why should the merchant attack *him*?

He would go and see Philip. With that conclusion, he pulled on a cloak against the early evening chill and left his room. It was only a short walk, but with his injured toes and sore kidneys, it was far enough.

The evening was fine, and the traffic was almost gone for the day. Soon the bells would ring for curfew and the gates would be slammed shut and locked, and another day would be ended. It was comforting to reflect that all the people were snug here inside the protection of the great city walls, the thousands of souls wrapped up like children in a nursery.

He was almost at the Paffards' house when he heard it. A shrill scream of horror and fear.

Combe Street

The priest stood stock-still, and he could feel the hairs on his scalp rising as the trembling scream faded on the cool evening air.

There was no power in his legs. He stood as though his boots were rooted in the muck of the street's surface, a terrible dread gripping him, because he was convinced that whatever had created that hideous sound was not human. It must be a creature from hell itself. And then his hand touched his cross, as though of its own volition, and with that first tingling sensation, his body reacted. He grasped it firmly, and holding it aloft, hobbled to the nearest house. It was the Paffards' dwelling. Father Paul pounded on the door like a man possessed. It was opened a crack by a most reluctant Gregory, and only when he recognised the blanched features of the priest did he pull the door wider.

'Father, get inside. What was that noise?'

'I have no idea,' Father Paul said as he stumbled after Gregory along the passageway to the hall.

'You saw nothing in the street?' Gregory said.

'No. I was walking along, and it was quiet. Most of the traffic's gone. It's late, you see. Most are at home.' He realised he was gabbling nonsense, and closed his mouth. 'Please may I have some water, or wine – anything,' he said thickly.

Claricia and Agatha entered, both pale, demanding to know what was happening, and though Paul gripped his mazer with both hands, still the wine almost spilled from the edge, his trembling was so acute.

A door slammed, and he looked up fearfully. Then there were steps, and a few moments later he was relieved to see Henry Paffard, cloaked against the night's chill. The cloak was above his ankles, and Paul saw the stain and tear clearly. He felt his mouth drop open.

The master of the house strode in, dropping his grey cloak as he came, looking about him with disdain. 'Well? What is all the fuss about?'

179

'Did you not hear the screams?' Gregory demanded as the old bottler bent and gathered up Henry's cloak.

'If that is what they were, we should be sending someone to ensure that no one from our house was hurt,' Henry stated. 'Where is John? *John*? Oh, there you are. I want you to take a stout staff and go out to see where that cry came from. Understand? Don't put yourself in danger. Now, where is Thomas?'

Gregory muttered something about Thomas being in his bedchamber, and Henry told him to go and bring him down. Father Paul was almost past caring by now. The wine had warmed and soothed his belly, and now he looked about him with his mind apparently clearer and calmer.

The sense of moderate well-being was short-lived, however, for Gregory returned in a hurry. 'Father – Thomas is missing!'

Paffards' House

Thomas had heard the scream, and at once his scalp crawled in terror.

He had never felt scared until the last week. Before that, he had been entirely secure and safe, especially in his home. His mother would always cosset him, the maids would indulge his every whim and pamper him, and even John would unbend slightly at the sight of him.

All that changed last week, and now, with that scream, he was thrown back into the terror of that night. He remembered the bodies writhing before the fire. Too late he had moved back into the shadows, but Gregory had seen him.

The look in his eyes terrified Thomas, and he would have fled, but Gregory hurried to him and held his shoulders, telling him to be calm, to be quiet, that he must never tell anyone, that this secret was between them, and them alone, and he must go to his bed now, and never speak of what he had seen . . . and Gregory's eyes had been as cold and dark as the water at the bottom of the well in the garden. Joan was already gone, and so Gregory didn't see her. He told Thomas once more to go back to his bed, to forget.

He hurried there, and when he was between the sheets, he firmly closed his eyes, trying to find rest and sleep, but he couldn't; the memory was too upsetting. And since then, whenever he knew Gregory was near, he could not help but duck away to avoid him.

Gregory scared him. He was scared of his own brother.

The scream cut into his thoughts like a sword stabbing butter. When he heard the horns, and shouting, it seemed to him that he had no choice. He must make his way to the hall, find Mother and Father.

Quickly, he scurried down the passage, but as he reached the hall, he heard voices, and paused to peer in from the shadows. There was a hole in the screen that separated the passage from the room, and by that he saw a man with his back to him. A man with a tonsure. A priest, he thought with relief.

Then he saw Gregory and the sight brought back his horror. His home wasn't safe! No matter what he did, he couldn't stay here.

All the thoughts tumbled though his mind in a moment, until he couldn't bear it any longer. He had to escape. Running silently to the door, he opened it – and bolted out into the night.

Cock Inn

Baldwin and Simon were talking to each other, for Sir Richard had engaged the serving wench in a conversation that had already progressed to the stage where she was giggling and sitting on his lap. Even Edgar, Simon noticed, had a bemused look in his eyes, as though wondering why the girl would find the hoary old warrior of any interest whatsoever.

That ended when they heard the first blasts on the horn. For a split second Simon, Baldwin and all the other men in the room were still, listening. Then Sir Richard sprang to his feet, and the squeal of dismay from his discarded wench was the signal for all to rush for the door. Simon and Baldwin were held up by the crush in the doorway itself, and then they were all running for Combe Street, ales and cups forgotten in their urgency.

Simon was a little ahead of the others, Edgar just behind him, when he came to the alley. He set his hand to the hilt of his sword as he pelted down it, partly drawing his weapon as he went.

There were four or five men already there, all grouped about a boy and two hogs. The hogs themselves were almost as terrified as the boy, and were backed into the corner, where they snuffled and grunted anxiously.

'What's the matter with the lad?' Simon demanded, irritated to have rushed all this way for nothing. He slammed his sword back in the sheath, still panting. 'Who is he?'

A woman with a round, sweaty face glared at him. 'The poor lad's been scared out of his wits, and I don't blame him. It's a miracle he hasn't been sent moonstruck!'

'Why?' Simon said impatiently, then glanced behind her to where she pointed. 'Christ's pain!'

Waves of nausea rippled through his frame, and he had to stand back, breathing deeply, to let Baldwin and Sir Richard get past to Juliana's body.

Paffards' House

Gregory raced back through the house again, hurtling up the stairs while the others ran about below, calling for Thomas all the way. He went into the bedchamber he shared with his brother, looking under the bed, behind the chest, inside the chest, but there was not a hair of the lad in there. His parents' room was empty, as was the maids' at the back of the upper part of the house. He even went to the windows in case Thomas had tried to climb on the roof, but they were all closed and barred.

Down in the hall again, he found his mother sitting with a cup of wine. Father Paul was seated on a stool, his face ashen. Gregory set off again to the rear of the house, to the garden and the outbuildings behind and opened the gate and peered out to where the body of Alice had lain.

'What's all the noise for?' Ben asked.

The sudden appearance of his father's apprentice made Gregory jump. He had forgotten that Ben slept out here at the back where the stock of tin and lead was stored, so that he could guard the valuable metals.

'It's Tommy. He's disappeared. Have you seen him?'

'No – not for a long time.'

Gregory ran back into the house. Agatha was in the hall too, now. He told them that he thought Thomas must have fled through the house to the front, and set off once more after the boy. John was with him this time, and the two ran into Combe Street, Gregory breathing fast as he stared about him anxiously.

'Master Gregory, don't worry,' John said. 'He'll be fine.'

'Where is he, though? If there is a murderer on the loose, Thomas could be killed too. You heard the Hue and Cry, didn't you? Where could he be?'

'I've not heard of many murderers having a need to kill little boys.'

Gregory would have snapped at him, but at that moment he saw the crush of people up ahead. He pointed, and John hurried with him along the stony roadway, both of them dreading what

183

they might find there.

Men and some women were staring into the alleyway, and as they reached it, Gregory spotted a small figure. 'Thomas!' And then, to his surprise, he saw his father standing a short way away.

'John, you take Thomas back to the house. He should be in his bed, not wandering the streets at this hour,' Henry Paffard said, and cast a look at Gregory as if to challenge him.

CHAPTER TWENTY-TWO

Alley off Combe Street

Baldwin saw Simon stagger and reel, and the moment he did so, he caught sight of Juliana.

There was a lantern nearby, and caught in its baleful gleam, he saw the alley as a series of little scenes. There was the sobbing boy, being hugged close by a woman, two pigs behind him, a man with a stick keeping them in their makeshift pen in the corner of the alley. There were two bailiffs, both ashen-faced, there were neighbours gathered to help as they might – and then there was Juliana.

She lay on her back, and at her throat there was a gaping maw, where a knife or sword had slashed. Blood had splashed all down her breast and skirts, and made them slick and foul. But the worst thing was her face. She had been rendered almost unrecognisable.

Baldwin approached her with a frown of concentration. Death held no fear for him. He had seen too many bodies in his life. As a young man he had joined the warrior pilgrims who set off for the Kingdom of Jerusalem to try to protect the last city, Acre, from the enemy's swords. There he had seen people slowly die from starvation and disease, or Mamluke weapons. Since returning to England and becoming Keeper of the King's Peace, he had viewed many corpses, and had witnessed judicial executions, as well as killing men himself. But even for him, this was a sight that shocked.

Juliana's murderer had hacked at her face as though in a frenzy. Her left eye was ruined with one stab, while another raked down her right cheek. But it was her mouth that made Baldwin stop short. Both lips had been cut away. One was missing, probably lying in the alley's mud and filth, while the lower lip hung, revolting, over her cheek. It was one of the worst cases of mutilation he had ever seen.

Simon was leaning one hand against the wall, head low as though he was about to throw up. Baldwin motioned to Edgar to take him away. It was bad enough here without Simon adding to the stench. When Simon had gone, Baldwin spoke to the man by the body.

'Bailiff,' he said, ' I am a Keeper of the King's Peace.'

'I know you, sir. I'm glad you're here.' The man was thick-necked and built like an ox, but at the sight of the body his voice had thickened, and there was a break in his tone.

'You must ensure that all the neighbours are collected. Has anybody sent in search of the killer?'

'There are men all over the alleys here.'

'The alley only has two entrances? Has no one seen a man about here?'

Sir Richard was staring down at the body. 'This is Mistress Juliana, isn't it?' he interrupted. 'I recognise her clothes.'

'I believe so,' Baldwin said.

'This boy came up from the city wall,' the woman

comforting him said. 'He said he was following his pigs when he heard her scream.'

'Can you tell me what happened?' Baldwin said, crouching before the boy. 'What's your name?'

The boy was shivering, his face grey, but he swallowed and nodded. 'I'm Rab. I was watching my master's hogs, and she screamed. I didn't want to come here, but the hogs went off and found her. I couldn't leave them—'

Baldwin held up a hand as the boy's voice became higher and more strained. 'Calm yourself. You were down by the wall then, and came up here?'

'Yes.'

'Then the killer must have headed back to Combe Street,' Baldwin decided.

'He may not have had much blood on him,' Sir Richard observed. 'If he got her in front of him, and slashed with a knife while pushing her away, the blood would have mostly missed him. He might have walked the streets and no one realise.'

'It all depends upon who was in the street at the time the first scream was heard,' Baldwin said. He looked up, past Sir Richard, and saw William and Philip Marsille approaching. Grabbing at Sir Richard, he said urgently, 'Stop them! For God's sake, don't let them—'

But it was too late. Baldwin saw their faces freeze in horror. Philip's expression became fixed and yellowish, until he looked like a corpse himself; William's reddened until Baldwin feared he might suffer an attack of choler and fall, but then the boy's face went absolutely white, and he tottered. Edgar caught him before he could fall, but then, as the people around the body and the bailiffs drew together to hide the remains of their mother from them, William happened to glance behind him.

'*You* did this! You killed her, you murdering bastard!' he bellowed at Paffard.

Baldwin ran to William before he could struggle free. Edgar had him by the shoulder, but before Baldwin could reach them, William had punched Edgar in the side of the face and was already yanking his arm away. Behind him, the sight that had enraged him were Henry and Gregory Paffard, Father Paul at their side, and even as Baldwin caught sight of them, he real-ised William had drawn his knife.

There was a short jerking motion from Edgar, a blow to the side of William's head, just above his ear, and William crum-pled to the ground. Edgar shot a look at Baldwin, then at Philip, as though daring Philip to try a similar attack, but Philip took one look at the grimly smiling man-at-arms and decided against it.

'Sir Baldwin, I think we should fetch Master William home,' Edgar said calmly.

Baldwin nodded. Simon was up and recovered, his back to the body of Juliana, glowering at the Paffards himself. 'You do that, Edgar. Hugh will help you. Simon, Sir Richard and I will speak to the Paffards.'

Paffards' House

It was good to stand near Henry's fire after the chill of the alley and feel the warmth seeping into his hands, Baldwin thought. His skin was growing thinner as he aged. He was falling apart, he told himself without bitterness.

It was natural. He was well into his fifties: his muscles ached after even moderate exercise, his right ear was grown deaf, and he could not stay awake through the night as once he had been able to. His body was giving up its strength. Yes, it was natural that a man his age should begin to show signs of decrepitude.

Father Paul stood near him, holding his hands to the fire, and Baldwin eyed him curiously for a moment before turning to the master of the house.

'Master Henry, it would seem that William believes you must have had a hand in the murder of his mother. I shall speak with him later, but for now, is there anything you would like to tell us?'

'It's nonsense! How could anybody believe that? I am a merchant in the Freedom of the City, not a cut-throat.'

'Why then should William Marsille make such an accusation?'

'Because he's a fool!'

'It is one thing to be a fool, and another to make scurrilous accusations, Master Paffard,' Baldwin said.

'It's because he hates us. That's why,' Gregory said.

'Why?'

'Because Father told them that he'd see them thrown into the gutter,' Gregory said.

Baldwin eyed the fellow. Gregory looked intelligent, but he was restless. His gaze moved on, away from Baldwin and on to the fire, then to his father, to Sir Richard, to the jug on the side-board – it was as though he found it difficult to maintain his concentration. Or was it a sign of guilt?

'Do you own their house?' Baldwin asked Henry.

'Yes – and I want them out. Those boys think the world owes them a living,' Henry said. 'Well, I don't. I want my property back so I can give it to someone who'll pay the rent. *They* haven't paid for weeks.'

'So you have told them they will lose their home,' Baldwin said. 'What else? They wouldn't accuse you of murdering their mother just because of that. And you wouldn't suddenly threaten them with eviction after weeks of no rent without some other motive.'

'They've been upsetting people,' Henry Paffard said. 'I told them they must leave the house because they have broken the peace. It is my duty as a responsible landlord to keep the peace between people living here.'

'That is still no reason to say that you killed their mother, Master Paffard. So what *is* the reason for that?' Baldwin insisted.

'Their mother came here earlier. She wanted me to go tonight to see her in that alley.'

'Why?'

'I don't know. How could I?' Henry demanded. Some of his old arrogance was already returning. 'The woman was lunatic.'

'Because she thought you guilty of murder?'

'Perhaps.'

'Why?' Baldwin asked. 'All around here say how well you treated your maid.'

'Yes,' Gregory sneered. 'Everyone is so impressed with my father. He was so generous, so kind to that maid.'

'Quiet, Gregory,' his father threatened. 'You don't know . . . You don't understand.'

'You allowed her to use your front door,' Baldwin said. 'That means she was more than just a maid to you.'

'She had been here many years. She'd earned the right,' Henry retorted.

Baldwin eyed him for a long moment. The man's manner intrigued him. He was waspish and arrogant, but there was another tone to his voice that spoke of some kind of internal conflict. He was a man to watch, Baldwin decided.

'They're jealous,' Gregory said. 'It rankles that they have to depend on us, while they think that they ought to be in here instead of us.'

'Why would the Marsilles think that?' Baldwin asked.

'Their father Nicholas was a friend of my father. After he died, his investments and properties had nothing behind them, he owed so much money. My father has been forced to protect them. That is why they infest that house. It's a matter of charity. We have looked after them with care, but we can't carry on if they offend all their neighbours.'

'That is why they hate you and your family?' Baldwin said, looking at Henry.

'Yes. They would pass around any scandalous lies to upset me.'

'And in so doing, guarantee that they would lose their home? It makes little rational sense to me,' Baldwin noted.

'You saw them!' Gregory said spitefully. 'They aren't rational. All the bad luck they attract, they blame on us.'

CHAPTER TWENTY-THREE

Marsilles' House

It was pitch dark outside now, and without a moon-curser in sight, Baldwin stumbled as they made their way to the Marsilles' home. Simon had to catch his arm.

Simon was still feeling embarrassed about his reaction to the body in the alley. He had thought he had grown accustomed to such sights, but the first glimpse of her face had sent his belly reeling, and the ales he had drunk in the Cock Inn had fought for release.

The entrance to the little house where the Marsilles lived was further up Combe Street, past the alley in which Alice had been discovered, and up the next. Along this squalid little way they went, until they came to a dog-leg, and it was just past this that Simon realised they had been walking along one of the walls of the Marsilles' place.

'God's cods,' he muttered as he looked at it. 'I wouldn't keep my cattle in a shed like that.'

It was no more than a lean-to, built against the side of a

more substantial building, and as Simon looked at it, he could see holes where the rotten planks of wood had decayed. There were patches of cob where someone had tried to fill in the worst of the holes in a vain attempt to stave off the elements. The roof of shingles was black and he suspected that it held many gaps between.

In the dog-leg, the alley formed a natural courtyard, and as well as the Marsilles' door, he saw two more in the adjacent wall as the door opened and Edgar let them inside.

William Marsille was sitting on a table, holding a cool, damp towel to his head, wincing, while his brother stood next to him, glowering at Edgar. Hugh stood behind him at the wall, wearing his customary frown.

Simon walked in and glanced about him with interest.

The chamber was small. There was scarcely enough space in it for a few men to stand; it was perhaps fifteen feet by six or seven, no more. The fire was a small heap of embers in a hearth, and the chestnut shingles must have been adequate to allow the smoke to leach out, because there was no chimney, nor even a louvre. To one side of the fire was a table, with three chairs about it, all good quality and entirely out of place with this chamber. There was a good iron-strapped chest, too, such as a merchant would use for his money, and a sideboard took up much of the outer wall. It must have formed a partial barrier to the cold, he thought. A ladder rose to the eaves, in which a series of loose boards had been laid, and up there Simon could see the palliasse on which the entire family slept. It was a miserable hovel, yet with furniture that would not have looked out of place in the Guild Hall, he thought.

'How is your head?' Baldwin asked.

His voice drew Simon back to the present, and he studied the boys. The older one, Philip, was a nervy youth who, in Simon's opinion, needed a damn good thrashing to wake up his ideas. William, on the other hand, even with his injury, was clearly a more mature individual, for all that he looked two years younger at about sixteen.

'I'm still alive. But if I keel over in a year and a day, I trust you will bring your servant to trial on my behalf,' he sneered weakly.

'You were about to attack a man. We could not allow that, no matter what the provocation.'

'I had intense provocation. He killed my mother.'

'Who did?' Baldwin asked.

'Henry Paffard.'

'Did you see him?' Sir Richard demanded. He had walked to the table and now sat, forearms resting on the tabletop.

'If I'd seen him, I'd have killed him,' William said. Wolf had wandered to his side, and now sat, looking up at him hopefully. He put a hand on the dog's head and stroked him.

'So it is only supposition?' Baldwin said. 'But he had already told you that you would have to leave this place?'

William looked up and about him with a wry grimace. 'Hardly a great threat, would you say? Yes, he sent his bottler, and said that he would see us all thrown into the street because of a tiny squabble between Emma de Coyntes and Mother.'

'What was your mother doing in the alley?' Sir Richard asked.

'Seeing Henry. She said that she knew something,' William told him. 'She said that it was to do with Gregory, and that Henry wouldn't want it bruited about.'

'What was it?' Sir Richard demanded.

'I don't know,' William said. 'She didn't tell us.'

At his side, Philip's head drooped. He was still deeply in shock, from the expression on his face, and Simon wondered how he himself would have responded, had he seen his own mother slain and mutilated in an alley. Not well, he concluded.

'So, could your mother have witnessed Alice being slain, do you think?' Baldwin asked. He was thinking of the tall priest again, wondering whether Laurence could have been there. It would have explained Juliana's reticence to talk about Alice's death, if the perpetrator was a priest.

'No. She would have said if she had . . . But she had been out when Alice was killed, so Henry might have thought she saw him do it,' William said.

'Or Gregory, if your story is correct,' Baldwin pointed out.

'Or, she saw nothing,' Sir Richard summarised. 'I think you are lucky you didn't get close to the merchant, boy. You could have injured him, and ended on the gallows tree. You have nothing to prove he killed your mother or his maid. There is no witness, no evidence, nothing.'

'Someone must know what she knew,' Philip said. 'Another maid, or a woman around here. They all gossip among themselves.'

Simon nodded and cast a look at Baldwin. The latter was watching Philip closely with that intensity Simon recognised so well.

'We can ask and find out,' William said. 'I will speak to all the women and see what they know.'

'You will leave them well alone,' Sir Richard growled in response. 'You almost landed yourself in very deep water tonight. Your mother is dead. You must concentrate on arranging her funeral and inquest, rather than trying to bring more mischief on yourself and your family.'

'Sir Richard is quite right,' Baldwin said, more gently to the two bereaved youths. 'You should avoid anything to do with the Paffard family. If Henry Paffard is hurt or injured in the next weeks, everybody will assume it was one of you. There is nothing you can do to escape the fact that all in this street know your feelings about Henry and his son. It is a shame your mother did not confide in you. Could it have been Gregory's affection for the maid, do you think?'

Philip suddenly looked up, his eyes narrowed. '*Gregory?*'

'We were told that he was a wastrel and had an affection for the maid.'

'Not him. It was his father. That man thinks he can use any woman in his house,' Philip muttered.

'My brother was in love with Alice,' William explained. 'He offered her his hand, but she told him she was happier with her rich merchant. With Henry.'

Baldwin gave a grunt of understanding. 'I see.'

'We won't be here long anyway, if they have their way,' William added.

He looked as though he had come to the end of his self-control and was about to burst into tears, Simon thought. He had an instinctive sympathy for the fellow. Glancing at Baldwin, he said, 'We will not allow that in the immediate future.'

'How can you stop him?' William demanded hoarsely. 'This is his house, and the only things we own are these pieces of furniture we managed to salvage. That bastard can have us thrown out tonight, if he wants.'

'If he wishes to make the Cathedral angry, he can try. We are here because we have been asked to come by the Precentor, and if Henry Paffard tries to evict you, he will incur my wrath also. I will personally visit him and have him change his mind,' Baldwin said firmly. 'If the worst comes to the worst, I will ask the Precentor to threaten excommunication.'

'You don't have the authority to promise that,' Philip said

ungraciously. 'You are a knight. A secular knight doesn't have the power to demand things like that of the Church.'

'Once *I* was a monk, and I travelled to the Kingdom of Jerusalem before you were born,' Baldwin growled. 'I was a fighting pilgrim in the Holy Land, and I have more authority in this than you can know. And besides,' he added, drawing his sword and setting it on the table where the peacock-blue metal gleamed wickedly in the candle-light, 'I can back up promises with steel, when necessary.'

Farm near Clyst St George

Ulric felt as though there were no more tears left in him as he dropped from his pony at the little farm.

A man's body was being dragged from the doorway by two laughing fellows, over to a pile of corpses. Sir Charles was still on his horse, directing the men with the wagon and carts. They must all be secured for the night behind the main farmhouse.

They had come down from the hill among the trees late in the evening, when many of the folk were in their houses eating their food. Quiet, domestic people, with only two older men and some youngsters sitting at table with their women, but a dog had set up a warning bark, and as Sir Charles' men poured into the yard area, men had appeared in doorways only to be cut down.

This was another of those places with little actual value. No gold, no silver. Only a little food. Nothing else.

'Ulric, fetch me something to drink,' Sir Charles called.

Nodding, Ulric dropped from his horse and made his way into a low doorway.

It was an old long-house. On the left he could hear cattle moving gently in their chamber, while to the right was the family's living space. Here he found a small barrel of cider, and

197

he had lifted the little cask to his shoulder, when he felt a hand on his arm. A man was behind him, and pulled him around, a blade resting on the side of his neck.

'I have been watching you, boy.'

It was the archer with the scar, the shorter one. Ulric had seen him earlier with a knife, laughing uproariously as he cut the throat of a little boy.

The archer pushed the knife slightly and Ulric felt his flesh move with the blade's point. 'I don't trust you. Remember that. You aren't one of us. If I see Sir Charles hurt, I will kill you instantly.'

There was a sudden pain at his neck, and Ulric gave a cry and staggered back.

'Oh, did the poor scanthing boy get cut?' the archer jeered. 'You'd best take the drink to your master, hadn't you? Wouldn't want him to go thirsty.'

Paffards' House

Father Paul remained sitting on his stool near the fire when the Keeper of the King's Peace and his companions left the hall. There was not a sound but for the crackling and spitting of the fire. All the men were engaged in their own thoughts. Father Paul saw Gregory staring at his father every so often, while for his part, Henry spent his time staring at the far wall as though seeing a picture on the pristine limewash that would answer all his life's problems for him.

For the priest, there was nothing else he could think of, other than the moments before Gregory had announced that his brother was missing: the appearance of Henry Paffard – almost, as it seemed – at the moment that the Hue and Cry was sounding out in the street.

He stood, feeling dizzy. It might have been his wound from

Sunday night, but he wasn't certain. He then made his way to the door without so much as a benediction. He was floating, a mere wisp of a soul.

As he passed the wall on which Henry's cloak was hanging, he could not help but touch it. The colour, the thickness, the feel: he was sure this was the same cloak worn by the man who had attacked and threatened him. At the corner, he saw the same little mark, the tear in the fabric that he had noticed while being beaten.

Outside, the air was cool and calming. He stood, swaying slightly. If he moved, he might fall.

Voices came from an alley. Not scary voices, just men talking, and he closed his eyes for a moment. He had to go and see. Lurching slightly, he crossed the road to where an orange glow showed that a lantern or two were illuminating something. There were more voices . . . and then he found himself outside the group of Watchmen and locals talking quietly. He was compelled to step closer and closer – until he saw the nightmare vision of his dead parishioner.

There was a rushing in his ears, and he didn't hear the men who called to him as he hurtled up to the open space of the street, and then, blessed relief, he could stop and take deep breaths, the cold air flooding his lungs and bringing clarity to his thoughts.

'Father, are you all right?' He recognised Sir Baldwin's voice, but could not answer.

There was a sparkling series of lights in his vision, and a blackness low and left, as though someone had removed all vision from that part of his eye, and then he felt his legs give way.

Sir Richard bellowed: 'HO, THERE! Grab him, Simon! Yes, take his arm.'

'What has happened to you, Father?' Simon asked.

'Not now, Simon. Let's get him to the Palace Gate – ach, no. Curfew has passed. Then to his church. Come, Father, you will be well enough after a short time.'

He was aware of hands at his armpits, strong hands that supported him as he floated along the street down to the South Gate, and in at Holy Trinity. Those same helpful hands assisted him inside his room and deposited him on his bed.

'Do you feel sick?' Baldwin was asking. 'Concentrate, Father. Don't go to sleep. Keep awake. Talk to me!'

'Water, please,' he croaked. His throat was parched once more.

'Here,' Sir Richard boomed, bending and holding out a cup.

He took it gratefully and drank quickly, slurping and spilling much of it down his breast.

'Easy, Father,' Sir Richard said, taking it away again. 'Sip, man, don't drown!'

Father Paul leaned back on the bed and closed his eyes. But no matter how hard he screwed them shut, he could still see the figure of Henry Paffard walking into the hall just after the sound of the horns and shouting outside. And he saw too the terrible ruin that had been Juliana.

'Father?' Baldwin said. 'What was it? What happened to you?'

The priest stared at the knight with wild eyes that seemed to see through Baldwin to a horror beyond.

'It was the devil. Tonight I have seen the devil himself. I must be in hell.'

CHAPTER TWENTY-FOUR

Paffards' House

The beating on the door was thunderous, and John the Bottler stood up sharply.

His first instinct was to go straight upstairs and stand outside his mistress's chamber door to protect her, but almost as soon as he had the thought, he squashed it. It was late, and any assailant would have to get past him here in his buttery.

Arming himself with the small hatchet he used for tinder, he strode along the passageway to the door. At the hall, he saw Gregory, standing with Agatha at his side, and John eyed them coldly. Once, only a short while ago, he had adored those two like his own children, but no more. Now he had witnessed for himself how Gregory and Agatha could behave, John would never be able to feel the same towards them. Still, he was glad when he saw Gregory usher his sister upstairs, take his knife and join John at the front door.

The hammering came again, and the two men looked at

each other, both anxious. John cried out, 'Who is that? What do you want?'

'This is Sir Richard de Welles, Coroner, and Sir Baldwin de Furnshill, Keeper of the King's Peace. If you want an easy life, you will let us in. NOW!'

John kept hold of his hatchet, but slid back the bolts at top and bottom and released the door. He slipped the latch and pulled it open a short way, peering out suspiciously. 'Well? What is it this time?'

The door was shoved wide by Sir Richard. Automatically, John lifted his hatchet, but the knight's hand gripped his wrist as he pushed the bottler from the door until John's back was against the wall, his arm still held in an iron grip.

'If you hold a weapon to me, my fella, you are threatening the King's Officer. You understand me? Now, go and fetch your master.'

Released, John nodded to Gregory, who sheathed his own knife. The bottler then scurried along the passage to the stairs at the far end, ran up them and made straight for the master's room.

'Who is it?' Claricia demanded.

'The knights again, my lady,' he said. 'They want to see your husband.'

'He's not here.'

John clenched his jaw. After a brief pause, he apologised. 'I must have missed him downstairs, then. I'll go and find him.'

He hurried back along the passage, reaching the stairs just as the door to Joan's room opened and Henry came out, tightening his belt. 'Well?' he said rudely, seeing John.

John stood back to let his master walk down the stairs, realising he still carried the hatchet. If he had the courage, he would slam it into his master's head right there and then.

* * *

'You took this long to realise?' Gregory sneered.

'Be silent, boy! I won't have my private business discussed like this. There are certain matters which should be kept in the house. They don't need to be discussed with all and sundry,' his father snapped.

'Don't need to be discussed? The whole street knows about you and Alice, Father! Only *you* think it's a secret still. No one else! Especially in this house.'

'Well?' Baldwin said. He had asked Paffard as soon as the merchant entered the room: 'Was the dead maid your lover?'

'I was very fond of Alice. She was particularly close to me,' Henry said. He gave another sigh. 'God's blood, man, don't you understand plain English?' He could have spat into the fire. This bitch-son knight was a lurdan if he didn't. He caught sight of Simon's cold stare and glared back. 'What?'

'Nothing,' Simon said quietly, but there was something in his tone that grated and Henry narrowed his eyes before turning back to Baldwin.

'Plain English I understand perfectly,' Baldwin said. 'So, you mean to say that you were taking advantage of this maid while she was under your roof?'

'I have the same natural desires as any other man, and she was willing.'

'Would she dare to refuse her own master?' Sir Richard demanded.

'I suppose you would reject the interest of your own maid or any other woman?' Henry scoffed. This was beyond belief! He walked to his sideboard, pushing John from his path, and poured himself a large cup of wine, pointedly ignoring the knight and his friends. 'I have taken many years to rise to my position, Sir Knight, and I will enjoy the fruits of my success whether you approve or no. It is nothing to do with you, nor to do with the Marsilles.'

'But they thought you might have had a hand in the murder of their mother. Did you?'

'She sought to blackmail me, I believe. As I told you earlier, the stupid bitch demanded to see me this evening. I didn't go.'

'Was it something to do with your affair with the maid?'

'I don't know. I didn't meet her, so I can't answer that.' He kept his eyes away from Gregory. The bitch had said it was a secret about *him*, hadn't she? He could guess what his son's secret was.

'So you did not go to that alley and kill her?'

'Eh? No, why would I? I wasn't going to pay her. More fool her, if she wanted to stand in the cold as night came on.'

'Who knew you had spoken to her? Who knew you were supposed to be meeting her?'

'How should I know? Perhaps all my household here knew, and Juliana's sons, I daresay. What of it?'

'Only this, Master Paffard: those who knew that she would be there are the people who could have tried to kill her. So from your own mouth, you must plainly be our chief suspect.'

Henry Paffard watched as Baldwin bowed and took his leave, Sir Richard and Simon following, and as they left, Henry cursed: 'Damn them, and damn her, the strummel patch! What are you two staring at? Get out of here!'

John and Gregory walked from the room, and Henry glared after them until he was alone in his hall, and only then did he cover his face with his hand and begin to weep quietly.

Wednesday after the Nativity of St John the Baptist[1]

Exeter Cathedral

Baldwin and Richard went to find Simon as soon as the sun was over the wall. Once they had breakfasted together, they left Edith and made their way to the Cathedral Close.

'You are leaving Hugh with Edith?' Baldwin asked as they walked along the road.

'I don't like the idea that there is a man killing women in the city,' Simon said. 'I have told him to stay here and look after Edith while we're here in Exeter. I don't think I'll be in any danger with you, Sir Richard and Edgar to protect *me*!'

'I would hope not!' Baldwin chuckled. He was thoughtful as they crossed over Carfoix. 'The Coroner will have to visit the scene of Juliana's murder last night,' he said.

'Have you any idea who could have wished to kill her?' Simon asked.

Baldwin sighed. 'To do such violence to Juliana speaks of a mind that is itself tortured. This murderer's heart must be completely without pity.'

'Why stab out her eyes and cut off her lips?' Sir Richard rumbled. 'That's what I don't understand.'

Simon said, 'It's as if the killer wanted to mark his victims. First Alice was stabbed in her breasts, now Juliana loses her lips and eyes. Alice, perhaps because of her affair with Henry Paffard, and Juliana because she was threatening blackmail. To stop her eyes from seeing, and her mouth from speaking.'

'Henry Paffard could have done that to Juliana if, as he said, she threatened blackmail. But why would he have killed Alice?' Baldwin wanted to know.

1 1 July 1327

It was a cool morning, and a thin mist hung above the river, he saw, glancing down to the water and beyond. His home lay over there. It was a grim way to spend his life, he thought, wandering this benighted city in search of a murderer, when all he wanted was to be at home with his wife. Still, he had to speak with the Precentor, if only to learn whether Father Laurence had left the Cathedral last night. Had he, in fact, been out and about in the streets? And if so, could *he* have had a reason to kill Juliana and mark her?

Wolf sauntered along at his side, although he disappeared to sniff at some of the tempting treats spread out on the cookshop trestles until an unimpressed cook's boy flicked his towel at Wolf's nose. The mastiff gave him a pained look as he turned away to follow Baldwin again, then darted beneath the trestle to scavenge a titbit. This time the boy aimed a kick at Wolf's rump, but the brute returned to Baldwin with a contented expression.

'What if Father Laurence had been detained inside the Cathedral for some reason? We'd have to look at Paffard more closely, eh?' Sir Richard said. He had consumed a brief snack to 'Keep body and soul together, eh?' before leaving Edith's house and Simon, seeing the expression on her face, felt sure that he was eating his daughter out of house and home. It was tempting to suggest that they all eat at an inn, but that would offend Edith. The suggestion that they should dispense with her hospitality would be insulting. Better to remain here a little longer.

'If he left the Close for any reason, then we would have to recommend that he be held in the Bishop's prison until his case could be heard.'

'Hmm. You think him guilty?'

'I am sure that he is concealing something from us, but what it is, I have no idea.'

'We should speak to the others who live in the alley next to the Marsilles,' Simon considered. 'Perhaps one of them saw Juliana leave her house, and noticed if she was followed.'

'A good idea, Simon,' Baldwin said.

They were soon in the Close, nodding to Janekyn at his gate, and to the beggars who plied their trade just inside the gateway. John Coppe was there, and smiled as Baldwin threw a penny into his pot. Coppe had been a fixture in the Close for all the time Baldwin had visited. A sailor, he had lost a leg in a brutal fight aboard ship and now begged at his accustomed spot daily.

Baldwin stopped and returned to Coppe. 'Do you know Father Laurence, the vicar?'

'Aye, he's known to me.'

'How would you describe him? Is he a genuine, kindly priest, or one of those who mouths good words but has no real interest in men?'

'Oh, you want to know how he treats a poor cripple, sir? I'd say he was one of the kindest vicars here. I've never heard a foul word from him, but once, when a horse was left grazing on the grass there and knocked an old widow's body from the cart she was resting in, waiting for her grave, he used some words then I've not heard since leaving ship. Apart from that, he's as mild in manner and speech as any I've seen. He's brought me food too, before now,' Coppe added pointedly. 'And ale.'

'Coppe, you are a disreputable vagrant who deserves the lash,' Baldwin said.

'Aye, Sir Baldwin. So, you'd like to share some o' your food with me?'

'I'll think about it,' Baldwin said, chuckling.

'What was that for?' Sir Richard asked as they carried on towards the Precentor's house.

'Just seeing if his opinion of the good vicar tallied with my own,' said Baldwin. 'And it does. Father Laurence struck me as a decent priest, not a killer.'

'Which is not a great deal of help to us, is it?' Simon muttered.

'Perhaps it is, and perhaps it is not,' Baldwin said. 'But I think the vicar would be well advised to remain within the Close for his own safety.'

They reached the Precentor's house, and were being greeted by a young clerk, when they heard the hubbub in the hall.

'What is the matter?' Baldwin asked of the clerk.

'It is one of our vicars, I am afraid. He has disappeared.'

Sir Richard rolled his eyes.

'I think that makes our case easier,' Baldwin murmured.

Talbot's Inn

Without his clerical robes, Father Laurence felt incredibly conspicuous, even though his tonsure was hidden beneath his cap and hood. With his height, he had to bend his head to appear more like others, and walking in that way made him feel still more as though everyone was staring at him. It was most unpleasant.

He had arrived at this inn late last night. There were many inns and taverns in the city, but he was known in almost all of them. The city of Exeter was not very large, and this was one of the few places that he had never frequented. It had a good reputation, so he had heard, but it so happened that it was close to the north wall, and this was an area the clergy rarely visited. So much the better now, it would seem.

Clad only in peasant garments he had purloined in the Dean's house from a pile of old servants' clothes that were intended for alms, he had been directed to the noisome little chamber out behind the stables, rather than the normal rooms. That at least was a relief. Sleeping out there with other poor folk who were staying the night, he felt sure that he would be all but invisible. He had curled up about his bundle of belongings wrapped up in an old chemise, and tried to sleep.

It was impossible. All he could see each time he closed his eyes was his beloved's face. He had loved, and his love had turned to misery. There could be no resolution for him. No return to his past life, no possibility of love. He couldn't bring such shame upon his Cathedral, for he loved it. No, he must give up all and find a new path in life. His adored had been so precious to him – but no longer. It would be insufferable to remain here now.

Insufferable, to meet, to speak with, and never admit his passion. Or to accuse. At least if he were to denounce his adored, there would be some sort of cessation with that exposure. Perhaps it would even ease his broken heart, just a little.

No, he must go. There was nothing else for it, since he had loved so strongly that he had willingly sworn to keep their secret, before he realised what the secret might be. And now he was bound by that oath. He had sworn on the Gospels, and could no more break it than fly, no matter how much he wanted to. The thought of her face, screwed up with such diabolical glee had almost struck him dumb with horror as she confessed to him. There were some women who took a delight in shocking, he knew, but never before had he been confronted by one. It was such a hideous experience . . .

The first dull gleams of daylight did not reach into this hovel, but the bellows of the stablemen and the clattering of buckets of drink for the horses was enough to waken a dead man. He was sitting up as his neighbours awoke, his bundle in his hands, staring ahead grimly. Only when they were all rising did he climb to his feet.

He decided to do without food, and instead made his way

along the roadway towards the East Gate, and there he joined the crush of folks preparing to leave the city.

It was there that he heard of the second murder, and he almost fell to his knees in horror.

This was no time for him to leave.

He must go back.

CHAPTER TWENTY-FIVE

Precentor's House

There was little that the Precentor could tell them when they finally arrived before him.

Adam was furious with himself. That *damned* fox-whelp Father Laurence! How could he reward Adam's kindness in this manner! When he was found, Adam would ensure that he had the worst of all possible punishments for this treachery. And now he had to explain and apologise to the good Keeper.

It was utterly in*tolerable*!

'My dear Sir Baldwin, it is with the very greatest embarrassment that I greet you today.'

'Precentor, do not trouble yourself,' Baldwin said firmly. 'I only wish to ease your difficulties in any way I might. Can you tell me when he disappeared?'

'Last evening. He was at Vespers and Compline of our Lady in the Lady Chapel, because I have checked with the Punctator concerned.'

Baldwin nodded. Punctators were stationed to mark off all

those who attended services to ensure that canons and clergy did not slacken in their duties.

'After that, nobody appears to have seen him. He should have returned to the house of the Dean, where he lived, but he did not arrive there. The Dean's steward assumed that he must have remained in the church to pray, but when he grew concerned at the lateness of the hour, he sent a novice to seek him. That novice had no luck in his hunt, and apparently Laurence did not sleep in his bed. He has disappeared.'

Baldwin saw the cleric behind Adam make a hasty sign of the cross, his face alarmed.

'He will have tried to leave the city, I expect,' Baldwin said resignedly. After this latest set-back, it seemed to him unlikely that he would ever make his way homewards. 'Have you asked the gatekeepers yet?'

'No. Of course,' Adam said, flustered. 'Luke, go and enquire of all the keepers, and ask whether they remember him leaving the Close.'

'If I may make a suggestion,' Sir Richard said in an unusually low voice, 'it may be quicker to send a boy to each of the city gates to ask if they saw a lanky great vicar. Where did he come from, Precentor? Where was his home?'

'He was from Marsh, over near Axminster.'

Sir Richard looked at Baldwin. 'What do you think?'

'He'd be mad to return home. It's the first place anyone would look for him,' Baldwin grunted.

'I think so, too. So he'll have gone to Topsham to the coast, that'd be quick; or he'll have gone down to Cornwall,' Sir Richard concluded.

Adam felt his mouth fall open. 'You think so?'

Baldwin smiled sadly. 'No, I do not. If he were to run, he would have taken the North Gate to head up to Somerset, I would imagine. The last thing on his mind would be to head further into the Bishop's See. He will wish to escape the Bishop's demesnes.'

Adam felt a cold clutching at his breast when he saw the grim expression on Baldwin's face. 'Why do you say "if"?'

'I fear that he may still be in the city. I only pray that he has not already been discovered,' Baldwin said.

Church of the Holy Trinity

Father Paul had slept badly.

The shocks of the previous day had been enough to weaken his mind, and every so often in his dreams a mare would bring a scene of horror: poor Juliana; the hessian-faced attacker in the cloak; the anguish of his almost broken foot; the punches, the kicks, and then, the appalling realisation as he saw Henry drop his cloak to the floor so carelessly that it seemed almost as if he knew the priest must recognise it and did not care. Henry Paffard was a member of the Freedom of the City, and a piffling priest was of such little significance in comparison, that a gesture like this clearly declared that Father Paul could go hang so far as Henry was concerned.

The mild-mannered priest raged at the conceit that could permit Henry Paffard to threaten him with exposure as a whoring hypocrite, and also to kill two women – for surely the murderer of the one was the murderer of the other!

His anger was so acute it nearly choked him as he sat beside his bedroll. His foot was enormously painful still, and throbbed sorely as though in response to his fury. In a growing city like Exeter, there were always one or two who were prepared to bully others in order to get their own way. All cities had the same mix of law-abiding, responsible citizens and irresponsible fools, but to commit a pair of murders, and flaunt it before a man who knew, assuming that he would not dare to denounce him, was an insult to Father Paul's robes. He could not allow Paffard to kill again. He *would not* allow it!

Gritting his teeth, he began to rise full of determination – but then there was a sudden knock at his door, and he stopped and stared at it with alarm. Before he could cry out, it opened and a tall man entered, shoving the door shut behind him. Under the hood his face was hidden, but the cloak was some dull, greyish colour.

'You don't scare me!' Father Paul declared, trying to hide his fear. 'I know what you've done, Master Henry.'

'Master Henry?' the man said with a dry chuckle.

Cathedral Close

There was no sign of Father Laurence, Baldwin was told. The South Gate had been closed correctly with the curfew, and there were two other men with the keeper there to confirm that there had been no cleric of Laurence's description seeking to leave the city in the hours before night. Both East and West Gates denied seeing him, and the only possible remaining exit, the North Gate, had been a problem because the porter had been unwell. A stomach-fever had overwhelmed him the previous day, and he had been forced to spend much of the evening and night near the privy. His son had shared the duty with a neighbour, but neither was reliable as a witness. Father Laurence could have left the city by that gate, and no one would have known.

A small group of freemen had gathered together in Carfoix before the sun had risen higher than the first quarter of the morning, and they were sent off to search for the vicar, with strict instructions to harm him no more than was needful to persuade him to return with them to the city.

Meanwhile, Sir Richard, Simon and Baldwin spent their morning speaking with men who had known the vicar, trying to learn more about the man.

If ever there had been a decent, reliable vicar, clearly he was Father Laurence. If it were not for one miserable old man who stated repeatedly that there had always been something about Father Luke he hadn't trusted, there would have been uniform praise for him.

It was a surprise to Simon. He had been taught at the school at Crediton, and the priests who educated him had been fine, intelligent men, but even amongst them, if a colleague had been discovered guilty of some offence, the others would tend to turn upon him. It was almost as though they felt the need of that release, to remind themselves that they were all ordinary men. And their comments upon another's behaviour could be vitriolic.

But this Laurence had inspired only affection. It made the idea of his being a murderer more than a little difficult to swallow.

'We are getting nowhere,' Simon said, after they had finished with the staff of the Dean's house and walked out to the Close. 'Should we not go and see the Sheriff and demand that a posse be sent to find this Laurence?'

'I would be reluctant to do so,' Baldwin said. He had been walking with his head to the ground, but now he looked up and around him with a face full of fierce concentration. 'He would be likely to try to send me to find the man, and I have a feeling that it would be unproductive.'

Sir Richard stopped and gazed at Baldwin. 'You think him innocent?'

'I am sure I do not know. But I begin to believe that in order to learn more about these dead women, we should be seeking a connection that is closer to them both. I could believe a mad killer trying to rape a woman as pretty and young as Alice; I can also imagine a man wanting to rape Juliana – but not then disfiguring her.'

'Perhaps this Laurence has become moon-struck?' Simon ventured. 'If driven lunatic, perhaps he . . .'

'That is what I cannot match in my mind. You weren't there when I questioned Father Laurence, but I tell you this, Simon, I saw no sign of madness. He was a calm, pleasant man. In every way he appeared a paragon of priestly virtue. If I had to guess, I would think him innocent.'

'Then where does that leave us?'

'Both these women were locals. They had lived and died within a few tens of yards of each other.' Baldwin began to walk again, this time towards the Bear Gate, and thence to Southgate Street. He continued as he marched, 'The more I think of them, Simon, the more it seems obvious that something must have connected the two, some motive for their deaths. One learned something – did the other learn it too? Or did she guess at it?'

'What of Laurence?'

'Others have gone to search for him,' Baldwin shrugged. 'They do not need us to assist them.'

'I shall take the message to the Sheriff,' Sir Richard said. 'If he wishes me to hunt down this priest, I can do so as well as you, Sir Baldwin. But I shall endeavour to ensure that Father Laurence isn't harmed, and indeed I will see to it that he comes back safely so we may question him further.'

'That is good,' Baldwin said, and grasped his arm. 'Be wary of the Sheriff, good Sir Richard. He is a devious, dishonest man.'

'What of it?' Sir Richard chuckled. 'I have the easier task, if you are correct and the murderer is actually here in the city still.'

Holy Trinity Church

Father Paul almost fainted when the hood was removed and he found himself staring up into the bemused face of Father Laurence.

'Me?' he asked again. 'Master Henry?'

'Forgive me, my friend,' Father Paul said, and fumbled for his stool. 'I must sit. My legs. Ach, my toes!'

'Father, you have no need to ask me for forgiveness, it is I who should ask that of you,' Father Laurence said, helping the older man to his seat. 'Let me fetch you a little wine.'

'No, not for me. I am fine. It was just the surprise. I had thought you were someone else.'

'Yes, a Master Henry. Who was that? Not Paffard, was it?'

'Yes. He is the devil himself, Father. He killed the maid Alice, and now he's killed the widow Marsille. Why he should do so, I cannot comprehend.'

Father Laurence's frown betrayed his doubts. 'Why should he do so?'

'He had been sleeping with his maid. Perhaps she was growing greedy? Whatever the reason, he must have killed her, and then Madame Marsille too. I think she saw him on the night he killed Alice and tried to blackmail him, or perhaps just confronted him to win a cheaper rent. Whatever the reason, he came here and threatened me, and beat me until I promised not to expose him.'

'He did?'

'Yes. He swore he would expose me as a womaniser. *Me*!'

'But that is madness,' Father Laurence said wonderingly. 'The man must be insane if he thinks he can get away with such acts.'

'He is rich,' Father Paul said scornfully. 'It is how men of his kind reason – that for every misdemeanour there is a price they

217

can pay that will cover their sins. Everything, they believe, comes down to money in the end.'

'What will you do?'

'I shall go to him and speak out if he will not confess. The inquest for Madame Marsille is today, and I shall ensure that no innocent can be convicted.'

'You are absolutely certain that the man was the murderer?'

Father Paul eyed him steadily. 'Who else could it have been?'

Laurence pulled a face. 'I don't know.'

'What made you run away, Laurence? Was it the same reason that made you go to the alley on the night Alice was killed?'

Laurence looked about him at the little room. It contained nothing – and everything. Possessions were few. There was the table, a stool, a palliasse, a chest for the priest's clothes, and a shelf on which his two bowls and a loaf of hard bread stood. So little, and yet everything for which Laurence had hankered most of his life.

Until that day he had fallen in love.

'My friend, please do not censure me,' he begged quietly. 'I have been a great fool. I have fallen in love.'

'To love is human,' Father Paul sighed.

'Not this love,' Laurence said grimly. 'This is the sinful kind.'

Alley off Combe Street

When Baldwin and Simon arrived, the Coroner was already making his summary for his clerk.

The gathering at Juliana's body was a sombre little group. The clerk sat once more, scratching his notes while the Coroner stood, looking decidedly queasy. His face made Simon feel less foolish for his behaviour last evening.

All those whom he had come to know in the last few days were there already. The Paffard household were clustered in a group, including Claricia, who stood apart from her husband, throwing him anxious glances every so often. Behind her was her bottler and the apprentice, Benjamin, and then the de Coyntes family, with Bydaud standing with his arm about Emma. The Avices were farther away, and six or seven men and boys stood between them and the two Marsilles.

On William's face was a look of uncompromising determination as he stared over his mother's body towards Henry Paffard. If no one else had been in his way, Simon was sure that he would have launched a fresh attack.

Simon wondered what sort of man Henry Paffard really was. He looked as though he was feeling the strain, with the lines standing out on his ashen features. His eyes had become sunken, and Simon was struck with the impression of a ghost.

Perhaps there was a ghost about here, he thought. The ghost of someone who had been betrayed, and who now sought revenge?

It was enough to make his heart feel as if it was encased in ice.

CHAPTER TWENTY-SIX

Rougemont Castle

The news that Sir Richard de Welles had arrived and would like a few words with him did not please Sir James de Cockington. 'Where is Sir Baldwin? It was him I expected to see.'

Sir Richard was standing in the doorway, while Sir James remained seated. It was a calculated insult; and one that Sir Richard had no intention of allowing. He crossed the floor to the cupboard and, gently pushing the steward aside, poured himself a large goblet of wine before he responded, hitching his hip onto the cupboard's top.

'You have several problems, Sir Sheriff. The Bishop is dead, you have two murder victims in your city, and you have news that the King's father, Sir Edward of Caernarfon, has escaped from Berkeley Castle. Also, a priest has run from the Cathedral. I can aid you with one of these. I will raise a posse to hunt down this Father Laurence and bring him back. The other matters are your affair.'

'You try to tell me what you will and will not do?' Sir

James stood. 'You will do as I command. *I* am the Sheriff of the city!'

'And I am Coroner in Lifton,' Sir Richard said, and drained his goblet before setting it down and idly walking towards the Sheriff.

Sheriff James was alarmed by the sight of the older warrior approaching, but dared not jump from his chair because that would display fear. 'You should make yourself available to me!'

Sir Richard stood over him, his eyes twinkling with amusement as he purred, 'Sheriff, are you going to threaten me?'

'I could have you arrested if you try to injure me! I am the King's man!'

'So am I, Sheriff. So am I. And we have enough to trouble us already without falling out. Do you see to Exeter, and I will go to learn what I may about this fellow, Laurence. I've met him, so I will know him when I see him. And Sheriff,' he added, 'when you are older, you will realise that to gain a man's respect, first you should respect *him*.'

Alley off Combe Street

'What do you think, Simon?' Baldwin muttered as the Coroner withdrew from Juliana's body.

Simon swallowed hard. 'I think I need to get away from here.'

Baldwin flashed a grin. 'What of the man there – see?'

He was indicating Gregory Paffard, and Simon turned to the boy in relief; it was good to be able to look away from Juliana's poor, ravaged features. The sight of the lipless face was deeply unnerving.

The fellow at whom Baldwin directed his attention looked as distressed as Simon felt. As Gregory looked up, Simon's gaze reached him, and their eyes locked for an instant.

'Baldwin, you're right;' Simon muttered. 'That fellow *is* more distressed than Juliana's sons. What on earth is going on?'

But Baldwin did not hear him – and when Simon saw Gregory turn and make his way out of the alley, he knew that he must follow him. Baldwin was busy listening to the Coroner while he spoke with a man who held the pig-boy tightly by the arm, so Simon pushed past those before him, and made off after Gregory.

The fellow led him away from the city and down to the wall itself.

'What do you want with me?' Gregory turned and demanded as Simon came out from the shadows of the alleyway and into the sunny patch of common land.

'That depends on what you can tell me,' Simon said.

Gregory was even more anxious and fretful at close quarters, Simon could see. All the while, his fingers played nervously with each other, while his face twitched and his eyes blinked with what was clearly a nervous reaction. Simon had seen youths before with that same kind of response – when they were worried, or when they felt guilty about something they didn't want to confess.

'I've nothing to tell you,' the youth mumbled.

'Where were you when Juliana was killed?'

'In our hall. With my mother and sister. And Father Paul from Holy Trinity.' This time, he spoke with more confidence, and the blinking slowed. Simon was sure that this was true.

'What of the other death – when your own maid Alice was murdered?'

'What of it?' Gregory challenged him, but there was less conviction in his manner, and his nervous tic was evident once more.

'Where were you that night?'

'I was at my home.'

'And the good priest?'

'He wasn't there, no.'

'Was anyone else there with you?'

'Well, we all were, sort of.'

'Explain, boy.'

'Don't call me a boy, you churl!'

As he spoke, Gregory stepped forward, fists clenched, and swung. Simon was ready for him. Moving his torso back to avoid the punch, he grasped Gregory's hand and pulled. The boy was already off-balance, and now he was drawn over Simon's outstretched leg. Simon turned just a little, bent at the waist, and the lad tumbled to the ground in front of him, swearing and spitting like an enraged cat.

'Shut up!' Simon said. He felt better for the brief engagement, as though the physical effort had removed the memory of Juliana's face. 'Now, answer me. You said you all were, "sort of". What does that mean?'

'What I said,' Gregory snapped.

He was about to rise, but Simon put his boot on his chest. Gregory tried ineffectually to shove his leg away, but Simon pressed harder.

'Say it again, then, boy.'

'We all went to the inn together, my father, mother, me, Agatha.'

'What of the maid, Alice?'

'She stayed at home. We were there for a meal. What, you think we'd bring our servants with us?'

There was a sneer of bravado in his voice, and he began that blinking again. Looking down, Simon saw that his fingernails were bitten, some of them to the quick. He truly was living on his nerves. 'Did you all stay there together?'

'Yes. Apart from Father, who had forgotten his rosary and went home to fetch it. After he came back, my sister and I returned to the house.'

'Was Alice there?'

'I didn't look for her. She was only a housemaid to me.'

'Fine: when you returned home, was *anyone* there?'

'The apprentice was hanging about in the hall. I sent him away. He's a fool.'

'I doubt your father would want a fool in his workshops.'

'The fact that Benjamin is still working for my father proves that he is hardly bright. He could earn more with any other pewterer – and learn more.'

'When your father left the inn, was it in order to tail the maid? She had been making love before she died, according to the inquest.'

'Of course it was.'

'And she was dead when you all returned,' Simon stated.

Gregory said nothing, but Simon saw his gaze slide away from him.

'So that is why you're so nervous. You think he's the killer too,' Simon breathed.

Alley off Combe Street

Emma de Coyntes refused to feel guilty. This death, while sad, was not her responsibility. It didn't matter how much Helewisia looked at her in that accusing way of hers, Emma wasn't going to be a hypocrite and pretend a grief she didn't feel. She hadn't liked Juliana, and the fact that the woman was now dead was no reason for Emma to alter her opinion.

Helewisia and Claricia both kept staring at her, as though she'd done something wrong, but none of it was anything to do with her, any more than the death of Alice had been.

Her conscience was clear. She felt her husband's Bydaud's gaze on her, and stared back. The sadness in his eyes made her want to go and hug him. But she couldn't. Not here, not now. Later.

Father Paul had stepped into the alley with a sense of dread engulfing him, as though the air here was somehow different from that in the rest of the city.

In some ways it was. The wind had picked up, bringing a constant reminder of the vats of excrement and piss out on Exe Island where the tanners worked. How any man could endure that life was incomprehensible to Father Paul. His eyes watering, he held a strip of his cowl over his nose and mouth as he went, but all the while that feeling of congestion in his breast would not leave him, and it only grew worse as he drew nearer to the group of men that comprised the inquest. 'Dear God, don't let me die before I right this,' he murmured.

The Coroner threw him a bored glance as he approached, and continued with his questioning. Father Paul saw Baldwin, and purposely kept his distance from the knight. He didn't like Baldwin's dark, intense eyes. They made him feel as though he should divulge every secret he had ever possessed, and it was an uncomfortable sensation.

Juliana was there just as he remembered her from last night. Blood had blackened the mud about her, and her ravaged features were hideous to behold. How cruel, when only yesterday she had been a vibrant woman in her prime.

But Father Paul wasn't here to see her. He had another purpose, and he would see it through. Licking dry lips, he blurted out, as loudly as he could: 'I know why this woman was killed. I know why they were both killed!'

'What? Who said that?' the clerk demanded, stretching his neck to peer at the crowd. The Coroner too was now staring.

'I spoke: Father Paul of Holy Trinity,' the priest said, walking bravely forward. He was shivering with nerves, but then he had been scared before. This was no worse than that horrible occasion when he had first stood up in front of his own congregation. 'I know who had reason to kill both of these women,' he repeated.

'You realise what you are saying?' the Coroner said.

Sir Baldwin had stepped to his side, and spoke into his ear. 'Father, I know you want to help, but reflect. This is a dangerous course on which you have embarked.'

'I know what I do and say,' Father Paul told him, and then he said, more loudly still, 'I accuse Henry Paffard of the murder of his maid and of the murder of Juliana Marsille.'

'Me?' Henry Paffard said.

'How do you answer?' the Coroner said.

Father Paul felt his lip curl in contempt at the sight of the merchant. 'Look at him!' he cried. 'Can any man here doubt his guilt? We must arrest him until he can be tried in the city court. He should be held securely so that the women of our city are safe. He killed Alice because she was demanding money from him, and then last night he killed Juliana. I know – I saw him arrive with his cloak on after Juliana's death scream.'

The Coroner turned his attention back to the priest. 'Seeing a man wearing a cloak is no proof of a crime!'

'He came to my church on Monday, two days since, and threatened me with exposure as a whore's gull and liar because he saw me giving alms to two poor women at my door. The man who threatened me had put on a sack to conceal his face, but he wore the cloak he wears now. Last night, when Juliana was slain, I was there in his house, and I recognised the cloak when he came home just after her death. It was the same as the one worn by the man at my house. I accuse him, therefore, of the murders.'

'Henry Paffard! I ask you again, how do you answer?' the Coroner repeated.

'I admit it. I am the murderer.'

Baldwin, watching him, saw how he resolutely lifted his chin, but did not look from side to side, neither at his wife, nor at his son and daughter. He looked very little like a criminal. Most felons would have moaned and expressed remorse, but Henry Paffard stood erect and bold, for all the world more like a martyr than a villain.

Baldwin narrowed his eyes thoughtfully. There was, he felt sure, something amiss with this confession. And when he glanced at Gregory, he saw something he had never expected to see on the youth's face.

It looked a lot like admiration.

Emma felt the shock rushing through her from her toes to her head. It was so powerful, she thought she must fall, and she rocked on her feet even as the murmurs spread through the crowds.

Henry Paffard had killed Juliana. Why? *Why?* It made no sense at all!

Emma could feel the eyes of Helewisia on her, and her face turned the colour of a beetroot with the knowledge that others were pointing and talking about her. The idea that Henry could have killed Juliana because of Emma's complaint was unthinkable. No. She was being ridiculous. The fact was, if Henry *had* killed her, it was for his own selfish reasons, not because of anything that Emma had said or done.

'Emma? Are you all right?' Helewisia had crossed the alley to her.

'Yes, of course I am,' she said, a little more curtly than she intended.

227

'You look upset. You cannot blame yourself. This wasn't your fault.'

'I know. And I thank you for your kindness,' Emma said with a sigh. 'I cannot be at fault if Henry decided to kill his maid and Juliana, can I?'

'There must be some reason for him to do something so extreme. Henry is usually so rational and shrewd.'

'Why cut off her lips?' Emma said, and shuddered.

'Because he wanted to stop anyone else threatening to talk about him? I don't know.'

'Talk about him?' Emma repeated. It was a thought. If Juliana had been going to speak up about having witnessed him commit murder, say, that would explain the mutilation.

'Poor Juliana,' Helewisia said.

'I will not change my thoughts about her,' Emma said rigidly.

'I think you should show more compassion and forgiveness now,' Helewisia remonstrated gently.

'She is dead. It matters little to her what I say or do,' Emma said sharply.

'You still offer no compassion, only pride?' Helewisia said coolly.

'I offer nothing at all. Juliana offended my daughter and me. Don't expect me to mourn her. I feel sorrow that she has died, but that is all.'

East Gate

Sir Richard de Welles was happy to be seated in the saddle once more. He beamed at the men about him as he ran his eye over them. A scruffy bunch of churls, but with the hearts of men of Devon, they would no doubt suffice.

It was not as though the task ahead was difficult, in God's

name. None of the porters at the gates had reported seeing a tall priest for a day or so, which meant Laurence must have been disguised. Or, at least wore a thick cloak over his clerical garb. All these fellows need do was ride on and see whether they could overrun a clerk on foot. Not a hard job, even in winter. Today, with the pleasant breeze and the sun trying to break through the clouds, it should be an agreeable task. Not even the prospect of a fight, he told himself sadly. It was always heartening to think that a manhunt could result in some form of struggle at the end of the day. Made the effort worthwhile.

Still, with a horse beneath him, the sun overhead, he was as content as he ever had been as he led the makeshift posse from the castle's street, into the High Street, and thence out by the East Gate.

There were two Sergeants with him, and two-and-twenty men. As soon as he was outside the city's walls, he commanded them to separate, and it was with only two men that he continued onwards to Heavitree. From there he intended to make a wide sweep up towards the north. He didn't think that the priest would have travelled more than ten miles if he left the city last night. Perhaps he could have covered slightly more, but if he had, news of the posse would soon reach all the small farms and vills, and the peasants would be on the lookout for a man with a tonsure. Ha! It wouldn't take long to catch him.

He had ridden four or five miles when he saw the first group of men.

Three of them lying at the side of the road – and all hacked and stabbed to death.

CHAPTER TWENTY-SEVEN

Rougemont Castle

Sheriff James de Cockington was silent as he walked into his hall. He took the proffered goblet of wine, and went to his chair on the dais without speaking. Sitting, he took a long pull of the wine, eyeing the group without expression.

In truth, he wasn't sure how to proceed. Henry Paffard stood with his head bared, his hands free, while two sturdy men guarded him. The priest stood, resolute and determined, and there was Sir Baldwin and his companion, and Simon Puttock.

'Sir Baldwin, I would be grateful if you would keep your hound at your side,' he remonstrated, seeing Wolf licking at his table.

Baldwin nodded to Edgar, who took Wolf outside. 'My apologies, Sheriff.'

James de Cockington paid him no heed. 'Coroner, speak, please. I am fascinated as to how this well-known and respected merchant comes to be in my hall.'

'He has confessed before the jury to the murder of the two women near Combe Street.'

'He has?' De Cockington looked at Paffard. 'So? Why did you do this?'

'I feel remorse, but I think my actions must have been caused by my arrogance and greed.'

'Arrogance I can believe – greed?'

Paffard shrugged. 'I did what I did. I will pay the price.'

'I fail to understand this. Can you not explain your reasons? No? Well, if you are determined to suffer the penalty, there is little I can do. You will be held in the castle gaol until such time as the next court, and then you will be hanged by the neck until dead.'

Paffard paled on hearing those words, but he did not demur, and obediently walked out with his two guards when motioned to leave.

'So, Sir Baldwin, it would appear the matter is resolved.'

'So it would seem.'

'And all because of this bold priest?'

'The merchant tried to silence me with threats,' Father Paul said. 'I would not permit that.'

'I congratulate you,' the Sheriff said. 'When there were so many clever minds set to learning what had happened and why, it took only a simple man in a tonsure to discover the truth. Is that not a lesson to us all, eh, Sir Baldwin?'

'It is fortunate that the fellow has admitted his guilt, is it not?' Baldwin said mildly.

'Why – do you think that makes him more or less guilty?' The Sheriff laughed. 'Perhaps, Sir Baldwin, it is time for you to surrender your warrant. A man of your age should not be struggling on with work of this nature. It is enough that you have had so many successes . . . *in the past.* Now you are so aged, perhaps you should return to your hall, retire, and enjoy the few years that remain.'

De Cockington smiled pointedly at the knight. He had never liked Sir Baldwin de Furnshill, and it was good to be able to score a point over him. Especially since he had seen to the exile of his own brother. Poor young Paul. He had liked the women a little too much, but that was hardly a crime, and he had been hounded from the city and the country, thanks to this scruffy Keeper of the King's Peace. No, he didn't like Sir Baldwin. Any embarrassment he could bring upon him would be worth the effort.

And Sir Baldwin's tight expression gratified him. He only wished he could see it grow into one of genuine pain.

Near Clyst St George

Sir Richard de Welles had been in many fights in his long life, and the prospect of another held no concerns for him. He had a sword at his side, and although his mail was back in his travelling chest at the inn, his padded jack was adequate for most blades, so he trotted forward to the bodies without fear.

All had died badly. Slashed and cut about, one with what looked like a nasty gash from a sword or axe blow, they had clearly been attacked by a strong force. Sir Richard saw a column of smoke to the south.

'These men are dead, there's nothing we can do for them,' he said, and beckoned his two companions to join him. 'Down there, looks like a building on fire. I'd guess there's a small band about here which has attacked these men and others. We need to ride and see what sort of number of men there are. You two with me?'

Both were locals, and the idea of felons wandering about lands this close to their homes was enough to stiffen their sinews. Soon the three were riding at a rapid trot towards the plume of smoke.

They had dropped down from Heavitree, and now the land lay flat before them, with dangerous stands of trees and small woods, from which ambushes could be launched all too easily. Sir Richard kept a wary eye upon them, looking for the sudden movement that could betray a bowman or a group of men-at-arms preparing to pull them from their horses.

There was no roadway, only dirt tracks, most half-smothered in mud after the last week's rains, and Sir Richard and the two riders made their way swiftly down to a farmstead that stood behind a small copse. Here, Sir Richard and his men stopped and stared ahead.

It was clear now that the men who were responsible for these attacks had military experience. It was plain from the way that one man stood outside the house, supervising the others in their tasks. Some were rolling barrels of ale along the track to carts, others carried sacks of produce. A man lay dead on the ground, his throat cut, while men took their pleasure with a woman, most probably his wife, nearby. Her moans could be heard from here.

Sir Richard's wife had been taken from him by the man who had been his steward. This man had raped and then murdered her, and Sir Richard had many times regretted his loss. No other woman would he marry, because no other could match her. To see this poor female sprawled in that undignified manner while men violated her, was insufferable. Sir Richard could no more tolerate leaving her to her fate than he could stop breathing.

He studied the men in the area with care, then said under his breath: 'You two get the woman and take her back to Exeter.' He encouraged his horse forward quietly until he was near the edge of the copse, then he raked his spurs along his beast's flanks and bellowed his loudest war-cry.

Drawing his sword, he burst through the trees in an explosion of mud and branches, only a matter of feet from the first of the men. The latter died before he could draw his sword, Sir Richard's blade hacking down through his shoulder. The group at the woman froze, the man on her gaping. Then there was a mad scrabbling as all of them bolted, trying to grab their weapons. Sir Richard spitted the man at the woman, before cantering to the rest of them. One had a sword: Sir Richard knocked it aside and slashed his neck. He fell, hands clawing at the blood as though he could stem the flow, but already Sir Richard was searching for his next target. The carter sat up on his board. Beyond was the fellow who had been directing the men.

With his horse prancing and wheeling at the smell of blood and the men's screams, Sir Richard had to fight to control the brute, but at last pulled his head about, aiming at the leader. He had taken advantage of Sir Richard's battles with his mount to run towards the farmhouse. Clapping spurs once more, Sir Richard hurtled after him. On the way he swept his sword round at the carter, trying to take his head off. He missed the man's throat, but his blade met the man's pate and he tumbled from the cart with his lifeblood spraying.

There were shouts from behind the house now, and Sir Richard rode round at the gallop. The leader had darted behind there, but Sir Richard wanted him. If he could capture the fellow, he would. If not, he would see him dead.

He slapped his rein end on the horse's rump, urging him on. The house was on his left, a small shaw to the right, and he pelted between them, out behind the house. There, he suddenly stood up in the stirrups and reined in, hauling on the leather until his horse's head was dragged back, chin to chest, before dragging the beast around and riding out of there as quickly as he could.

Behind the house were at least thirty men-at-arms, and some were already mounting to pursue him.

Gatehouse to Rougemont Castle

'The atmosphere in there was suffocating me,' Baldwin said to Simon, exhaling in a long breath as they came into the open air.

'The man does not like you,' Simon said.

'Our antagonism is mutual,' Baldwin replied. 'I detest the fellow. Hold! There's the Father. I would speak with him for a moment or two.'

The man he referred to was already under the narrow way of the castle entrance, and he and Simon hurried to reach the limping priest before he had descended the path that led to the High Street.

'Wait, Father, could we speak with you?'

Father Paul turned reluctantly. Baldwin was surprised by this: he had expected to find the man happier to speak. After all, he had succeeded in making the murderer admit his crimes.

'Father, I would be grateful to speak with you, if I may.'

'I have much to do, Sir Baldwin – including a congregation to prepare a Mass for. I trust you can be swift.'

'I would merely appreciate your view as to why the man should have thrown his life away.'

Simon and Baldwin fell in alongside the priest as he hobbled along, Edgar and Wolf following after.

'It was clear to me, when he threatened to expose me as a womaniser, that he was fearful of exposure himself,' Father Paul said. 'He thought he would be able to destroy me. What he did not realise was that I was less anxious about my reputation being harmed than he was of being discovered as a murderer.'

'But he broke in upon you, beat you . . . Did he say anything else?'

'Only that I was to forget everything I saw that night.'

Baldwin frowned. 'Why conceal his face when he wanted you to forget him?'

'To kill is so repugnant, he must be lunatic. Don't look for logic.'

Simon too was puzzled. 'Tell me, Father, when you were in his house, did it seem as though he was tortured with guilt, or that he was teasing you? He must have known you would recognise him somehow.'

'No, he just walked into the house and effectually ignored me. Paid me no heed.'

'That is curious,' Simon said. 'I've never known a man behave in such a manner. I could understand his boasting to you about the fact that it was him, if he thought he had you fully in his power, and I could understand his being ashamed – contrite, even – but to ignore it altogether is most peculiar.'

'You must ask *him* about it,' Father Paul shrugged.

'When did you decide to come and accuse him?' Sir Baldwin enquired. 'You did not appear to feel so strongly last night.'

'I had a long think about it last night, and prayed before going to the inquest. It seemed plain to me that the matter was too important to be left. How could I live with myself, were another murder to be committed and a third woman die?'

'Very true,' Baldwin agreed thoughtfully. 'You think he could have killed again?'

'Of course. Murderers are like wolves. They find attack difficult the first time, but once they have a taste for meat, they kill again and again. Henry Paffard was surely a man of that nature.'

'It is incomprehensible to me,' Baldwin said slowly, 'that a man with so much money, with his position and status, should either commit such crimes himself and not pay another, or that he would willingly confess, rather than deny everything and rely on allies and friends in the city to protect him. What was he thinking of?'

'He is perhaps a more honest man than others you have met,' the priest responded shortly.

'More than that,' Simon put in, 'is why he should have killed the women. The first, we heard, was his lover. There is no evidence that confirms she was in any manner a threat to him. Nor the second, this widow Juliana – so why kill them?'

'I don't know. But when a man has confessed to the murders, it seems pointless to question his motives.' At that, the priest hurried off along the High Street, clearly glad to be away from them and their questions.

'There is more to this,' Baldwin said. 'I should like to speak to some of the others along Combe Street. In particular, the rest of Paffard's household. There must be some explanation for his bizarre behaviour.'

'What bizarre behaviour?'

'Well, confessing to a crime he didn't commit – I should have thought that was strange enough, wouldn't you?'

Near Clyst St George

Sir Charles of Lancaster had been sitting by a fire chewing at a piece of meat so hard and leathery, it made his teeth ache. Hearing the commotion and screams from the front of the farm, he had sprung to his feet, and then, when young Aumery ran around the side of the house, he had thought at first that they were being pursued by the whole posse of the county. He roared orders, shouting for his horse, and shoved the last of the dried meat into his mouth as he ran to the horse-lines.

It took a moment only to leap into the saddle, and he was drawing his sword free even as Sir Richard turned and rode away.

237

'*To me! To me!* Ulric, you too!' Sir Charles bawled, and then was spurring his beast onwards, scattering stones and clods of grass as he galloped past the house, noting those of his men who had died with rising anger. There was a man there, Nick the Bakere, who did not deserve to die in the dirt. He was a good, loyal servant of Sir Edward of Caernarfon, and should have seen his old age. Instead this bastard intruder had killed him.

Sir Charles could see the large figure up ahead now. He bent lower over his mount's neck, and used the flat of the blade to urge his beast to greater efforts. The man in front was clearly a knight, but Sir Charles's horse was fleet, and he had a feeling that he would soon catch the fellow. Then, if he wanted to live, the man would have to surrender. Sir Charles had no intention of leaving someone wandering around to spread the news of him and his men.

Pursuer and pursued rode under a stand of trees, and out to a coppice behind, and then they were thundering along a road in a small vill. Looking about him, Sir Charles recalled this place – it was Clyst St Mary, a small community he had bypassed yesterday. There looked to be too many men about the place, and in any case, he had wanted to head straight down to Bishop's Clyst. Those who supported the new Bishop deserved to pay for their lack of integrity.

He jabbed his spurs again as they drew out of the vill, and then they were riding along the little causeway that headed almost due west, pointing like a lance at Exeter. He could imagine the place already. First there was Heavitree with its old hanging tree, where a gibbet stood to prove to all travellers that this city was a place where the law ruled. It was always good to see a man hanged from a tree. It showed that others were safe.

They wouldn't have to ride that far now. Before they were halfway over the causeway, Sir Charles saw the man ahead glance over his shoulder to check on his whereabouts. If he had been less of a threat, Sir Charles would have left him, but the safety of his men lay in the balance. He had to catch him.

The other man's horse looked as though it was slowing. Sir Charles allowed himself a smile of glee as he began to draw up to the rump of Sir Richard's horse, wondering whether he should prick the beast's backside, to make it jump and throw its rider, or whether he should simply kill the man and take his horse. It looked a good, sturdy brute. It would have to be, to carry this fat bustard so far, so swiftly. 'Halt, man, halt! Yield!'

He was so engrossed in his thoughts, he did not notice that they were almost over the causeway, and that ahead were two more men with a woman. It was Sir Richard's men with the woman they had rescued. Only at the last moment did he real- ise his danger. He slowed, but it was already too late, and a hail of stones was flung at him. One struck his shoulder, and he cursed aloud at the pain, and then a second hit his horse's head over the eye, making the beast stumble, rearing and whinnying in anger. Sir Charles fought to control it, but had to lean forward to save himself from toppling, and then the horse was on the ground again, and as he looked up, he felt Sir Richard's sword- pommel bludgeon him about the head.

As he hit the ground, a wash of silence flooded over him, and it felt as if the roadway had swallowed him.

CHAPTER TWENTY-EIGHT

Paffards' House

Gregory was in the hall when his mother appeared in the doorway.

'You look at your ease there,' she said. She traced a finger along the door's jamb, essaying a smile. It made her pale face look ghastly.

'I am,' Gregory lied. There was a dull ache in his heart, if he was honest. He had no desire to see his father executed. After all, the same blood flowed in their veins. Henry was a member of the Freedom of the City – surely there was something his friends could do to have him released into Gregory's own custody? But even as he had the thought, the boy rejected it. The court would have to come to judgement on the matter, and there was not a man in the city who would consider releasing a self-confessed murderer.

Gregory could do nothing to help.

'Why did he kill Juliana?' Claricia asked.

Gregory frowned. 'What do you mean?'

'What could she have said that would justify his murdering her? I suppose the maid had become tedious for him. Your father always liked variety. That was why he stopped coming to my bed, I think. He thought me boring after so many years. So instead, he began to use the whores at places like the Cock, and then he seduced Alice and other maids.'

'He is a lusty man, Mother,' Gregory said wearily.

'Yes. Much more so than you. You have no desire for a wife?'

Gregory felt a flash of alarm in his breast. 'Me? Now? I have so much to do, I don't need to worry about women as well. Please, you must leave me. I have a lot to think about.'

'Yes, of course,' she said, and fixed him with a sad, understanding look as she withdrew from the doorway.

Only a short time later Agatha walked in. She smiled, wandering around the room, finally approaching him from behind, and he felt her fingers on his back with a tingle. 'You are tense, brother. Is it me?'

'Yes,' he said harshly. 'It has nothing to do with Father's position, nor the way Alice and Juliana have died. What do *you* think?'

She chuckled, the bitch. 'Aren't you glad? You're master here now, brother dear.'

He shook his head. 'No. I'm just the caretaker until he comes back.'

'Comes back?' she repeated with a kind of wondering amusement.

Just then, they heard knocking on the front door, and Gregory motioned Agatha to leave. She waved at him, smiling, and hurried out of the hall. Gregory had felt his face ease at the sight of her, but then he heard John talking, and his face resumed its previous expression of anxiety.

Near Clyst St George

Sir Richard ensured that Sir Charles was disarmed, taking two daggers and his sword, before going over to the white-faced woman.

She had lost her wimple when the men were raping her, and now her dark hair was wild, clinging to her tear-stricken face like a veil. She had bright blue eyes set in a narrow face.

'Mistress, I am sorry we didn't get to you sooner. What's your name?'

'I am Amflusia. My husband was Cenred. They killed him. And my boys, my little . . .'

She surrendered to her tears, shoulders shaking with her sobs, and Sir Richard turned to glower at Sir Charles's prostrate body.

'Mistress, he will pay for his crimes. Believe me.'

Paffards' House

A short while later John came into the hall, and Gregory saw that Sir Baldwin and his friend Puttock were with him.

'Can you not leave me alone?' he groaned. 'You have taken my father, what more do you want?'

'I am sorry, Master Paffard,' Baldwin said, 'very sorry about your father. It must be most distressing to see him surrender in such an undignified manner.'

'It was a shock, yes,' Gregory said. He was remarkably still. 'I don't know what to think. I'd had no idea he could have been responsible for such terrible crimes. It is difficult to know what I should do for the best at present.'

He heard another knock at the front door, and motioned to John to answer it before rising with an ill grace and offering his guests a cup each of wine. He didn't want to be here. It was just his sense of propriety and loyalty that made him remain.

Someone had to keep an eye on the business while his father was in gaol, until he could be released.

Released! What a ridiculous notion! His father was in gaol because he had confessed to killing two women. There wasn't the remotest likelihood that he was ever going to be set free! He'd be held there until he was thrown before the Sheriff's court and given the only sentence he could truly expect. Like any felon, he would be taken out to Heavitree and the public gallows, and there he'd be held while the rope was tied at his throat, and then he'd be pulled up, kicking, to dangle for however long it took to die. And Gregory would have to pay men to grab his legs and pull, to try to minimise his father's suffering.

But then he thought that perhaps local people would see his father's crimes as so heinous that no one would want to ease his pain. Gregory might be forced to help kill his father himself.

Baldwin was talking, and he had to push all thoughts of his father's execution to the back of his mind. 'I am sorry, Sir Baldwin,' he said, clearing his throat. 'I was wool-gathering. What did you say?'

'I was only saying, that if you have need of a pleader, I know some experienced men.'

'That is very kind of you, but I think it would be to little advantage. After all, he has confessed, and in any case, the accused man is always denied a lawyer. You know that. The innocent have no need of a man versed in the law.'

He spoke with sarcasm. It always seemed to him that if a man denied his crimes he should also be granted the benefits of a pleader to make his case as best as he could. It was surely unreasonable that only the prosecuter should have the services of men trained in the law.

'It seems curious he should have been responsible for these murders,' Baldwin said thoughtfully, as though the idea had

243

MICHAEL JECKS

only at that moment occurred to him. 'After all, there was little threat to him from either woman, surely?'

'You need to ask *him* that,' Gregory said. He had returned the jug to the sideboard, and now walked to his chair again. He sat just as John entered the room again. He held a message in a scroll.

Gregory took the scroll and glanced at the seal. It was from Master Luke the Goldsmith, and Gregory frowned at it for an instant before breaking it and reading the letter.

'The rats have begun to leave us,' he said without mirth. 'The first merchant who finds that he is now unable to assist us in our business. Well, so much the better. I wouldn't want to see him making money with us.'

'The first?' Baldwin asked.

'He won't be the last. All those who now feel distaste for any dealings with my father will be sending similar letters, although I hope others will couch their phrases more inoffensively. This tarse Luke tells me that his house will do no business with mine until my father has paid for his "gross and obscene crimes". And what then? I suppose I should be grateful that he will deign to work with us again!'

He screwed the note up and hurled it at the fire. It caught almost immediately, as it rolled away and sat at the edge of the hearth, a ball of yellow flames. Gregory could have wept for the ruin of his father's reputation almost more than for his impending death. Henry Paffard had never been a man to inspire great friendship. He was too arrogant and too aloof. But he had founded this house on firm respect for himself and his acumen. Since that was lost, there would inevitably be a lessening of the family's status. They might even lose much of their money.

'Master?' Baldwin said. 'Can I help? You are deeply troubled, I see.'

'It is going to be a hard time for me and my family,' Gregory said. He remained staring at the fire. The ball had turned into a sphere of glowing embers, and he thought how apposite that was: like his family, it had flared briefly, and now was no more.

Strange how things turned out. Only a few days ago he would have welcomed the idea of the closure of the family's business; it would have left him free to make his own life without the baleful presence of his father watching over everything he did. But in reality, what else could he do, but continue with the business he had been taught, the craft that he had learned from the age of seven? He was a pewterer, and his father's mercantile ventures had created a thriving business for him to drive forward. Yes, it would have been better if Agatha had been born a boy and older than he, so that she could lead the business, but she had not.

He would do all he could to run things as his father would wish, Gregory decided. Which meant he must go and see him. There must be a number of things that Henry would wish to discuss with him.

'Master Paffard?'

He looked up. He had quite forgotten that Baldwin and Simon were there. 'I am sorry, sir. I am too confused. Please excuse me.'

'Of course,' Baldwin said. He rose, Simon with him, and the two men walked from the hall.

Gregory covered his face in his hands, but today he had no urge to weep.

He was merely steeling himself for the ordeal to come.

Outside the Paffards' House

John did not escort them as Simon and Baldwin walked to the door. Baldwin opened it and began to walk down the steps, when Simon heard a slight noise from the shop-front. He glanced inside. There he saw the maid, Joan, standing and sweeping with a great besom, carefully moving between piles of lead ingots and shining tin, stacked in piles waist-high.

On a whim he went in and said, 'Maid, are you well?'

'Yes, I thank you,' she replied with a duck of her head.

She was a pretty enough little thing, Simon thought to himself. Large, anxious eyes, set in a sweet face with rosy cheeks, she had the kind of looks that would tempt many a man to sweep her up and cradle her in his arms. He had always found small, compact women like her attractive, and she would never lack for admirers, he was sure.

'You must have been sad when the master was taken away,' he said, seeing her stillness.

She stared at him, and for a moment he wondered whether the loss of her master had left her deranged. The impression was only strengthened when she began to shake, her shoulders jerking spasmodically. It was some time before he realised that she was laughing silently.

'Maid?'

'I cannot help it! I am so happy, to know I'm safe at last! He will never come to my room to take me at night after this. Never again! You ask if I am sad? No. Never! He can rot in *hell* for all I care,' she said with a horrible determination.

'He raped you?'

'Every night since Alice died. I was under his protection here in his house, and he should have guarded me, but instead he . . . He forced me to submit. He is evil!' she spat.

'What of his son? Are you safe from him?'

'Gregory? Oh yes, I feel entirely safe with him.'

'So the son is not the same as his father. That is good.'

Quick as a flash, she said, 'You think?'

Simon was bemused. 'What do you mean?'

Joan shot a look at the door, then at Simon, wondering whether she dared speak. This man looked kindly enough, but she was loath to trust any man after recent experiences. She had already said too much. If Gregory were to overhear her comments, she could be thrown out on the street once more, looking for work. A vision of the stews appeared in her mind, and she muttered, 'I must return to my duties.'

'One moment, maid. Tell me – I swear I will keep your part secret. If you have something to say about your master, you should tell me. We don't want any others harmed. Do you doubt Henry was guilty?'

She shook her head. 'No. I cannot.'

'Very well. But before I leave, let me ask you this: when you found your friend's body on Saturday, why was Alice outside? What was she doing out in the alley? Did you hear anything about that?'

'Master Henry came back before all the others, I know – I saw him. *And* heard him and her upstairs in her bed,' she said, her lip curled primly.

'I see.'

'He had no shame – not that she minded. She was happy to do as he wanted. She boasted about her affair with him. Not just with me, but with others in the house, in the street. All over. As though he was going to make her his wife. She thought he would buy her a house and give her servants. The fool.'

'She loved him? Or simply played the whore?'

'She didn't mind his attention,' Joan said. Her head was hanging, and she was embarrassed and ashamed to be speaking of her dead friend in this way.

'Who else knew?'

'Master Henry never bothered to hide his passion. All knew, even his wife.'

'And on the night you found Alice, you heard them upstairs, and after that you went for the bread? But where were all the others, then? Surely Master Henry would have been anxious that his wife could return and find him rolling on the floor with their maid?'

'I think the mistress would not come back, exactly for that reason,' Joan said. 'She knew what Master Henry was doing with Alice, and didn't want to see proof of it. So she stayed in the tavern and hid her head. Later, Master Henry returned to the inn, and she could come back with him when she was sure it was safe, I suppose. No wife would want to be confronted by the sight of her husband with another woman.'

'What of Master Gregory? Did he not say anything?'

She blinked and looked away.

'Maid, please. Trust me.'

'He wouldn't say anything. He *dare* not!' she hissed, and fled out and up the passageway.

'Oh,' Simon said helplessly. The girl was plainly distraught, but he had no idea why still.

Baldwin was waiting at the end of the street, so Simon hurried on down the steps, closing the door behind him, and went to join his friend.

'Did the maid have anything useful to tell you?' Baldwin asked.

'Only that her master was in a loving grapple with Alice on the night the girl died. And then she was sent out to buy food. Just as we've heard.'

'So the last person seen with the maid was Henry.'

Simon shrugged. 'Who else would it have been? He admitted to the murders.'

'Yes.'

'But something is niggling at you?' Simon said.

Baldwin gave a sour grin. 'You too?'

'It seems entirely out of character for the man to confess,' Simon said with his hands held out. 'He allowed all in his house to realise he was swyving his maid, and then took up with Joan the minute Alice was dead. He acted with the arrogance and lack of shame of a lord exercising his rights over his peasants – and then confesses to a double murder with no apparent motives. It makes absolutely no sense.'

CHAPTER TWENTY-NINE

Near Clyst St Mary

It was a groggy Sir Charles who woke to the sunshine on his face. The warmth and beauty soothed his aches and pains when he opened his eyes. He was near a causeway over a little river with boggy banks, a village at the other side.

And then, all at once, a thundering pain exploded in the side of his skull, enough to make him close his eyes and give a hissed curse.

'Awake, eh? Glad to see it, sir.'

That booming voice . . . Suddenly Sir Charles remembered the chase, the alarmed knight, the two men and woman, the stones flung at him, and then the crushing blow that felled him from his horse. He attempted to spring to his feet, but his hands had been bound, his legs were too enfeebled after the attack, and his sword and daggers were gone.

'It would appear that you have me at your mercy, sir,' he said. Sir Charles had the gift of apparent mildness to conceal simmering rage. It had been a useful asset in the past, and he kept his voice low and calm now as he studied the knight before him. 'I am Sir Charles of Lancaster. I do not think I know you.'

'No reason why you should, Sir Charles. I am Sir Richard de Welles, Coroner to the King at Lifton Hundred,' Sir Richard responded with a smile. 'I trust I didn't break your head?'

'You hit me hard.'

'Aye, well, Sir Charles, it was necessary to slow you down a little. And now, since we have a few miles to ride, it'd be best for us to get under way.'

'Oh?'

'Aye, you will be glad to hear that you're to be taken to Exeter. You and I will be talking to the Sheriff before long, I think. He'll be keen to hear all you have to say on matters of interest. Such as the damage you've done to the Bishop's lands.'

'What damage have I done?'

Sir Richard looked at him, and the smile remained, but grew hard and cold. 'Sir Charles, you may think me some vill's fool, but I know about the rampage you and your followers have been set on for the last days. And with the death of the Bishop, I think there's enough there for me to consider you a felon, along with your men. Especially if I learn you were up at the Bishop's lands near Honiton when he was killed.'

'Me?'

'Luckily there were many witnesses of the attack, so we should soon know whether you were involved, eh? You will find that the men of Devon can be determined when they decide to punish those who've attacked their Bishop.' Sir Richard narrowed his eyes as he peered back the way they had come. 'But first you will be tested for the murder of this good woman's family, and for her rape.'

'Let us hurry back, then,' Sir Charles yawned, glancing at Amflusia without interest.

'Perhaps we should,' Sir Richard said. 'How many men were there with you?'

'Back there? Five-and-thirty or so. There were some good fellows you killed, too. I don't like to see good men slaughtered.'

'Nor do I. So, there, we have something in common, eh?' Sir Richard said equably. 'Now, let's get you on your beast so we can ride to Exeter.'

'I doubt me I can ride yet,' Sir Charles said. He winced as he looked up at Sir Richard, and rolled over to try to lift himself, but the effort made him gag and retch.

'Ach,' Sir Richard muttered. 'Come, boys. Help the knight upon his horse. So, Sir Charles, tell me: you had so many men to raid the Bishop's lands, but why would you wish to do so? Do you have an unreasoning dislike of Bishops generally, or just ours?'

'Only yours. He was a member of the Berkeley family, the ones who kept my King prisoner.'

Sir Richard looked at him with a measuring eye. He was no fool, and just now he was wondering what sort of man Sir Charles was. There were plenty who deplored the capture of Sir Edward of Caernarfon, himself included, but to kill a Bishop, and then to ride about the land despoiling all those manors owned by the Bishop, were the actions of a simple felon rather than a knight. After all, once the Bishop was dead, there was no need to maintain a campaign against him. This knight could have returned to his home, but instead chose to launch a series of attacks – in the hope of making profit, or Sir Richard was a Moor.

'So you killed the Bishop because his brother was a Berkeley? For that you were prepared to roam about the countryside steal-ing whatever took your fancy?'

252

'It was laying waste the lands owned by the Bishop. We wanted to bring home to the people here how much damage the Bishop has caused by his betrayal of his King.'

'Oh, I see,' Sir Richard said happily. Many men were content to believe his buffoonery when he put on his show of being a rural knight of limited, even bovine intelligence, but in reality his mind was as sharp as any. And now he was calculating how many of the men Sir Charles had at his disposal would be competent to attack manors like Bishop's Clyst and others. Of the men he had seen so far, at least thirty seemed capable of creating merry hell in even a large manor.

'Would you help me to my horse?' Sir Charles said thickly.

Sir Richard nodded to the two men with him, and then it was that the situation changed.

As the two went to Sir Charles and took his arms, Amflusia was standing a short way away, watching Sir Charles with terror in her eyes. Something had caught her attention. She goggled with horror, frozen to the spot, and then managed to scream.

A whoop, two blasts on a horn, and suddenly a mass of men and horses appeared at the farther end of the causeway, and thundered towards Sir Richard.

He saw Sir Charles's hand dart down to one man's belt, and suddenly there was a sharp scream, and the man clutched at his breast. Sir Charles had grabbed his dagger and stabbed him. The second man was only a farmer, and he leaped away from the path of the dagger's blade. He had a long knife at his belt, but for a man like him to draw and fight a knight would take more courage than he possessed. Lunging for his horse, he grabbed the reins and threw himself into the saddle even as Sir Richard drew his own sword.

Yet even as he did so, he saw that the men from Sir Charles's force were halfway to him already. He must fly, if he was to save himself.

Hastening to his mount, he saw Amflusia.

She stood gaping at the approaching men. Her mouth worked soundlessly, and her eyes were fixed with a terrible certainty. She was lost, if they were to catch her.

'Woman? Mistress? Amflusia, COME HERE!' Sir Richard bellowed, and grabbed the second man's horse. It was no racing thoroughbred, but it would suffice. He lifted the woman about the waist and flung her onto the horse. The latter, realising this was no time for delay, set his ears back and cantered off up the road. Sir Richard had bare moments. He took the reins of his own beast, threw his leg over the saddle, and then drew his sword, holding it carelessly in his hand as the men approached.

'Sir Charles, I look forward to our next meeting,' he said, before spurring his mount on, back towards Exeter.

Rougemont Castle

The Sheriff was irritable as he stamped his way along the corridor to his hall. He had plenty to do, what with the news of Sir Edward of Caernarfon's escape and the death of Bishop Berkeley. The two matters, equally shocking and terrible, were cause for much thought. But as yet, Sir James had been granted little time for quiet reflection.

This evening the food had been late from the kitchen; his guests (a more tedious set of wastes of good skin he hoped never to have about his table again) were first boorish, then downright repugnant when drunk – which they were, right speedily; his tumblers, intended to lighten the mood after he had delivered some unpalatable home truths about the way the city of Exeter had been managed so far and how *he*, Sir James, was going to see it alter its way for the future, were also late, and it was very late when the guests began to filter from his hall, some blaring their disgust at the idea of the additional taxes, other meandering about, dazed from wine or from dismay, he didn't care. All he knew was, he wanted them out.

The sudden appearance of the man in his doorway as he was ushering the last guests out of his home, was enough to make him groan. Not another damned fool who wanted to petition him for some favour or other.

'Tell him to go away and come back tomorrow,' he growled to his steward, but the man would not listen. Gabbling some garbage about finding a small force attacking the Bishop's lands, he approached the Sheriff.

'Shut up! No, I said *shut up,*' the Sheriff repeated loudly. Sir James did not like having strangers in his hall at the best of times, and this man would not have looked out of place in a pigsty, with his filthy clothes and pink, anxious features. 'Calm down, you fool, or I'll have you thrown into the gaol for disrespect!'

'Sir Sheriff, sir, it's Sir Richard de Welles. He sent me on ahead to warn you.'

'Warn me of what?'

'There is a host outside the city walls, Sheriff. Sir Richard captured their leader, but when a large force came to fetch him back, we had to run. We only just got here with our lives,' he added, as though worried that the tale was not sufficiently gripping.

'Tell me all,' the Sheriff sighed.

Cock Inn

Baldwin was glad to sit in the inn and rest his legs and mind.

Simon sat at his side, plucking at his sleeve. 'I have had an idea, Baldwin.'

'Speak!'

'Think, Baldwin – and not like a noble knight, but like a felon. Imagine you are a killer. You kill to save yourself trouble, to protect your reputation, perhaps even for the joy of killing, women in particular. It would add a spark to your lovemaking, to know you are going to kill a maid later. You do not care a fig for how your actions may affect others. You do all you can to serve your own interests. It is more likely that you would "remember" suddenly that your apprentice had been there at the moment the girl died, or that your other maid had been jealous of her from the first, and that *she* had killed Alice. The last possible thought in your mind would be to announce to the world that the deaths were your responsibility, and to accept the charge against you.'

'What are you getting at?'

'You can smile at me, old friend, but I think the merchant knows who committed the murders, and is determined to protect that person, rather than see him hanged.'

'So you think it must have been his son?'

'If I had to lay money, I'd place it on Gregory's head. The maid in there was reticent about him, but she indicated that there was something evil in his past, too.'

'And at last Henry Paffard has managed a decent, unselfish deed, whether he wanted to or not. Well, well.' Baldwin stretched his aching body. 'It is a good theory. I like the idea that Henry would put his name forward in that manner.'

'But you doubt it?'

Baldwin considered. 'It is not that I doubt it, it is that I doubt he will ever admit it. Whatever happens, he won't retract his confession now, unless he knows that his son is safe. And if Gregory did commit the murders, he may yet be found out. So Gregory cannot be safe.'

'Nor can anyone else!' Simon pointed out. 'But what if the boy is innocent? If the merchant was mistaken, then he will die and the true felon will walk free. That is an idea that sticks in my throat, Baldwin. And would in his too.'

'What do you wish to do about it, then? The only safe remedy would be . . .'

' . . . to find the man actually responsible,' Simon finished. 'Henry must help us.'

He would have continued, but for the sudden arrival of Sir Richard. With a bellow that must surely have been audible from the Precentor's house, he marched in. '*Ale, a quart, over here*! And bring me a capon and bread. I have a hunger that would be meet on a lion!'

'Sir Richard, I hope you had a good day? Did you find the priest?' Baldwin asked.

'No. But I found a gaggle of murderers. Even caught one for a while.'

'What?'

'Aye.' Sir Richard was looking towards the door as he spoke, and now his face grew sombre. 'And I found a woman there. They were raping her in turn, with her man's body beside her. I swear, if I find Sir Charles on the road, I will have his liver for that.'

'Sir Charles?' Simon repeated.

'Sir Charles of Lancaster, aye,' Sir Richard said, and then he became aware of the effect of his words upon his friends. 'What? D'you know the man?'

CHAPTER THIRTY

Bishop's Clyst

Sir Charles had not enjoyed capture, and now that he was back with his men, he swore he would not allow it to happen again.

'Sir Charles? Are you ready?' The men were mounting their horses and ponies.

'Yes, Ulric, my friend,' he said. He did not smile.

Ulric had little experience of battle, Sir Charles thought, but he'd been making up for it in recent days. On the surface, he was all Sir Charles needed – a right-hand man who was devoted to him, just as he himself was to Sir Edward of Caernarfon.

Still, he was fully aware that Ulric's devotion was equivocal at best. Ulric must know that his future without Sir Charles was likely to be brief and painful, but the fool could decide to throw himself on the mercy of a posse, were he to be caught. That was why the others didn't trust him – and neither did Sir Charles. Ulric's continued presence here was based upon one act: his protection of Sir Charles against an assassin. That act, and a certain amount of self-interest, since if Ulric were to make off, he would know that Sir Charles could count on his men to find him and bring him back – and he had already seen how they treated their enemies.

Besides, Ulric himself had brought news of the Bishop's movements – so that they could slaughter James Berkeley and all those in his entourage. It was entirely his responsibility that the Bishop was now dead. He would never dare submit himself to the clemency of the Church. Not after ensuring the murder of one of the Church's chief princes.

Sir Charles could understand his position. Some years past, Sir Charles had returned to England to beg for a pardon. During his exile he had wandered over Europe, first hoping to join a lord's host, then thinking he might join the Teutonic Knights with their crusades to colonise the heathen lands to the east, but all had come to naught. Eventually, desperate, he had taken the fearful decision to plead with the King to be permitted to return, and he had found his entreaties successful. His good name had been restored, his life renewed. He had not expected such largesse, and he would be eternally grateful. There was nothing he would not do to serve the man who had given him so much. That was why he was here, that was why he would fight and destroy the Bishop and his lands: because the brother of Berkeley had captured his King and held him in his gaol at Berkeley Castle.

Bishop Berkeley had paid for that crime, and soon his brother would too.

However, Sir Charles felt he had come to a crossroads in his campaign.

His force was reduced. Only two and thirty men-at-arms remained, along with carts and sumpter horses to carry their winnings. They had been lucky: the death of the Bishop had been achieved with ease, and now they were laden with gold and plate from him and the manors they had overrun. All lands controlled by the Bishop of Exeter had been their target, and they had laid waste all the manors east of Exeter; but now that Sir Richard de Welles had found Sir Charles, it was plain that it was time for them to move on. Sir Charles must plan how to contact Ulric's merchant in Exeter, this man Paffard who was to take all the treasure and exchange it for cash. In the meantime there were other manors, and plenty more to take, both in treasure and in food.

He raised his hand and waved to signal their advance, and the gentle murmurings of the horses were smothered by the squeak and rumble of the carts. Together, the noises made a deafening cacophony, with the jingle of the chains, the complaints of leather harnesses, the thunder of the wheels rolling over rough ground . . . These were the sounds of war, to his mind. The proof of men on the move.

They would ride north and east, away from the city, and head for the little farmstead which he had thought would make a good point of ambush. Now the big knight had discovered him, there was no doubt in his mind that the men of Exeter would soon be after him, and he needed to deter them.

Within a short period, Sir Charles hoped to have destabilised those who supported the new regime. With God's grace, they would be forced to surrender before too long. And when that happened, Sir Charles would be granted a new position, perhaps.

A man who had helped rescue his King from gaol and reinstate him on his rightful throne could anticipate a reward that was fitting for a king-maker.

Cock Inn

Baldwin and Simon exchanged a look.

'We have met Sir Charles before,' Simon said. 'First on pilgrimage to Santiago de Compostela, and he joined us on our return from Galicia.'

'Is he a friend to you?' Sir Richard asked directly.

'I would not willingly kill him,' Simon shrugged. 'He was a good companion.'

'Well, he's turned rebel,' Sir Richard said, and explained about the dead at Clyst St George and all about.

'That is indeed grim news,' Baldwin said.

'Aye. Tomorrow we will be forming a posse to ride to find him and his men, and then we will force them to fight.'

'We shall ride with you,' Baldwin said, and Simon nodded.

It was a sad task, Simon thought, but if a man like Sir Charles turned to murder and robbery, he would not expect to escape. Especially when one of his victims was the Bishop himself.

'Was he ever evil?' Sir Richard asked. 'There are some men whose greed will not allow them to rest, I know – is this Sir Charles built from that mould?'

Simon shook his head. 'I don't think so. He was most certainly ruthless. I saw him fight a number of times, but he tended to be loyal and decent. He did battle against those who were intolerant and cruel, mainly in order to help others. I am surprised if he has returned to cause injustice himself.'

'He was always a strong man,' Baldwin said, 'and oftentimes those who are most tested in battle can become inured to the pain of others. But if he was leading this gang of men, I fear he has gone too far along the road of arrogance.'

'Aye. Well, he was there and his men were raping the widow while her husband's body lay beside her, still warm. A terrible scene.' Sir Richard took a glum sup of ale. 'So! Come the morning we shall ride again, gentles. It's only a shame I couldn't find sight or trace of Father Laurence.'

Simon said, 'Ah! We hadn't told you.'

'Told me what?'

'He was innocent, my friend,' Baldwin explained. 'Henry Paffard has confessed to the murders, so there is no need to seeks out Father Laurence. His only crime is ecclesiastical, for running away from his job at Exeter.'

'Oh.'

'So you can forget about the good priest.'

'Henry Paffard, eh? Good God, I would never have thought him capable of such deeds. Still, a man can never be certain what his neighbour will do, can he? And I suppose a fellow like him – rich, powerful, used to taking whatever he wanted whenever he wanted it – is similar to a knight like Sir Charles. Once he turned bad, he couldn't help himself. You take one thing, and next time you want something, you think how easy it was last time, and take it again.'

'Perhaps,' Baldwin said. 'He might have found the second life easier to take, possibly. But Simon is less sure. He believes Henry is innocent and is protecting his son by confessing.'

'Oh?' Sir Richard said, turning his shrewd eyes to Simon. 'And why do you think that?'

'I won't go through all that again,' Simon said with a vague feeling of grumpiness. 'I know it hardly seems rational, but—'

'On the contrary, it seems extremely rational to me,' Sir Richard boomed. 'And if it were true, I would be anxious to see that justice was done. I dislike the idea that the man who is guilty of killing those women should go free and another take his place at the gallows. That would definitely offend me sense of justice.'

'Well, if you can think of a means of persuading Henry

Paffard to tell the truth,' Baldwin told him, 'I would be happy to help you. But for now, I think we should bring the Precentor up to date with all that we have discovered.'

Rougemont Castle

Sir James de Cockington walked back and forth, a mazer of sycamore wood chased with silver in his hand. His steward was with him, and periodically refilled the Sheriff's cup, but apart from that he was silent. He knew better than to interrupt his master while Sir James was in one of these moods.

Sir Richard's report had given him scope for much careful thought. It was a terrible dilemma for any man to confront: to support the attempt of Sir Edward to win back his rightful throne, or to show support for the new, young King Edward III, Sir Edward's son. It was crucial that he made the correct choice. The wrong one would lead to disaster on all levels; the right one to him retaining his existing position, and possibly enhancing it.

There was still no news of Sir Edward of Caernarfon since his astonishing escape from Berkeley Castle, and the lack of information was driving Sir James to distraction. He *needed* to know! If Sir Edward was free, and intended taking up his throne again, Sir James must clearly throw his weight behind him, but if he was simply meandering over the land with little more in his mind than escape to the Low Countries or France, he would surely never be able to return. When his Queen had invaded England the previous year, all she had with her was an honour guard of perhaps a few hundreds of Hainault mercenaries, if what Sir James had heard was true. Yet for all the paucity of men, her ambitions were clear.

She had set sail for England, and not one naval ship obeyed the King's command to fight her at sea. When her men reached the coast, of those sent to prevent her landing, all turned to her side. Her forces grew daily, and she led them across the country, giving thanks at churches, spreading coin like water amongst those who gave her their adulation; none would stand in her path, other than those who wanted to join her. It was a glorious, bloodless invasion, and had ended in the capture of her husband as he rode from one castle to another in the wild lands of Wales.

If Sir Edward were to declare himself King again, how would others in the realm respond? Sir James considered the nobles who ranked in his immediate vicinity. He had no doubt that Lord Hugh de Courtenay would remain four-square behind the Queen; he was still bitter about his treatment by Edward, seeing his estates eroded as the King sought to reward others at his expense.

The same must be true for those who remained up on the Welsh Marches. There were enough there who had seen their lands and titles stolen in order to advance friends of the King. Few would forget how Despenser, Edward's beloved favourite, was allowed ever more licence to threaten, bully and rob them of ancient customs. Likewise the Scottish Marches. There the great barons would not wish to see Sir Edward return. He had caused them nothing but sorrow, with his incompetent handling of the Scottish wars.

But in the middle of the kingdom it was harder to predict how the lords and barons might respond. There were many who disliked the old King, but were not yet persuaded by the new regime. Queen Isabella was adored, but her choice of Sir Roger Mortimer as her adviser and, most believed, lover, had set a lot of men's noses out of joint. They believed that she should have remained chaste. Selecting an avaricious bastard like Mortimer as her lover had injured her position, for she was still married to the King. Adultery was a crime for an ordinary mortal, but for a Queen there was an especial significance. A Queen who took another man to her bed was worse than others, for she could pollute the blood-line of the King.

How would they respond? He considered the lower nobles, the knights and squires of the country, and pondered afresh at the thought of the numbers of men required to free the King from his prisons. First there had been an attack on Kenilworth Castle, one of the strongest fortresses in the realm, and then an assault on Berkeley. Both involved significant forces. There were plenty of men who thought that if they helped the King return to his throne, they would be rewarded.

And now there was this new group wandering the countryside, if that gross deofol Sir Richard de Welles was to be believed. Didn't bear thinking of. Led by Sir Charles of Lancaster, they had already killed Bishop James, apparently, and now were spreading misery wherever they went, all over all those lands associated with Bishop James. Ravaging an enemy's territory was normal enough, but to do so to a Bishop was unusual, to say the least.

Sir James set his jaw. It was impossible to make a decision. He could not commit himself until he knew how the wind was blowing.

But he might be forced to, if the posse left in the morning.

Precentor's House

It was growing late when Simon and Baldwin walked with Sir Richard up to the Palace Gate, and thence up to the Precentor's house.

Adam Murimuth received them in his hall with cordiality, but he was drawn and exhausted, and Baldwin thought he looked as though he really needed to go back to his bed and lie there for a week to recover from the strain of the last days.

'I am well, I thank you,' he responded when asked. 'I am busy with the management of the Cathedral's resources.'

'One problem must be the outlying manors,' Baldwin said.

Adam nodded and rubbed his eyes. 'It is a matter to which I have given some thought. There is so much to be done at this time of year.'

'Have you heard of the outlaws laying waste to the Bishop's manors?' Simon asked.

'Sorry?' Adam asked, peering vaguely at him. 'What outlaws?'

Sir Richard cleared his throat and began telling him about his capture of the leader and then the man's escape.

Adam sat back, his face blanched. 'This is dreadful! Thirty of them, you say? Where did they come from!'

'The men who supported the King and released him from gaol were from the middle of the kingdom,' Sir Richard told him. 'I would assume that these fellows came from there too.'

Adam listened with a frown of concentration as they spoke of the Dunheved brothers and others who had been involved in the Berkeley attack. 'Any men you need, or horses and weapons, you must let me know,' he said. 'I will happily assist you in all ways.'

'There is some good news,' Baldwin said after they had discussed the force they would need. 'You can at least set your heart at rest over Father Laurence. Henry Paffard has confessed to the murder of the two women over at Combe Street.'

'Paffard?' Adam said, shocked. 'Why on earth would he do that? He is a respected man, in Christ's name! He has everything most men could want.'

Baldwin looked at him and shrugged. 'Some men will try to take more, no matter what they already have. Perhaps this man is formed from that mould.'

It was possible, but it made no sense. Adam could not help

but think of Paffard's wife and family. The relatives of self-confessed killers never had a good time of it. Often they were reviled by others, sometimes even attacked in the street. He hoped the Paffard family would be safe.

He would send someone to speak with them. That would be best.

CHAPTER THIRTY-ONE

Paffards' House

Claricia hugged her arms about her as she sat rocking near the fireside. Gregory was somewhere in the house – perhaps at the workshop with Benjamin the apprentice. He appeared to have taken a new interest in the business now that his father was in prison. It was a pity the boy had never shown such a fascination before. Things might have turned out differently if he had.

It wasn't fair to blame her boy. She knew that. It was Henry's fault for being so free with other women. Why kill them though – *why*! Henry had certainly demonstrated his ability to inflict pain on her over the years – but it was the searching for new flesh that had tormented her.

She had known about Alice, of course. Just as she had known all about Clara and Evie before. But she had always managed to find something to make the girls leave before now. Clara, she had discovered, was a liar and a thief. Even Henry had lost all affection for the girl when his money was found in her bed, along with a prized brooch. And Evie had been even easier. In those days Claricia had not yet lost her confidence, and she made it plain to Evie what would happen to her if she didn't leave: she would find herself without a home. Claricia had been younger then, of course, and Henry hadn't worn her down so badly. It was before he started to take his belt to her regularly, and she had still felt sure that she could retain his affection, perhaps even make him love her again. Of course, it hadn't happened. He still came to her bed, but that was a mechanical urge, not from love. He wanted new conquests. One wife would never be enough.

Claricia sighed to remember the early days of her marriage, before serving girls and whores entered Henry's life. He was a man of strong passions. That was the truth of it.

She heard a shout in the street, but it did not distract her from her mournful thoughts. There was another shout – and Claricia frowned and turned to look at the door as though there could be some form of response from that direction.

Agatha passed by the doorway, and peered inside. Seeing her mother, an expression of blank contempt settled upon her face. Claricia flinched. Agatha had always thought her a foolish, incompetent wife and mother, and there was nothing Claricia could do that would change her mind.

At least Thomas was loving and affectionate. She had been up to check on him a short time ago, and he had been completely dead to the world, his darling little face frowning as though he was running after a friend. She had seen that look on his face so often when—

There was a loud crashing sound, and the house seemed to rock, the old timbers reverberating. 'What on . . .?'

She rose to go to the front of the house, when John came hurrying from the buttery. He put a hand out to stop her, and suddenly she could hear voices, raucous laughter, a jeering shout. Up in front she could see Agatha, pale in the passage's dim light.

'Mother,' she began, but John again held up his hand.

There came another thunderous sound, and this time it was accompanied by crunching and splintering. John went to his buttery and came back gripping his hatchet. He stepped beyond Claricia and curtly ordered Agatha to return to her mother. After a moment she obeyed, and stood beside Claricia, the two women watching John edge forward cautiously, his hatchet held out before him.

A final crunch of wood, and the door was thrown open. Outside, John saw a crowd of men all orange and hideous in the flickering light. He bellowed incoherently, motioning with his weapon, but they laughed at him.

'Out of the way, old man!' one of them shouted, brandishing his torch. A second beside him held a lump hammer in one hand, a skin in the other, and he drank, dribbling wine, as the men guffawed.

Claricia was convinced that John was about to be murdered before her eyes. She had to clutch at Agatha for support.

Only to feel her daughter stiffen and draw away.

There were too many for John alone. He couldn't hold them back, not with one little hatchet.

It was not only men, either; he could see women behind them – some of the whores from the stews, one or two women from the street – plus a few urchins hoping to see a fight. All had the appearance of devils taunting the damned, their faces demonic in the red firelight from a bonfire near the houses. There were four women, dancing with two men, all of them drunk. A couple were kissing and fumbling against a wall.

These were the dregs of the city, John thought angrily. Scum:

ill-educated and foul-mannered bitch-clouts, all of them. They did not deserve to live in the same street as folk like the mistress. Claricia Paffard was a saint compared to this filth.

'We want them out, all of them!' a man bellowed.

'Their old man was a murderer, and we want them out before they copy him!'

'Bring them out, strip them, *tar them*!' a woman chanted, and others began to take it up, until everyone was clenching their fists, shouting the words.

John gripped his hatchet firmly, turned quickly to see that Gregory had come down and stood now with his mother, an arm about her shoulder, while Agatha gripped his arm and waist, her face turned to the crowds with horror and fear. Then she reached up and buried her face in her brother's neck.

'Begone, you fools! There's no one here deserves your violence,' John tried, but the two men nearest pushed forwards, the man with the skin swigging from the open spout as he came. The man with the torch grinned wolfishly when he caught sight of Agatha.

'That's more like it,' he said lecherously, and would have gone to reach for her, but John slashed at him, and he dropped the torch, grabbing his forearm and staring in dull disbelief. 'You prickle!'

The other swung the hammer, and John had the wit to duck, but even so the maul hit his shoulder, and the head thudded into his flesh. He didn't feel the bone shatter, but he knew he soon would if the man tried another attack. He dived down, thrusting with his hatchet, and was gratified to feel it slip into the man's thigh, then grate on bone. Pulling it back, he crouched low, warily, eyeing the two men. Then he was aware of another beside him, and thought Gregory had joined him, until he shot a look and realised Benjamin the apprentice had come. He had

271

a pair of cudgels, and swung them hopefully, narrowly watching the two men. Gregory had disappeared.

From somewhere overhead there came the three blasts of a horn, and John breathed a sigh of relief. That Gregory might have gone to an upper window to blow the alarm for the Hue and Cry had not occurred to him. There was a murmur, then a series of cat-calls and insults, but it worked. Suddenly the folk outside realised that the Watch would soon be with them, with their long iron-tipped staves, and they would be likely to ask questions about the people and what they were doing there.

For a moment the mob stood still, and John reckoned that his life was held in the balance, but then there was a bellow, and John saw two priests hurrying up the stairs to the door. They entered, and the mob gradually broke up, the man with the ripped forearm glaring at John as though memorising his features for later.

'Thank you, Fathers,' Claricia called, her voice trembling.

Agatha had gone. John wondered to where.

'Are you all uninjured?' Father Paul asked, his eyes wide with alarm. He saw the torch, still smouldering on the floor, and picked it up. 'The fools! They could have set fire to the whole city!'

'Please, Fathers, stay here a while and have some wine,' Claricia said. She stared at her ruined door. 'They may come back if you leave us.'

'The Watch will soon be here,' Father Paul said. 'They will serve to protect you. But until then, yes, a little wine would be exceedingly pleasant.'

Claricia nodded, and then began very quietly to weep. Paul took her and walked her to the hall.

John was suddenly as weak as a newborn kitten, and would have dropped the hatchet, had not Laurence reached out and rested a hand on his shoulder.

'You did well, my friend. A Hector at the gate.'

John didn't know what that meant, but he did recognise the priest. He bowed, and went to fetch wine, and as he strode to his buttery, he saw Agatha coming down the stairs. She saw Laurence, and stopped.

As John poured wine, he heard Laurence say, 'Hello, maid,' with a kind of brittleness in his voice.

Second Thursday after the Nativity of St John the Baptist[1]

Marsilles' House

Philip Marsille woke early the next morning with the smell of burning still in his nostrils. Here, at the wall with Combe Street, the daub was broken away at the base, and where the wattles were exposed, the smell of the bonfire had come in to him. The screaming and shouting had been terrifying, and he had been convinced that there would be a battle, here outside his house.

He rose, carefully so as not to wake his brother, and walked to the table.

When Alice had rejected him, he had gone mad for a while, he thought. The woman he adored, whose feet he would have kissed, had no feelings for him. In his passion, he had decided he must leave, and that he would go to war with the King, but when there was the reality of a fight nearby, like last night, he was too scared to go and pitch in.

He missed his mother. She had always tried to instil in him a strong code of honour, such as his father had possessed, but Philip hadn't absorbed it. Or perhaps it was the shock of all the things that had happened in the last weeks. First Alice being

1 2 July 1327

273

found, then hearing they would lose their house, and Mother dying like that. Poor Mother! All she ever wanted was to see her sons do well, and they'd failed her.

William was clever. He would be all right, with a little luck. Perhaps he would learn his own trade. But it was certain that he was better off without a coward for a brother. Philip should be the master of the house since their father's death – he was oldest, after all. But the chill reality was, he was too afraid. Of life, of the world, of other men. In fact, he was useless.

He threw an old cloak about him, and pulled on a hat, making his way out to the street. Walking often aided him when he felt miserable, and never had he felt the need for comfort more than now. He wandered up Southgate Street, and when he reached Carfoix, deliberated a moment about keeping on going up to the North Gate and perhaps continuing out of the city, leaving forever. But a small gathering at the High Street outside the Guild Hall took his attention and he went to see what they were doing.

It was a posse, he learned. A number of men were called upon to help Sheriff James de Cockington hunt down a group of trailbastons who were ravaging the episcopal estates, and who were themselves probably guilty of the murder of the Bishop himself. Apparently many others had been killed too, he heard, and he suddenly had a flash of brilliance.

Seeing the Sergeant on his sturdy rounsey discussing the men present, Philip called up to him. 'Sir, can I join you? I want to be part of the posse.'

'Where's your sword?'

'I have none.'

'Horse?'

'I . . .'

'Yeah, right. Piss off, boy, and when you have something to offer, that's when you can come back, eh?'

It was his laughter that sent Philip on his way. He walked on until he came to the East Gate, and there he stood staring out at the lands down towards Heavitree. That was where the felons were. He ought to go and see if he could find them himself, fight them himself, and maybe bring news back to the Sergeant. Show him he had been a fool to refuse such a competent guide and fighter.

Except he wasn't. He had no weapon, as the man had said. As for a horse, he couldn't afford a day's fodder, let alone the beast itself. Like the man had said, he was only a boy.

Sunk in dejection, he turned around and headed homewards.

Rougemont Castle

The Sheriff left his hall with his goblet in his hand. Draining the wine, he tossed it to a servant, who fumbled the catch, dropping the valuable pewter on the ground.

'If it is marked, have it mended,' Sir James de Cockington said to his steward. 'You can have the man pay for the damage.'

He stood on the mounting stone while grooms brought his beast, and then mounted and surveyed the men all about him.

It was a goodly-sized posse. More than fifty men were gathered on horseback before him in the castle's inner ward, and none were the foolish old dolts one expected at this time of year. Usually the hale and hearty types would be held back for their work in the fields, but today he had forced the Watch to scour the city for younger, strong lads who knew how to handle a sword. Apprentices, the sons of richer men, some men-at-arms from the castle's garrison, and of course Sir Baldwin, Sir Richard, and their friend Puttock, were all there. All competent men.

'My friends, today we go to hunt outlaws. These men are wolf's heads. They have murdered your Bishop, and they have ravaged his lands, killing his peasants. They will do the same to us, if they come here. Make no mistake about that. So our duty is clear. For the defence of the city, for the protection of our families, we must find them, and arrest those we may, and kill those we cannot. Are there any questions? No? Then we ride: first to Bishop's Clyst, and thence to see where they have ridden.'

He raised his hand, gave a wave to indicate that they should move off, and then as he urged his great palfrey into a trot, the cavalcade began to fall into line behind him.

Some distance to the rear, Sir Richard was talking to Simon. The big knight rode in a casual manner at the best of times, but today he was at his ease, and he leaned back, giving space to his belly, which rested on the crupper.

'Ye see, Simon,' he said in what he fondly supposed was a conspiratorial whisper, 'what ye have to bear in mind is that the fellows down here don't need too much in the way of training. You point 'em at the enemy, and they'll fight all day. All the same, they are, the fellows down here in the wild lands.'

'Hardly wild,' Simon bridled.

Baldwin chuckled. 'He means compared to the delights of Lifton, Simon.'

'Lifton has much to commend it, aye,' the knight agreed. 'There's good land about there, and the water is clean and pure. Makes a man grow. Some grow old.' He chuckled to himself, and Simon winced, knowing a witticism was about to appear. 'Y'know, I was talking to a man there, just an ordinary peasant, you understand, and he looked so old, I said to him, "How old are you, fellow?" and he answered that he was, "Ten and three score, Sir Knight." And I thought that sounded odd, so I said to him, "Hey?" I said. "Ten and three score? Why not three score and ten, fellow?" And you know what he said? Eh? Ha! He looked at me, and he said, "Because I was ten before I was three score!" Eh? You understand? Ha!' He roared with honest delight.

Simon muttered unintelligibly under his breath, and Sir Richard glanced at him smilingly, and nodded, without hearing.

Baldwin guessed at Simon's comments, but his own deafness made it difficult to hear anything while they were surrounded by the racket of the horses' hooves, the chatter of the men, the squeaking of harnesses. Edgar was at his side, which was a relief, but even though he was so close, now that he spoke, Baldwin had to cup his hand to his ear to try to hear him. As he did so, Wolf yelped as a hoof came too close, and Baldwin's horse jinked sideways.

'Wolf, get out,' he called, then cupped his ear again. 'Eh?'

Edgar moved closer. His customary smile played about his lips, but his eyes were hooded and alert. 'There are plenty of men here with skill with weapons, but few who have actually been in combat, Sir Baldwin. I think we should be very cautious when we approach this group. If it is Sir Charles, he will know how to bait a trap.'

'A good point,' Baldwin said, glancing about the men in the column.

They were riding spread well apart, with some jogging along three or four-abreast, bunching up, while others were single-file or in pairs. Trying to organise such a group would not be easy in an emergency.

Baldwin peered through the rising dust towards the Sheriff. Sir James de Cockington was no fool, but he would take offence at any idea presented by Baldwin. Sir Richard too was a dead-end. The large knight had not yet been insulted by the Sheriff, but it was obvious that Sir James disliked any companion of Baldwin's, and he would be sure to have noticed that Sir

Richard had been with him when they first arrived in Exeter, and had remained with him ever since.

'Edgar, we cannot speak to the fool who leads us, but we can take precautions. Do you ride to the right flank and go ahead to spy the roadway, and I will take the left.'

'With respect, Sir Baldwin, I think I would prefer to remain with you,' Edgar said.

Baldwin watched his mouth as he spoke. This deafness was infuriating! 'No. I will ride with Simon and keep our eyes open on the left. You ride with Sir Richard. Simon is not so experienced in this work as me, and Sir Richard's eyes are not so sharp as yours. Keep your eyes open, remain alert, and with luck we shall be safe.'

CHAPTER THIRTY-TWO

Venn Ottery

Sir Charles had been up before dawn, preparing the ground.

The land about here was clear, and while he had made a decision not to upset the farmers in the vill, he would not allow any of them to escape the place in case they might run to warn any approaching force that he was here.

His dispositions were simple. The vill was held overnight by him with twelve of his men. The peasants here would see only that small group, and as soon as he left the place, he would ride eastwards, along the straight lane until he reached Sog's Lane. This small track led between two high hedges until it passed down a slight dip and through between a shaw. On either side the bushes and trees rose high. And that was where the bulk of his men would be waiting.

In the north, Sir Charles had often been forced to ride with Earl Thomas of Lancaster to pursue the Scottish raiders, and he intended to use their own tactics if he could. He had seen how devastating their attacks had been.

For now, he would enjoy a leisurely breakfast. There were eggs and bacon, cold capon and pottage along with good bread, and he sat down with a wooden trencher on his lap to watch the distant horizon. From here there was a good view of the land to the west if a man was up high, and he had a fellow stationed in an elm not far from the farm. With him, Sir Charles was confident he would receive good warning.

It was possible that he would remain here for a day or more and see nothing. But if he had to bet, he would think that the fat knight who had caught him would not be prepared to give him up so easily. No, Sir Richard would want his head.

Sir Charles chewed his bread and ignored the weeping and complaints of the women from the farm while his men enjoyed their rest.

Clyst St Mary

Sir James de Cockington rode up to the causeway with a sense of nervous anticipation. There were places here where a force could possibly attack a man, he thought.

He beckoned his squire. 'Men could be set to hide beneath the low walls here, and then spring up to shoot arrows into us when we ride along the causeway. Or they could be waiting, hidden in the trees all about here, and as soon as our men are on the causeway, they might block both ends and attack us like that. Should we send a small force out first to see whether the passage is safe, do you think?'

Edgar had been trotting off on the right flank with Sir Richard, and now both rode up at the canter.

'Sir James, this was where I caught him and sadly lost him again,' Sir Richard said, glowering at the roadway as though it had itself betrayed him.

'I was just deliberating as to whether to send some men to ensure we were safe in the vill up there,' Sir James said.

Edgar shook his head. 'He will not have remained here after his capture. He will have moved further away, hoping to avoid capture or to find a better location for an ambush.'

'Where?' Sir James asked.

'East of here. Nearer the hills.'

Sir James eyed Edgar. 'You are very sure of yourself.'

Edgar smiled. 'I am experienced in war.'

'A knight, are you?' Sir James asked with a sneer in his tone. 'I am a knight, you see, and yet you, I believe, are a mere man-at-arms.'

'That is correct,' Edgar said, and his smile broadened. 'I am sure you have more experience than me. So, Sir James, please, you go in front of all of us and test the safety of the causeway.'

'It would be a mistake for me to go,' Sir James said quickly. 'The captain of a host doesn't risk himself unnecessarily.'

'Then I shall go, Sir James. If I die, pass on my best wishes to Sir Baldwin.'

He jabbed his heels at his rounsey's flanks and was off in an instant, the beast cantering along the causeway, kicking up the dust.

'Arrogant puppy,' Sir James muttered, ignoring the fact that he was younger than Edgar by almost ten years. 'He needs some of that assurance knocked out of him.'

Sir Richard snorted. 'I don't think you understand his skills, Sir James.'

'Such as?'

'He was crusading in the Holy Land while you were still being told which end of a lance to hold.'

'Really?' Sir James eyed Edgar's disappearing figure. 'A

shame he never learned manners while there.' Or you either, fat man, he added silently to himself.

Combe Street

Philip Marsille walked along the road carrying a small bundle. In it was a loaf of bread, two eggs and a piece of ham that was going off. It was all he could afford.

His rejection by the posse that morning felt like the final disaster. He could not even discover whether he was suited to fighting. It seemed as if nothing could leaven his gloom.

The sight of Father Laurence ahead in the road made him grunt a greeting, but he would have passed straight on if he could.

'My son, I am sorry about your mother,' Father Laurence said haltingly.

The priest looked at him as though he needed Philip to ease his own distress, the boy thought. Well, he had no time to bandy words with those who wanted comfort from him; no one would give *him* any.

'Why? You didn't kill her,' he said roughly.

'There were enough would have been happy to think I had,' Father Laurence said. 'There were many thought I killed Alice.'

'What would you expect them to think?' Philip snapped. 'You found her and didn't tell anyone. It made you look guilty. And then you ran away, too.'

'No. I was always here.'

'But hiding. You should be at the Cathedral. Why aren't you there now?'

'I will return soon. I behaved foolishly, and I will have to accept my punishment,' Father Laurence said sadly.

Philip looked at him. He had no sympathy left for others after the murder of his mother, but he did at least sense a kindred misery about Father Laurence. 'What will they do?'

'I have missed many services at which I should have been present. That is a serious crime. So, I have no doubt that my food for some weeks will be of the plainest, and I will have to undergo a some form of contrition. It is the way of the Church.'

'Don't you feel you deserve it?' Philip said. He couldn't keep the scorn from his voice, but when he saw Laurence's face, he was sorry. The man looked so ground down.

'Oh yes, I deserve it,' the vicar said hoarsely. 'And much more than the Church will even impose on me. You can have no idea.'

Philip shrugged. 'Well, take the punishment and be glad it's not worse, then.'

'Perhaps I should.'

'What do you want, Vicar? Absolution? I can't give you that. Go to the Cathedral.'

'I know. I am sorry.'

They were just passing the Paffards' house, and the bonfire from last night was still smoking. A scorch-mark ran up the limewashed wall of the nearby De Coyntes' property, and it struck Philip how close those flames had been to his own bed. Fortunate, it was, that someone had moved the bonfire further away from the houses.

Then Philip sensed something else. It was the vicar. He was staring at the Paffards' house with a kind of longing that Philip understood only too well. And suddenly he realised what the priest was so guilty about, and why he had to come back here. Philip had loved Alice, and Father Laurence was also in love, but it was with someone who could not return it, perhaps.

'Was it Alice?'

'Eh?' Father Laurence asked distractedly.

'You loved her too, did you? I asked her if—'

MICHAEL JECKS

'God, no!' Father Laurence said, and lifted his hand in the sign of the cross. 'Me? Never her, no.'

'But you looked, just then, as if you were missing someone, as I miss her.'

Father Laurence was already moving away from him, and in his eyes was a haunted expression, as if he had been accused of the murders again. Philip opened his mouth to speak, but the vicar suddenly turned and fled without saying anything more.

Philip watched him go with bemusement. There had been no reason for him to react in that manner, he thought.

He turned to go back to his house, and saw Gregory and Agatha at their door.

It was only when he was in his alley that he realised that in Gregory's eyes he had seen a similar misery to that in Father Laurence's. And the implications of *that* made his belly lurch.

Venn Ottery

In the middle morning's sun, Sir Charles remained sitting out in the yard, his eyes closed, making the most of this period of inaction. He knew, as a warrior, that such moments were all too fleeting.

'Sir Charles! Sir Charles!'

The sudden cry had his eyes wide in an instant. 'Ulric – what do you see?'

Up in the top of the elm the lad was leaning out dangerously, his head jutting out towards the west. 'At least fifty men, all on horseback. I can see their dust.'

Sir Charles trusted Ulric's eyes. If the lad said there were fifty men out there, he was almost certainly right. There was no need for Sir Charles to try to climb the tree as well.

He rose, stretched, and began to issue his commands. 'Ulric, get down, fetch your mount. You men: douse the fires! You two: leave her alone and fetch your arms.'

Gradually he gathered his men together, two still tying their hosen after their rape of the woman from the farm. There was a little boy, who had been used as their servant for all the last night while his mother was spread out for the men to enjoy, and Sir Charles leaned down to him now. 'Boy, I want you to run away. Do you understand? Run.'

The child stared back with his eyes wide in terror. He daren't move, and Sir Charles rolled his eyes.

'Kill his mother, and perhaps he'll run. Go on!' Sir Charles called to his men, then: 'Torch the house.'

There was a flash of steel, and a gasp as the woman was stabbed through the heart. Her son gave a whimper, and as one of the men booted him, he began to stumble away. Sir Charles irritably jerked his head, and the man drew his sword. Only then, at last, did the boy start to run, almost tripping, and then pelting faster and faster along the roadway.

'Good,' Sir Charles said with satisfaction. 'Now, load all you need, and let's be off.'

He lazily climbed onto his horse, and with a glance behind, set off at a walk. They made their way along the easterly route, and soon came to Sog's Lane. There, at the top of the lane Sir Charles halted his men again. There was a solitary oak in the side of the road, and Ulric climbed again to the top.

'Wait until they have seen us,' Sir Charles said. 'We want them to chase us.'

De Coyntes' House

Emma had completed the majority of her morning duties and with her maid Peg, had carried the washing tub out to the alley and up-ended it.

There was a narrow channel in the middle of the alley that took the waste away, and the tub's water was adequate to clear most of the ordure left in the alley overnight. Someone had emptied their chamber pot into it. Probably the boys next door, she thought, glancing at the hovel where the Marsilles lived. They had no idea of decency. Most people would walk a few yards from their door to empty their pots, but like all young men, these two lived only to please themselves.

She walked down the alley now, and stood staring at the still-warm embers of the bonfire from the night before. It made her shudder to think that any stray sparks could have set the entire block ablaze. She, Bydaud, Anastasia and Sabina could all have died in that, had it taken hold. No one who had ever seen a fire in a city would ever forget the horror of the flames licking at the walls, the way that the roofs caught light, thatch or shingles, it didn't matter which.

Helewisia had not spoken to her since the inquest. Fine, if that was how she felt. Juliana had insulted Sabina, and that was all there was to it. If Helewisia wanted to be offended on a dead woman's behalf, that was fine.

What really interested Emma was why Henry had cut Juliana's lips off. To stop her talking, of course – that was the inference – but that was intriguing, because it implied that there was someone to whom he wanted to impart the message.

Emma looked up and down the street, and when she saw Claricia Paffard on her steps, in a sudden burst of compassion, she walked along to speak to her.

'Madame Paffard? I was very sorry to hear about your husband.'

'My husband is lost to me. He is no more.'

'But you must know that nobody blames you or your family. It is not your responsibility if your husband takes to such a course.'

'You think so?' Claricia said. There was anger in her eyes, and Emma could only think that she was still trying to come to terms with the shock of learning that her husband was a killer. It must have been very difficult for her.

But there was no shame or humility in her eyes. All Emma could see was a raging anger, as if she thought her husband had merely let her down, and the obloquy of his crimes was nothing whatever to do with her.

It left Emma feeling chilled to the bone.

CHAPTER THIRTY-THREE

Venn Ottery

The column had already found two other bodies by the side of the road, much as Sir Richard had the day before, and Baldwin looked down at the two youths with a horrible sadness in his heart. Both had been captured in the fields and slain where they were. Baldwin had seen them because of the rooks which had congregated, the foul carrion. They rose in a black mist when he clattered nearer.

They had ridden quickly enough from the River Clyst, and now were almost at Venn Ottery, a modest manor with three small houses and a reeve's hall. A chapel finished the complement of properties, and while there were some columns of smoke rising from between the houses, unusually there was no one about. Apart from one tiny figure running straight at the column itself. Baldwin left the bodies and rode with Simon towards the head of the column, his eyes all the while on the road ahead to ensure that Sir Charles did not have an ambush ready.

When he reached the Sheriff, the child's interview was already complete.

'The men have just left. This little fellow saw them packing,' Sir James said, his voice raised so that all could hear him. 'They must be just the other side of the vill, not far. They have carts, so will be impeded. We shall ride hard to them, and when we reach them we shall destroy them all. Good. Prepare to ride. We shall be moving at a swift pace.'

'Sheriff, that is good news,' Baldwin put in, 'but we must be aware of their movements in case of an ambush.'

'There is a scant baker's dozen of men,' the Sheriff said carelessly. 'This lad was able to count them.'

'Where are the others which Sir Richard saw yesterday?' Baldwin demanded.

'Ridden off, I daresay, or gone on ahead. No matter. We have a third of them here and will wipe them out,' the Sheriff said. 'Why, Sir Baldwin, you don't fear them, do you? This will only be a short action, I promise you!' He laughed and set off.

Baldwin clenched his jaw against the insult, but he did not have time to protest further. The column was already moving off along the lane, and more than a couple of men glanced at him with grins, as though they were enjoying the Sheriff's joke at his expense.

'Simon, when we are past this vill, keep close to me,' Baldwin said and waved to Edgar. In the Holy Land Edgar had been his Sergeant, and now he returned to Baldwin's side and took up his post to protect Baldwin's flank, Sir Richard with him, and he nodded in the direction of the houses. 'They're burning the place.'

'I know. They are doing everything they could to tell us they're here,' Baldwin said. 'It is like the men who used to prey on travellers in the Holy Land. They would sometimes set a trap such as this. Allow one or two victims to escape, burn what they left . . .'

'Then what?'

'Let us see,' Baldwin said grimly. They were all riding at a steady pace now. 'Sir Richard, stay with us. We shall form a guard. If there is an ambush, we must charge their flank and force them to run.'

'Aye,' Sir Richard said, and his hand went to his sword-hilt, testing the blade's pull from the scabbard. He suddenly bellowed to two men in the posse. 'You, and you. Come here. You will remain with us, and if we charge, you come with us. Clear?'

It had been a pretty little hamlet once, Baldwin thought to himself as they rode into the yard area in front of the larger of the houses. What remained of the Reeve lay before his door, butchered. Wolf wandered over and nudged and sniffed at a dog that also lay nearby, his back hideously bent where a savage blow had cut through his spine. Baldwin called Wolf away, and he came with a last reluctant prod, as if unwilling to believe the other was dead.

More bodies lay scattered about. Baldwin counted five, including the poor naked woman beside her door. The boy had gone to her, and crouched at her side, wailing. Three of the houses were already smoking, and one had thick, greenish-yellow smoke pouring from the roof where the thatch was ablaze. In the warm air, the smoke rose quickly, but then drifted away southwards. It was a relief that they would not be riding into it.

'They're ahead! Less than a quarter-mile!'

The shout from in front made Baldwin look up with alarm. He saw Sir Richard give a wolfish grin. 'There's a trap, then,' the big knight said, nodding happily. 'As you thought, Sir Baldwin.'

'Why? What makes you think it's a trap?' Simon asked.

'They will have seen us coming,' Baldwin said through gritted teeth. 'They saw us and yet waited until we were certain to see them. And now they can persuade the Sheriff to give chase until he is inside their trap and cannot escape.'

'Christ's cods! So what can we do?'

'Follow me!' Baldwin said.

Venn Ottery

Sir James de Cockington rode ahead with anticipation thrilling in his blood. The bastards were just up at the corner of a little lane, couldn't possibly escape, not with the posse so close behind them. And it was good odds, with four or five men to every one of theirs.

'Keep up! Come on, charge the devils! These whorecops won't live to murder another farmer!'

He was at the lane's turn, and leaned into the corner, raking his spurs along his horse's flanks, and now he saw them all again. Slightly fewer, as though some had slipped to the hedge at the side, but their wagons were up there in front, at the far side of a small wood. He drew his sword. 'Take their carts, then kill them all!' he bellowed, and hurtled down the incline at the gallop.

A snap and whicker, and a whistling noise – and he was sure that he heard a man's cry – but as he had the thought, a rider was overtaking him, a short man, bent almost double, on a grey rounsey. Sir James was about to feel irritation when he saw the man rise from his saddle and drop, a foot caught in his stirrup, and Sir James saw the wicked crossbow bolt in his forehead.

291

Then he saw that behind him and the rest of the posse, a pair of carts had been pushed into the road. Their escape was blocked, as was the road before them. And on either side archers were standing, picking targets with lazy precision.

He crouched lower, eyes wide with sudden terror, as the bolts and arrows began to fly, and over the rushing roar of the wind in his ears, he could hear the high whinnies and screams of men and beasts as the missiles slammed into them.

Simon and Baldwin were at the rear of the group as the main column began to gallop, and at the first shriek of pain, Baldwin bellowed and pointed to a thinner part of the hedge at the side. He cantered to it, and leaped through, Simon close behind him, Edgar and Sir Richard side-by-side behind, and found himself in a pasture. There, ahead, he saw the trees, and in the midst of them were a number of men.

'Quick!' he roared, and thundered straight at them. Somehow three others had joined them in their diversion, and now they all spread out into a loose line as they crossed the field, hurling clods of earth and grass into the air as they went.

For Baldwin, any nerves had fled as soon as the first arrow was loosed. After that he knew only rage that felons, no matter whom, should dare to attack him and his companions. He felt the wind in his hair, the tug and snatch of the cloak at his throat, the reckless abandon of his horse, the weight of the sword in his fist, and let the savage glee of warfare take him. Bent low over his horse's neck, sword held high, he raced towards the nearest man.

The ambushers were concentrating too hard on their victims in the lane to notice him, and when they did, it was already too late. Baldwin's first blow hit an archer in the middle of his breast, and as he fell from Baldwin's sword, he saw Simon had killed another, while Sir Richard was bellowing and cursing, whirling with his beast as a man tried to flee his fury. Then Baldwin and Edgar were in the trees and for a moment it was a close thing. Baldwin's blade seemed to be alight with a cold blue flame as he stabbed a man, then hacked at another. An arrow thrummed past his ear, too close, but then Edgar had the bowman with a slash to the throat, and he fell in a spray of blood. Another was about to fire at Simon with his crossbow, but Wolf seemed taken with the same frenzy as his master, and ran in low, biting his legs. The man fell, and Wolf towered over him, his snarling mouth at the man's throat, and he squealed in terror until Simon came and slew him.

It had been a quick action, but already the men from the road were pouring into the woods, and of the twelve or more of those who had lain in wait, only two were still living. The other side of the woods was not so secure. The enemy was in there, and arrows whistled and thumped into the trees about them as they rallied.

Baldwin and Edgar rode on until they could see a break in the trees, and there they halted. A few arrows whacked into the trees nearby, but there were too many twigs for an archer to aim with accuracy. A twig could throw a clothyard off by feet even at short range.

'Where is the Sheriff?' Baldwin bellowed, trying to bring some order to the madness about him. '*To me!* Where is the Sheriff?'

There was no sign of him in the road. A few men were still struggling together, but even as Baldwin stared, he saw Sir Charles's men running up with knives, and soon all the members of the posse which had charged into the ambush with Sir James were dead. Farther back down the lane, Baldwin saw the remains of the column the Sheriff had led from Exeter so light-heartedly earlier that day. They had retreated, and now streamed back away from the fight. A few, perhaps five or six, stood watching from the top of the road at the corner. Apart from them, and Baldwin's small team, the Sheriff's entire column was dead or had fled.

'He is here, enjoying my hospitality, Sir Baldwin,' Sir Charles called, and Baldwin peered through the trees. 'Would you like to join him?'

'Sir Charles? Is that you?'

'Aye. It is good to see you again, my friend, but I would have wished it were under better circumstances.'

'I agree with that,' Baldwin said. He jerked his head and he and Edgar rode back to where Simon and Sir Richard stood still on their horses. The other three were also still there waiting, and Baldwin gestured to one, then pointed up towards the remaining men, who still waited nervously at the top of the lane at the corner. 'Go to them and tell them to charge when they hear us begin to fight,' he whispered. The man nodded and galloped away.

'What is that, Sir Baldwin? Seeking assistance? There is no one near here. I conducted my spying with the greatest of care, I assure you,' Sir Charles called.

Baldwin motioned now to Edgar, flattened his palm and lowered it in dumb sign. Edgar nodded, and was about to drop from his horse when Sir Charles laughed.

'Do ask Edgar to stay there, Sir Baldwin. I can see you both, and I would so hate to have to fire this crossbow at him before he has had a chance to leap upon me.'

'Greatly though I enjoy our conversation, I think I must leave you,' Baldwin said, peering through the screen of leaves to see the man.

'Please don't do that. I would be very sorry to have to hurt this fellow any more,' Sir Charles called back, and there was an edge to his voice as he spoke.

'Who?' Baldwin said.

'It . . . It's me, Sir Baldwin,' Sir James de Cockington called.

'Is that the Sheriff?' Sir Richard bawled.

'Yes, it is me.'

'Aye, right. Then you'll know that we don't tend to suffer felons to barter with a man's life, eh?' he yelled.

'That has been the rule, I know, but there are times—'

'I am a King's Officer. I'm the Coroner for Lifton, the King's manor. I am very sorry, but I won't negotiate with a man holding a blade to a Sheriff's neck.'

Sir Charles spoke again with an oily sweetness. 'Sir Richard, I appreciate your candour. So, would you prefer me to slit his throat now?'

'Aye. Do that and we'll discuss matters when I have you tied and ready for thc ropc.'

There was silence for a moment, and then, 'If you mean to provoke me, you won't succeed.'

'No? Good,' Sir Richard said. He glanced at the others about him. 'This fellow will not allow the Sheriff to survive. The body would be too much baggage to carry with him. So he'll kill Sir James as soon as he may. Nor will he release him willingly. If we negotiate, he will look for advantage . . .'

'I want you to surrender your arms to me and then you can ride away. I will take the good Sheriff with me as far as the border with Somerset, and then I give you my word I will release him.'

Sir Richard smiled grimly. 'In a hog's arse he will! That whoreson will kill Sheriff James as soon as he may. If we throw down our weapons, he'll kill us. Even if he let us ride off, he'd use our weaponry on others. We can't allow him to escape.'

Baldwin looked from him to Edgar, who nodded agreement. He glanced at Simon.

Simon was troubled, but he gave his assent. 'We both know Sir Charles, Baldwin. He's bold, resourceful and determined. I can only think of the bodies by the roadside all the way back to the Clyst. And he has killed the Bishop and despoiled the Bishop's manors as far as Petreshayes. No, we cannot allow him to escape.'

'Very well,' Baldwin muttered. He raised his voice again. 'What do you wish us to do, then?'

'Throw all your weapons here into the roadway. Then you may mount and ride away.'

'You expect us to throw away all means of defence?' Baldwin laughed. He looked at Simon and Sir Richard, and they nodded and began to sidle away.

'You can remain here and haggle if you prefer. I would like to return home, however.'

'Where is your home now?' Baldwin asked.

'I live far from here,' the response came. 'I won't be visiting again for some time. Now, your weapons?'

'Wait,' Baldwin said. He turned to the others. 'DISMOUNT!' he shouted, but then added: 'Slowly, and keep your weapons ready!'

Louder again, he said, 'WE ARE COMING!'

'We'll hold our fire,' Sir Charles said.

'Sir Baldwin, don't surrender!'

It was the Sheriff. His tone of anguished trepidation was enough to incite in Baldwin's heart a sudden and unexpected sympathy for the man. 'Don't hurt him, Sir Charles. You know I cannot allow you to escape if you harm him.'

'Come and throw down your weapons.'

Baldwin glanced about him. His companions were spread

out, but he was uneasily certain that the men with Sir Charles would have each of them marked, and they would be ready with their bows, preparing to fire as soon as the posse came closer.

'Come, my friends,' Baldwin said.

CHAPTER THIRTY-FOUR

Venn Ottery

Sir Charles lay with his chin in the dirt, staring through the stems of a blackthorn hedge at the men who slowly approached. This was not how he wanted to finish his ride. It was a great shame that Sir Baldwin and Simon should have been sent after him, but there was nothing to be done about it now. Two former travelling companions were now his enemies, and that was an end to it.

'Stop there,' he shouted when the men were near the road. 'Throw your weapons into the roadway. All of them.'

He had over twenty men still. Five were injured and out of the fight, two were scratched and keen to kill those who had hurt them, and three lay in the road. In compensation, there were eight of the men from Sir Baldwin's column lying dead, and the Sheriff was here with him, sitting quietly with a knife's point resting under his chin. He was not moving, but watched the posse approach with a terrible certainty. He knew that Sir Charles could not allow any of them to escape.

Sir Charles waited until the men were almost at the hedge, and then turned to issue the command to kill them.

At the same time, the Sheriff knocked his hand away and sprang up. 'Sir Baldwin, beware! It's a trap – they will kill you too!'

'Get down!' Sir Charles roared, and would have opened him from gut to gizzard, but before he could, two arrows were loosed into Sir James de Cockington's back, and exploded through his chest and belly. He coughed, and blood dribbled from his chin as he fell to his knees, staring at the two barbed points, before toppling to the ground. Sir Charles clenched his fist, striking Sir James's body three times in impotent rage, and then swore viciously and continually as the arrows and quarrels flew over his head, but it was all to no use. The men with Sir Baldwin were in the road, concealed behind the carts that still littered the place.

There had never been a situation in which Sir Charles had felt at such a loss. Even while abroad he had always known where his escape could be effected. Today, no such avenue occurred to him. His horses were at the rear of the pasture with Ulric, while down there in the roadway with the carts were his winnings. The treasures he had accumulated from the episcopal manors were packed upon them. He could escape, perhaps, but only at the cost of losing all he had gained.

He had no choice. Giving an incoherent roar, he leaped down into the road himself, bellowing to his men to follow him. There was a man before him, and he swung his sword, only to have it clash with Sir Richard's, then it was knocked away, and he and Sir Richard circled warily. He could hear crashing and shouting, screams of agony, and a terrified man's last shrill scream, before he concentrated utterly on Sir Richard. There was a moment of serenity, almost, and then he drew his sword up and into the St George guard, and waited, watching.

Sir Richard launched himself forward, and Sir Charles could have laughed at the clumsy attempt. This fight would be quick, then, with so old and portly an opponent. He turned fluidly and knocked the sword aside with ease, only to find that it wasn't there. Sir Richard had reversed his manoeuvre at the last moment, and Sir Charles almost spitted himself on the up-turned point.

It was a caution. A knight as old as Sir Richard must surely have had the expertise to survive many dangerous encounters. Sir Charles warily tested his parrying with his point, without exposing himself too greatly, and then lunged. His blade was almost at Sir Richard's belly, when his sword was effortlessly flicked from its path, and Sir Richard's point came straight for his throat.

He withdrew again. This opponent was surprisingly competent, he thought, and as he did so, he heard a sound that sent a shaft of ice into his bowels. A horn, and he could feel the ground rumble beneath his feet. Glancing up the lane, he saw seven more horsemen pounding towards him and his men.

''Ware the men!' he bawled, but his men were not trained warriors. They were competent in a mêlée, or against peasants, when armed with war hammers and axes, but they had not been trained to stand in line with lances fixed against a foe this deadly. One dropped his weapon, and was instantly slain by his opponent, a second wailed, turned, and fled. He was cut down by Sir Richard as he passed, and then the horses slammed into the men remaining, their breasts used as rams to batter at the men, while blows were rained down upon them. Men were crushed against each other, had their skulls broken by axes, were stabbed and hacked at with swords and knives, and in only a few moments, ten were dead, another seven wounded, and being forced back while the horses herded them into the edge of the roadway.

'Surrender!' Sir Richard thundered.

'Go swyve a sow,' Sir Charles responded. 'Your father did.'

Baldwin approached, his sword bloody, a great rent across the front of his tunic. 'Sir Charles, surrender or we will have to kill you. I would not do that, for memory of the times we enjoyed in your company.'

'I will not surrender. What, give up now so I can hang from a tree like a common churl?'

'The city of Exeter will give you a good hearing. You need not die here.'

'I will not submit to a pair of rural knights with the dregs of Exeter to back them.'

'Then guard yourself,' Baldwin said.

Sir Richard interrupted him as he raised his sword. 'Sir Baldwin, he is mine. I would not have you kill a friend. Leave him to me.'

'Sir Richard, you have a most dangerous opponent.'

'Sir Baldwin, I watched this man's fellows rape a poor woman yesterday. My wife was killed by a faithless, dishonoured coward and as I killed him, so shall I kill this. Without aid.'

Baldwin hesitated, but the cold rage in Sir Richard's eye was impossible to ignore. 'Very well,' he conceded, and withdrew.

De Coyntes' House

It was already beginning to edge towards twilight when Bydaud de Coyntes made his way along the street towards the alley and his home.

He had a strange feeling as he approached them. A kind of reluctance he had never known before. It was almost as though he was fearful that there might be another body outside the house when he reached it. Nonsense, of course, but even so, he could hardly help himself from looking about him, his eyes going straight to the piles of rubbish that lay against the wall of the houses in the street, hoping not to see any limbs or a face staring back at him.

He was tired today. Perhaps it was the effect of two broken nights' sleep in the last few days, but he thought it was more than just that. There was a new nervousness about him at work. The excitement of new opportunities.

It was yesterday that the first of the merchants had come to him, a shifty-looking man in his late fifties with a shock of unruly white hair beneath his cap, and narrow, keen eyes that moved about the tiny shop like a bird's looking for a morsel on which to pounce.

'We have been reconsidering some of the city investments and other works,' the man had said without preamble.

'Yes, sir?' Bydaud had replied.

This was no ordinary merchant entering to have a word; it was a senior man from the city, one of the four stewards, and with his patronage a poor merchant like Bydaud could hope to make a much better living.

'We do not like what we have heard about Henry Paffard. There is no place in the city for a man who has confessed to murdering women, and no place for him to share in decisions about the future direction of the city. If you were to be asked, it may be possible that you could join the Freedom of the City in his place.'

'I would be honoured.'

'I hope so. Not many cities would consider bringing in foreigners, but we are a more progressive city, I like to think.'

He had continued to outline some projects already under-way, and Bydaud was keen to help with each. He had the contacts with France and the Low Countries which the city needed, and in a short time all was agreed. The steward left him and said he would be back as soon as he had discussed the matter with his companions in the council.

As good as his word, he had arrived this very afternoon, and in a short while, Bydaud and he had agreed their contract. Bydaud knew he would make a little less money on these voyages than he would usually, but he was also convinced that the prestige would be worth it.

'What of Henry?' he asked at one point.

The steward looked at him appraisingly. 'You prefer us to take this business back to him?'

'No!'

'Good. Then that is all.'

For the first time, Bydaud thought his decision to come here to Exeter was about to pay off. The money which this deal would bring in would help, but it was the idea of additional business that attracted his attention. There was potential to make much more in the longer term. Especially just now. The city was going through a period of expansion, with the new cathedral building and renovations to the city walls, and these men were offering him a percentage of all that effort. With luck, in a year or two he would be a member of the Freedom himself, every bit as important as Paffard ever had been.

It was a glorious future.

Venn Ottery

'Sir Richard, for a fat man you can move swiftly,' Sir Charles panted. His eyes were fixed on Sir Richard's. To fight a man, it was usually necessary to watch his movements. Sir Richard's legs hardly appeared to move at all, but his arms could dart about with blinding speed, and the sword's point moved fastest of all, as Sir Charles knew. It was the eyes of the opponent that betrayed the assault.

There! The blade slid towards him, and Sir Charles had seen the tiny narrowing of Sir Richard's eye just before. To make certain, he waited a little, and then saw the eyes narrow again in the same way. That was his mark. That was Sir Richard's giveaway sign. And that would be his doom.

Sir Charles slid backwards, avoiding a cart's wheel on his way and a dead man's arm, allowing a hint of anxiety to tweak his eyes and brow. He retreated before that swift-moving blade, the cold, angry face of his opponent, until the little telltale narrowing came again, and this time Sir Charles whirled, wrenching his sword-hand up, blade pointing at the ground, knocking Sir Richard's sword away, and then while Sir Richard's belly and breast were exposed, he completed the manoeuvre, his blade arcing up to Sir Richard's throat.

An easy feint, that, he thought, as his blade was thrust up, but again it was blocked, and Sir Charles had an icy conviction that this man would kill him. He was far superior in swordsmanship.

There was a scream, and then suddenly, four horses were thundering towards them all. Sir Charles stared as Ulric rode straight at him, leading a spare horse by the reins, keeping his own between Sir Charles and the others, while other horses ran wild amongst the men, distracting them all.

'Good man!' Sir Charles managed as he slammed his sword into the sheath and hurled himself into the saddle. It took him only a moment. He had been riding and training with horses since he was seven years old. Now he snatched the reins, bending low over the horse's neck, and raked his prick spurs along the brute's flanks, feeling the surge of power beneath him. The huge beast seemed to take flight like the bolt from a crossbow, galloping straight off along the lane away from the men. There was one man who stood in their path, but a blow from a hoof sent him crashing into a cart, a great bloody welt on his face. And then the road was clear.

He spurred and slapped reins to the horse, and saw that there was a corner ahead. He leaned into it with the mount, and at the other side the mud was thrown up in great gouts; splashes hurled at his face, on his lips, and he must wipe them away, concentrating all the while on the surface ahead, avoiding any potholes or branches that could turn his beast's leg.

A glance behind. Three men approaching. All riding well, low and eager. Good. They would be easily ambushed, then.

Ulric was white-faced. He must know that if he was caught by the posse, he would be killed, Sir Charles thought. But it could be that he was scared of the ride. Sir Charles didn't know how many times Ulric had ridden at full gallop. This might be his first time. A whistle, and he saw a clothyard arrow drop into the road's hedge. So they had almost the distance, then. Soon he'd be out of their range and their line of sight. A hedge, and he crouched lower, and took it in one explosive leap that felt as though a tub of black powder had gone off beneath them both, and then there was a massive, jarring crash as they hit the ground again, and Sir Charles was turning, wheeling his mount with him, then riding back.

The first man was over a moment early, and as his beast's forelegs hit the ground, Sir Charles's sword was out, and he skewered the rider, his blade ripping through the fellow's belly; a second man was over, and Sir Charles had little time to recover. He slammed the guard into that man's face, and he went down, unconscious, thrown to the ground while his horse careered away.

Then it was the third. This one was a youngster, and in his eyes was the terror of death as he came over the hedge. Sir Charles took hold of his arm as he landed, and ripped him from his saddle, hurling him to the ground. He stabbed the boy in the throat, still holding his arm. He let go as the life left the fellow. He noticed a large red birth mark on the back of his hand. 'Marked, eh?' he said with a grin. 'You were cursed from birth!'

His horse was prancing about, and Sir Charles had to get it under control.

'Ulric?' he called.

The boy was sitting in his saddle still, stunned at the sudden battle, panting, his eyes as wild and anxious as his beast's. 'Yes?'

'Get that man's shirt and jack off,' Sir Charles snapped as an idea came to him.

It was bold and dangerous, both of which made it appealing, and he smiled as Ulric set to work.

CHAPTER THIRTY-FIVE

Paffards' House

Claricia Paffard watched her youngest son, little Thomas, as he entered the hall. Gregory was in the passageway and, on seeing him, the boy ran over to her and hid behind her.

'Gregory!' Claricia called. 'What on earth have you done to upset him?'

'Me? Nothing. It must be Father,' Gregory said. 'What is it, Thomas? Are you worried?'

Thomas said nothing, but clung to Claricia; she could feel him trembling. She looked from one to the other.

'I don't have time for this,' Gregory said. Then he burst out: 'Mother, we must plan for the worst. I still do not understand what Father thought he was doing when he confessed, but the business is already suffering. I've had several notes from other merchants telling me that they don't want to have any more trade with us. I fear that the—'

'Gregory! You are the head of the house now. It is your part to resolve these problems,' she said sternly.

'Mother, I—'

'You have never enjoyed the work. Well, that is your fault and your shame. Your father created this business from nothing. He has a reputation of being the best pewterer this side of Bristol, but you never tried to emulate him. Now you can at least try to win back a little of the respect of the people of this city.'

'How should I set about it?'

'If you are so feeble-witted, speak with your sister. She at least has a good mind for the business,' Claricia snapped.

Gregory stared at her for a short while before spinning on his heel and storming from the room. She could hear him as he stamped up the stairs.

'And what of you, little man?' she sighed, turning to Thomas. 'Are you so upset because your father is in prison, or because your brother now holds all our lives in his hands? It is a fearsome thing, is it not?'

She could weep, if it were not for the jubilation that would keep leaping through her frame at the thought that Henry was in prison. He could no longer shame her or hurt her, while he was safely shut up there.

Thomas gave her a great hug, his small arms about her shoulders, and then he hurried from the room, and Claricia heard the front door slam behind him.

There were steps a moment or two later, and John appeared.

'John, wait. It was only Thomas. He has gone into the street to play.'

'Will he be safe?'

'At this time of day, I think even I would be safe out there,' Claricia sighed.

John went to the sideboard and poured her a little watered wine, which he passed to her, but she did not sip. Instead she sat staring reflectively into the fire.

'Mistress? Do you want some food?'

'I am not hungry. I am just tired. So very tired.'

'He has not been a good master to you,' John muttered.

'He was a foul womaniser and I do not regret his imprisonment,' she said with venom.

'It was his lack of respect I found so troubling.'

'He had none for me. Not even when I was with child.' She wept.

'I know,' John said quietly.

When she was young, she had been so pretty. Much like her daughter Agatha now. John had been steward to her father, Sir Geoffrey of Uplyme, and when the master's wife died soon after the birth of their second daughter, John had been given the care of both children. He had hired the wetnurse and drynurse, as well as having charge of the hall itself, and some responsibility for the lands about.

It had been a marvellous time. John had enjoyed all his years there. His master was often away, and that meant that John had the pleasure of the children and could manage the estates as he saw fit without interference or interruption. Being in such constant control did lead to some friction when Sir Geoffrey returned, of course. John almost resented the way that the master would look through all his decisions and question some of them. But the feeling soon left him as he returned to the girls.

Claricia's sister died, sadly, when quite young, falling from a horse. The brute broke his leg in a rabbit-hole, and she was thrown, landing on her head. Death was instant. John, who had been there on her first day, carried her home on her last. He had mourned her deeply, and even Sir Geoffrey had commented on his devotion, but to John it had felt as if he had lost his own daughter.

When Sir Geoffrey had died during the battle at Roslin, it was natural that Claricia should marry. And Henry Paffard had then appeared a good, solid foundation for a family. Not too old, an apprentice with a good trade, and there was a certain thrill about marrying a man who was not a member of the knightly class. She knew no one else who had done so. But then she knew so few others who had no money, no parents, no brother to help look after her.

'Thomas is troubled,' she said now.

'Mistress, there are some things you may not be aware of,' John said.

'About Thomas?'

'No, about your husband,' John said. 'You see, he had been sponsoring rebels.'

Venn Ottery

The men who trotted up a short while later were peasants from Sir Baldwin's posse, Sir Charles saw with pleasure. They had a cart, on which one body already reposed, and now they were looking for others.

'Go on, boy,' he urged.

He and Ulric had stripped the man whom Sir Charles had clubbed, and the loose-fitting chemise and hosen were a good fit. On his head he wore a cowl and hood to conceal his features. His own clothes they had draped over the moaning body, and then Sir Charles took a rock from the hedge and beat at the head until the dying man was unrecognisable. It took some while, and Ulric had stood away while Sir Charles worked, his face drawn with distaste.

'Get them,' Sir Charles said, pushing the lad on.

'Over here!' Ulric said, waving.

The two men from the posse clambered from their horses

and thrust themselves through the ruined hedge. 'Sweet Mother of God,' one said.

'They lay in wait for us,' Sir Charles said.

This was the moment he had feared. A posse was formed usually of those from a near vicinity, and usually could know each other well, but he was hoping that such a large group as this would contain men from all over Exeter. He and Ulric were wearing other men's clothes, and he hoped that all the posse members would be so tired after their day that they wouldn't care to notice who else was with them. It was still a risk though, and he held his hand on his belt, near his dagger, while the two men glanced at the bodies.

'Ah, well, best get them loaded,' one said.

Sir Charles glanced back at the men further up the lane. 'Why don't you go back and tell them to get started?' he said to the other. 'There's no point them waiting for us. We'll soon be done here, anyway.'

'Very well,' he said. He pushed back through the hedge and was soon mounted and trotting back to the rest of the posse.

Sir Charles breathed a sigh of relief. That meant that they could dawdle along behind the others, and with luck escape detection. He bent and helped the other man carry the bodies to the cart. There they hefted them up on the back, Ulric standing on the cart itself to receive them and to heave them into position.

'For a knight, he did a lot of work,' the posse man noted, glancing at the fingers of the man clad in Sir Charles's tunic. They were black and grimy, horny as a dog's pad.

Sir Charles said nothing, but when he had a moment, he thrust his own hands into a muddy pool to simulate a peasant's.

When all was done, they gathered up the horses and set off after the rest of the posse. They were none of them in a hurry.

311

Sir Charles pulled the hood over his face and rode with his head down, like a man exhausted after his labours.

They would follow the others into Exeter, and speak with the merchant Paffard about money for Sir Edward. And then he would find out what he could about Sir Baldwin and that fat fool Sir Richard. He had a burning urge to see them both suffer for their theft of his treasure.

Marsilles' House

William was at home, sipping cold pottage left over from the day before when Philip entered that evening.

'Where have *you* been?' William asked grumpily.

'Watching the murderer of the girl Alice,' Philip said with cold passion. 'And probably the killer of our mother.'

William put his bowl down on the table. 'What are you talking about? They were killed by Paffard – we know that already – and he's held in the gaol.'

'What if he isn't guilty?' Philip said.

William eyed his older brother with a wary disdain. 'You've been drinking, haven't you? Have you spent what little money you had?'

'Some of it.'

'When you know I have nothing?' William grated.

Philip gave a gasp of exasperation. Reaching into his purse, he brought out four pennies. 'Here's half for you, if you're so desperate!'

William took them and stared at them. With one or two of these, their mother's final days would have been easier.

'I was going to join the posse this morning. They refused me.'

William asked pointedly, 'You've done something stupid, haven't you?'

'I met with Father Laurence and spoke with him.'

'The vicar who ran away? Where was he?'

'Out in the street here. And you know what I learned?' Philip ran a hand through his hair. 'I think he is a guilty of the "old sin".'

'You do realise I haven't the faintest idea what you're talking about?'

'I think he is a sodomite. And so is our neighbour Gregory.'

'*What?*'

'Don't you understand anything, Will?' Philip said, disdain rasping his voice. 'You know the penalty for a sodomite: death. So in order to protect his son, Henry Paffard was prepared to do anything. Perhaps that's why he killed Mother – to keep her silent so Gregory would be safe.'

'In that case our mother's killer is in gaol and will pay for it. Thank God for that.'

'And meanwhile his son will run our lives and can throw us from our home at any time.'

William looked about him at their meagre possessions. 'We can find another place, Phil.'

'And the man who now has power over our lives is a sodomite, Will. Think of it! A sodomite who was responsible for our mother's death and who could destroy us as well! Are you really prepared to allow him to ruin us?'

'Look at us, Phil: we're already ruined. There is little enough he can do to us, is there? Let's just get out of here.'

Philip sat down in a seat, and said no more. But inwardly, he seethed. If William thought he was going to lie down, roll over and forget that their neighbour and landlord had ruined their lives, he couldn't be more wrong. Philip would find some way to bring justice to that shit Gregory Paffard *and* the priest.

MICHAEL JECKS

Exeter

It was a mournful group that rode back to Exeter that evening. The carts with the belongings of the Bishop would no doubt be gratefully received at the Cathedral, but the mood of the crowds at the East Gate was sombre when the bodies on the carts became visible. There were so many!

Baldwin and Simon had gathered together all their own wounded, and these were arranged in the carts, the dead tied to any available horses. Sir James's body itself was at the head of the column as it reached the city, led by his herald, and as they passed under the gate, there was a shocked silence. Even hawkers and beggars were stilled as they turned up the castle street towards Rougemont.

Baldwin and Sir Richard rode up the narrow way, but as Baldwin saw Simon, he told him, 'You go to Edith, old friend. One of us at least should try to have a pleasant evening. Our time will be taken up with seeing to all these men.'

'I'll find a barber for you, and send him to the castle for the wounded,' Simon said immediately. With all the arrow-wounds, they would have need of a good surgeon.

'A good idea,' Sir Richard said, his usual strident tones quite muted.

'Are you quite well, Sir Richard?' Baldwin asked, not for the first time on their ride homeward.

'Yes. I think so,' he replied. It had been a hard day. He had killed two men in the fighting, and it was a sobering experience, as always, to take life. But there was more to it than that. 'You know, I had an intense rage against that fellow,' he said. 'It was as though he was the man who killed my wife, and that today I had a chance again to visit punishment upon him.'

'Perhaps this will allow *you* to rest, and to leave *her* to rest,' Baldwin said.

'I think not. The memory of my wife will always be with me, I hope,' Sir Richard said quietly, pain apparent in his voice.

Baldwin nodded, but he could not understand. This strange, complicated man, with his enormous appetites for drink and food, was yet still so devoted to the memory of his wife. And it only added to Baldwin's affection for him. After all, as he told himself, he was scarcely less complex himself.

'Open the gates. Your Sheriff is here!' he bellowed at the castle. And slowly the great gate began to creak wide.

Baldwin rode inside, the line of carts following him, their wheels thundering over the drawbridge. He dismounted, watching the last of them entering the East Gate, and the last few members of the posse, plainly nothing loath, broke away at the bottom there, and trotted off along the High Street.

Inside, he remained on his rounsey with Wolf, and he noticed that Sir Richard had dropped from his horse and gone over to a woman in tatty clothing, her dark hair matted. That, Baldwin assumed, must be Amflusia, the woman he rescued from Sir Charles yesterday.

There were many carts. Those holding chests and trinkets that Sir Charles's band had stolen from the Bishop and others, were segregated in a corner nearer the gate, and as soon as they all were parked, there began the foul task of unloading all the dead and arraying them on the ground, in order that they might be identified. There would need to be an inquest over all these poor souls, he told himself, even as his eyes took in the sight of Sir Charles's body.

'Dear God, what happened to his face?' he breathed horrified. The man had been beaten so violently that his nose was crushed, his jaw smashed. Even his own brother would not recognise him in that state.

The carter was helping two others to haul the bodies from

the cart. 'Him? He was their leader. I think the men who caught him made sure he was dead. Must have hit him with a rock.'

'A rock?' Baldwin said. He was about to leave and had in fact opened his mouth to speak to Sir Richard, when one of the other riders peered, frowning at the line of men.

'What is it?' Baldwin said. There was a strange quickening in his blood. He knew that something was wrong.

'This is Perkin. I recognise the birth mark on the back of his hand, look! But these were his clothes,' the man said, bewildered.

Baldwin glanced down. The fellow was pointing at a man in an ancient cotte and hosen. 'Are you sure?'

Sir Richard had joined him. 'Those are the clothes of the man who rode at us and saved Sir Charles.'

'Yes,' Baldwin said, and walked to the body in Sir Charles's clothes. 'And I don't think this is Sir Charles, either!'

CHAPTER THIRTY-SIX

Second Friday after the Nativity of St John the Baptist[1]

Exeter Cathedral

Simon could not help but look up at the soaring columns and arches high overhead with a feeling of apprehension.

It was true that a man had to die some time, and equally true that the best place in which to die was undoubtedly a church, best of all a cathedral – but somehow that reflection was of little consolation when the next moment could bring a large rock tumbling onto his head. Simon knew, of course, that masons were magicians with their tools and their knowledge of balancing stones one atop another. However, he had seen magicians in the street who had signally failed to achieve their little deceptions, and he did not wish to learn that one of the masons involved on this project had similarly much to learn.

He had felt safer yesterday riding against Sir Charles.

1   3 July 1327

There were so many stories of cathedrals whose spires and towers had collapsed. Ely and Salisbury, for example . . .

'Simon, concentrate!' Baldwin said.

He returned his gaze to the vicars presiding over the service.

It had been a sad little gathering that had met last night after their return. As soon as Baldwin had told the city's guards about Sir Charles, he and Sir Richard had hurried to the Cathedral. Adam Murimuth and the chaplain to the castle had discussed the funeral, and had agreed on the terms for the service to honour the Sheriff. Baldwin had heard that on top of the costs of the wax for the candles and other expenses there were to be payments of eight pence to each canon present, four to each vicar, a penny to each of the annuellars and a halfpenny to each boy. But first there must be the service for the dead Bishop, and they were all in here now to witness that.

'So, you are sure?' Simon said.

'There can be no doubt,' Baldwin said. 'Sir Charles escaped. I believe he is here in the city.'

Simon grunted. 'Why?'

'Hush, Simon.'

The body of Bishop James was up near the altar, that of Sir James de Cockington a few yards behind. Both had been carried in with great ceremony, with canons and vicars in their solemn black gowns and caps all holding candles. Baldwin, in a moment's cynicism, wondered who would be paying the bill for all the wax: the Cathedral for the Bishop, the estate for Sir James. It was quite likely, he decided, that the estate of the Sheriff would end up paying twice, because the Cathedral was still desperate to make sure that they earned enough money from every activity.

As Sir James was brought in, his face exposed so that all

could see him, his herald led his procession. More vicars, and annuellars were with him, although no canons. The funeral of the Sheriff was a glorious moment for the Cathedral, but his must not overshadow the Bishop's, and so it had been agreed that the Sheriff could come to the church and lie here for a day, but that the Bishop's funeral would go ahead as planned.

The herald, carrying Sir James's sword upside down, point at the ground, was one of the few in the room who appeared genuinely affected by the death of his master. He had tears flowing down both cheeks. A man losing his master was always in a terrible position, as Baldwin knew. There was no son in Sir James's family to take over a loyal servant, and whoever was promoted to the Shrievalty was unlikely to want a servant from his predecessor. He would bring his own men with him.

It was a poignant thought.

'What is it, Baldwin?' Sir Richard said.

'I was thinking. When I was in the Holy Land, I heard of monarchs from the past who had their slaves buried with them in their heathen pride, and it strikes me that our English lords leave their own retainers in perhaps a more troubled position. It was the reason for Sir Charles of Lancaster's original descent from grace, after all. Once, he was a loyal servant of his lord, Earl Thomas of Lancaster, but when Earl Thomas lost his head after Boroughbridge, and his lands were sequestered by the King, Sir Charles was one of many knights who found that he had lost all. His home, his hearth, his food and his duty. All a knight possesses, when his service is taken away, is his horse and his sword, and these Sir Charles took with him to France to find a new life.'

'Aye, well, the man will be found and hanged. You can ask him about it then.'

'There are others worse than Sir Charles.'

319

But it was astonishing that he should have dared kill a Bishop. Even with his fearless attitude to the world, that was stunning to Baldwin.

Paffards' House

Agatha Paffard rose late that day. When she entered the hall, it was empty, and it seemed so much a metaphor for her own existence that she felt a sob tear at her breast. It was only with an effort that she could swallow it down. She would not show the world how utterly meaningless her life was.

Because her life was a sham. All through her childhood she had dreamed of marrying and being 'happy ever after'. It was the way that girls were brought up. The idea that one day they might be married to a cruel man who would be happier finding women on the streets, and who would beat his wife for complaining was not totally strange, however, for all women knew a man like that. Agatha herself because she saw it every day in her father. She hated him.

Yet she hated her mother more. Claricia was scared of her own shadow! She deserved the contempt in which she was held. She should have been more firm, not only for her own sake, but for that of her children too.

Agatha knew her brain was better than most men's. It was an enduring sadness that she could never take over the family business. And stupid, too, because while she adored her brother, Gregory was not suited for matters of finance and organisation, whilst Thomas would never be academic or capable with figures. And a good manager of a business, a good merchant, needed those skills in spades. Here she was, the one member of the family who had the competence to take over from father, and she was the one who was exluded by the mere chance of sex.

CITY OF FIENDS

She knew she was intolerant, argumentative, and she gloried
in it. Her dread was that one day she might grow to be like her
mother. Better that she should never marry, than that! Perhaps
Claricia had not been that way when she was younger, but it
was no good to look at her and think how she might once have
been. It was how a person developed and grew that mattered,
not how much promise they had exhibited long ago. Many
could show promise: it was how they lived up to their potential
that signified. Well, Agatha had more promise than any in her
family, and her mother was drained of all purpose.

It was no surprise. She had been forced into a life that was
repugnant to her. She knew, as well as Gregory and Agatha,
how her husband had made use of the maids in the household.
Agatha herself had been out in the street when Henry had paid
money to one of the whores. She had seen him, drawn into a
tavern by the giggling wench, and Agatha had felt as if she
would be sick. Luckily she had not been alone that day. John
had been with her, and he kindly drew her away and back
homewards.

Agatha bit her lip with disgust. That a man like her father,
with all his wealth and intellect, should be so prey to his own
urges beggared belief.

'Sister, are you all alone?'

'Yes, Gregory, but don't let that stop you coming in. I was
only enjoying some intelligent conversation.'

'Alone? I thought conversation meant at least two people.'

'Intelligent, I said, brother dear.'

'Ouch!'

'You see? Even you can understand me sometimes. Rarely
enough, true, but occasionally.'

'Why do you have to be so mean to me all the time?'

'It's hard to know where to begin – or how to describe the

reasons in a suitably vacuous manner such that you would comprehend.'

He laughed.

'You do realise the state of our business?' she said, not looking at him.

He groaned. 'You know that if I could, I would gladly pass the business to you – *if* there is one still, once Father is dead.'

'There would be a business if *I* were in charge,' Agatha said immediately. 'But as matters stand, we have less than three months. That will be how long I expect you to survive without Father at the helm.'

'Why is it you have such a lousy opinion of me?'

'You know I don't. Not really.'

He chuckled. 'Your contempt for my intellect is as vast as the oceans.'

'Well, if you're going to put it like that . . .'

He was stony-faced. 'Do you really think I'm that dull-witted? I couldn't ever manage to make pewter like Father, I know, but I could learn the mercantile trade, surely.'

'Again, it is hard to know how to respond to that. I wouldn't want to patronise you – that means talk down to you, by the way – but I—'

He flushed angrily. 'I was being serious.'

'Brother, dear, you have many wonderful attributes,' she said, 'but when it comes to the trades that Father has arranged, you would have little idea how to negotiate them, even if you understood where the profit would come from.'

'I'm no fool!'

Agatha looked at him. His face worked, and he looked as though he was going to burst out with a curse, but he couldn't. He knew he would lose her favours if he did so. That was the thing. She had such control over him. When she saw him turn and stamp from the room, she had a little frisson of pure delight.

She arrested him in his tracks when she called, 'Oh, Gregory, don't forget to ask someone to come and mend the front door. There's a bit of a draught coming in today.'

He paused, his back to her, and then marched on out of the room.

It gave her a spark of joy to see him so angry.

Paffards' House

In the yard behind the house, Thomas was kicking his pig's bladder in a desultory fashion against the wall. The bladder bounced high over his head, and slammed into the vegetables, cracking a stem of kale, and he looked guiltily towards the house, but no one was there to observe his casual vandalism, so he scurried over, liberated the ball from the vegetables, and began to kick it again.

At least his brother and sister weren't out here. He didn't feel safe around either of them. Gregory was scary. Had been, ever since Thomas saw them in the hall that terrible day. It was all right, Gregory had said, and he shouldn't be scared, but Thomas was old for his years, and he found it very unsettling.

He kicked again, and the bladder bounced back, rolling to stop at the storeroom where John kept his barrels. It was the sort of place Thomas would have liked to play in, but John always had the door locked against thieves. Anyone could break through the garden's gate, he had said, to steal their ales and wines.

Thomas went to the shed and picked up his ball.

Benjamin reckoned that there was less chance of someone stealing the ale than of their taking the lead or tin from the workshops, but Thomas had heard him say that old John was a fool who thought only his barrels were valuable, and didn't understand the true amount of money a man could win for even a single ingot of tin.

Thomas stood at the wall, his ball in his arms. There was a little crack in the wood at the bottom of the panel, and he stared at it for a moment. It was quite round, gnawed into a hole about the size of his hand. Smaller than his head. He put his hand to it and pulled. A piece of the rotten timber came away in his hand.

Then he heard someone enter the garden, and he stood back quickly.

But that hole interested him. Sometime he would have to go back there and have a look at it. He reckoned he could open it up a bit more, and see if he could squeeze into it and make the storeroom into a hiding-place for games.

With Gregory behaving as he was, he might want it as a place to hide in, in earnest.

Exeter Cathedral

The incense was cloying, and thick in Baldwin's throat. He was glad when the service finally ended and they might return to the fresh air. Especially since he was on fire to catch Sir Charles.

As they came out, they were hailed.

'Good gentles, God be with you!'

Sir Richard turned and Baldwin was surprised to see him pull a face when he saw Adam Murimuth hurrying to them. He saw Baldwin notice his expression and muttered, 'I can't feel comfortable about that priest. Every word I say seems disrespectful before him. Can't tell him any of me jokes.'

And a good thing too, Baldwin said to himself. Aloud, he added, 'Good day to you, Precentor,' as Adam stopped, puffing slightly.

'And to you!'

'Good to see so many folks in there, eh?' Sir Richard rumbled happily, as he and Simon trailed after them.

Baldwin heard his comment, and looked about him at the houses of the Close. There *were* so many, and all of them, he knew, filled with men. No women, no wives existed here in the Cathedral Close. Only countless men.

'You will excuse me speaking frankly, Precentor,' he said, 'but it struck me as sad to see two men without a woman to mourn them.'

'There were many men to mourn them,' Adam murmured. 'The good Bishop will be speeded on his way, I hope, and will soon be received into Heaven.'

'Amen,' Baldwin said.

'It is terrible to see the Sheriff die. What news is there of the outlaw responsible?'

'We believe he may have escaped into the city, and all the men of the city's Watch are looking for him,' Sir Richard said. 'They know the places a man may hide.'

'He has caused a terrible void at the heart of the city,' Adam said.

'A new Sheriff can be found with ease,' Sir Richard said carelessly.

'It will require careful thought. All too often the Sheriff is shown to be corrupt.'

'Without casting comment on the late incumbent, I think few could dispute that,' Baldwin smiled.

'The city needs a strong man to take up the duty,' Adam sighed.

'I am sure you will find that the post will soon be taken up by a strong man,' Sir Richard said with a chuckle. 'Nature abhors a void, as they say.'

Baldwin smiled. 'Sir Richard, you are a constant source of

surprise. But you are correct. The emptiness will soon be filled, probably by a member of the de Courtenay family. There are many there who would desire to take on the position.'

'For reasons of service to the people?' Adam asked hopefully.

'No, for reasons of profit and corruption,' Sir Richard snorted. 'There aren't many left who consider the aid they may give to others, Precentor.'

They left him then, marching on together to the High Street.

'I still think it sad that there were no women to mourn in there,' Baldwin said.

'Aye, well, there has been enough thinking of men without women recently,' Sir Richard said more quietly.

'Sir Richard, you must not think I was passing comment on you,' Baldwin said. 'I was merely thinking of the Bishop and the Sheriff without a woman to grieve their passing.'

'It's all right, my friend. I didn't think that you were associating them with me,' Sir Richard said. 'But I *was* thinking of my wife when I was fightin' with that man Charles, and the poor woman I saved from his men. There are too many who are prepared to make use of any disturbance for their own advantage.' He looked over at Baldwin, and for once his face wore no smile. 'And that is why I am anxious to see him captured or killed. He's outlaw, so any can take his head off.'

'I will aid you as I may,' Baldwin said.

'It ain't just him, you realise. It's all to do with the release of Sir Edward of Caernarfon. While he's abroad, men like Sir Charles will try to return him to his throne. And that must mean more farmers killed, more widows made, more women raped, more orphans. I don't wish to see that.'

Simon whistled. 'And you were yourself a keen supporter of the old King.'

'Aye, Master Puttock,' Sir Richard said. There was no twinkle in his eye. 'But I am a still more keen supporter of the people in my own manor, and they will suffer if there's more bloodshed.'

Simon nodded, thinking of his own family. He hated to think that there could be war down here. In the last months he had seen rioting in London, and the murder of his friends. War had trampled the land with battles, sieges and death, and he wanted no more of it.

'It would be better that they were both captured quickly,' Baldwin said. 'Sir Charles is unpredictable – and while I supported Sir Edward, and was loyal to him and to my oaths, now I would prefer that he continue to remain in safe custody, rather than he should be loose, and persuaded by others who have their own motives.'

He was filled with displeasing thoughts, paying scant attention to the people who pushed and shoved about him, feeling an irrational anger – although whether it was focused at Sir Edward of Caernarfon, at the new King, at Sir Charles, or someone else, he could not tell. Perhaps it was Sir Charles, because he had disturbed Baldwin with his murder of Bishop James, who was by all accounts a thoroughly decent man and priest, and by his support of men who could rape and slay for profit. Sir Charles had always been a troubling companion, ever prepared for violence, but to see this man whom Baldwin had quite liked, a man who had a great strength of character and was himself a loyal friend, become outlaw for these appalling crimes, was depressing.

'What are the Watch doing about catching Sir Charles?' Baldwin muttered. He must accept the fact that he could not permit Sir Charles to live.

Not after murdering the Bishop and the Sheriff.

CHAPTER THIRTY-SEVEN

Marsilles' House

Philip Marsille was convinced he was right about Laurence and Gregory. There must be some way of proving his point, and he stood in the street, at the corner of the alley, for much of the morning, his eyes on the Paffards' door, in the hope of seeing Gregory.

It was almost the hour of the midday meal that he saw the fellow at last.

Gregory came from the house looking like a boy who had seen his favourite puppy killed, rather than a grown man. His father was in gaol, that was all – it was better than being orphaned, and Philip felt little sympathy as he levered himself upright and set off in pursuit.

In his mind, he saw Gregory beaten and bruised, kneeling at his feet, begging for forgiveness, pleading, offering money and treasure, perhaps houses too. The vision was delicious. And completely unrealistic, Philip knew. He had no idea what he intended to do. All he knew was, he needed revenge against the family which had killed his mother. He deserved justice, and if there was no other justice to be had, he would have to find it for himself.

Poor Juliana. Dying like that, alone, but so close to home in a shit-filled alley. The guilt of being absent when his mother needed him was a torch burning in his breast, consuming his soul.

It was clear Gregory was not thinking about being followed. He walked up Southgate Street to a small shop where there was a smith expert in making locks for doors. Soon Philip heard him shouting, demanding to know why his money was not as good as any other man's, but the locksmith's responses were too quiet for Philip to hear. When Gregory came out, he stared about him wildly, as if expecting a fresh disaster to strike him even now. He held his hands up to the heavens, and strode towards a tavern, diving inside like a man who needed a drink badly, and Philip was sorely tempted to enter with him, but rather than be observed, he waited outside.

He did not have to wait long. Soon, Gregory reappeared with a fresh determination. He strode up to Carfoix, and thence down along Southgate Street. But instead of heading to his home along Combe Street, he continued towards the massive gate itself. The inner face of the gate was ancient, much patched with fresh stone, but Gregory ignored it. Instead he went to the side, to Father Paul's church.

Gregory knocked on the door, and Philip threw himself to the other side of the road before he was seen. There were so many men and women streaming into the city along this road that concealment was easy enough. He saw the door open, and a moment later Father Laurence came out, pulling a hood over his head. He remonstrated with Gregory, apparently, but Gregory was obviously past caring, from the way he reached out to the vicar – but Laurence drew away, as though in revulsion, and Gregory's hand fell to his side. He looked crushed.

That was the moment, just a moment, when Philip felt a sharp sympathy flare. These two unfortunate men loved each other but could never be happy. On their faces he saw the same misery he had felt last Saturday, when Alice had rejected him . . . Then the moment passed, and instead he saw two men – unnatural, horrible men – whose lives were condemned. He had heard enough of priests, after all. He knew that they were often perverted. It was what came from having so many men living together in unnatural proximity, without women on whom to work their natural desires.

He didn't care. These two were despicable. That was clear to the meanest intelligence.

At that moment, Laurence and Gregory moved away together, both of them striding quickly up the hill again. Philip hurried after them.

City Gaol, East Gate

Baldwin was reluctantly persuaded to join Sir Richard and Simon in a tavern. They chose a small wine shop called the Goose's Flight on the High Street, but none of them was greatly cheered even by the good quality wine on sale. They all felt sombre after the funeral and their reflections afterwards.

'Come along, Sir Baldwin,' Sir Richard said. 'There's little chance of finding Sir Charles in this city, even if we are very lucky. The Watch and bailiffs are looking for him. They know what they're doing. We'll have a bite, and then go and help them as we may.'

Despite his cheery words, it was Sir Richard whose mood was most noticeably at odds with his usual good humour. He was angry that he and the others had all failed to kill Sir Charles when they had the opportunity, and the suspicion that Sir Charles had ridden into the city behind him left him simmering with anger. The man was making fools of them, or so Sir Richard felt.

The acts of the gang were disgraceful. He felt no sympathy for those whom he had killed or captured, ready to be hanged at the next opportunity, any more than he would have had for a fox that got in amongst his chickens. But the knight – he was more dangerous as a symbol: he was prosecuting a hard war for the man whom many still considered to be the rightful King. Including himself, he confessed wryly.

Baldwin, he could see, felt similar conflicts. They both had ties to Sir Edward of Caernarfon, after all. They had both given their oaths that they would do all in their power to support him, and at the last had failed.

'It will soon be over, Sir Richard,' Baldwin said, catching his eye. He tipped up his cup. 'With luck Sir Edward will be recaptured soon, and all these difficult choices will be gone.'

'Until then, I am left feeling like a knight who's not fulfilled his purpose,' Sir Richard said heavily. He gulped at his wine with a scowl. 'Where's that bastard Sir Charles now, I wonder?'

'Well,' Baldwin said, 'there is one thing we could do which might distract you. Visit Henry Paffard.'

'What are you suggesting?' Sir Richard asked. 'That he was forced to confess the crimes when he didn't commit them?'

Baldwin shook his head. 'There was no compulsion that I saw. He freely admitted to them.'

'Then what're you saying?' Sir Richard asked, frowning.

'Only that I do not understand his motives.'

'Oh, "motives"!' Sir Richard rumbled. 'I should have realised *that* word would rear its ugly head. You look for motives like a maid looks for raisins in her pudding, man! Little morsels to add sweetness to the tales of woe which you and I must hear. Perhaps it was sex, perhaps it was money? Who can tell what that diseased mind conceived of when he committed his deeds? No, believe me, old friend, when I say that you will win no accolades by seeking further truths about this man Paffard.'

'Perhaps not,' Baldwin said. 'But I would still know whether there was some reason why he should make love to Alice and then slay her, or why he would cut the lips from Juliana?'

'Don't forget that he stabbed Juliana in the eyes too,' Simon reminded him. 'Was this to indicate no talking and no looking? Or no talking about something she had seen?'

'Perhaps. But so far as we know, the women were neither of them a threat to him. If they were to accuse him, he could conspire with lawyers to have them imprisoned for their defamations. He was a rich, powerful man.'

'He felt guilt, perhaps?' Simon tentatively suggested.

'Guilt for killing the women?' Sir Richard said. 'Perhaps. Probably not though. His manner was perfectly composed. If I had my guess, I should say it was the certainty that his friends in the city would not hang him.'

'So you think he admitted to crimes, knowing he would be safe?' Baldwin said. 'Surely if he intended not to suffer the punishment, he would also have attempted to evade the suffering that comes from confessing to a crime? What would be the point of admitting that he was a murderer, in the hope he would be later found innocent?'

'Unless he thought he had no choice but to do so,' Simon said. He was frowning as he considered the implications of this. 'If he thought that someone else would be in danger . . .'

Baldwin caught his breath. 'Simon – that could be it! Perhaps he felt he was protecting his wife, or his sons, or daughter.'

'What's the reason for him doin' that?' Sir Richard mused.

Simon said, 'If someone had threatened his children unless he confessed, if he thought the threat were credible, that might make him admit to the crimes. But more likely it's because he thinks the murderer was someone close to him. And he sought to protect them.'

'And so the name Gregory comes to mind again,' Baldwin said.

Exeter Gaol at East Gate

When the man unlocked the trapdoor in the cell's ceiling, Henry Paffard had been dozing on his bench, trying not to think about the scurrying of rats' paws overhead.

In his home, Henry had rarely seen a rat. They were a nuisance when they managed to gain access to the grain store, or the flour, but they were not apparent most days except as a distant sound, as they tried to gnaw through a rafter, or when someone found a pile of droppings. Here, he had already discovered seven distinct creatures. Perhaps he should name them? He had the names of certain men in the Freedom of the City who merited being allied with rats.

'Please come down,' he said sarcastically as the gaoler stood peering in at the trapdoor. 'If you wish for wine or food, you are welcome to all I have.'

Baldwin pulled the trap wide and gazed down into the room. 'A repellent cell. It must be chill down there.'

Beneath the gaoler's chamber, the cell was little more than a pit with rock walls. Damp ran down into a channel that ran along one wall and away. It was a foul, repugnant little space.

'I believe most gaols have a similar elegance and style,' Henry said coldly. 'I had not anticipated the bed of an inn of quality when I came here.'

'You have enough food?'

'There is some greyish slop which my gaoler appears to consider has the merits of ambrosia.'

'Has your wife not brought you anything?' Simon asked.

Henry looked at him. 'If she has, I haven't seen it. I will ask her next time she visits. I will make sure of it!'

'We wish to speak with you. Come outside,' Baldwin said.

'I am honoured. But what could you wish with me?' Henry asked warily.

'We want to know why you lied to get yourself put into prison,' Baldwin threw over his shoulder.

Henry Paffard felt as though the walls of the gaol had collapsed about his ears.

Marsille' House

William had been at the row of merchants' shops in the High Street all morning, but there was no job going for an untrained youth. Since his mother's death the goldsmith had found another woman to run his house and taken on an apprentice and had no need of William. The latter was back at the bottom of the pile, and he returned home demoralised with the conviction that the world was determined to serve him ill.

He walked inside, his belly rumbling. Hunger was a terrible thing, and he had nothing to eat. He went to the cupboard where they had stored food before, but it was empty, and he stood staring at it with real desperation. He and Phil had lost everything. The only thing saving them was the generosity of the Paffards, Henry in particular, and with him in gaol after confessing to murdering their mother, that support was likely to end. No matter what Gregory must feel about William and Philip generally, the fact that his father was in gaol for their mother's killing was bound to affect him.

The hunger actually hurt – a sharp stabbing in his stomach.

It seemed as though his entire belly was caved in, and he wondered how much worse it would get as he began to die.

Once he had been given a loaf by Claricia Paffard. The thought sprang into his head that he could perhaps go to her again now. Maybe she would show him some mercy. Perhaps once she would have. But now their two families were associated with the horror of murder. William's family had provided the victim, while Claricia's husband was in gaol because of the death. Still, Claricia would feel remorse for her husband's crime, surely?

Filled with a ravenous resolve, he walked the short distance to the Paffards' house. Outside and staring up at it, he had a sinking feeling.

It was so large and imposing. No matter how brave he was when talking to others about how he would fight to make his way in the world, make his way in this city of his, there were times when it seemed impossible that he would ever manage. How could he, when he was starting with no father to guide him, no business, no profession or trade?

Slowly, he mounted the steps and made to knock on the door, but then his hand fell away without striking, and he stepped down again, kicking at stones in the street. His hands in his belt, he kicked again. He was a fool! Better that he and Phil should leave the town and go somewhere else, where they were not known. There were opportunities on the moors. They could both make their way to the rough lands, and eke out a living scraping tin from the ground. He had heard of men who had made vast sums in gold doing that. And as miners, they were servants of the Crown, so safer than other peasants.

Idly, he followed the pebble. It had gone into the alley where Alice's body had been found. He kicked the stone again, trailing after it disconsolately, past the place where Alice had lain.

There was nothing for either of them here in Exeter. The city was unforgiving towards men like them.

There came a rattle and squeak, and he saw that his stone had hit the gate that led to the Paffards' garden. It was ajar, and William could not help but set an experimental hand against it. There was a muted protest from the metal hinges, and then the wood submitted, and he found himself peering around it.

The garden was filled with small barrels and sacks, and his mouth watered to think of the food that must lie within. It was unfair that his belly was so empty when others had such plenty. He stepped in, warily looking about him. A second step, and his eyes were fixed on the barrels and sacks, thinking of the riches that lay inside. Surely those sacks held grain or flour, and the barrels contained pickled fish or salted meats, perhaps even almonds? The temptation was too profound. He could not help but submit.

He took a couple of quick paces, and bent to a barrel, and at that moment he was struck with the consequences of a theft here. Not only would he run the risk of eviction, the final disaster for Philip and him, but there was the probability that Gregory Paffard would prosecute him in the Sheriff's court and see him executed for the theft. No man could be permitted to rob another, and a fellow who stole from his neighbour's home was always considered the worst of all thieves. No one was safe from a drawlatch; such men caused alarm throughout the city.

No. He shouldn't do it. He was about to release the barrel when he heard a gasp, and turning, he saw the figure of the maid, Joan, in the doorway. Just behind her was John the bottler.

'What are you doing here?' John demanded loudly.

William shook his head, but guilt was in his steps as he walked backwards towards the gate. 'I was only trying to see Gregory, your master.'

'By walking in through the garden door? If you wanted the master, you should have called at the front door, like everyone else,' John said, advancing threateningly.

William backed away and took to his heels. He didn't stop running until he was back in his own house. There, he stood staring about him, filled with utter despair as the hunger gnawed at his belly.

CHAPTER THIRTY-EIGHT

Combe Street

Sir Charles walked up Southgate Street with a deliberately dragging step. He knew that men like Sir Baldwin were capable of recognising a man by his gait, and he had no desire to hand himself over to the other knight so easily. He reached Combe Street, and Ulric tugged his sleeve.

'This is it?' Sir Charles asked.

'Yes, sir. It's the street where Master Paffard lives.'

Sir Charles gazed about him with that open, smiling demeanour that had so distracted his enemies over the years. This was a good street. There were some shabby little buildings, true one little more than a hovel in which he would not have kept his pigs, but there were some great places on the north side, and he felt sure that Paffard's house would be one of these.

Ulric's arm came up to point out the house. Sir Charles placed his hand atop Ulric's wrist and jerked it down. 'No need to tell people what we do here,' he murmured, still smiling.

He told Ulric to wait, and made his way across the street,

avoiding the pony and cart that threatened him as he went, and he glared at the beast, wondering if it was one of the carts that had been taken from him yesterday. He didn't recognise it, however and on the board at the back was a pair of sacks that looked as though they were filled with flour. Not the gold and plate he was missing so grievously.

To think that this time yesterday he had been rich, he thought as he climbed the stairs. Well, with luck soon he would be able to get his hands on some money and then got out of this damned city. That would be good. He knocked loudly.

He would have liked to have exacted some form of revenge for the defeat inflicted upon him by Sir Baldwin and Sir Richard, but that would have to wait. Until Sir Edward was back on his throne perhaps.

The door opened, and he found himself looking into the face of an older man. 'Good day. I would like to speak with your master.'

'Master Gregory?'

'No, Henry Paffard,' Sir Charles said. His smile was unaltered, but he was aware of a sinking sensation in his bowels. 'Is he not here?'

'Sir, I fear Master Henry is in gaol for murder. He's waiting for his trial.'

'Who is responsible for his business now?' Sir Charles said, all trace of a smile eradicated.

East Gate

Simon had seen many men come from within a gaol, and generally such men looked unprepossessing and weary, all too often blinking in the flare of sunlight like blind men miraculously granted their sight again.

Henry Paffard was not like them. He strode out with his head high, and while he had no means of keeping himself clean, he had somehow contrived to avoid soiling his clothes or face. And he looked as easy in his mind as he had two days ago, before he confessed.

Either he was mad, Simon concluded, or he was a very extraordinary man indeed.

'I don't understand what you are saying,' he said coolly as he looked from one to the other. He shot a quick, eager look up the hill to Rougemont as if hoping for rescue.

Baldwin frowned at that. 'It is not the day of your hanging yet, Master Paffard. Although that will be soon enough.'

'Perhaps,' Henry said. He turned back to Baldwin with a slight puckering between his eyebrows. 'Well?'

'We wish to know why you say you killed those women.'

'Oh, is that it?' Henry said. He looked at them in turn again, a slight curl at his lip. 'And what then? You will offer me my freedom? Or food?'

'You said in there that you would be speaking to your wife about food,' Sir Richard said. He had a broad smile on his face. 'That is like a man saying that he'll go to the butcher to complain about the chop he ate last night. Except you can't, can you? If she won't come to visit you, you won't ever be able to chastise her again.'

'I am sure I will.'

'Why?' Baldwin asked. 'Why are you so certain that you will be able to escape your fate?'

Henry said nothing. Why should he tell them that when Edward was throned King again, with the help of his loyal subjects, pardons would be granted to those who had helped him. These fools had no idea. Just as they couldn't understand why he had taken it upon himself to accept responsibility.

'You see, we may be as foolish as you think us,' Baldwin

said, 'and that means we will be likely to make a silly assumption. For example, I may well believe that you confessed because you were intending to prevent another man from being accused. From all I have heard, you would be unlikely to do so unless the man at risk of being caught and punished were close to you. Man or *woman*, of course. It could be a wife or daughter – but it is more likely to be a son, I think.'

'So you think, eh?' Henry managed. The knight's words had hit home hard, and he had to force himself to keep looking at Baldwin without displaying emotion.

'It is clear enough that you don't want to die, I think,' Baldwin said, his head cocked to one side in appraisal. 'You have not submitted to despair, as men will when they are to die. You look like a man who has determined to shame himself, but you don't expect to die. I have no idea why.'

'I am a man of integrity.'

'No. You are a man of business,' Baldwin said harshly. 'They are different men, from different worlds. And your life is to end soon, with you unremarked as a felon, who deserves no sympathy.'

'I will be freed. You will see.'

'Really?' Sir Richard said. 'By whom, eh? The world is busy with other matters, Master Paffard. Not many wish to exert themselves on behalf of a fellow who murdered women. I had to slay a man yesterday because he joined others to rape and kill on the Bishop's manors. He helped to kill a woman too. No one raised a finger to help him either, so don't think anybody will to save you.'

Henry stared, and his mouth fell open a little. 'What man did you kill?'

'One of a gang of felons. Sir Charles of Lancaster led them. We destroyed them east of Exeter yesterday.'

'It's not true!'

Baldwin shook his head. 'If you were hoping for Sir Charles to come and save you, your hope is forlorn. Sir Charles fled. His carts are here at Rougemont, and he is a fugitive.'

'Sweet Jesus!' Paffard said, and in his eyes there was genuine horror. He turned and walked from them, back into the gaol, then down the ladder to his cell. 'I have nothing more to say to you. Any of you!' he roared. 'Leave me to prepare myself for death.'

Paffards' House

Sir Charles was led through to the hall. Claricia and Agatha were there, Claricia sitting, Agatha standing at her back.

'You are Madame Paffard? Henry Paffard's wife?' Sir Charles asked.

He was aware of the old man behind him, but was unconcerned. John wore no knife. If need be, he could have the elderly bottler dead before he could turn and run to the door. Sir Charles knew his abilities only too well, even after his mistake with Sir Richard.

'I am. Who are you?'

'I am a friend of his. Sir Charles of Lancaster.'

'I do not know you. If we owe you money, sir, I—'

'More than mere money, my lady, but it will do for now.'

'Then you will be disappointed. There is none.'

'Your husband promised me and my companions plenty, if we were to—'

'He could have promised you the sun and the moon and all the stars in the heavens, but it wouldn't change the fact that we have nothing. His business has failed in recent months, and while he was hoping for something to rescue him,' Claricia said, 'it too failed.'

'I was the rescue,' Sir Charles said. 'It was my business that was to have helped. And there is still time.'

He was unsure how far to unburden himself. This woman looked frail and agitated, while her daughter was a hard-faced harpy, from the look of her.

'My husband is in prison for murdering two women. He will never be released.'

'He may be proved innocent in court.'

'He has already confessed.'

Sir Charles shrugged. He had known others walk free after being found at the scene with the blade dripping blood still gripped in their hands.

'Where is he being kept?' he asked.

Marsilles' House

William was still standing in the chamber when there came a loud knock on his door. With a sigh of annoyance, he opened it wide. 'Well?'

There were three men outside, all rough, hardy-looking types. One pushed past William and snorted as he looked about him. 'Come on!'

'Who are you? What are you doing?' William demanded.

'You're being thrown out. Don't piss us about or it'll be painful.'

'No, Master Paffard told us we could stay. You've made a mistake. We're allowed to stay!' William said with desperation.

'Well, we've been told to get you out. We were told today. Now, out of my path, boy.'

'It's a mistake. Come with me now and speak with Master Gregory. Leave my things and come with me!'

William had grabbed the man's wrist, where he had taken hold of a chair. This man must surely see it was a mistake! The Paffards wouldn't throw them from here, not really.

343

The man turned lazily and swung his other fist into the side of William's head.

It was as if he'd been hit with a club. A dull thud set his teeth rattling, and his legs wobbled as though their muscles were turned to blancmange. He collapsed to his knees, gripping the table, eyes wide.

'You don't listen, do you? We were called to Paffards' place and told to get you out. You're not wanted any more, boy, so like I said, piss me about and you'll regret it. Now, out of my way!'

Talbot's Inn

Gregory Paffard had remained in the tavern for an age after Father Laurence left him, but he didn't touch the ale before him. It tasted sour, just as did everything that touched his tongue today.

Until only a short while ago, he had been a contented, successful young man. What, was it a year, or more, since he had realised? Perhaps longer, but it was not until he and Agatha had met with Father Laurence that he truly understood the horror of his situation. He could never be happy. Laurence had told him. The bastard didn't even shed a tear, showed no sympathy. Nothing. Just a blank face that concealed his true feelings.

Gregory groaned. He was cursed! All his life he had craved love, and now he had found it, now he had learned how glorious and fulfilling it could be, he was to be deprived of it. That was what Laurence said: Gregory must part from his lover forever. They must be separated, Laurence told him, for the sake of their eternal souls. Perhaps a life of penance could save them.

He was himself God's finest joke. A man with free will who willingly chose a path of heretical crime.

Leaving the ale, he rose and staggered from the room. The coolness of the air outside acted upon him and he felt as though he was a little mad. People looked at him differently, he was sure, with a kind of horror, as if he wore the leper's cloak. There was nothing for him. Better to go and hang himself. Suicide was a sin, true, but no worse than the one he had already committed.

Standing at the corner of the High Street and Cooks' Row, he had to clutch hold of the nearest wall to support himself. A wave of nausea washed through his body and he wanted to spew. It was only the looks of curious passers-by that stopped him. He forced himself upright, and was about to walk off, when Benjamin hurried up to him.

'Master Henry wants you to go and visit him, sir. He said it's very important you go right away.'

Paffards' House

Thomas kicked the ball again.

There was nothing he liked as much as this. A sunshiny day, with a ball and a wall to kick it against. He booted it hard, and it catapulted behind him, narrowly missing his head, which made him laugh in exhilaration as he chased the ball, and kicked it again. It went high, hit the wall and fell in among the herbs. He looked quickly over his shoulder to make sure Sal hadn't seen it, but there was nobody there in the doorway, and he scuttled over to it, his quick pang of guilt soon forgotten.

He played a while longer before the ball soared high, and then landed again beside the bottler's store-shed.

Thomas walked to it, and knelt again. That broken board was so tempting.

Joan said, 'So, still trying that piece of wood?' She had come out quietly with an armful of clothes, which she was soaking in water from the well, and she chuckled to see his look of comical alarm. Both were recovering from their fears of the last few days.

He sprang up and clutched his ball to his breast as though it was a shield against any adult recrimination.

'Don't worry, Tommy. I won't tell him. I don't think it's as dangerous as he says anyway.'

Gradually the hunted look left his face, and he wiped at his cheeks, aware that they felt very hot after his exertions. He returned to kicking the ball, but every so often his eyes went to that appealing gap in the timbers, and at last he couldn't resist another look.

He went and peered inside. There was something gleaming dully in the gloom. Perhaps if he just got his arm in . . . But no, it didn't reach.

With a look at Joan, he began to squirm his legs in first, to get in there and find out what it was that lay beneath.

And then he screamed.

CHAPTER THIRTY-NINE

Marsilles' House

Philip had given up. He had followed Gregory and Laurence up the street to Bolehill Lane, but there he lost them among the milling crowds. Giving up, he walked into an alehouse and drank a quart of strong ale, then bought a meat coffin from a cookshop and ate it on his way back down the road. That was the last of his money, so carefully saved.

On entering the alley to his house, he stopped, aghast. 'Whatever's happening?' he cried.

All their furniture – the chairs, table, cupboard, everything – was sitting out there in the filth. 'Will! Where are you? What on earth is going on?'

There was a rattle at a door, and he saw Emma de Coyntes peering at him.

'Philip, I am sorry,' she said. 'I had nothing to do with this, you have to believe that. They have ordered that you be evicted. You haven't paid them rent for a long time, and they are demanding that you leave.'

'Who is this "they"? The Paffards wouldn't do this to us. No! Is it Gregory?'

It made no sense. Had Gregory ordered their eviction before he left his house, before Philip started to follow him down the road?

'I don't know. William was here, but he's run off, I don't know where he's gone.'

'Will's gone?' Philip was staring at her. He could not understand what was happening, and then it was as if a hammer had struck inside his brain, and he was filled with a righteous fury. 'Who said they could do this? Isn't it enough that they have already seen us ruined?'

'It wasn't their fault, Philip,' Emma argued. 'Look, come inside with us for a little while. There's nothing out here for you. You know that Henry—'

'Not their fault? No, but they haven't helped as much as they could have,' Philip snarled. The anger was making his heart feel hot, like steel at the forge. It seemed to him that it must burst from his chest at any moment. 'My father was a good friend to Henry Paffard, and where does it leave us? Deserted, left in the street, our belongings all gone. What sort of a friend would treat his friend's family in such a way? My father thought he was leaving us in the care of someone who would protect us. Now my mother's dead, my brother's fled, and look at me! *No* future, *no* trade, *no* chances of making a life for myself, let alone for any other. Not that there is another, now Alice has died.' His voice broke with grief.

'Come in here,' she said again. 'Please, calm yourself before the bailiffs hear you and have you taken for breaking the peace.'

'Go with *you*? It was you who complained to Paffard about us in the first place. It was you telling tales about my mother that us caused to be threatened with eviction, wasn't it?'

Emma flinched.

'Well, I congratulate you, Mistress de Coyntes. You've succeeded! You are rid of us at last.'

She bridled, her own rage ignited in the face of his attitude. 'You want me to apologise? When your mother was so rude to my little Sabina that she cried for an hour afterwards? You expect everyone else about here to run after you – to dish out money and food and gifts – but when your friends try to have a quiet time of things, what do you do? You insult us and annoy us, and think you can just get away with it, don't you? Well, you can't.'

'That's it, is it? You asked me in because you were feeling guilty about us, nothing more. No sympathy or genuine Christian charity, just scared for your own soul. Well, I hope you can live with yourself after this, woman, because you'll get no sympathy from me when your life is altered.'

'Our life altered?' she jeered. '*My* husband is a *good* provider for us.'

'What does that mean?' Then he gasped. 'Do you insult my father now? Have you no shame, mistress? You would insult a dead man to his son?'

'Oh, in God's name, boy, take a look at yourself. Listen to yourself! A beardless boy with no means of earning a living, and all you can do is snarl and make a show. If you were half a man, you'd go out and achieve something without others constantly having to do it all for you!'

'Do what for me? Forcing me to lose my home by complaining to my landlord?' he demanded.

'Oh, get out of here, *boy*! Go on! Take your rubbish and clear off. This isn't your home, not any more,' she spat, pointing down the alley.

He turned from her and strode away, ire lending wings to his feet, but as he reached the road, the tears were already stinging. There was no way Philip would allow them to fall. He was too proud for that. It was little enough, perhaps, but his pride was all he possessed now, and he would not give it up.

There was a cart rolling past the entrance to the alley, and he waited until it had gone, and then marched on resolutely to the Paffards' house, where he ascended the steps and knocked loudly on the door.

John the bottler appeared in the doorway after a long wait, and Philip swallowed and asked to see Gregory.

'He's not here just now, master. He went out this hour past.'

'Then may I speak to Claricia?'

John nodded thoughtfully, and shut the door. After another wait, he returned and jerked his head inside, down the passageway.

Philip followed him along the flagged way until they came to the hall. Inside Philip saw Claricia sitting huddled.

'John said you wanted me,' she said without looking up.

'Mistress, all our belongings are in the alley. Your son had men throw us from our house . . .'

'Not Gregory, no. It was me,' Claricia said. There was no emotion in her tone.

'But why? We cannot survive without a home, mistress.'

'Remember the old friary up beyond Saint Nicholas's Priory? Since the friars moved out beyond the walls, there are places to sleep there.'

He knew that area. The friars had taken down the stones to move them to their new friary. What was left was a miserable collection of rough chambers constructed of old boards and planks, with sometimes a waxed cloak thrown over the top. The poorest of the city lived there, the beggars and drunks who could find no other place to rest their heads.

'You would leave us there? What have we done to you?' he pleaded.

'You have done nothing,' Claricia said. She lifted her faded eyes to him, and he saw that they were red from weeping. Her cheeks were sunken, and she looked as though she had become an ancient crone in the last two days. 'It is not you, master, it is us. My husband. He has ruined you. When your father died, Henry took the money left for you, and invested it for his own advantage. I know it has happened before, and it will again, but today it means you have nothing because my husband took it all. And I cannot repay you. That would impoverish my son. It would take my daughter's dowry and leave her without a husband. So, for my family to survive, yours must be utterly ruined.'

He stared, uncomprehending, wondering how she could be inventing all this. And then he saw the papers on the table behind her. 'You mean this? He stole all our money? What of the house? Our gold?'

'It is gone, Philip. All gone. Henry took it all and lost it.'

Exeter Gaol

Gregory paid the gaoler to let him see his father, and was soon inside, wincing at the stench, but then he burped as some of the ale returned. He reeled a little passing down the ladder, but his father didn't notice.

'Father?'

Henry Paffard looked at him and said nothing for a moment. Then, 'I have been told that Sir Charles of Lancaster's men were killed and that he's gone on the run. Is this true?'

'Yes. They were caught over east and mostly killed, from all I've heard,' Gregory said.

He could hardly believe the change in his father. Henry was grey about the face, and whereas in the past he had always been a strong, resolute man with the suave manner of a lord – because in many ways he *was* a lord to the people of Exeter – now he looked like a common churl from the streets. His was the first family among those of the rich men who ruled the city, and his assurance and patrician manner had served to add to that aura. And all now was gone.

'Then we are ruined, Gregory. My money was invested in Sir Charles and the others. God's ballocks, I was so *stupid*!'

'I don't understand.' Gregory was close to hiccuping, and had to put a hand over his mouth as another wave of ale washed up through his system. The atmosphere in the cell made him feel as though he might choke.

'You understand *nothing*, do you?' his father groaned. 'I promised to help the men who have released Sir Edward of Caernarfon from his prison. I was going to be repaid handsomely, and you would have gained a knighthood when he returned to the throne. Think of that, my son! The first of our family to be raised to the chivalry! And now Sir Charles – the man I thought would come here and save me – is dead, and that means all I paid to him is also gone. We are lost, Gregory.'

'You have been a traitor to our King?' Gregory said disbelievingly.

'We only have the one King. This boy on the throne is no more our King than you are,' Henry growled. 'He deposed his own father, at the behest of that bitch his mother and her lover. They have no right to say the boy is King. Only God has that authority.'

Gregory passed a hand over his brow. He was sweating. 'Why are you here, Father? Why did you confess?'

Henry looked up at the ceiling of the chamber. Like him, it was old, worn, on the verge of collapse. 'It seemed the best thing to do.' Then: 'Gregory, I know it was you – you who killed Alice. Why did you do that, son? She wasn't hurting you, was she? I suppose you heard she wanted a house of her own. She would not have damaged our family. I thought if you were captured for the crime, you might be slain too quickly, but that if I confessed, I could count on the men of the Freedom to protect me, especially since I knew that Sir Charles was on his way. That was what I *thought*,' he said bitterly.

'You *knew* Sir Charles was here?'

'Of course I did! I sent him messages with Ulric. How else do you think he would know when the Bishop was on his way to the manor at Petreshayes?'

'But . . . you were going to set him upon the Bishop? Why?' Gregory's eyes were stretched wide.

'Can you imagine how much money there would be in that? I was going to win back all I had paid with good interest.' For one second, Henry looked animated.

'But . . . a *Bishop*!'

'Oh, I would have been pardoned on my deathbed. It was all arranged. The new Bishop would be approved by our King, once he had regained his throne and removed his son, and the new Bishop would be more amenable to my part in the over-throw of his predecessor.'

Gregory could only stare. He had never realised that his father was so ruthless.

'But I still don't understand. Why did you confess in the first place, Father? Why not just deny it all?'

'Because I couldn't see you in gaol, Gregory. Dear Christ, don't you realise? I know all about you, you're my son. My *son*! I knew you killed them both. I couldn't see why, but you were obviously guilty. If they'd arrested you instead of me, you would be dead by now!'

'But I had nothing to do with any of it, Father. Please believe me: *I* didn't kill them.'

Henry stared at him, and in his eyes Gregory saw his own despair mirrored perfectly.

'You mean I did all this for nothing?' he said brokenly. 'Sweet Jesus!'

Paffards' House

John was in his buttery, but he could not settle.

It was most curious. Since the deaths of Alice and Juliana he had felt a kind of heightened tension, as though his life was edging towards its climax. A not unpleasant feeling. He had lived a good life, after all. A life of service and duty, which meant much. There were so many who sought only their own self-advancement, through corruption or theft. He was proud to be different.

The air was warm, and he took off his heavy robe, setting it on his hook. As he did so, his keys were pulled from his belt, and he took them up, placing them on the protruding peg in the wall. He often rested them here – it was a convenient place so he wouldn't forget them.

Then he eased himself down on his stool, back against the wall, legs on a small cask, and closed his eyes. He did feel enormously tired today. A rest would not hurt . . .

High Street

'Why are we here?' Simon asked as Baldwin and he walked to the Guild Hall and entered, Sir Richard following.

'There must be some reason for Henry Paffard to have confessed to two murders that he did not commit,' Baldwin said. 'If we can find out why he would do such a thing, that motive may itself help us with resolving these matters.'

'Go on,' Sir Richard boomed, gazing about him with approval.

'If he was protecting his son, for example,' Baldwin said. 'If his son were to confess, that would lead to a speedy resolution.'

'Seems unlikely to me,' Sir Richard decided. 'The man is typical of a newly rich merchant – a nasty piece of work and dishonest too: little better than a picklock. The sort of churl who will only speak when his clerk's beside him counting the number of words so they can charge later.'

Baldwin grinned, then: 'You don't think he would be loyal to his son? Paternal love is a force in its own right, after all.'

'From the look of him, no,' Sir Richard said bluntly. 'He struck me more the type who'd stab his own son if he thought he could sell the skin to a tanner for tuppence.'

'I wonder . . .' Baldwin said. 'I have known men like this before, and while they show little affection in public, in private they can be as devoted as any.'

'Even men as stiff and unbending as that prick Henry? You saw how he was just now.'

'Yes,' Baldwin said simply. A clerk in a corner of the main hall directed the three to a house a few doors along the High Street. At one side of it was a shop – clearly successful from the number of men standing at the wares. Beside this broad front was a dark door, where Baldwin knocked; a maid ushered them into a large room.

This was a modern house filled with all the trappings of wealth. The timbers were new, the oak a shining gold, the daub all limewashed until it sparkled, while on one wall a series of paintings showed the religious sensitivities of the owner. A large sideboard was filled with silver and pewter, and the glass in the window showed how the owner could afford the best. Not for him mere waxed sheets. He had paid a plumber to fit the glass together to stop the draughts.

When he entered, it was to this panel of bright glass that he walked, as though to ensure that they all noticed how splendid his house was.

He was a short man, but very lithe and taut as a bowstring, Simon thought. With his rich tunic and coat with fur at throat and hem, he could have been a lord, especially with the jewelled rings at his fingers. He had a narrow, contemplative face, under grey hair, with kindly eyes set deeply, and he looked like someone who would be hard to shock or even surprise. His complexion was slightly pale, as though he was recovering from a malady, but there was no shaking or tension in him.

'Sir Baldwin,' he said with a short bow.

'Master Chepman. I hope I find you well?'

'As well as can be hoped with the state of the kingdom,' the merchant replied. 'How may I help you?'

Simon remembered meeting this man some years before, during the Christmas celebrations, but it was clear that life had been kind to him since then. When Simon met him last, Luke Chepman had been setting out as a new member of the Freedom. Now, he gathered, Chepman was one of the four stewards. As such he was one of the most powerful businessmen in the city. There were few who wielded as much authority.

'We are here about Henry Paffard, Master Chepman.'

'Oh, yes. An unpleasant character. Did he really kill those women?'

'He says he did.'

'I know. That wasn't what I asked,' Chepman said with a thin smile.

He went on to tell them all he knew. 'I have never liked Henry. He is one of those men who tempts you to count your fingers after shaking hands. Exceedingly ruthless, even for a merchant used to dealing overseas. Such men have to be used to negotiate with some of our most difficult clients – but in his case, he would always appear to strive to get the better of a man for no other reason, I believe, than to demonstrate his own superiority. How often would a merchant ask to be reimbursed for the cost of candles while tallying his cargo! Henry did that to me once. Only once, mind,' Chepman said with a small smile. 'Besides, I am fortunate in that I am rich enough now to be able to ignore men like him. But he is clearly in real trouble this time. Murder is a serious business.'

'He confessed.'

'Which did surprise me. The Freedom would have done all it could to protect him.'

'Would it still?'

Chepman smiled again, but there was a depth of cynicism in his eyes. 'Sir Baldwin, would you defend a man who told you that he had killed your wife? No. Juliana, whom he claims to have killed, was the widow of a friend of Paffard's. Nicholas Marsille was not so very competent at his trades, but he was a man of his word, and respected. Their family was popular, and it was a shock when Marsille died suddenly.'

'How did he die?'

'There was no foul play, if that is what you mean! He saw a woman drop a babe into the road, and being Nicholas, he wanted to help. A horse was coming close, and Nicholas leaped into the brute's path to save the child. As a result, he was himself killed. It was just an unfortunate accident.'

'But little remained of his estate to pass on?'

'There were many who were prepared to help the family, naturally. But Nicholas had long worked with Henry Paffard, and when he died, Henry volunteered to help. He said that he would see to all their debts. And he did. He arranged for all Nicholas's debts and outstanding payments to be paid. Some, no doubt, tried to take more money than they were entitled to. I know that Henry tried to protect Juliana and the others from that. I saw men who were prevented.'

'But you had suspicions, from what you say?'

'Nothing firm. But the family seemed to lose all their treasure. And now they are living on the charity of the Paffards. To me, it seems curious.'

'So you believe that Henry Paffard took their money deliberately to rob them.'

Chepman shrugged. 'Sir Baldwin, this is the purest speculation, of course.'

'And let me speculate further. You think that he might have admitted he killed the women because he was ashamed and felt his guilt?'

'No – I doubt he was at all worried about them. I don't believe he feels any guilt about the fate of the Marsilles,' Chepman said, and coldness had crept into his voice. 'I think that the whole idea of guilt is hard for him to comprehend. No, he confessed because he felt it was just another deal and he expected to escape. He never thought the great Henry Paffard would remain in prison.'

'But he would have to!' Simon expostulated. 'How could he think he would get away with this?'

Chepman looked at him. 'An example would be Sir Hugh le Despenser: he was guilty of stealing from people for many years, Master Puttock, and he carried on doing so, without concealing his thefts, and without any punishment. I do not doubt that Henry Paffard believed he could get away with it too.'

CHAPTER FORTY

Cock Inn

'So, brother,' Philip said as he saw William sitting on a bench by the wall. 'I hope you are well?'

'You know about the house?'

Philip sat beside his brother and took up his drinking horn. It held a rough, sour ale that to Philip's mind was probably off, but he drank it anyway. He had need of it today. 'I know of them both.'

'Both?'

'I spoke just now to Madame Paffard with a view to trying to talk her into letting us stay, but she said no. And then she began to tell me how her husband had stolen all our money. Our father left us with plenty to keep us, Will. It was Paffard who embezzled it all. And the superb irony is, not only did he do so, but then he made us take his own hovel and pay him rent. A perfect theft.'

William looked at him. 'And he got away with it? He robbed us blind and walked away?'

'And now he'll die, but we'll still be poor,' Philip nodded. He drank more of the ale. 'This tastes better if you drink enough,' he mused.

'Enjoy it while you can. I can't afford another,' William said, eyeing the remains of his drink with regret. 'That's the end to my money. My last farthing.'

'What will we do, brother?' Philip said.

'I wish I knew.'

'If I could find a sword, I'd go to the King.'

'You've said that before, but you still don't know one end of a sword from the other,' William pointed out.

'That's unkind.'

'It's still true.'

Philip passed him the drinking horn to finish. 'I think we should find out if we can recover even a little of our money, Will. I don't want to die knowing we were robbed and our mother died in poverty without trying to do something about it.'

'What can we do?'

Philip frowned. 'We could speak to Gregory. I was trying to follow him this morning because . . .' Memory of the look in Gregory's eye came to him, and he murmured, 'There may be a way we could persuade him to give us money.'

'Who?'

'Master Gregory. I think he may be willing to pay us to keep quiet.'

Paffards' House

There was a squeal at the rear of the house, and John leaped up, disorientated for a moment. Then he yawned, rubbed the sleep from his eyes and hurried off to find the source of the noise.

In the garden, he found Joan comforting little Thomas.

'What is it with the boy?' John demanded, still feeling the effects of a shattered rest.

'He fell over, that's all,' Joan said, wiping at the lad's face. She did not look up at him.

'Was he playing in my shed? Or beneath it? It's dangerous there, as you know.'

Joan shook her head. 'Of course not. He was being sensible and careful, but something cut him when he fell.'

'Oh. Is he badly injured?'

'A nasty cut in his knee,' she said. 'There must have been something there.'

'Where was it?'

'There, by your storeroom,' she said, pointing with her chin.

John walked to it, and prodded carefully with his foot. 'Ah, it's a piece of metal from an old barrel,' he said. He bent and picked it up. With his back to them, he frowned. 'You should take him inside, and wash the wound with egg-white, Joan. The metal is rusty, and we don't want the boy to get lockjaw.'

Joan agreed. She had seen a man lose his leg from a small scratch before. This was deeper than a scratch, and possibly more dangerous. She bundled the shivering Thomas up in her arms and hurried inside, sitting him on the table in the brewery, where there was a copper of hot water, and she moistened the edge of her apron in it and dabbed it on his knee.

Thomas sniffled and moaned, but Joan wiped until she was satisfied that the worst of the mud was cleaned from the wound, and then she went to Sal and took an egg, breaking it into a pot and using her fingers to smear the white all over the wound. She wrapped a strip of linen about it and stood back to eye the results.

John was in the doorway. 'It was a bad cut, wasn't it?' he said to the boy: In his hands he held a rusted piece of metal that might have been a cooperage band a long time ago. 'It must have fallen from a barrel many years ago. I am sorry, Master Thomas. I should have seen it, and not left it to hurt you.'

He gave him an apple, smiled in a fatherly manner and walked away.

'There you are, pet,' Joan said, and she cuddled the boy. But she had a frown on her face. The wound on Thomas's knee was one with very straight edges, as if cut by a sharp blade on Sal's table, not by a rough piece of rusted metal. But she had enough on her plate already without searching for a shard of sharp steel.

Exeter Gaol

'Father, in God's name how could you believe I'd have killed them' Gregory hissed. 'Why'd I have done that?'

Henry sighed heavily. 'It was hard to see you like that. I know you didn't realise. Perhaps it was Thomas who brought it all home to me – how you spent all your time with Agatha when you were little, whereas Thomas is always happier outside with a ball and sticks, playing rough and tumble and getting into mischief. I should have seen it before, but I never thought a son of mine would turn out this way.'

Gregory was hot, and there was a stickiness about his upper body that was horribly uncomfortable. 'I don't even know what you mean,' he said, his throat dry.

'You will have to marry and hope that this . . . this aberration ceases,' Henry said.

'Father, I cannot help my love any more than I can help breathing,' Gregory said quietly.

'No, you don't love,' Henry said, shaking his head. 'You cannot. This perversion is not love.'

'Father, I . . .' It was a shock to know that his father had guessed his secret, but that Henry would have confessed to protect him – that was extraordinary. 'I feel the same as you do towards your women, believe me.'

Henry fixed his son with a furious stare. 'You speak of things you have no understanding about, Gregory! A man and a woman, they *should* have feelings for each other. They *should* enjoy their lust. It's natural – *normal*! But men? No. It's against every law of nature and—'

'Men?' Gregory blurted.

'I know about you and Father Laurence.'

Gregory could think of nothing to say, other than, 'Laurence is a priest.'

'He's an unnatural and depraved bitch-son to tempt you. Has he . . . Have you . . .'

'We have done nothing. And will do nothing,' Gregory added flatly. The heat was gone, and now he felt as cold as if the chamber was made of ice. His head was swimming.

'You swear this?'

Gregory turned away. For a space all that he could hear was his own heart. He had to think quickly. 'I swear it,' he said. 'I saw him today and he said we must not meet again. I agreed with him.'

'Then at least the sodomite shows some sense,' Henry said. His voice was cool again, his mind already on other matters. 'Now, Gregory, you will have to take over the business, at least for now. And you will need to find me a pleader to argue my case in front of the Sheriff, and—'

'He's dead. We have no Sheriff.'

'Christ's soul! Are you serious?'

'Sir Charles killed him.'

'This could be disastrous for me. I can't stay in here! I have to get out!'

'All the men who could fill his place are in the north with the King,' Gregory said soothingly. 'There will be no court for some time.'

'Hell's ballocks! I'm not rotting in here while they play with fighting in the north! Find me a pleader, Gregory,' Henry said. 'And not some prick-for-brains like the arse in the Guild Hall! I want my freedom back. I cannot stay while they wait for news of a replacement Sheriff.'

'I will do what I can,' Gregory promised.

Henry looked at him, and in his face there was some of the old fire again. He ran his fingers through his hair. 'I am here because I thought I was protecting you. And you tell me you are innocent of the murders. In that case, who *did* kill those women?'

'I had thought it was you, Father,' Gregory admitted. 'I didn't hurt either of them. I promise, if I can find the real killer, I will prove you were innocent and have you released.'

'Perhaps,' Henry said, but there was a cynical smile on his face. 'Except you forget that I have actually confessed. I was fortunate that I wasn't dragged to the Heavitree gallows that same day. Trying to win my release will not be easy.'

'I'll tell them that—'

'That I lied to protect my son? Because I thought you were a murderer, or a sodomite?' Henry asked sarcastically. 'Since both offences will have you hanged, I should be cautious before I used such an argument in public, Gregory.'

Gregory embraced his father and then withdrew from the gaol. Outside, he bent over and threw up, the sour taste of the pints of ale revolting. He wiped his mouth with his sleeve, feeling hot and shivery, but cleansed.

Despite all his problems, at least he was free. His father, on the other hand, might well die soon.

CHAPTER FORTY-ONE

High Street

After leaving Master Chepman's house, Baldwin and Simon were about to head up towards Carfoix when Sir Richard crossed the road and called to them to follow him. He dived down a little alley near St Petrock's Church. Halfway down there was a little door, upon which he knocked; when it opened, he plunged inside.

Simon exchanged a glance with Baldwin before following him down a flight of stairs to an undercroft. To their surprise, they found themselves in a large chamber, once used as a storage room, with a bar set out and benches placed all around the walls. A heavy-set landlord with a square, scarred face stood at the row of barrels wiping his hands on his shirt.

'My host, a trio of your best ales,' Sir Richard called from the entrance, and strode over to a pair of benches.

The landlord, grumbling to himself, obeyed the knight as Simon and Baldwin sat opposite him.

'Ah, this is a good tavern. I was here once and a man who was visiting saw another fellow who looked just like himself, except he came from Bordeaux. Could have been brothers, apart from that. Anyway, this foreigner frowned at the local, and said, "Tell me, fellow, did your mother ever travel to Bordeaux? You look so much like me". And the Devon man looked back and said, "No, but my father often did". Eh? You see? Hah!'

Baldwin smiled thinly. Sir Richard's sense of humour had clearly returned. The big knight leaned forward, elbows on his massive knees. 'Well? I would think that Henry Paffard deserves all he gets if he remains in gaol.'

'He is one of the most deserving fellows for a prison I could have thought of,' Baldwin agreed.

'Even in a city like this, there can be few men who would take advantage of his wards to the extent he has. He has robbed them of everything,' Simon grunted.

Sir Richard leaned back and surveyed the other two. 'So, are ye saying we should allow him to die on the rope, then, even though he is innocent of the murders, because he's done things in his time that make him fully deserving of the rope?'

'No,' Simon said firmly. 'I don't think so. I wouldn't mind his execution because I don't like him, but it isn't my place to make a judgement.'

'No, and I'm glad it's not mine either,' Sir Richard said firmly. 'But I am more exercised by the other aspect of this whole sorry affair, which is, that if Paffard *is* innocent, we still have to find the actual murderer.'

'It is of no matter to me what happens to Henry Paffard,' Baldwin said. 'All we have heard shows him to be a ruthless cheat, an adulterer, a bully, and a thief. But I will find the killer of those women, no matter what. If it was him, so much the better. But if another, I will do all in my power to capture him instead.'

'Then we need to return, I think, to the places where the women died and see if there is something we missed,' Sir Richard said. He looked up as the landlord approached with three jugs and cups. 'Thank you, host. Your ale is always a delight to a poor fellow with a raging thirst.'

Simon took a cautious swig of the ale. It was strong, sweet, and very easy to drink, he found.

Baldwin took a sip and coughed behind his hand. 'Dear God in heaven, that's potent!'

'Hmm?' Sir Richard took a deep quaff and smacked his lips. 'Ah, as good as I recall from my last visit. Host, you keep a good barrel in your hostelry.'

'Thank you, sir.'

'So, gentles, how shall we go about this?'

Baldwin looked at Sir Richard's round, honest face, and considered. 'As you say, we must return to that location. It is clear that the murderer was someone local. But why commit two murders within a few yards of each other? It makes little sense. And a motive is entirely lacking. The maid, Alice, was not disliked by any that we have heard.'

'Except,' Simon ventured, 'Claricia Paffard must have felt some resentment towards the woman who had ensnared her husband, mustn't she? It is one thing for a man to take a wench in a tavern, but inside his own house? How very humiliating for her.'

'She was very quiet.' Baldwin recalled again the time when his wife Jeanne had been similarly silent after his infidelity. The hurt he had inflicted had caused her to withdraw for some time.

Sir Richard grunted agreement and stretched his legs,

draining his jug and holding it up for the landlord. 'How would your wife respond, Simon?'

'She would be driven to hurling plates and cups at my head, I think,' Simon grinned.

'But Claricia seemed to have been ground down by her husband,' Baldwin said. 'Her manner was that of a woman driven to extreme despair. Would you agree, Simon?'

'I suppose so. She was certainly all but silent whenever I saw her,' Simon nodded. 'And always in the background.'

'And if she had developed an extreme hatred for the maid who was the cause of her humiliation, she might just take it into her head to murder her,' Baldwin said. 'Alice was stabbed in the breasts – perhaps as a comment on her sexual incontinence? If Mistress Paffard wished revenge on her rival, that might be a way to resolve it.'

'What of the second woman?' Sir Richard asked.

'She was mutilated too, was she not?' Baldwin said. 'She had both lips cut away as though to stop her talking, but she was also stabbed in the eyes.'

'Perhaps Madame Paffard heard that the woman was gossiping about Alice and Henry, and she felt so ashamed and embarrassed that she killed Juliana in a manner designed to put others off from talking of the affair.'

'There is the one problem,' Simon reminded them. 'The priest. Father Paul saw Henry Paffard return wearing that cloak just as the alarm was given about Juliana's death.'

'Aye,' Sir Richard agreed sombrely. 'That is an indication that Henry Paffard was the guilty one.'

'No,' Baldwin said thoughtfully. 'It only means that he returned to the house after the murder. We don't know exactly how long after, nor do we know who else could have been out at a similar time. Anyone could have donned his cloak. But surely it was a man who attacked the priest. Even a priest would be able to tell the difference between a man and a woman, surely?'

Simon nodded. 'So, I suppose we should return to the street now and ask him. Only Father Paul can help us there.'

'Very well.' Baldwin sighed, closed his eyes and finished his cup.

'You wish for no more to do with the matter?' Simon queried as they rose and left the tavern.

'I wish only to return to my home and to see my family,' Baldwin said truthfully. 'We have been forced to travel too much over the last years. For my part, all I wish for now is a peaceful time in my home. I would even surrender my position as Keeper. I no longer need such onerous duties.'

He looked up at the sun, and felt the heat on his face. It felt good, and he thought again of his wife Jeanne, her brilliant red-gold tresses, her beauty, and he felt only a sad certainty that no matter what he wished, his life would never be a quiet one.

Paffards' House

Back in his buttery, John the bottler set the rusted piece of metal on the bench, looking behind him into the passageway to make sure that no one was watching him. Then he carefully reached into the fold of his tunic where he had hidden the dagger.

The blade was smeared and clotted with dried blood, and he eyed it with distaste. He must clean it back to the dull steel and then get rid of it. He couldn't keep it about him. Ever since that damned Keeper had described it in such fine detail at the first inquest, he had known he must dispose of it. How it had come free, he didn't know. He had carefully pressed it beneath the shed's floor, safe with the other secrets there, in the certainty that no one would ever find it again. But here it was. Perhaps young Master Thomas had been playing there again. John had done all he could to dissuade the lad from going near the shed, but he was a boy, and boys tended always to go where they were not permitted. The little brute could have pried a board loose and tried to worm his way inside, even after all the warnings. Then, when he cut himself, the movement of his legs had brought the dagger out to the open, where John had found it. Or maybe it was only the action of rats pulling it out.

It was fortunate that he had discovered that rusted cooperage nearby to explain the injury.

John replaced the blade in his tunic and considered. There was one good aspect, of course. If the boy had been trying that, he had at least probably convinced himself that he should not play there again. And that was all to the good.

All the same, he would take a hammer and some new wood to where those lower planks had rotted. He didn't want any more incidents like this.

Exeter Gaol

Sir Charles and Ulric arrived at the gaol after purchasing some bread and cheese and eating it on their way. It was as they were passing down the next street, Sir Charles following Ulric, who knew this city better than he, that he caught sight of a face he recognised in the throng ahead. He bent his head, so that his hood would better shield his features, and broke up a piece of bread, stuffing some into his mouth, like a famished peasant with a late lunch. He was turned away as Sir Baldwin and the other two passed by, his hands at his mouth with the bread in them, and while he watched carefully, there was no sign of their having noticed him. They were too involved in their own discussion.

Still, it had been a close-run thing, and he felt his heart pounding as he swallowed his bread and followed Ulric.

The gaol was beneath a grubby little cell with a studded door, set into the wall beside the East Gate. Often a gaoler would allow a prisoner to meet with friends, for a slight consideration. Sir Charles had but few coins in his purse and what he did have, he didn't want to share.

He walked up the road towards the castle, and found some gravel in the interstices between the rocks of the wall.

Ulric waited outside. When Sir Charles knocked at the door, there was a surly grunt from the gaoler, who appeared to have been snoozing. 'What is it?' he yawned.

'I want to speak with the prisoner.'

'Oh?' He looked Sir Charles up and down, his eyes lingering on the swollen purse at Sir Charles's belt. 'Why should I let you see him?'

'Because I will make it worth your while,' Sir Charles said. 'Shall we go inside?'

The man hesitated, then saw Sir Charles weighing the purse in his hand. It appeared to give him an incentive, and he opened the door to a small chamber that had a trap-door in the floor.

'He is down there?' Sir Charles asked.

'Aye.' The gaoler was eyeing his purse. 'A penny to see him.'

'A penny?'

There was a belch and a nod from the man, and Sir Charles made a show of unwillingly untying the thong that held his purse to his belt. 'Well, open it up, then,' he muttered.

The gaoler turned and fumbled with the bolts, soon having them open. He lifted the trap, just as Sir Charles swung his purse. The stones and coins hit the man's head with a dull, wet crack, and he pitched forward into the prison. His neck broke with a dry crack as he hit the stone floor.

'Who is that?'

'I am Sir Charles of Lancaster. I'm here because you have made a real hash of things, haven't you?' he said amiably as he began to climb down the ladder. 'We need to talk, Henry.'

CHAPTER FORTY-TWO

Combe Street

As he walked home, slightly unsteadily, Gregory Paffard was filled with a new purpose. Not only was he now the effective master of the house, he was also the only man who could save his father.

But Henry had been right when he pointed out that Gregory could scarcely claim that his father had confessed to the murders in order to cover up for his son. That would lead to the rope for both of them! Worse, if people believed that Gregory had been committing sodomy, it could mean a pyre.

There must be another way to get him released, and all the way home, Gregory tried to think which of the pleaders would be best for his father. It must be a man experienced in matters of this complexity. A murderer who confessed and then denied his guilt was a rarity.

'John!' he called as he entered, slamming the door shut behind him and throwing hat and cotte to the ground.

'Where is my mother?' he demanded when he saw Joan in the hall with Thomas.

Thomas looked up at him with a look of terror, quickly duck-ing behind Joan.

'What is it, little one?' Joan asked. She was quiet, and held Thomas closely, Gregory saw.

'Thomas? Come to me,' Gregory said. He squatted, as he would before a puppy, beckoning with both hands in as welcom-ing a manner as he could. 'Do as I say, Thomas. I am the master of this house now.'

His brother turned and rammed his face into Joan's arm. She looked down and threw an accusing glance at Gregory.

'I've done nothing to him,' he protested.

'Leave him, please,' Joan said. 'He is alarmed. It's all the murders. Death and his father in gaol. Plus he's hurt himself.' She gestured at the bloodstained bandage about his knee.

'That's not my fault,' Gregory spat, rising. He was tempted to go to Thomas and pull him from the maid, but his legs were still wobbly. Instead, he strode from the room. The buttery was empty, and he drew off a large cup of ale from the barrel, drain-ing it in one draught.

'I think you've had enough,' Agatha said, as he refilled it. She had approached from the stairs, and now stood leaning in the doorway.

With her full body, Gregory thought she looked like a goddess. She was painfully beautiful sometimes.

'Brother, dear, you need to get a grip,' she said.

'I'm fine,' he said, but he knew his voice was thicker than it should be. 'It's Thomas. He's terrified of me.'

'You know that he's been like that since last Saturday?' she said and looked at him.

He remembered. The feel of soft flesh under his hands, the smooth, inner thighs parting for him. 'Oh, God, Agatha!'

'Yes. I think he saw everything. Are you surprised he's a bit alarmed? Perhaps you should have a word with him.'

'Thomas? I would never hurt him! Thomas is . . .'

'Our brother, yes. How was Father? Ben said you went to see him.'

'Worried. He wants a pleader.'

'Who will you send?'

'Christ knows,' he muttered. He reached for the barrel again, but glancing at her, threw the cup aside. 'John! JOHN!' he bellowed, and stormed through the house, finally finding the bottler in the kitchen yard.

'Master?'

'I need you to go to our clerk and find out who is the best pleader for the courts. We have to try to liberate Father from the gaol. His confession was an error. It was only to try to protect . . . well, me. He thought I had committed the murders, and wanted to save me. But I didn't.'

'No?'

'Of course not! How could you even think that! I had nothing to do with them. Either of them. So, John, we need to get the best pleader we can.'

John stared at him, and there was something unnerving about his gaze. Gregory was aware that the bottler was deliberately intimidating him.

'Well?' he said coolly.

'I will ask Madame Claricia first.'

'Then do so and hurry up about it! Or you will find you are no longer bottler in this house!' Gregory snapped.

And then John did an astonishing thing. He stepped up close to Gregory and glared at him. Gregory was forced to retreat under the threat of those fierce eyes.

'You need to remember that I am the servant of your mother:

not you, not Master Henry, not anyone but her. And I will make sure that she is happy with your suggestion before I leave her alone in this house. If you don't like that, you'd best go and fetch the pleader yourself, *master*.'

And, shaken, the only thing Gregory could do was nod his agreement.

Exeter Gaol

Sir Charles of Lancaster climbed the ladder with a smile still fixed to his lips, but his mind was racing and filled with anger.

The fool had not achieved anything he had been instructed to do! It had been his place to simply gather in some money to pass to Sir Charles to help support the Dunheved brothers. That was all. But instead, the fool had forgotten his promises and his duty of responsibility to Sir Edward of Caernarfon. He'd got a little money, so he said, but the damned fox-whelp had gone and got himself arrested for murder. Because he had admitted these crimes!

Sir Charles reached the top of the ladder and pulled it up after him, lowering the heavy trap-door to the cell, and tugging the bolts over.

'You do realise that the success of the whole enterprise depends upon money?' he had said to Paffard.

The man was already cowering by then. 'Of course. But what would you have me do?'

'You should have kept out of gaol until you had paid us!'

'Can you free me? All you need do is get me home again, and I can present you with the money I have. There is a chest in my house. It's a large chest, and it contains my store of spare funds. If you take me there, I can pay you.'

'Where is the key to this store?'

'Here! I have it here.'

Sir Charles eyed him doubtfully. 'Where is the chest? Anyone might have taken it.'

'No, no, it's safe.'

'Where?'

Henry Paffard was no fool. He opened his mouth to speak, but then he closed it again. As soon as he gave away the location, he knew that his personal value to Sir Charles would reduce to nothing. Worse than nothing: he became an additional liability, and Sir Charles would not want to leave a stray soul behind when he left.

'Did you not hear me?' Sir Charles smiled. He set his hand to his sword and slowly drew it. It gave off a whisper of steel as it came free, and Sir Charles held the tip pointing at Henry's head. 'I asked you where it was stored.'

'In my hall,' Henry declared and stared at him defiantly. 'Beside the fireplace there is a wooden chest. Behind that is a door in the wall. The money chest lies inside.'

'And the key?'

Henry curled his lip. The key was on a thong about his neck, and he slowly pulled it from his chemise and held it up, reaching around with his hands to untie it. But then he rolled and lunged away, trying to escape.

Sir Charles did not hasten. He stepped after Henry, and then stabbed once, leaning his full weight on the blade.

So now, here he was, with a key bound about his own neck to a chest in a house to which he had no access. All in a city in which he knew he was being hunted.

He closed his eyes and set his jaw. Just for a moment, Sir Charles was exhausted. The last days had worn away at him, and there was a cold certainty building in his heart that no matter what he did, he would not live to see Sir Edward of Caernarfon back on his rightful throne.

Then he snorted deeply, like an old war-horse sniffing fire and blood, and stiffened his back.

He was Sir Charles of Lancaster. He had survived too many battles in England, France, Guyenne and Galicia, to allow one more set-back to throw him.

Opening the door, he walked out as if leaving his own front door, turning and closing it gently behind him as he went, and then looked about him for Ulric.

The boy was a short way down, near the friary on the High Street, and Sir Charles strode over to him.

'Come, we have to get over to the other side of this city again,' he said gruffly, and then he suddenly saw a woman in the road before him.

She was dark-haired, wearing a scruffy tunic, her matted hair framing her horrified features.

Even as she began to scream, Sir Charles ran straight at her: she took the full force of his blow in her face, and hurtled backwards into the road.

The screaming had stopped. But in its place there were shouts and bellows, and a horn blew.

'I think,' Sir Charles said as he ran, 'you will need to hurry yourself, friend Ulric, if you want to live to see tomorrow's morning.'

Paffards' House

The bottler made his way to his mistress's room and knocked gently on the door.

When she called out, he entered.

She looked terrible, the poor lass. Hardly surprising after the way things had gone just recently, but still, it was very sad to see her like this.

'Mistress, your son has asked if I can go to find a pleader.

Your husband has changed his story, and now denies his murders.'

She look at him pretty sharply at that. 'What do you mean, changed his story? How so?'

'Apparently Master Gregory spoke to him and it transpired that Master Henry confessed because he thought the felon was your son. Now he's been told that he's innocent, he wants to save himself.'

'It was impressive that he had the desire to try to protect Gregory, if only for a short while,' she said. 'I didn't think he had it in him.'

'You don't want me to find a pleader, do you?' John asked, and there was a faint tone of surprise in his voice.

She smiled sadly and walked to him, placing her hand on his cheek. 'Dear John. You don't understand me, do you? You think only of the insults and shame he has brought to me.'

'All the time,' John said gruffly.

'But I still cannot discard him without making an effort to save him. He is my husband, and I owe him the debt of chivalry. After all, I was the daughter of a knight. I understand duty. It is a painful duty, but it is mine. So yes, please, go to the pleader and see how we may have my husband released.'

'Yes, mistress.'

'You never know, John,' she added. 'Oftentimes a man can change. He can become reborn – with luck.'

John nodded, but as he closed the door and left the room, he was thinking that the main way he wanted to see Henry Paffard change was with a knife in his belly.

He was almost back at the buttery when he realised that he did not have his keys on his belt.

CHAPTER FORTY-THREE

Combe Street

William and Philip had been standing there long enough for the shadows to move from almost overhead to point to the east, and William knew that it was at least one hour past midday. The bells were the only way to measure the passage of time generally, but he had always spent time watching the movement of the sun and the play of the shadows, and could tell the hour with great accuracy.

Shadows. That was what his life had become. No work, no money, and now no home either. He was like one of the shuffling tatterdemalions in the streets, the boys and men without homes and no means of supporting themselves. There was that man he had seen before, the old tramp with his cloth bag containing his belongings gripped to his breast, his ragged beard and his constant look of terror making him fearsome rather than fearful. He was a shadowman, always hiding in the darker corners, rarely daring to show himself in case he was persecuted, or worse.

William shuddered. Perhaps Philip was right, after all, he thought. Maybe they should just leave Exeter and find themselves new lives elsewhere.

The door to the Paffards' house opened, and William felt Philip punch his shoulder to warn him. But it wasn't Gregory who descended the steps.

'Leave him,' Philip said.

'He may know something,' William hissed. 'Like, where Gregory is!'

Philip reluctantly agreed, and the two followed John as he crossed Southgate Street and went on up to the Bear Gate of the Cathedral.

William felt hunger gnawing further into his belly. At the bottom of the gate was a stool where an old woman begged, and she held out her hand hopefully as they passed. It made William imagine how he would look in twenty years' time, if he would be taking her place there at the gate. The beggars here had to pay good money to be able to keep their posts, he knew. He wondered how much.

'Sir? Sir – John, sir,' Philip called, and the old bottler turned with an enquiring look in his eye.

'What?'

'Master Gregory, sir. We wanted to speak with him. Is he at home?'

John looked over their heads towards the house. 'Aye, he's there,' he said at last, 'but I don't think he'll want to see you.'

'But he's ordered us to be evicted,' William said.

'Aye. I had heard.'

'It's not fair!' William said hotly.

Philip placed a hand on his forearm. 'Sir, will he see us if we ask?'

'No. I'm sorry, boys.'

'You know,' Philip said, 'that his father stole our inheritance? All we want is something to help us start up again. Is that so wrong?'

John bared his teeth in a flash of ferocity so sudden that William couldn't help but take a step back.

'Look, boys, you know and I know that Master Henry took your father's money, business and house – everything. So let's not beat about the bush for the deer. Send in the hounds. You want to stay in your place? Gregory won't let you.'

'His mother said we were a reminder and an embarrassment.'

John gave a twisted grin. 'She said that? It's true: Gregory won't want you hanging around because you'll remind other people what his family did to you. You understand? A man has to trade on the value of his own word here. You take away his word, and his business will fail. And right quickly, too. You are the constant reminder to any clients that he cannot be trusted. They will think that Master Gregory doesn't pay his debts even when under oath to the widow of his friends. So he will try to keep you as far from his door as he can – and if that means he has to pay sailors or roughs to beat you up – or even kill you – he'll do it.'

'Would he pay us to go?'

John laughed. 'He's a rich man. Rich men don't get to be rich by giving away money. Paying a man to beat you or kill you is one thing; paying you blackmail to go, that is a bad investment. Henry taught his son well.'

'Then there is nothing we may do,' Philip said angrily. He rested his hand on his dagger's hilt.

'Aye, the world is a cruel, sad place,' John agreed, 'when a man can rob another and profit by it. But that is the way of the world now. There is nothing a man can own or enjoy that another cannot take from him.'

He left them then, but didn't offer them godspeed or good fortune. What was the point? They had lost everything.

Paffards' House

Sir Charles stood in the alley beside Henry Paffard's house and listened carefully. It was hard to hear anything over his own stertorous breathing, but Sir Charles was never anything if not cautious.

Ulric he had told to run as fast as he could up to the North Gate, and escape. With his guilty look, he should soon be seen and caught, and since Sir Charles intended to be away from here in short order, when Ulric was caught, his testimony would come too late to help the Watchmen to capture Sir Charles.

Speed was essential if he was to escape, however.

The front door had looked most appealing, but should there be any dispute about his right to enter, he would prefer by far that it should happen in a less public location than the front of the house, where passers-by could all too easily be called upon to come and assist the family. So now he stood and waited a moment or two until his heart had stopped pounding quite so alarmingly, and his ears could still detect no sounds, and only then did he set his hand upon the wooden latch of the gate and test it. The lever lifted, and he pushed ever so gently. Sometimes these rich merchants would have dogs to guard their homes, and he had no desire to be mauled.

There were no hounds present. With relief he opened the gate until a short squeak alerted him to a rusted hinge. He slid through and closed the gate behind him. A small garden area was revealed, with the house on his right. No one was visible there, nor at the outbuildings behind. He gripped the hilt of his dagger and strode towards the rear door, opening it and going inside. There was no need for concealment now. If someone saw him he must silence them as swiftly as he could.

There was a brewery, then a large kitchen, and he hesitated there, hearing two voices.

He chose the route of arrogance. Sheathing his knife again, he stepped into the room, looking about him at the mess and smoke as though disgusted.

'Who are you?' the cook demanded.

'I'm here to see your master,' he said, 'but no one is about. Do you know when he will return?'

'You walked in without the master?'

'Your bottler let me in, Cook. Do you know when your master is to be back, I said?'

'No.'

'Very well,' he said, and passed through to the hall.

The room was empty, as he had hoped. He saw the chest at the wall, and pulled it away with a single yank on the handle. There was indeed a door set into the wall, sealed with a small padlock. He tugged at the key about his neck, hoping as he did so that there were treasures in here, and not coin. It would be hard to escape with a chest full of heavy coin.

Still, this was not the time to worry about that. He pulled the key's thong in two, and took the key to the lock. He thrust it in and turned it, and opened the door. It was dark inside, but went back some distance. He reached in and felt about. There was nothing.

He sat back on his heels. The chamber was empty. If once there had been money or treasure or gold, it was gone. Probably because Paffard had been an incompetent businessman, he had frittered it away, or perhaps he had lost the money at gambling. For whatever the reason, the money was gone. And Sir Charles was in trouble.

There came a sound from behind him, and Sir Charles whirled, rising to his feet as he did so and catching sight of a little boy's startled face. The lad looked like a faun meeting a hunter. They stared at each other for a split moment, and then the boy had turned and was gone, a flash of hosen and green shirt.

'God's cods!' Sir Charles swore viciously, and took off in pursuit.

Southgate Street

Simon could not help but feel that he would be better off spending time with his daughter and grandson than traipsing about the city from gaol to merchant, to church and thence to God knows where. The murder of the two women was sad, but it mainly served to remind him of the dangers of the city and the risks all took every day.

His musings were interrupted by a growing clamour from Carfoix.

'What, in Christ's pain, is that?' he said.

'I don't know,' Baldwin said, 'but it sounds as though the Hue and Cry has someone.'

'They're coming down here,' Sir Richard said. He was standing with his vast legs wide apart, thumbs in his belt. And then he stopped and peered ahead. 'Can you see who's being chased?'

It was impossible to make out what was happening. There was a clot of humanity in the road, and carters and tranters were already shouting furiously at the men to clear the roadway.

'No,' Baldwin said helplessly, and then he saw a man break away from the crowd to remonstrate with a carter. 'Hey, you!' he called to him. 'Who do you hunt?'

The man with his long staff paused. 'The man they're calling Sir Charles of Lancaster. He was up at the East Gate. Punched a woman, and laid her senseless, and ran on down this way. Been running after him ever since!'

'You're sure he came down here?' Sir Richard demanded. 'We haven't seen him.'

'He could have taken any of the alleys,' the man panted.

'Sir Baldwin, you carry on. I am keen to see that this bastard doesn't lay a finger on another woman,' Sir Richard bellowed. 'I'll go with this man.'

'Very good,' Baldwin said. 'Edgar, you go with them and see if you can help capture Sir Charles. You should recognise him as fast as I would.'

Edgar nodded and was soon off with Sir Richard and the man, who was a bailiff. There was a roar as Sir Richard approached the gaggle of men milling near the Bear Gate entrance, and then some order was restored.

'Come, Simon,' Baldwin said. 'Let us go and speak with the priest.'

Simon nodded, and they continued down the street, but as they came to Combe Street, he spotted Father Laurence. 'What's *he* doing there?' Simon asked.

Combe Street

There was no sense in protracted arguing. Both brothers sensed that this was the end of their road. There was nothing they could do to recoup their losses. They slowly made their way back to the Paffards' house, as if drawn by a magnet, and there they stood in the roadway.

Philip could never remember such a confusion of spirit. All his soul was baying for revenge upon Henry Paffard, but the merchant was out of reach in the gaol.

'Where can we sleep tonight?' he wondered aloud.

They had no money to pay for board and lodging, and tonight they must leave the streets before the Watch appeared and began to ask difficult questions of them.

William said nothing, but stared at the alley along which their hovel stood.

'Will, it's pointless. We cannot go back. It isn't our home any more.'

'Only a couple of years ago, we were rich, our parents were happy and content, and we had a future. Now Paffard's stolen it all. Not just our money, Philip, he's stolen our lives.'

His brother was right, Philip thought. They had nothing remaining of that happiness. And as to what they could do now, he had no idea.

Just then, he heard a door open, and looking up, he saw Gregory Paffard in the doorway of his house.

It was as though the sight spurred him into action. Without conscious thought, Philip began to walk, his body filled with a total, all-consuming purpose. He could not have put it into words but the intention was there.

Gregory had already run down the steps, and had set off in the direction of Southgate Street, Philip only a matter of paces behind him, when Gregory suddenly stopped with an audible gasp.

Philip took no notice. He drew his knife in one fluid movement, held it aloft for a moment, then grabbed Gregory's shoulder, whirling him around.

There was a shout, an inarticulate cry, and Philip stood looking into Gregory's frightened expression for a moment, and then his knife swooped down. And as it did, a man came, and thrust Gregory aside.

He was in the way, and there was nothing Philip could do as

he saw Father Laurence's face appear before him. There was a second in which all time seemed to stop. Philip could see the priest's face in front of him, the eyes half-closed in anticipation – no fear, no terror, but an acceptance – while his knife appeared to be fixed in space.

But then it descended, slamming into the priest's chest with a thud that could be heard in Father Laurence's voice as a little grunt, and Philip felt his fist tug the blade free again, and stared with horror at what he had done.

There was a scream, and when Philip looked, he saw Agatha at the door to the house, an expression of horror on her face. But her eyes were on her brother, not the priest.

Father Laurence smiled at him, a patient, forgiving smile, and then he turned and walked three paces before he stumbled, and then simply collapsed, like a falling tree. He was already dead before any could reach him.

But Philip had heard him say those words. As he stood with Philip's knife in his breast, he looked up at Agatha, and murmured, 'I still love you.'

CHAPTER FORTY-FOUR

Carfoix

There was a rushing of men all about as they searched alleys and side streets to find Sir Charles. Sir Richard was used to this sort of work, but even he was growing despondent as the sun crept around the sky. There was a moment when he thought he saw a man furtively creeping along, but when Edgar went and questioned the fellow, he was only a hunch-backed peasant on his way home.

'What d'ye think?' he asked Edgar.

'It would be a miracle to find him now, if he's still here. He found a place to hide yesterday after he reached the city. He must have an ally here, or someone whom he can trust. Without knowing who that is, we are searching for a single straw amongst many.'

Sir Richard nodded. Then he said, 'Hold! If the fellow knows someone here in the city, perhaps it was one of the men who had joined him in his gang?'

Edgar nodded. He wore a supercilious expression, but Sir Richard didn't care.

'So, if the fellow was with him in his gang, it was someone who left here a few days ago when Sir Charles first approached this city – someone who disappeared and has recently returned.'

'Yes. That is possible.'

'Aye, better than nothing, as you might say,' the knight said with satisfaction. He turned and led the way to a watchman.

They were explaining Sir Richard's reasoning when a boy hurried up. 'The gaoler's dead, sir,' he said.

Sir Richard glowered at him. 'What?'

'Someone has killed the gaoler and the prisoner, sir. They're both dead in there.'

'That, friend Edgar, is why the man was at the East Gate – it's near the gaol. Now, Watchman, is there a man of the sort I described – who left the city before the death of the Bishop?'

'There is one young feller. He left the city almost a fortnight ago,' the man said. He had a healthy three-day growth of beard, and when he scratched his chin, it rasped. 'We can try him.'

'Where?'

'Down behind Smythen Lane.'

'Take us there.'

Paffards' House

Thomas ran. He pelted hell for leather through the house, through the kitchen and out past the brewery to the garden behind, but here he could not see anywhere to hide, and he hesitated only a moment before thinking of the shed.

It took only a moment to rush to the broken slat, jerk with his hand, and wriggle inside the cold, dank interior – and only just in time.

He saw through the broken plank the man who ran out, closely pursued by Joan, who was shrieking at him to know what he was doing. He turned to her, and as Thomas watched, the big knight struck her once on the side of her head, and she tumbled down to the ground, her wimple awry.

Sir Charles threw a harried look about the yard, and then began to trot to the workrooms at the rear. It was when he was almost there that Thomas squirmed about a little to look, and his foot caught on something. It was sharp, and scratched at his leg, and he instantly thought of rats.

Rats. Their sharp teeth that would gnaw through a wooden beam, that would score even a metal plate, rats were everywhere, and the memory of John's words about rats eating through a boy's leg in a moment, that was enough to make him whimper to himself. He dare not squeal, he dare not kick and scream for help, because the man he had seen robbing his father's hall would come and find him. He must lie still, even if the rats ate through his leg. Better to be eaten alive than found by that horrible man.

He could not help a muffled sob though, and feeling something sharp again, he cast an eye behind him in the gloom.

And then he screamed for real, and fought his way through the hole once more, just as Sir Charles reappeared.

Thomas didn't care. He raced back into the house – getting as far away as he could from the grinning face in that dark hole, the grinning face of the skeleton in shreds of clothing.

Smythen Lane

The house to which Sir Richard was directed was a small, shabby affair halfway down the narrow street, and as the knight strode along the cobbles, he was thinking about the man he sought.

If it was the one who had ridden off with Sir Charles after the fight, then Sir Richard had seen him when he rode at Sir Richard with a spare horse for Sir Charles. At the time, Sir Richard had gained the impression of a slender youth with a brown thatch of hair. Not the sort to inspire fear in a man. Sir Charles, of course, was a different matter.

'Edgar, this man is not as dangerous as Sir Charles, I deem. You and I should be able to capture him. But if Sir Charles is with him, we need to worry about him first.'

'I understand,' Edgar said. He had a nonchalant attitude, but Sir Richard had seen Edgar fighting often enough to be assured of his skill and speed.

The watchman knocked hard, and Sir Richard grasped his sword. There was no answer, and he told the man to break down the door. 'We can't let him run out the back,' he snarled.

Under the combined efforts of the watchman and Edgar's boots, the timbers were soon broken in pieces, and the three men rushed into the small building.

'You, upstairs,' he shouted to the watchman. To Edgar, he jerked his head. 'You, with me out to the yard.'

They hurried through the place. There were only two rooms downstairs, and in the second a family was eating, sitting on the floor. They said nothing as Sir Richard and Edgar hurried past, a group of four children and two adults, all with the same thin, weary faces, eyes grown enormous from starvation.

Outside they found a tiny yard, and Sir Richard immediately spotted a man struggling to climb over the rear wall. Sir Richard blundered on, but Edgar overtook him, springing up onto the wall and flinging himself over.

He had left Sir Richard behind. There was the sound of running feet and Edgar set off after him on his soft leather boots. A figure darted left, and Edgar followed.

The man was clearly in view now. A thin fellow, with a haggard expression and clothes that spoke of days and nights in the open. Edgar smiled to himself. This would be easy.

He lengthened his stride. Edgar was well-fed and fit, and the man he chased was neither. Already he was flagging, and Edgar slowed slightly too, keeping a watchful eye on him, to ensure that this wasn't a feint designed to mask a sudden attack.

It was not. Ulric suddenly tripped and fell headlong. Edgar drew his sword and waited for him to recover. Ulric sobbed in the dirt where he lay, his face inches from a pile of horse droppings. They were behind the fleshfold, and the roadway was a darkened mass of excrement, made more liquid by the urine of all the cattle that passed by.

'I wouldn't want to be lying there myself,' Edgar said.

'Kill me here,' Ulric wept. 'I can't live on.'

'Why?'

'I was with Sir Charles and his men when they killed the Bishop. I will be hanged anyway. Please, just finish it.'

He looked up, and Edgar saw the resignation in his eyes. It was strangely touching. 'How did you meet with Sir Charles?'

'Henry Paffard paid me to take a message to him. It told Sir Charles where the Bishop was and where he was travelling next. Sir Charles used that to hunt him down and slay him. I'm guilty of being a party to that. And then, I was with him when he raided the Bishop's mansions, too.'

'Did you dislike the Bishop for a reason?'

'Me? No! I thought he was a good man – like the last, poor Bishop Walter. I used to work for him and I liked him. I was only a messenger – but when I had delivered the message, I was stuck with them.'

'Why do you think Henry Paffard was involved with Sir Charles?'

'I heard Sir Charles say that the treasure he'd collected was to go to Paffard, and the money he paid was to support the old King, Sir Edward of Caernarfon.'

Edgar gazed at him, his eyes narrowing. 'You know that Sir Charles went to see Paffard today?'

'Yes. I was outside the gaol when he went in.'

'He killed Paffard.'

'*No*!' Ulric's face crumpled as he took this in. 'So I can't even prove he used me as a messenger? I am ruined!'

'Where is Sir Charles now?'

'I don't know. We were going to Paffard's house when the Hue and Cry started behind us. He told me to come up this way, but I wanted to go home first and hide. I hoped I would be safe, but nowhere is safe now.'

Edgar lifted his sword, and Ulric flinched, shutting his eyes before the final blow.

'Oh, in the name of Christ,' Edgar said. 'Killing you would be like strangling a kitten. Go in peace, boy, and don't take dangerous messages again.'

Ulric slowly opened his eyes and stared in amazement. 'You mean it?'

'And lie, boy. When someone asks you where you've been, say you went to visit a friend in Tiverton or Tawton. Say that you were away drinking all the time. After all, Henry Paffard cannot accuse you of joining in the gang now, can he? And Sir Charles will have more on his mind than your offences. I think you will be safe. I won't punish you more.'

Combe Street

'Sweet Mother of God, Phil! What have you done!' William screamed. He watched as the body of the priest kicked twice in its death-throes and then was still. 'Quick! Let's get away from here!'

There was a shriek of horror from a few yards away, and while William knew he ought to move, to grab Philip and bolt from this road, his legs wouldn't respond. His mind was slammed into a blankness so intense he could not conceive of escape.

'You go, William,' Philip said. He was not looking at the priest, but at the smug face of Gregory Paffard. 'You didn't hear that, did you? Father Laurence still loved her. Not you!'

'I never thought he did love me. Is that what you thought? You poor fool,' Gregory jeered. 'And now you've killed him. You've made my life easier, Philip. Thank you.'

'Phil, come on! You can't kill him, you have to get away from here! With me, now.'

William was close to sobbing as he pleaded with his brother. There was something so ineffably grim about the idea of remaining here, while the bailiffs and porters and Watchmen all congregated. They would die, both of them. That was when he realised. Philip *intended* to die here. He was not going to run away, because his mind was wholly bent upon the man before him. His aim had been to kill Gregory, and while Laurence had taken the blow intended for his victim, the error had not deflected him from his original purpose.

'Phil, no!' William groaned, but he could see he was too late.

Philip's face wore a look of tragic determination. His was a mind torn by the loss of the woman he had loved, as it was by the death of his mother. And now, the representative of the family that had impoverished him and ruined his mother's last days was here before him. He stepped forward, slowly, like a cat stalking a bird.

'You should go,' Gregory said. 'I am entitled to protect myself, churl. You come for me, you strummel patch? Worthless whorecop. What do you want from me, eh?'

'Your life,' Philip said, and crouched, his knife before him. 'You can at least afford that.'

'You realise that there are thirty men and women at least

watching you right now? This is not self-defence, Philip. It's you attacking me – unprovoked, too. You will never escape from here, you piece of shit. You can't hope to kill me!'

'I will.'

And William watched as Philip moved forward inexorably, his lethal blade sweeping from side to side. William saw Gregory pull out his own dagger.

That was when William heard another bellow as Baldwin and Simon came running. There was a snarl, and Wolf rushed up, but before William could respond to the dog, he felt a fist thud into his back, and was sent sprawling as John sprang over him, and with his hatchet in his hand, he hacked at Philip's head.

'No!' William shouted in desperation as Philip seemed to shiver, the hatchet embedded. He dropped his knife and turned, falling to his knees as he went, and William saw Philip's eyes go to him for one moment, before they rolled up into his skull, and his body collapsed.

CHAPTER FORTY-FIVE

Paffards' House

Sir Charles saw the little gegge take off again, and he gave chase with a grim determination. If the bratchet got to the road, young as he was, he could call the Hue and Cry, and Sir Charles had had enough of running. He sprang over the body of the maid he had struck, and ran into the house again, past the rooms and into the kitchen, where the cook stood at the far end, a heavy knife in one hand, a cleaver in the other. She looked pale and slightly waxen as she stared at him with determination, but said nothing.

He was frozen for a moment. Then, 'If you try to leave the house I will kill you, woman,' he snarled, and carried on along the passageway. There was a wailing sound; it came from upstairs. With a smile fitted to his face, he went to the stairs and climbed as silently as possible. The steps were of wood, great square sections cut diagonally and pegged to a pair of flat sheets behind. They were immense and solid, and there was no squeak or creak to give him away as he ascended cautiously to the upper passage. There he stood a moment, listening. There was a scuffling sound at the front of the house, and he made his way there, stepping slowly and carefully. A board moved under his foot, and he heard a piercing screech as it rubbed against a wooden peg, and at the same time, all noise in front of him ceased.

There came the sound of a shutter sliding down its runners, and Sir Charles ran on into the room. At the far side, he saw Thomas, standing at the open window in the bedroom, the large bed against the wall on the left.

'Away from the window, boy,' he said. 'Don't try to shout, because I'll throw you out if you do. I won't have that.'

Thomas clung to the string that held the shutter in its place, and stared wide-eyed at the man who approached him, step by careful step.

The little fool must have been soft-minded, Sir Charles thought to himself.

'Now, little man, you need to tell me something. Your father was looking after money for me. I have to have it to take it to some friends. Can you tell me where he kept his money? He told me it was in the hall downstairs, but the cupboard is empty. I don't know where else it might have been moved.'

Thomas shook his head.

'It is all right, boy. It is my money. Your father was looking after it for me.'

He was almost at the boy now, and he made a quick lunge, but even as he did so there came a red-hot searing pain in his right flank.

'God's cods!' he roared. He darted away and turned, expecting to see a man with a sword. Instead it was a woman. 'You stupid bitch!' he snarled, and drew his sword.

He knew her. It was the pathetic lurdan of a wife of Henry

Paffard. She had got her husband's sword from somewhere . . .
Sweet mother of God, but she'd struck well, just as he was
bending over – and the thrust had slipped up above his hip and
into his guts. He knew from experience that wounds in the belly
would often go rotten and lead to an agonising death. She
would pay for this!

The boy was shrieking and squealing. It was not to be borne!
He aimed a blow at the boy's head, but missed, and he knew in
that moment that he had only a short time. Glancing down, he
saw that blood had already stained the whole of his side and
thigh, and he could hear a rushing sound in his ears. 'Damn
your noise, boy!' he rasped, and as she stabbed at him, he
knocked her blade away, thrusting forward at her. But his
strength was leaving him, he knew. He caught something, but it
may have been just her gown, untied as it was. He felt his blade
catch, and then he saw her move away again, and he was left
standing, panting, while she moved to the door, the sword in
both hands, pointing at his belly.

He couldn't run. Not now. But he wouldn't surrender.

She called to the boy, and Sir Charles found his head was
falling as Thomas edged around him, eyes fixed and terrified.
He felt tired. Must have been that run here from East Gate, he
thought to himself. And then his eye caught sight of the blood
on his leg, and he remembered he had been stabbed.

Looking up, the woman was at the door, holding out her
hand to the boy.

With a last effort, Sir Charles grabbed for Thomas and
pulled him to his side. He held the sword's point to Thomas's
throat. 'You have killed me, woman,' he hissed. 'Now I shall
kill your boy.'

Combe Street

Baldwin and Simon pushed John away from the bodies of Father Laurence and Philip. Both were dead.

William crouched in the dirt, tears rolling down his cheeks as he stared at his brother. He would have fallen on his brother's breast, but the sightless eyes made him pause. There was something that was not of his brother in them, as though his brother's body had been emptied of all Philip's soul and was now filled with a demon instead. It was Philip no more. Even his corpse had been stolen from him.

With an inarticulate bellow, he sprang up and ran bare-handed at Gregory.

He was arrested in his onward rush. An arm went about his chest and swung him backwards off his feet. He could only lie on the ground next to his brother, retching as he tried desperately to catch his breath.

Before him, when he managed to gather his courage and his spirits, he saw Gregory sniggering. William tried to clamber to his feet, to leap at him again, but a boot was placed on his chest and pushed him back.

'Get off me!'

'Speak respectfully, boy,' Baldwin said. 'You are captured. Calm yourself, because I will not allow you to rise until you are calm.'

'I will avenge my brother!' William said, trying to shove the boot away, but he stopped at the sight and feel of the peacock-blue blade that rested so lightly upon his Adam's apple. He swallowed, and felt the steel prick his skin.

'You will stay there, William, until I have decided what to do with you. Master Paffard, would you object to asking one of your servants or an apprentice to go and seek the Coroner? With luck he will not be far away.'

'With all my heart,' Gregory said, and strode towards his house.

'Now, Master William, you may rise. Don't roll that way, the last horse left evidence of his passing. There, that's better. Now – up, please, and clean yourself.'

His calm manner, both respectful and magisterial, was enough to make William nod and obey. 'I won't try to kill him now.'

'Nor at any other time, I hope,' Baldwin said. He still held his sword, but less threateningly. 'What was this about?'

'We learned today that the Paffards had stolen our inheritance. That's why we've had to scrimp and save as best we could. Our house had to go, not because of debts, but because we were robbed. Those people in there have taken everything we had, and now they have even taken my mother and Philip.'

His eyes filled with tears as he looked at his brother's body.

'What do you have to say, bottler?'

John looked at him and said truculently, 'I saw a man trying to attack my mistress's son. What else should I do, sir? I stopped him.'

'With an axe,' Baldwin noted. He glanced at John's belt. 'You never wear a knife, do you?'

'I have little need. All my knives are in the house. Who would try to attack me, or rob *me*?' he sneered. 'Now, can I go?'

'You just killed a man,' Baldwin said.

'In protecting another. You saw that. Philip Marsille was attacking Master Gregory. You saw him move forwards and try to slay Master Gregory.'

'Yes. I would have used the back of the axe to hit him and

401

stop him, however,' Baldwin said. 'There was no need to kill him.'

'Perhaps you are more experienced in such affairs.'

'Perhaps,' Baldwin agreed.

'It's not fair,' William said. 'Philip was only trying to avenge us. They *robbed* us of everything. All we had, they took from us. It's not justice that Philip was killed.'

'It's not justice?' Simon shouted. 'There's a dead priest there, boy, *that* is not *justice*! Your brother behaved like a felon, and he paid the price here on earth. You have to pray that a priest will perform the last rites over him and save his soul, because otherwise he's beyond salvation!'

'God wouldn't punish him for an accident. And Laurence died happily. He was miserable.'

'Why?'

'Well, Philip thought he was a sodomite with Gregory, but Laurence loved Agatha. He said so as he died. It was the last thing he said. And Gregory couldn't even leave that. He had to taunt Philip even with that.'

'I heard,' Simon said. He looked over to where Gregory had returned and stood contemplating the two bodies in the road-way. 'You! Paffard! Come here.'

'Why? Do you wish to take my words already? Shouldn't we wait for the Coroner?'

Baldwin said, 'We shall hear your testimony as soon as the Coroner arrives, but there's no point in standing out here. William, and you, Gregory, come into the house now.'

The bottler looked as though he was about to refuse entry to William, but all were startled by the sound of Thomas's voice, overhead, screaming high and shrill.

Paffards' House

The room was whirling slowly. It was just as Sir Charles remembered when he was young, and very drunk. In those days, to shut his eyes had been hazardous, and now the same sensations were assailing him. And he was so very tired.

'Move. Out of the way, woman,' he said, his words slurred.

She stood with her sword ready, but in her eyes there was only terror for her son. 'Leave him – take me,' she entreated. 'He's so little.'

'He's more valuable than you,' Sir Charles said. He moved around her, so his back was to the door, and then made his way, step by halting step, along the corridor. 'Don't forget, I can stab quick as a snake, and he's dead. You can do nothing to stop me. One mistaken move, woman, and you lose your son.'

He was almost at the stairs, when he heard the running boots below, and he felt a small thrill to know that this was finally his end. They wouldn't let him leave. Casting about him at the hall, he noted the woodwork. It was good work-manship, he thought dreamily. Perhaps if he had been trained as a carpenter, he would have been happier: with a skill that did not involve fighting, with a livelihood that did not depend upon killing.

He stood with his back to the wall as Baldwin came rushing up the stairs. Mistress Paffard was still to his right. 'Mistress, please have your son back,' he rasped. The pain in his side was growing. It was as if the whole of his right side had been seared in a forge, and it felt worse inside than out. He was dying, he knew, but he also knew it could take hours of agony.

'Sir Charles, please submit,' Baldwin said.

'Sir Baldwin, I have known happy times with you,' Sir Charles said. 'From Galicia, to the Isle of Ennor, to Cornwall, we were companions for many miles. I think you know me well enough to know I will not throw down my weapon. It's not my way.'

'Nevertheless, as Keeper of the King's Peace, I demand that you yield.'

'Damn you!' Sir Charles managed, and smiled. It was easier to do that than to lift his sword. He used both hands, and charged at Sir Baldwin.

Baldwin stepped to the side and as Sir Charles ran on, Baldwin thrust his sword forwards and up, so that the point entered Sir Charles's neck just above the collar of his tunic, and the blow pierced his spine. His body clattered to the ground at Baldwin's feet.

Paffards' House

They congregated in the hall while the jury arrived to view the bodies. There was a subdued atmosphere, and Baldwin was as aware of it as any. He had another man's blood on his hands now. There had been many times in the past when he had been forced to kill a man, but rarely had he been so aware of the shame that came with a killing. Sir Charles had not been a threat to anyone, he was sure. The man was already more than half-dead.

'Are you all right?' Simon asked.

Baldwin glanced up. He had been staring at his sword, which was wiped clean of Sir Charles's blood, but which he had not resheathed since the short fight. 'Yes. Only regretful that another man had to die.'

'There have been too many already,' Simon said. 'Still, I think Sir Charles was glad it was you. He knew you wouldn't miss.'

'Perhaps so,' Baldwin agreed. 'He certainly did not try to protect himself. Even a child could have done more to parry my effort.'

'He didn't want to,' Simon said.

Baldwin had not considered that. It was some sort of relief to think that the man had been willing to see Baldwin as the agent of his death. And a responsibility, too.

A knocking at the door caused him to look up. The familiar bellowing voice could not be mistaken, and a short while later Sir Richard was in the hall with them.

'Well, Sir Baldwin, I think we are closer to the truth about Paffard now,' he said when he heard that Sir Charles was dead. 'This feller went to the gaol, and there he managed to murder Henry Paffard. Aye, I am sorry, Mistress Paffard, but he had to silence your man. Paffard himself was giving information to Sir Charles. It was his messages told Sir Charles where the Bishop was goin' to be. That's how he knew to kill him. From what we heard, it was their plan to liberate the Bishop's treasure and gold to help the Dunheved brothers and Sir Edward of Caernarfon. That much money would buy them a lot of support.'

Baldwin nodded. It was a simple enough plan, but could have been strikingly effective. If the money had been successfully brought to the Dunheveds, it would have purchased them many more men.

'What now?' Simon said.

Baldwin sighed. 'It will take time to document all that has happened today.'

Sir Richard sucked on his teeth. 'I think you should be cautious before writing anything down. If news of Paffard and Sir Charles's plan was to become common currency, there could be repercussions. With a new Sheriff needed, we could have a hard man placed here, charged with cowing the city to ensure that no similar plots could be entertained. I would think it'd be safer to forget much of what has happened.'

'If the Coroner is in agreement,' Baldwin said. 'I shall ask him.'

Sir Richard nodded and then, his expression softening, he gestured towards Wolf. 'You ought to be careful there, Baldwin. Before long, you will lose your hound, at this rate.'

'I think that boy is desperate for a dog of his own,' Baldwin agreed.

In the corner of the room, Wolf was sitting very upright, Thomas before him, and Wolf's paw on Thomas's shoulder. As Baldwin watched, his dog very gently bent his head and rested it on the boy's shoulder, his mouth working quietly.

'That's his sign of highest affection,' Baldwin noted. 'He can give no higher praise.'

'I'm sure that the boy will be most grateful,' Simon said drily.

Baldwin grinned, and then walked over to the boy. Wolf looked up, and would have gone to Baldwin, but he held up a hand and frowned briefly, which was enough to make Wolf remain where he was. 'You like my dog?'

Thomas shot him a look very quickly, then hid his face in Wolf's neck.

'He's a good fellow. Brave, but kind. It's what I always look for in a dog, whatever the type. Have you never had a dog?'

'No.' Claricia walked over and lifted her child. 'My family hasn't had dogs. Henry didn't care for them.'

Thomas was silent. He was still remembering the man who had caught him, who had held him so tightly. And then, he also remembered that horrible skeletal smile under the shed.

'There's a dead man under the shed,' he said. 'I thought it was trying to hold me there with it, Mother. I was so scared!' And he burst into tears.

'What?' Claricia asked. She tried to pull him away, but he clung on tightly. 'What did you say?'

'Out at the yard, where the shed is – a skeleton. I was hiding there, and I felt this hand on my leg, Mother, and I was scared, really scared!'

She stared at the men in the room. There was a silence, and Baldwin sheathed his sword. 'Master Thomas, could you show us where this was, if we come with you?'

CHAPTER FORTY-SIX

Paffards' House

Thomas felt a shrinking sensation as they all walked through the passage, out past the kitchen, where Joan was being fed warm broth by a solicitous Sal, and out to the yard behind.

'Where was it?' Baldwin asked gently.

Thomas stared at him. His tongue clove to the roof of his mouth, and he could say nothing. Instead he tried to cling still more tightly to his mother.

'It's all right,' she said, but he knew it wasn't. Nothing was right at all. Not since the day his dog had been killed, not since the day he saw his brother in the firelight. Not since his father said he had killed those ladies. Nothing ever could be right. He began to sob quietly.

There was a whistle, and Thomas peered out from the protection of his mother's neck. He saw Wolf come out and sit by Baldwin, and Baldwin crouched, and spoke without looking at him.

'A big dog like this will always protect the people he loves,' he said. 'And there is no one he loves more than small boys. Did you know that? It's because they are more fun. They play, and they like to cuddle the dogs. You should come here, and let him guard you.'

Thomas gripped his mother more firmly.

'A dog like this can make you feel all your troubles are leaving you,' Baldwin said. He rose and moved away.

Thomas held on, but Wolf was looking about him in an interested manner. He sniffed idly at some grasses. When Thomas looked over at Baldwin, it was clear that the knight was expecting him to climb down and hug the dog again. It was tempting, but he couldn't. Even as he watched, the dog was ambling towards the shed where he had hidden. He gave a little cry, and hid his face again.

'Was it there?' Baldwin asked, looking at the shed. 'Was it there, Thomas?'

'There's nothing there but my ales,' John said.

Thomas looked at John, and felt again that fear he had known all those years before when his dog had been killed. There was something in his eyes that terrified Thomas. He couldn't speak.

Baldwin followed his dog towards the shed.

'There's nothing in there,' John said again. 'Come, I'll show you.' He walked to the door purposefully, unlocked it, and opened it with a flourish. 'See, sir?'

Baldwin entered, and Thomas watched, shivering slightly. He wanted Sir Baldwin to see the body, but he daren't show him, not himself. That would be awful. The skeleton underneath was terrifying, and John was even worse.

He saw Baldwin come out again, and the knight shook his head, smiling. 'There's nothing in there, Thomas. It's perfectly safe.'

'There's nothing in there, master,' John repeated as he closed the door and locked the padlock again. He looked straight at Thomas. 'Nothing at all. You just had a nasty dream.'

The people with them began to move away. They all thought Thomas had been making up his story, that he had dreamed it all, just as John said. Thomas himself could not hold John's gaze. Instead his eyes went to Wolf, who was sniffing at the side of the shed. The side where his plank had come down.

Baldwin was about to call Wolf away, but decided to inspect the side of the shed, where Wolf was sniffing with keen interest. 'Simon? Could you come here a moment?'

Suddenly there was a flash of steel as John brought out a dagger from beneath his robe. It gleamed wickedly in the sun, and Baldwin had to move back with a muttered oath as it almost sliced his robe. Thomas saw him stumble, and then recover his poise and draw his sword, but before he could attack, Edgar had clubbed John over the head with the pommel of his own sword.

Paffards' House

John was brought to with a bucket of water from the well thrown over his face. He came to spluttering, angry, and with his head aching badly, momentarily confused as to where he was, and why he was lying on a bench. He tried to sit up, but his hands were tied, and it was impossible to do so without help. Edgar was there, and he pulled on John's arm to haul him upright with all the grace of a miller heaving a sack of grain.

'You have much to explain,' Baldwin said sternly.

The knight was before him, and John recognised the other two knights, Sir Richard and Sir Reginald, the city's Coroner. Gregory and William were here too, staring at him with loathing. But it wasn't to them that he looked.

'I have done nothing but serve my mistress.'

'You have done her a great *dis*-service. You say that this was all at her instigation?'

'No. I was acting without her.'

'Then what do you tell us?' Sir Richard demanded.

'She was Evie – a maid. She was a strumpet, a right forward wench,' John said. He was tired and his head hurt, but he wasn't going to submit to these fools. 'She was waggling her arse at the master, and my mistress was upset. So I removed her. I thought it would stop him – after the earlier one.'

'What earlier one?' Baldwin asked.

'Clara. She was the first wench Master Paffard started to swyve in the house. Before that, he just made use of the bitches down at the stews. I know – I saw him there. I was with Agatha when she was little, and we were trying to walk past, but he was lustful and went to spend himself with one of those whores. In front of his daughter! She didn't realise, I hope, but what if she were to tell her mother what she had seen? Eh? It was shameful! And the mistress must have known. She's a very intelligent woman, my mistress.'

'I am sure she is.'

'So when he started to make his use of the maids here, I saw it must stop.'

'You killed this Clara?'

'No. She was lucky. I took things and made it seem that she had stolen them. I showed the things to my mistress, and she was happy to tell Master Henry. He wasn't going to keep a thief in his house, so he threw her out the same day.'

'But Evie was different?'

'She wouldn't have been so easy. She was a shrewd little vixen, that whore. She had Master Henry so tightly bound round her little finger, it's a miracle her finger didn't fall off. She had him paying for new clothes for her, for necklaces, and rings. And all at the time he was ignoring his own wife. The poor mistress was forced to watch all this. And when she complained, did he listen to his rightful wife? No. He beat her with a belt. She was in her bed for days, and the only one allowed in to see her was Evie. She took up the food and drink. That was cruel of the master. I swore then that I'd never let my mistress be so foully treated again.'

'So you killed this Evie?'

'I didn't want to. She found me when I was putting things in her room, same as I had with Clara. Said she was going to tell Master Henry, and that I'd be forced out of the house. And then she began to bait me about it: she jeered at me, saying she'd get a better man for my mistress, a man who was more virile than me. Said I'd always wanted to lie with my mistress, and that was why I was so pathetic. Sir, I couldn't tell you half what she said.'

'And you couldn't bear her words?'

'How could I? Saying I would lie with Mistress Claricia? That would be like bedding my own daughter. I have looked after her since her birth, all the time while her mother died, and her father, and then her sister. I helped her through all that, and when she married, I helped her again. And ever since, I've been here.'

'So you killed for her. How did you bring Evie to this grave?' Baldwin asked.

'I killed her in her room, and when all were busy in the shop or out, I took her body down to the pantry and wrapped her in a sack, then carried her out to my shed. It took no time at all to lift some planks and install her beneath. And I would have been clear, except a dog came into the yard and started trying to get to her. That and the rats.'

'What of the smell?' Baldwin asked.

'It was winter. The chill kept that away. The privy was nearby, and that smell covered the other.'

Baldwin nodded. 'And then you began to suspect that Alice was behaving in the same way?'

'She was worse. She didn't want little trinkets, she wanted a house of her own. And Master Henry was going to buy one for her! All that money on a house? He used to have a chest of money behind the wall in the hall, but he took it and used it all to buy a place in Stepecoat Lane, which was to be hers.'

'What happened to it?'

'It is still his, I think. You should ask him.'

Sir Richard and Baldwin exchanged a look. Baldwin continued, 'How did you manage to kill Alice?'

'She was a fool. That day she flaunted herself at the master again. He went with his family to the inn to have a meal, and she persuaded him to come back and lie with her while the others were eating. He did, too. He came back under pretence of forgetting his rosary. He and she were loud, very loud. And I became more and more angry the longer they went on. He didn't care what anyone thought; he didn't care if it broke his wife's heart. He didn't care what I must think either, hearing him whoring away, when he knew I adored my mistress. No! So I sent her out into the yard to take a message to the apprentices, and followed her and killed her. It was easy, so she didn't suffer. Later, I took her body out into the alley and left her there. She had company.' He laughed. 'There was a dead cat.'

'What of Juliana?' Baldwin said.

'She went to the master and threatened to tell about his family's affairs.' John's eyes went to Claricia, and then to Gregory.

'What of it?'

'How do you think my mistress would feel to know that everyone was pointing at her behind her back and laughing at her? All her friends, her neighbours, all the people about her here, knowing that she was being made a fool of and could do nothing about it?'

'How will they all feel to think that she held a murderer as a bottler in her household?' Sir Richard said.

'Why did you cut away Juliana's lips?' Baldwin asked.

'She was going to talk about my mistress all around the city. I wanted to show that people couldn't get away with that sort of behaviour. So I showed them. All of them.'

'And you stabbed her eyes.'

'Because she had seen . . . She said she had seen things.'

'You admit to slaying three women. And you killed Philip Marsille tonight as well,' Baldwin observed.

'I would do it again, gladly, for my mistress. You think it is easy to watch the child you have raised being insulted in that way?'

William pushed his way past a surprised Sir Richard. Baldwin reached for him, but William did not try to advance further to hurt John. He stood staring down at him.

'When you have the opportunity to consider,' he said quietly, 'you can reflect on how you destroyed my life, and my brother's, and my mother's, just to satisfy your notions of "loyalty". You can never repay me the harm you have done. I will go to your trial and I will accuse you, and when you hang, I will stand with the executioner to make sure no one goes to ease your suffering. You will take a long time to die.'

John looked up without expression. This cur had no idea what suffering was, he thought, and he shrugged and turned away.

But then he heard a rustle of skirts, and saw that Claricia was at William's side.

'Master Marsille,' she said quietly, 'if this house has been bought in Stepecoat Lane, I hope you will accept it as a gift from me, in proof of my good intentions towards you.'

She then faced John. 'As for you, I reject you utterly. You must have been infected with a demon to have thought that I could ever support you in this. To kill those girls, those women! It leaves me with a feeling of utter horror that I have shared a house with you.'

'Mistress . . .'

'I do not know you. You are nothing to me.'

'Mistress, please!'

'Gregory, Agatha, come with me and—'

'Mistress, you must not desert me!' John called. He roared now. 'Mistress Claricia, if you don't want the worst secret loosed, you will not leave me!'

'There is nothing else you can say that can harm us more,' Claricia said.

'You think so?' John said. 'Ask your son, then, and your daughter, mistress! See what they think. See Agatha's face? How she blushes? Like an innocent maid, not at all like a wench who knows the pleasures of a condemned lust, is she? And your son! Look how he pales!'

'What are you saying, churl?' Gregory managed. He stepped forward threateningly, his hand on his dagger.

'You'd kill a man bound, would you? How brave! But I am speaking the truth, as you know, Master Gregory. Beware! If you attack me, it'll be on your soul.'

'It would weigh on my soul as much as slaughtering a rabid dog,' Gregory said. 'You are nothing. I will not defile my hands with your blood.'

He turned and marched away, his mother and sister following.

'Enjoy your bed, then! Enjoy your unnatural lusts!' John

bawled after them. He collapsed back on the bench, his head pounding, the rage still making his blood boil. He couldn't believe that they would dare to desert him. He had given the family everything, the utmost loyalty, the devotion of a slave. And in return they would willingly see him hanged.

Well, if he was to hang, he would see that they suffered too. He stared after them as they disappeared into the house.

'I want to see a priest,' he demanded. 'I will confess all you want, if you let me see a priest and make my confession on the Gospels.'

Claricia was still carrying Thomas as she entered her house. She stumbled slightly over the paving slabs on the way in, but it did not stop her in her dazed journey.

'Mother,' Gregory called, but she gave no indication that she had heard.

Claricia's world had collapsed about her. Her son and daughter were guilty of incest – a crime against God as much as men. She could not take it all in. Her husband's treason, his betrayal of her and the family, his plotting with the murderer Sir Charles, and now his death . . . the attempted murder of her two sons . . . There was no sanity in the world.

'Mother?' Gregory called again.

'I do not know you,' she whispered, cradling Thomas's head at her shoulder.

Gregory glowered. 'You don't believe him, do you? The old fool doesn't know anything – he made that claim to upset you, that's all. I've never done that with Agatha, Mother!'

She should have guessed. When she had seen those secret looks between her two older children, she should have sensed that there was something going on between them. It was obvious now, but before, when she was always so fearful of being punished by Henry for the slightest offence, she had not had time to worry about Gregory and Agatha. Incest! It was a terrible word. All would get to hear of it and they would shun her, and Thomas as well as the others. The family faced financial ruin already. This would push them into abject poverty.

At the door to the hall, she turned and faced her eldest son. Her face was drawn into a rictus of pain and grief.

'Leave me!'

CHAPTER FORTY-SEVEN

Paffards' House

Baldwin and Simon took hold of John's arms and took him out through the house to the front door. In the hall, Simon saw the figure of Claricia sitting on a chair near the dead fire, Thomas still in her arms.

Closely followed by Sir Richard and the other members of their party, they went out, through the front door, and into the street.

It was early evening, and the scent of woodsmoke was all around. Simon snuffed the air, feeling as though a great weight had fallen from him. To be out of that house was a marvellous feeling. It was as though the walls themselves were permeated with misery.

'Baldwin, I don't ever want to go back there.'

'I do not blame you for that.'

'It is a good house,' John said. He was walking resolutely, his head up, looking about him like a man who was at ease with himself and off for a walk on a pleasant evening, enjoying the sights and scents about his home.

'It was,' Sir Richard corrected him. 'Until you decided to kill all the servants.'

'I only sought to protect my mistress. I was always a most devoted servant.'

'Aye. I believe devoted servants can be the most dangerous of all,' Sir Richard said.

'You make fun of me?'

'No. There is nothing amusing about this situation. You have brought ruin upon your house, but no more than your master. Henry Paffard has done as much.'

'He was a fool,' John scoffed, 'to think that he could forever get away with his behaviour. No man can own all the women in a city, but he seemed to think it was possible.'

They were already at the end of the street, and Baldwin pulled John with him down towards the church by the South Gate. Baldwin opened the door, and they all passed inside. Baldwin and Simon remained at the rear with their prisoner and the watchman, while Sir Reginald walked up the nave towards the figure of Father Paul kneeling at the altar. Sir Reginald cleared his throat gently, to indicate that the Father had company.

'Yes? What can I do for you?' Father Paul asked tiredly, breaking off from his prayers.

He was not feeling well, and now he was seized with a great emptiness and sorrow. The death of Father Laurence had quite shaken him. He had thought that God's will should be visible all about, but the events of the last week had disturbed his equilibrium, and just now he was less sure of his faith than he had ever been.

'Father, we need you to let this man put his hand on the Gospels and swear to tell us the truth.'

'Why? Why do you need to know the truth? The truth is, good men have died!' Father Paul said with great bitterness.

'Father, you are unsettled,' Baldwin said kindly. 'We will leave you and find another priest. I am sorry to have troubled you.'

'You haven't troubled me. It's my good friend Laurence. His death was so pointless.'

'He tried to save Gregory Paffard's life,' Baldwin said.

'For what? Why should God allow Laurence to die like that so that another may live? Who is to say that the saved man is more worthy than Father Laurence?'

'Not I, Father – and yet God did. Who are we to assess His means or His plans?'

Father Paul stood. 'You speak truth. But I don't know that I can work towards His aims any more. I am too tired of this world and the endless battles.'

He took up a volume of rough-edged pages, and holding it carefully in both hands, walked up to them. 'So, then, John,' he said, and held out the book. 'Put your hand on it.'

'I swear I shall tell the whole truth,' John said.

'Begin,' Sir Reginald commanded.

Cock Inn

Bydaud drank well in the Cock that night. He was feeling cheerful. More men had come and demanded his services, and whereas a week ago he had been close to bankruptcy, now he was being feted by many of the richer elements of the mercantile class in the city. There were risks, as he knew. A man's reputation could be destroyed as swiftly as it could be built, usually more easily, too. And those who were even now keen to establish links with him because of the destruction of the House of Paffard, would be just as keen to discard him and go to a newer, fresher face. There was no loyalty in business. Only self-interest.

But he would not consider the possible pitfalls ahead. He was enjoying himself now, for the first time in many weeks, and he intended to make the most of it. He had seen the group of men bringing John from the Paffards' house, and he was sure that it boded well for him. Paffard was over and done with.

Still, he must return to his wife and see what she had prepared for his meal. He finished his drink, slammed some coins down on the bar, and made his way homewards.

There was a crowd gathering outside, and he wandered through them all, beaming beatifically. The world, to him, had a roseate hue tonight after a half gallon of the Cock's best ale. It was only a miracle that an alehouse of that nature could brew their ales so well. They had the same ingredients, so he imagined, as most others, and yet there was a sweetness and maltiness to theirs that quite outstripped all the others he had tasted in the last year.

As he went along the street towards his home, he gradually became aware of a shouting from behind him, and when he glanced over his shoulder, he saw that there were more and more men following along behind him. At least thirty, although his eyes were a little hazy. He wondered what they could be doing out here, before he realised that the leading men were the two whom he had seen the other night at the Paffards' house. One still had his forearm bound with a piece of filthy cloth where John's hatchet had opened it. Bydaud could see it quite clearly by the light of the flaming torch the man held in his good hand.

There was nothing in the way of firewood here for them to light, he thought to himself, so what could they be intending to do? And then he realised that they were set upon the destruction of Henry Paffard's house!

With a squeak, he set off homewards as fast as his legs would take him. These men had tried to break into the Paffards' house only two days before, and tonight they looked as though they intended to finish their job.

'Oh, Christ Jesus!' he muttered to himself, and was for a moment nonplussed. Should he go home, or fetch the Watch? Home, of course. He couldn't leave Emma and the girls all alone with this mob. He hurried his steps, and then, as he ran up the alley, he saw William.

'Quick, please, go to the Holy Trinity, fetch the Watch and those knights,' he panted. 'These fools may try to burn the house again, and we'll lose the whole street!'

Church of the Holy Trinity

Baldwin and the others had already heard John's confession regarding the two maids Clara and Evie, and how he had killed Alice and Juliana Marsille, but now he began to talk about Gregory and Agatha. Baldwin listened for only a short time, before deciding he needed hear no more.

'Simon, I cannot listen to this,' he muttered, and Simon nodded and left with him. Sir Richard and Edgar joined them.

'A shameful business,' Sir Richard said as they stood outside the church.

'I am shocked to hear it,' Simon said gruffly. 'The idea of incest is not unknown in some of the farther distant valleys near Cornwall, but here, in a Christian city?'

Sir Richard eyed him with a benevolent smile. 'Me dear fellow, there is nothing you can find happening in the most pagan of lands which ain't goin' on in the middle of the biggest cities in this kingdom. Wasn't it you told me of the necromancer trying to kill the King by stabbing pins into a wax figure? At least incest doesn't normally end a man's life, eh?'

'Clearly the boy Thomas has seen something of it, from the

way he hid from his brother and sister,' Baldwin hazarded. 'It is sad to think that his own innocence has been shattered in this way.'

'Aye,' Sir Richard said, and would have continued, had not Simon pointed up the road. 'What is that up there? It looks like the boy William.'

William ran up and drew to a stop, pointing back the way he had come. 'Please! There is an angry mob outside the house again. They look as if they're going to set fire to it!'

They could all hear the sound of chanting and singing, and a sudden bellowing. 'Come!' shouted Baldwin.

The street was already in an uproar by the time they reached it.

Simon found himself looking at the men and women of the mob. 'Baldwin, I don't like this. It is too much like London last year. And Bristol when the city was under siege.'

'There are only forty or fifty men,' Baldwin noted.

'Forty or fifty swords could make me lose a lot of weight,' Sir Richard considered. A man walked near him with a torch, and Sir Richard took it from his hand. He gave the stunned reveller a beaming smile and walked on, leaving the man bemused. 'Come along, then, before they get rowdy.'

'Rowdy?' Simon repeated, gazing about him at the men.

The two men at the front of the crowd were rousing the worst elements into a frenzy of hatred towards the Paffard family.

'Look what they did to me!'

The ragged slashes inflicted by John were displayed to increasing anger amongst the people there.

'Come along, Sir Baldwin,' Sir Richard boomed fussily. He pushed his way onwards, and the others followed in his wake like small boats trailing behind a ship. The people parted for them, until they were in the front. And Sir Richard did not hesitate, but carried on up the steps to the door. 'You fellows know who lives here? Aye, I thought you did. He is dead. He was killed this afternoon. All there are in here are the women-folk of the house, and the children. Are you all bold enough to make war on women and children? Come, now. Disperse before the Watch is called to you.'

'We want them out, and then we'll fire their house!' the man with the cut arm yelled.

Sir Richard cast an eye over him. 'Edgar, do you think you could silence him?'

Edgar nodded and moved off while the man continued haranguing the crowds. Simon watched him uneasily, while the two knights moved together slightly. Wolf was with Baldwin, his hackles rising.

There was a roar from the people, and the man before them raised his injured arm again with a fierce yell. He pointed at the house. 'So, let's get at them!' he screamed, but as he turned to rush the house, he found himself staring into Edgar's smiling face.

The man raised his fist to punch Edgar, but Edgar was a trained fighter. The punch he landed on the man's chin hurled him backwards a yard. He looked bewildered at the force of the blow, and shook his head like a drunk trying to clear the wool from his wits, while two others supported him, and then he was about to lunge at Edgar when there was a sudden lull.

Simon turned to see that the front door had opened. In it stood Claricia Paffard. She was clad in a white linen tunic that made her look otherworldly in the light of the torches, almost like an angel. At her side was Thomas. Her head was encased in a tight cowl, and she looked at the people filling the street with a kind of wonder. 'What do you want with me?'

There was a stillness. The man Edgar had hit was feeling his chin with a look of bewilderment, and others were shamefaced. It was one thing to attack a building, but quite another to hurt women and small boys. At the back, Simon saw two men look at each other and turn away. Hopefully more would soon disperse, and the matter could be forgotten. It was only fortunate that they had come out of the church in time to prevent a serious attack, he thought.

And then Gregory appeared. 'What do you want with us?' he demanded imperiously. 'Do you think you can attack us because my father has died? I will have my place in the Freedom before long, and when I do, I'll see to it that each and every one of you here tonight is punished.'

Simon could have cursed the fool. His words were inciting the crowd to violence even more efficiently than the rabble-rouser in front of Edgar. Shooting a look at Baldwin, Simon could see that he too recognised the danger, and was urgently indicating to Sir Richard that they should push the boy inside.

There was a stone flung, which crashed into the wall near Gregory's head. All at once, Gregory's face changed, as though he suddenly realised his danger. Another stone was thrown, and it smashed into his shoulder, making him lurch backwards. He gave a cry, and Claricia turned to reach for him. Before she could do so, however, Edgar had swept her off her feet, and drew her away with Thomas.

And that was when the crowd surged forward. Baldwin and Sir Richard were thrust aside, Baldwin knocked from his feet before he could draw steel, and Sir Richard took up his position above him, his own sword in his fist, saving Baldwin from being trampled. Simon managed to push his way to the side of Sir Richard, and clasped Baldwin's forearm, lifting him from the ground. Then all three, with their weapons ready, tried to make their way to the doorway, but could not beat their way through the press.

Gregory had disappeared. Simon hoped he had made his way inside, but could not be sure. There was the sound of breaking wood, and then hammering as the mob tried to break into the house. Simon saw a section of the wall to the side of the door gave way under the efforts of six men with hammers and picks.

Uppermost in Simon's mind was Agatha. She was only a young woman, and with a drunken throng like this, she would certainly be in danger. It was unthinkable that a girl so much younger than his own dear daughter Edith could be left to fend for herself against so many, and he shoved his way towards the hole in the house wall.

Someone had clambered inside and removed the door's bar, and now it was thrust wide, and there was a shout of victory as men tumbled in. Simon was among them, and he ran ahead hoping that he might reach the girl before the crowd. He was the seventh man to hurtle along the passageway, but then, when he reached the hall, he saw it was too late.

Agatha and Gregory lay on the floor, entwined in a pool of their own mingled blood.

CHAPTER FORTY-EIGHT

Second Saturday after the Nativity of St John the Baptist[1]

Precentor's House

Adam Murimuth poured the wine himself that morning. He was grateful to these men for their efforts in the last week, and it was a sign of his respect that he brought the drinks to them.

'Sir Baldwin, Sir Richard, Simon, I can only say that I and the Cathedral are indebted to you for everything you have done. It is sad indeed that this affair should have come to such a pass, but at least you have resolved it. I trust you are all well now? You slept well?'

Baldwin nodded. It had been some time before the crowd had been induced to leave the street. Some men were still wandering about the house trying to find the caskets of jewels and diamonds that were rumoured still to be lying in profusion all over the house. They had to be forcibly ejected by Edgar and

1 4 July 1327

MICHAEL JECKS

two Watchmen. Baldwin and the others had come here to the Cathedral Close for safety. There was a distinct impression that more violence could ensue, were they to try to find their way to an inn. Random members of the mob could try to seek them out, and none of them were willing to risk that.

'You are sure that it was not the intruders who killed the two?' Adam asked as he took a mazer of wine for himself. He had used all his goblets for his guests.

'Quite certain, yes,' Baldwin said. 'The injuries that killed them were entirely consistent with the knife that Gregory held in his hand, and it fitted the sheath about his waist. Simon was there almost immediately, with the leaders from the crowd. No one would have had the time to place the sheath on his belt, and I myself saw that belt about his waist, and the sheath and the knife earlier in the afternoon.'

'So they killed themselves from shame, do you think?'

Simon shook his head. 'No. I think Gregory so loved his sister that he would not see her ravaged or slaughtered slowly by the crowd. And then, in his grief, he took his own life.'

'Terrible, terrible,' the Precentor murmured. 'To think that such awful events could take place here. It makes one think that it should be recorded. Such things should not be forgotten.'

'I believe, with respect, that there is no need to record what has happened this last week,' Baldwin said firmly.

'I am sorry? I do not understand.'

Baldwin looked at Sir Richard and Simon, both of whom nodded. 'We have been discussing this already, Precentor. If we allow news of all this to be bruited abroad, we run the risk of inciting more people to violence. This began as the treachery of Henry Paffard. He was keen to make money by selling his Bishop to a known mercenary. If news of that murder is allowed to escape to the wider world, and people realise that Sir Edward of Caernarfon is free, they may rally to him, even perhaps allow him to raise a force about him. Then again, if the Berkeley family realises that their kinsman was murdered in revenge for their holding Sir Edward, it will lead to further ramifications. I would avoid that, if at all possible.'

'I cannot conceal Henry Paffard's murder!'

'He died in prison. Any death in prison is usually considered to be from natural causes, be it from cold, hunger, thirst, or an injury. He suffered an injury. I should leave matters at that.'

'What of the mob violence towards the Paffards?'

Sir Richard spoke up now. 'This is a good city, Precentor. The people here are not so unruly as some. They were incited to fury by a few hotheads, but that is an end to it. I think you will find that they will be as calm and sensible as you could wish. This ain't London, after all.'

'I see. And you are all sure of this? Well, very good, then. I am only glad that the character of poor Laurence is rescued without a stain to besmirch it. Although I still do not know what he was doing there in the alley when Alice was killed.'

Baldwin shook his head. 'We will probably never know.'

Cathedral Close

After they had made their farewells to the Precentor, Baldwin was in a pensive mood as he walked with his friends up towards the Broad Gate. He had been struck with the same question as Adam, and as he walked, he became more and more convinced that there must be a clue somewhere to Laurence's feelings.

At the gate, he waved the others on, and stood inside the gateway. He didn't have to wait long. Janekyn Beyvyn was in his chamber, and when he realised Baldwin was outside, he hurried out, wiping his hands on a cloth.

'Sir? You wanted me?'

Baldwin sucked his teeth for a moment, then said, 'Would you walk with me a moment, Janekyn?'

'If I can keep the gate in view. I have my job to do, sir.'

They strolled along. Horses roamed here, cropping the grass over the graves, and two boys were playing chase in among the slabs.

'Janekyn, I have thought much about the night of that first murder. It strikes me as peculiar that Father Laurence would have gone out into the town, then when he saw the dead girl, come running back to the Bear Gate. Why wouldn't he have gone to the Palace Gate, for that would have been nearer? And then something else struck me: he would have assumed that all the gates would be closed. He would have naturally known the hour when the gates were locked. It was a miracle that any was still open, wasn't it? He was fortunate.'

'Yes? I don't understand what you mean.'

'If he thought all the gates would already be closed, it is clear what his purpose must have been. I mean, he must have already decided that he was not going to come back that night. It was only the shock of seeing Alice dead in that alley that made him return. Otherwise, he was going to flee the city that same night.'

'You think so?'

'Oh, I think we both know it. I remember you saying that there were two men on that gate that night. One was a friend of Laurence's, wasn't he? Who could be relied upon to open the gate for him?'

Janekyn said nothing, but his pacing was slower now as he listened, and his face had taken on a similar appearance to the chips and blocks of rock that lay all about.

Baldwin continued: 'I do not recall his name – nor do I wish to. But it is plain enough to me that Father Laurence was a popular man amongst the clergy. The porter at the gate too liked him. As did Father Paul at Holy Trinity. All seem to have been struck with him. And yet he was a sad man who was determined to leave the Cathedral and the city. That astonishes me, frankly.'

Janekyn licked his lips. He cast a look over his shoulder at his gate, and then turned to Baldwin with an eye half-closed as though measuring Baldwin in some way. At last he nodded, as if he had passed some test.

'Sir Baldwin, I remember you from years ago when we had all that trouble here in the Cathedral. You were straight with us all then. I don't see as you've changed much over the years, so I'll tell you. There were several of us here knew how unhappy Laurence was. He didn't want to be a priest: he was a strong, happy soul, who would have been contented as a peasant with a small plot to plough and work. And the worst of it is, he could have been that by now.

'I don't know what made him come back, but I know why he left. He was in love. The girl Agatha who died at her brother's hand – he was going to ask her to run away with him. So he went to see Agatha that afternoon, full of mustard, but she refused him. Cut him right down. Running off with a renegade priest wasn't good enough for her, see. So he went to say goodbye to Father Paul, and after, he went back to the house one last time. I think he walked up the alley to be near her, but hidden. He could stand in there and imagine her only a foot or so away, the other side of the wall. But he never saw her.'

'Instead he found a dead woman.'

'More than that, sir. He found a dead young thing who was the same age as Agatha, and who had a similar face and build, from what I saw at the inquest. I think he might have thought it *was* her.'

'He thought the dead girl was his beloved?' Baldwin said with a flash of insight. 'Of course, in the gloom of the alley, it would easy to mistake her.' He should have thought of that. 'So he ran back here in shock?'

'To the gate where he knew the porter,' Janekyn nodded. 'He was just lucky that it was so early in the evening.'

'And you knew all this?'

Janekyn lifted an eyebrow. 'If I'd heard, I'd have told the Precentor in the blink of an eye. No, I was told all this by my porter on the day Laurence ran. He was anxious about him after all that.'

'I see. I am grateful to you, friend Janekyn. You have eased my mind a little on the matter.'

'Little enough,' Janekyn observed. 'It is sad to think Laurence is dead. But at least he died in protecting another. That's good. But it's a miserable twist of fate that the man he was saving was such a coward he killed himself so soon after.'

CHAPTER FORTY-NINE

Second Tuesday after the Nativity of St John the Baptist[1]

Cowley Ford

When he reached the bank of the river by the ford, Ulric stood and stared at the fork in the road, wondering which way to go.

He had been lying low in the city since being discovered by the strange servant, and every day had brought him a new moment of terror. There were so many there who might recognise him. Only yesterday at a cookshop, he had seen a man who had been in the posse. Ulric had been so alarmed, he had fumbled the change in his purse and dropped two pennies, and the man had himself stepped on one of the coins, picked it up and passed it to him.

Ulric had been so shocked, his hand had shaken like the ague. 'I drank too much last night,' he said, but he was sure that the man had seen through his little fiction. The fellow's eyes

1 7 July 1327

had been on him all the way along the street, he could sense it, even if he hadn't followed him. But that meant nothing. He could have paid some urchin to trail after him, and perhaps even then was preparing a group of sturdy citizens to come and capture Ulric for his part in the murder of the Bishop . . . But no one had come, even though he had sat up in his room, waiting. At any time they might break down his door and crash in to capture him, but nothing happened.

It was this morning that he decided he must make the move and flee the city. He had wrapped up his spare shirt into a bundle, along with half a loaf of bread and a lump of blueish cheese, and as soon as the gates were open, he was on the road.

His way was easily chosen. He would go to Tiverton and see if he could find work. Or Crediton. Both were goodly-sized towns, so he'd heard. Perhaps he could start a new life there. Get employment in a shop. His skill with a pen would help him.

Tiverton or Crediton. He stood, frozen by indecision. Then, with a flash of simplicity, he chose north. At least with Tiverton he wouldn't have to cross this river and get his feet soaked.

'Hello.'

Turning, he saw a young woman. She was a pretty thing, with her hair straggling from beneath her wimple.

'Hello,' he said. She was familiar at once. 'You used to work in Paffard's house, didn't you? I was apprenticed there. Ulric.'

'Yes,' she said with a wary politeness. A look of pain crossed her face. She didn't want to remember that place. 'Where are you going?'

He pulled a grimace. 'North.'

'Oh?' She glanced at his meagre pack. 'Me too. I'm going home. A friend died, and I don't want to stay in the city.'

'Where is home?' he asked.

'A farm,' she smiled. 'North. Can I walk with you?'

Ulric smiled back, and the two began their journey. It was a pleasant day, and Ulric had almost forgotten his fears when he heard horses approaching from Exeter.

'What is it?' she asked, seeing how he blanched.

The horses were on them, riding at an easy canter. Two men, one knight with a thin beard that travelled about his jaw, and his servant was the man who had caught Ulric on that fateful day. Ulric sighed. This was the capture he had feared. He felt a sob rise to choke him, and was about to drop his pack, when the two men rode on past, and off into the distance. But as they passed, Ulric was convinced that the servant had looked at him and winked.

'Are you in trouble?' Joan asked.

'I don't know. I don't think so.'

'Perhaps if you wanted, I could go with you,' she said. The thought of return to the farm was not appealing. Memories of her father's strap lingered, even while she was determined to get away from Exeter.

'I'd like that,' he said.

It brought a glow to her face that he thought was exquisitely beautiful, and later, when they sat to share his food, they sat very close together.

Stepecoat Street

William Marsille entered the house for the first time that morning.

He weighed the key in his hand as he opened the door and stepped inside, looking about the room with a feeling of unutterable emptiness. It was good to know that he had a place to live, but that was scant compensation for the loss of home and family which Henry Paffard had caused.

There should be a mother in here with him, and Philip, too.

They should have been able to join him here with happiness. If all the money which his father had left for them had been given to them, they would have been able to enjoy a glorious time here, but they were gone, and William was the sole survivor of his family.

Walking through the room, he peered out at the tiny yard area. Still, while small, there was space for a few vegetables. It would suffice.

Claricia had been determined to give him this place. At first he thought it was simple guilt which made her want to give it up, but then he began to wonder. If this had been intended as a love-nest for her husband's young lover, it would scarcely hold pleasant associations for her.

Up a ladder, there was a bedchamber over the fire. He climbed up and stared at it, then clambered in and lay on his back. There was nothing here. All his belongings were lost. Cupboard, table, chairs, all had been broken up for a bonfire outside the Paffards' house. But at least with a house he could start afresh.

There was one thing of which he was absolutely certain, and that was, no matter what, nothing in the world could ever make him copy Gregory and kill himself. No. To end a life was the greatest cowardice.

And he was no coward. He was son of Nicholas Marsille, and he would build a business to rival any in the city.

Paffards' House

Without the servants it seemed loud. Thomas could hardly imagine why, because with fewer people about the house, it should have been quieter, but no matter.

Sal was still there, even though Joan had left, and she seemed to have cheered up considerably since the disappearance of both the younger maids. Thomas didn't know why. But she was also nominated, or believed herself to be, his guardian, and she made his life cruel. Every time he played with his hoop in the road, he could count on her to shout to him just because a horse was coming, or a cart or some men and women. He could see them! He wasn't a baby!

Today there was a curious feeling about the house. Ever since his mother had returned from the shops, there had been a kind of tension in the air. It didn't bother him unduly – it wasn't like the bad atmosphere in the old days. It was more a feeling of excitement, rather like a feast day. Except it wasn't, he was sure.

When a knock came at the door, Thomas was worried. He still remembered the other knockings. Callers to let them know a maid was dead, others to try to barge in and burn the house down. Callers scared him. As soon as he heard this one, he ran to his mother in the hall.

'Why are you here?' she asked sternly. 'Should you not answer the door, Thomas?'

He looked up at her, and as the knock came again, he buried his face in her lap. A mute appeal for protection.

'Oh, very well, child,' she said. 'Come with me.'

Picking him up and resting him on her hip, she made her way to the door. Unbarring it, she pulled it wide, and Thomas saw a man with a sack. It wriggled alarmingly.

'Here it is, mistress,' the man said, lifting the sacking and passing it to her.

'I thank you,' she said, and the fellow was gone. 'Thomas. This is for you.' She set him down on the ground, and passed him the sack.

He didn't want it. He stepped away from it, eyeing it suspiciously.

And then he heard a little sound, and his heart leaped.

Because the noise was a sharp whine. Like a puppy's.

Furnshill

Baldwin cantered up the last part of the roadway with his heart lightening.

It was always the same when he came home. There was a vague sense of anticipation that bordered on fear, in case Jeanne or one of the children had fallen sick, perhaps died even, but that could not be drowned out by the feeling of utter joy he felt on seeing his house again, the long house with the great hall, the solars, the stables, the neat pastureland before, the trees behind. It was a scene of rural perfection. He knew that he was the luckiest man alive to possess this manor, and there was not a day when he woke here and didn't think of that.

'Home, Sir Baldwin,' Edgar said.

'And I am as glad as a king ever was to see his palace,' Baldwin said. 'I will never again willingly leave my house and family. There is no task, no function that could tempt me away from here. All I love is right here.'

Edgar looked at him with a grin. 'So, until the next time you are called away, we can rest?'

'Edgar, old friend, I shall relinquish my duties as Keeper of the King's Peace,' Baldwin said. 'How can I continue in that role when I do not fully believe that the King is on his throne? This boy, Edward III, may be more callow and incompetent than his father. And if there is any steel in the committee of regency running the kingdom, it will be due to Queen Isabella and Sir Roger Mortimer. And I trust neither. No, Edgar, it is time for me to accept that at my age, I am too old for this position.'

'So we shall retire at last?'

'Aye, my friend. We shall hide ourselves in obscurity here in Devon. And at last, perhaps, find peace.'

And so saying, he whipped his rounsey into a gallop.

Road to Bristol

It was a hard and weary ride to the King, Adam Murimuth knew. He had only just set off this morning, and already, some thirty miles from Exeter, he was regretting the impulse that had made him agree to be one of the delegates with the messages telling the King about the death of the Bishop and the Sheriff. There was no escaping the fact that the journey would take a long time.

But he did at least have some ideas that had been fermenting at the back of his mind, and now, on the road, he would have time to consider their implications.

For some years he had been maintaining his little journal, and the exercise had been rewarding. It was not in any way a great chronicle, but a series of notes and jottings. He had started when he was about thirty years old, as an exercise in memory, reminding himself of the things he had been doing on certain days and while it had been useful – and he could not deny it, enjoyable too – it was of such little meaning as to be irrelevant. If he stopped today, it would not be noticed.

Which was curious, in so many ways. Here he was, living through a momentous period in the history of the realm, and all someone looking at his journal would note would be the order of service at his Mass, the food he disliked at table, or the catty remarks he made about certain companions in the choir. This was no way to be dealing with the great matters of moment that were being played out all about the kingdom.

No, what he should be attempting was something on a grander scale entirely. Something that had sweep, and that would entrance and educate. Something that would show the world what a marvellous thing was this creation of God's. Something people could refer to for information, perhaps. And in its pages, he would record the truth. No concealments like the latest sorry adventures in Combe Street. He would have the facts of Henry Paffard's criminality, the horrible truth of his bottler, the sorry acts of his children. No, perhaps not. Little could be achieved by tales of ordinary men and women and their secrets. But to tell the story of the kingdom – that would be an undertaking of importance. As befitted a . . .

He smiled at his pride. A journal was surely all he could manage. But there were such attractions to attempting a chronicle. A book that would tell the tale of the history of the last years. Perhaps he could go back a short way, and speak of Edward II, and then tell of the shameful way in which he lost his crown and throne, that unhappy monarch. A chronicle that would certainly be of instructive use . . .

It was indeed a glorious idea.

And today was a day of wonderful inspiration. For it was as he settled beside the fire that evening, that he had another excellent idea.

He had been musing for some time about how to broach the death of Sheriff James de Cockington. It was sure to upset the King, for finding suitable souls to take on such positions was increasingly difficult. The Sheriffs were a difficult bunch. Some were honourable, but for the most part they were aggressive and corrupt. They took what they could from the people and extorted money from all those who were forced to go to them for justice. It was no way for the realm to administer the law.

But once in a while a knight proved himself honourable. A good, kindly man with a sense of fairness and integrity – that would be a man to make a rare Sheriff. If he could temper the loss of one Sheriff with a recommendation of a replacement, he would make himself popular.

And Sir Baldwin would, Adam felt sure, make a perfect officer for the King.

To find out how Baldwin de Furnshill's adventures began, read on for an exclusive excerpt of *Templar's Acre*, the thrilling new novel from Michael Jecks and a prequel to the Knights Templar series.

PROLOGUE

29 May 1291

The creaking of the ship was familiar.

As he began to come to, the sound brought back memories of his first voyage, and for one glorious moment he dreamed he was on his way there again – en route to Acre – a year ago, before the catastrophe.

Still only semi-conscious, he listened with half an ear to the thunderous crash of waves against the hull, the wind singing in the sheets, the flapping of flags, the moaning of the timbers. And then he heard the whimpers and weeping all around him, one man sobbing uncontrollably, and he remembered where he was, and his eyes snapped open at the terrible memories that flooded back. He would never sleep again in case he dreamed of them.

The broken bone in his leg hurt like hell. Each movement of the ship made it shift, and he felt the jagged edges grating. The scar at his cheek pulled, and the burns on his limbs shrieked for butter or grease, but Baldwin paid them no heed.

In his mind's eye he saw it all again: the flames, the shattering of buildings and bodies, the dread assaults, the devastation. He saw the corpses lining the roads, he saw his little dog, Uther, and he saw the men of whom he had grown so fond: Ivo and old Pietro, Jacques, brave Guillaume, Geoffrey of the sad eyes. All those who had endured the last hellish weeks with him – and then died. And he sobbed unaffectedly as he recalled the disaster that had overwhelmed them all. No tears would come, but he felt the grief must throttle him.

Then he saw *her* again: Lucia, his love; his mistress, with her black hair and olive skin; her calm, trusting eyes . . .

And his heart could no longer contain his desolation.

BOOK ONE

PILGRIM, MAY 1290

CHAPTER ONE

It was his first experience of battle, and for Baldwin de Furnshill it was made all the more hideous by his sea-sickness.

The screamed alarm came while he was asleep, dozing in the sunshine with the other pilgrims on the deck, and from that first wakening, he had stood gripping the shrouds against the rolling and plunging of the ship as the two enemy vessels came on relentlessly towards them. It was like watching the hounds chasing a deer, seeing these two closing up ever nearer. As the seas rose before them, and the pilgrim ship hurtled down one wave's flank, only to bob up once more, he saw that their pursuers were now only a stone's throw away.

A whistling thrum – and he flinched. A quarrel flew past, missing his face by mere inches, only to thud into the mast. He turned and stared at it. The vicious barbs had sunk so deep, they were almost hidden in the wood. He imagined it would have passed clean through his skull, had it flown true. The thought made the hot bile rise to sear his throat, and he crouched, anxious that another might hit him.

He was not yet seventeen years old; if those galleys caught his ship, he was sure to die before his birthday. Sixteen was too young to die, he thought wildly. He didn't want to die like a coward, but he had never fought in a battle, and he stared about him in a panic, thinking there was no escape from a ship. Then another quarrel hissed past – a second narrow escape.

'Get down, you lurdan!' a man rasped behind him, and suddenly he was flat on the deck. 'Want to get yourself killed?'

Wiping at his eyes as they filled, Baldwin shook his head speechlessly. What was he doing here, in the middle of the sea, with pilgrims and crusaders? He must have been a fool to put himself in this position. But he had to pay for his crime. He prayed that God would pardon him for the murder after his pilgrimage.

If He let Baldwin live.

He shivered uncontrollably as he waited, lying under the protection of the wale.

There must have been three hundred men on board – Christians all, of course, many of them crusaders who had taken up the cross from Antwerp, from Paris or Hainault, a few like himself from England, some mere pilgrims – but they all waited with the same dread, listening to the whack of slingshots and arrows plunging into the wood. Occasionally there was a soggy sound as a missile hit a man, followed by a groan, shriek or curse. The Venetian shipmaster shouted commands as he tried to evade their pursuers, and hoarse bellows from the ships overhauling them were audible over the whine of the wind in the sheets.

All the young man knew was a paralysing terror: not of death or dying, but of failure. His failure.

He shouldn't be here, curled up like a child on this wildly rocking ship. He was the son of a knight, not some low-born bastard-whelp from the coast. His place was on a horse, winning renown and glory at the point of his lance. He ought to be riding behind his knight, a squire or sergeant, bringing a horse to aid his lord, fighting with the other men-at-arms. Instead, look at him! There was no honour in dying here. He had sworn his oath to help defend the Holy Land in hope of his own salvation, and he hadn't even reached the coast yet. These pirates were attacking while they were still on their way.

The reflection was enough to make him grab for the sheer and pull himself upright. A hand reached to drag him back down, but he shrugged it away. It was old Isaac, the pilgrim who had shared his meals from the day they first took ship. Well, Isaac could crawl and hide, but Baldwin would prefer a quick death from an arrow than a coward's end.

The other ships were close now. Even as he rose, he saw a grapnel fly through the air, and threw himself to the side to avoid its hideous barbs. It caught at the ship's wale, and he saw the sailor who had thrown it pulling hard, two of his companions grabbing the rope and helping draw the ships together. The first saw Baldwin, and he smiled – a fierce curl of his lips that sent ice into Baldwin's spine.

He tugged at the metal hooks to release the grapnel and throw it into the sea, but the weight of the men hauling at the rope meant he could make no impression on it. He stared at it, despair flooding him. And then he cursed. He wouldn't submit without a fight! Drawing his sword, he hacked at the rope. One, two, then a third blow – and there was a crack like snapping timber, and the rope parted, the loosed end lashing back. Baldwin saw it whip at the pirate's arm, and lay the man's flesh open to the bone. He screamed and fell, and Baldwin felt a savage joy. He bared his teeth and waved his sword over his head, taunting them, until a pair of arrows passed close by.

But now the pilgrims and crusaders were with him, and they were firing their own arrows even as the two ships came closer, and Baldwin roared defiance as he saw a sailor topple, struck by a lucky shot. It was only then, as he stared at the sailors on board that ship, that he realised that they did not look like the Muslims he had expected.

These pirates weren't their enemy. With a sickening lurch, he realised that they were fellow Christians.

The flag of Genoa flew at their masts.

The man beside Baldwin fired a crossbow, swore to see it miss his target, and bent to span it again. He shoved his foot into the stirrup, catching the string on his belt's hooks, and straightened his legs until the bowstring was held on the nut. He hastily dropped a quarrel into the groove, aimed, and fired, muttering to himself as he missed again, and lowered it once more to go through the reloading sequence.

The pirates were very close to the larboard side of their ship, and he could see their grim faces: dark, bristle-bearded, savage men, with blades glittering in their fists. The men on his ship began to yell insults, screaming their contempt for the sea-raiders. Baldwin joined in, bellowing abuse with words he barely understood.

The man beside him had reloaded. At this range he couldn't help but hit a pirate Baldwin thought – when the bowman coughed and lurched, his head striking the wale with a sickening thud. Baldwin instinctively assumed that it must have been a roll in the ship's gait that had made him lose his footing, but then he saw the fletchings of the quarrel protruding from the man's neck, and turned with shock to see that the second ship was even closer, on the starboard side. Her crew were already leaping up onto the wale-piece, and some few had landed on the deck and were hacking about them at the terrified pilgrims.

That was when saw the man with the crossbow, his eyes fixed upon Baldwin as he lifted his weapon to aim.

His bowels seemed to melt within him. All was slow as though, coming close to death, the very fabric of nature and movement of time had been slowed by God. It was punishment for his crime. God was giving him time to appreciate his destruction, as if He had chosen to demonstrate just how feeble were his own puny efforts. God was watching as this ship, full of His servants, was overrun, and Baldwin could do nothing to save himself, nor would God save him. His body was grown listless, his limbs leaden. There was no escape from a crossbow's bolt.

All was futile.

He had travelled all this way in order to reach Acre, to participate in the defence of the last enclave of Christianity in the Holy Land. It was Baldwin's task to help destroy the ungodly hordes of pagans and help drive them back whence they came. And in return, he hoped to win peace from memories of Sybilla, and the body of her lover. In those seconds, staring at the crossbow's quarrel, he remembered this. He remembered the oath taken at Exeter Cathedral, the journey to the coast at Exmouth, then the voyage to English Bordeaux, followed by an overland trip to the Mediterranean coast, where he had caught this ship. All those miles, all those leagues, only to see it end here.

The crossbow was aiming at his heart. He knew it, and in those last moments, Baldwin offered a prayer for his soul. 'Dear Father, accept this soul, undeserving as it may be, and allow me to join You in Heaven. I beg . . .'

He saw the point of the quarrel gleaming with a cold, blue wickedness, and then a man shoved him, bending to grab the crossbow from his fallen companion's hands, and in that moment a roaring sound came to Baldwin's ears. And just for a moment, he thought he was dead. For a moment.

Then the crossbow moved imperceptibly, and the man at his side gave a yelp of agony as the bolt plunged into his back, through his belly, and slammed into the timbers before him. He snarled, turning past Baldwin, and loosed his own crossbow at the ship behind him. The face of the bowman at the ship's rail suddenly gushed blood and fell back, and the man beside Baldwin sank to the deck, coughing and swearing.

And still Baldwin stood, incapable of moving, his sword useless in his hand as he stared at where the bowman had been.

He did feel, truly, as if he had already died.

Or that his soul had – and had been renewed. He felt as though all that had gone before had been taken away by that bowshot, as if it had taken his sins and foolishness with it.

Michael Jecks
King's Gold

1327. One kingdom. Two kings. Only one can rule.

As the year 1326 draws to a close, London is in flames. King Edward II is held prisoner, and the mercenaries and rebels led by the vengeful Queen Isabella and her lover, Sir Roger Mortimer, are in the ascendant.

While the richest in the kingdom fight over the spoils of the invasion, the Bardi family, bankers who once funded the King, are in a quandary. They must look to their own future with the Queen as the mob rampages over the city, steering a careful course between rival factions. But money can tempt the heart of even the most honourable, and in this age of corruption the bankers must guard their lives, as well as their coffers.

And guarding the deposed King on behalf of Mortimer and the Queen, Sir Baldwin de Furnshill and his friend Simon Puttock find themselves, once again, entangled in a tightening net of conspiracy, greed, betrayal and murder.

Paperback ISBN 978-1-84983-083-6
Ebook ISBN 978-1-84737-903-0

Michael Jecks
The Oath

Amid the turmoil of war, nobody's life is safe...

In a land riven with conflict, knight and peasant alike find their
lives turned upside down by the warring factions of Edward II,
with his hated favourite, Hugh le Despenser, and Edward's
estranged queen Isabella and her lover, Sir Roger Mortimer.

Even in such times the brutal slaughter of an entire family, right
down to a babe in arms, still has the power to shock. Three
further murders follow, and bailiff Simon Puttock is drawn into
a web of intrigue, vengeance, power and greed as Roger
Mortimer charges him to investigate the killings.

Michael Jecks brilliantly evokes the turmoil of fourteenth-
century England, as his well-loved characters Simon Puttock
and Sir Baldwin de Furnshill strive to maintain the principles of
loyalty and truth.

Paperback ISBN 978-1-84983-082-9
Ebook ISBN 978-1-84737-901-6

Coming June 2013 from Simon & Schuster

Michael Jecks
Templar's Acre

The Holy Land, 1291.

A war has been raging across these lands for decades. The forces of the Crusaders have been pushed back again and again by the Muslims and now just one city remains in Crusader control. That one city stands between the past and the future. One city which must be defended at all costs. That city is Acre.

Into this battle where men will fight to the death to defend their city comes a young boy. Green and scared, he has never seen battle before. But he is on the run from a dark past and he has no choice but to stay. And to stay means to fight. That boy is Baldwin de Furnshill.

This is the story of the siege of Acre, and of the moment Baldwin first charged into battle.

This is just the beginning. The rest is history.

Hardback ISBN 978-0-85720-517-9
Ebook ISBN 978-0-85720-520-9

SIMON &
SCHUSTER

London · New York · Sydney · Toronto · New Delhi ·

A CBS COMPANY

IF YOU ENJOY GOOD BOOKS,
YOU'LL LOVE OUR GREAT OFFER
25% OFF the RRP ON ALL
SIMON & SCHUSTER UK TITLES
WITH FREE POSTAGE AND PACKING (UK ONLY)

Simon & Schuster UK is one of the leading general book publishing
companies in the UK, publishing a wide and eclectic mix
of authors ranging across commercial fiction, literary fiction,
general non-fiction, illustrated and children's books.

For exclusive author interviews, features and competitions log onto:
www.simonandschuster.co.uk

*Titles also available in **eBook** format across all digital devices.*

How to buy your books

Credit and debit cards
Telephone Simon & Schuster Cash Sales at **Sparkle Direct** on **01326 569444**

Cheque
Send a cheque payable to *Simon & Schuster Bookshop* to:
Simon & Schuster Bookshop, PO Box 60, Helston, TR13 0TP

Email: sales@sparkledirect.co.uk
Website: www.sparkledirect.com

Prices and availability are subject to change without notice.